Advance Praise for Matthew Clark Davison

"*Doubting Thomas* moves co[...] sionately among races, gend[...] other human conditions. A [...] vigor, this liveliness, would [...] any writer; the fact that it's Matthew Clark Davison's first is a clear indication of marvels yet to come."
— Michael Cunningham, Pulitzer Prize-winning author of *The Hours*

"*Doubting Thomas* by Matthew Clark Davison is wonderfully insightful and tremendously generous of spirit. A book for our age in that it masterfully navigates the emotional terrain of real people with real affection for each other, who are trying their best to do the right thing by those they love. That they do this across differences of race, sexual orientation, class, and culture is a part of the book, of course, yet this isn't some intellectual exercise. The book's characters are terrifically alive and kicking, constantly surprising, dismaying, and delighting us."
— Alice LaPlante, author of *Turn of Mind*

"How do you go on after one rough year, after the end of a relationship, an illness in the family, and a false accusation, which leads to multiple betrayals from the community that once nourished you? Matthew Clark Davison's absorbing, electric *Doubting Thomas* knows that just when you think the losses are behind you, more are on the way, and yet some losses are entangled with unexpected offerings: a fresh way to see, a chance to be of purpose again, and an invitation to love. A searing, candid debut."
— Paul Lisicky, author of *Later: My Life at the Edge of the World*

"*Doubting Thomas* is a phenomenal gift; a complex and careful layering of the inherent intersectionality of personhood, and a testament to the transcendent possibilities of storytelling. Heart wrenching and mending, Matthew Clark Davison proves in these pages that, in the hands of the right writer, a novel's humanity and craft can amplify one another to matching exaltation. *Doubting Thomas* reveals Davison as the preeminent among such writers, from whom the rest of us are lucky to learn."

—T Kira Madden, author of
Long Live the Tribe of Fatherless Girls

"An electrifying debut. *Doubting Thomas* is one of those novels where you return to passages again and again to see exactly how the author pulled off an ingenious sleight-of-hand. Matthew Clark Davison is a force to be reckoned with."

—Armistead Maupin, author of *Tales of the City*

"A wrenching professional crisis becomes the occasion for a man to reckon with everything that made him who he is—the loves of his past, his family, the very job he's in danger of losing. Is it possible to emerge from such a moment with hope and an open heart? The extremely talented Matthew Clark Davison offers an answer in the form of this very beautiful novel."

—Ann Packer, author of *The Dive From Clausen's Pier*

"What's so enviable, so thrilling in *Doubting Thomas* is how deeply realized these characters are . . . not just Thomas but every character brims with rich detail, nuanced psyche, the beautiful paradoxes of soul and being that make us human."

—Patrick Earl Ryan, author of the 2020 Flannery O'Connor Award-winning collection *If We Were Electric*

"In all my years of reading, I've never quite encountered a book like *Doubting Thomas*. What is seemingly a book about scandal and betrayal becomes, in Davison's skilled hands, a prismatic view of one man's grappling with the complexities of family, community, history, memory, and self. *Doubting Thomas* is nuanced, layered, detailed, and incredibly touching. In short, this is a fiercely complicated story, beautifully told."

—Zoela Renee Summerfield, author of
Every Other Weekend

"In Matthew Davison's *Doubting Thomas*, a gay man is accused of molesting one of his students, and is forced to turn his world inside out. With much grace and a deep understanding of both parenthood and friendship, Davison has meticulously chronicled love—wild and brotherly and even marital—into one man's battle to understand himself. Sex too—a treat for the sensuous."

—Terese Svoboda, author of *Great American Desert.*

"From the shock of the first sentence, through heart-rending twists and shifts, right through to the end, *Doubting Thomas* is a compulsively readable, brilliantly assured novel. Matthew Clark Davison creates such indelible characters, you'll miss them when you close the book."

—Justin Torres, author of *We the Animals*

DOUBTING THOMAS

MATTHEW CLARK DAVISON

AMBLE
PRESS
ANN ARBOR

2021

Print ISBN: 978-1-61294-199-8

Amble Press First Edition: June 2021

Printed in the United States of America on acid-free paper.

Cover design by Ann McMan, TreeHouse Studio,
Winston-Salem, NC

Amble Press
PO Box 3671
Ann Arbor MI 48106-3671

www.amblepressbooks.com

This novel is a work of fiction. Names, characters, places, and
incidents are the product of the author's imagination.

For Jon and Paul, my first two loves.

And for Barbara Ellen Clark and Robert Davison, for giving me brothers.

"Put your finger here; see my hands.
Reach out your hand and put it into my side.
Stop doubting and believe."
—John 20:26

"Whether the citizen lives or dies is not
a concern of the state.
What matters to the state and its records is
whether the citizen is alive or dead."
—J.M. Coetzee, *Diary of a Bad Year*

Chapter One

Wednesday
May 1st, 2013

A single word printed over the picture of Thomas and his fourth-grade class asked *Pedophile?* There it hung in Times New Roman bold, staring up from the online edition of the newspaper. He remembered the day that photo had been taken, only a year ago, when one of the parents snapped the candid shot as he and the kids lined up for a field trip beneath the oaks on the school grounds just as the Portland spring had started to give way to summer and geraniums had begun to dot the forest floor.

His body buzzed with a foreign set of sensations as he sipped mint tea. Only one other time, in college, had he felt something similar, the first of his HIV test results. Fear, yes. A tamped-down terror that buzzed in his chest, prickled and dampened the skin of his forehead, his scalp. Just as the mint had started to calm his stomach, another wave hit him as Thomas stared again at the on-line photo on his phone. His students' eyes were covered with black bars, the kind he'd seen thirty years ago on naked people in medical dictionaries when he and his older brother James were kids and would sneak away from the children's lit section and into the science room at the library.

Thomas clicked to *Contacts*, then *Family*, then *James*. Before the first ring, his older brother picked up, said hello. Up until now he hadn't told any of his family because up until today, even with all of his lawyer's warnings, he didn't believe there'd be reason.

"There's an unfortunate work situation," was all Thomas managed, imagining a national newspaper picking up the local story and James seeing it first. "If anyone contacts you, don't comment. And don't mention anything to anyone else in the family, especially the girls."

Just then, his lawyer, Jerome, pulled into Thomas's driveway and honked the horn. "More later," Thomas said, cutting his brother off. He got up and grabbed his rain jacket from the back of the chair, made his way to the door.

They met in Mercy's office first. Then in the vice principal's. Now it was time for the town hall. Once inside the recreation building, they walked toward the room normally used for school presentations. The arrangement of the space mimicked his own classroom, with a wall of windows opposite the entrance. A podium usually stood solo in front of all the glass, which never made sense to Thomas, because it backlit rather than highlighted the speaker. In his classroom, the same area was where his kids had circled for story time that day nearly a month ago. Here, two tables were assembled and angled at forty-five degrees to each side of the podium. Between the tables and the entrance, they'd put out seven rows of chairs. Thomas and Jerome had been instructed to sit at the table on the left, Lisa and Conrad Jay—Toby's parents—near the investigation teams on the right. Thomas pulled his phone from his pocket. His nephew had texted a moment before, *Another state votes to allow gay marriage!*

Victory! Thomas quickly typed and sent before turning off the ringer.

Thomas and Jerome took their places just before the Jays sat down. Had there been a judge sitting on a riser, the room would've resembled a courtroom instead of a community forum or town hall: Thomas with his lawyer on one side, one of the sheriffs and the district attorney and her team on the other. It struck Thomas that Mrs. Jay's dress looked like a man's oversized oxford shirt, and she kept playing with the built-in belt. She'd worn the same dress to the King Farmers' Market the Sunday morning after they'd hosted the fundraising party for the scholarship fund. Like the Jays, many Country Day parents lived in the West Hills, which was a considerable drive to northeast, and Thomas had been shopping at that farmers' market for years without ever encountering Country Day-ers. King's, unlike the other outdoor markets, had opened a month early this year, in April instead of May, so it drew a larger crowd.

He remembered the awkwardness as he and the Jays had looked into each other's canvas bags. Mrs. Jay talked about melon, about heirloom versus hothouse tomatoes, about kale—which kind is best, which to avoid, as if she were an expert on organic food instead of a person who led a sales team. She seemed relaxed, in charge. Her eye contact reassured Thomas that the incident with her husband from the fundraising party had gone unnoticed. In fact, the tone of their conversation reminded Thomas of her occasional appearances at her son Toby's bi-monthly parent/teacher conferences (which Conrad usually attended, solo), where her contributions seemed both urgent and meaningless, as if she were playing a game—not of domination, but certainly something to do with control. She needed to lead. If Thomas started in on Toby's social skills, she'd redirect to his reading comprehension. Her manner was compelling, convincing, as if by rerouting she'd uncovered the topic that everyone wanted to discuss all along.

This made Thomas wonder if it had been his own meekness that kept him from calling her right after the other incident— not the one at the party, with her husband, but the one in the classroom with her kid. The sheriff's report showed that Toby had said something after school that same day—the Friday *before* the fundraiser—and the Jays still invited him.

No matter what the order of events, he couldn't blame them for inquiring, even if they should've called sooner. Maybe it took the weekend to sink in? At the very least, it must've been confusing. If Toby, who didn't usually lie, indeed came home and told

3

them, as they claimed, that "Thomas touched my pants," they deserved to hear an explanation. But they'd been given one. The same one by several witnesses. Why hadn't that been enough? What were they doing here? Unable to think of another reason they'd taken this route, pushed it this far, Thomas could only think of the other incident: Conrad's dumb kiss at the fundraiser. He regretted not having said something then, too—to her—right then and there, at the party, and if not at the party, the farmers' market. But he had doubted himself.

Lisa Jay possessed a particular combination, a peculiar set of qualities that, individually, Thomas dealt with well: power, wealth, sincere directness, and a strange, almost masculine beauty. Having worked with kids of high-performing parents for years, and having grown up with his father, Thomas knew how to deal with alphas.

Mrs. Jay's particular mix, the ever-shifting emphasis on one or two traits over the others, and the relentless-seeming need to drive the narrative, threw him off, not because he found it distasteful; he didn't. He found it alluring. Sexy? Not only that, but Thomas wasn't completely sure she'd seen the kiss between her husband and himself, and if she hadn't, mentioning it would have caused trouble rather than alleviated it.

So, it had come to this. Now the parents and legal professionals arrived in ones and twos. Thomas watched Jerome as he arranged documents on the table. The faces of the parents looked dim, as did the room, which Thomas knew would stay that way until noon. The sun needed time to angle through the evergreens shading the building. He reached into his pocket and grabbed the Ziploc he'd filled with chalky pastel antacids. He'd been chewing on them for a month. He placed one in his mouth. It slowly dissolved as people packed themselves in. The clock showed ten. The facilitator said, "Time to get started." Jerome pulled files from a leather folder as Thomas sipped at a bottle of water, cleared his mouth of the bits of antacid, then took out his notebook and pen and braced himself to endure. Thomas scanned the rest of the space. Who were all these people? He only recognized about a dozen of the parents from his current class and previous years, all looking—not at him—but at their phones (this morning's headline?) while waiting for things to begin.

At their table, the Jays were joined by Mercy, Thomas's friend and boss, Head of School, who'd come in with Toby's psychologist and one of the sheriff's investigators. As they whispered to each other, Thomas recalled how he'd bumped into the Jays a second time that Sunday, the morning after the fundraiser, at the market. The first time at the fruit stand. The second time, they tasted pies at the bakery's tent. He'd said something silly about their outrageous price, like, "Is the crust made of gold?" to Mr. Jay, whose clean-shaven face appeared too white in contrast to his blackberry-stained lips. Then, "What a fun night last night. The food? Those oranges in the vodka tonics? Did you buy them here?"

Thomas should've known something had shifted, transpired between their first and second meeting, but he'd been too distracted, too self-conscious. He rarely ran into parents after work, unless on purpose, so he didn't think twice about what he was wearing until he noticed that Mrs. Jay, standing by the plexiglass display case full of pies, looked right at Thomas's groin. He wore his baggy weekend pants. They were too loose, and he hadn't worn underwear. A pause opened between them and then lingered. Mrs. Jay lifted her gaze to meet her husband's, but he stared down at his own bare wrist, as if he'd wished he'd worn a watch. Thomas waited, then tried to shift things by mentioning how well Toby had done in his group report. "Such a team player," they'd agreed, before Mrs. Jay said the impatient grandma was watching Toby, so they'd better get back. It seemed her mood had turned, from surprised to angry, and Thomas chastised himself. Maybe he shouldn't have gone to the party. He definitely shouldn't have gone upstairs alone with Conrad. He even swore at himself for leaving the house without wearing underwear. Still, he would have never guessed this from that.

∾ ∾ ∾

Mercy welcomed the parents. The sheriff painstakingly recounted each of the steps they'd taken in the investigation. Stubble covered Mr. Jay's face, his graying beard almost white against a Mediterranean complexion, his lips pale pink. He used his right hand to adjust the gold watch now on his left wrist. *Coward,* Thomas thought, as Conrad Jay kept repositioning himself, slouching, lowering his chin to chest—as if to shrink—as if to fit into his wife's shadow.

Mrs. Jay shifted her gaze between her husband, Toby's psychologist, Mercy, Jerome, the District Attorney, and the DA's assistant, who had taken over the role of facilitator. Up until today, Thomas had spent too much time wishing he could know Mrs. Jay's thoughts, get insight into what she hoped to prove. Now all he could think was *how dare she. How dare she punish me for the sins of other men.*

"The Jays aren't vindictive, they're confused," Thomas had, up until today, insisted to Jerome. He'd even been so stupid as to blame himself, playing and replaying Toby's solo section of his group report, when the class burst into applause. Toby froze then, too. The unexpected applause—like the unexpected laughter—derailed him. Thomas chastised himself for not mentioning the incidences, but, how could he? It didn't occur to him. Besides, mentioning them only explained Toby's behavior, not his parents'. Up until today his refrain had been, "The Jays give a lot of money to the scholarship fund. Toby is a kind kid who knows his parents love him and shouldn't be made to suffer because adults are making mistakes."

Jerome never wavered. Each time Thomas said something to defend them, Jerome replied, "You're caught in their web and you can't see it. Whatever the formal outcome, your life as you knew it will be over."

Nearly a month had passed since the incident. Three weeks since the call that forced Mercy to put him on leave. He'd endured two solid weeks of interrogation after interrogation, formal and informal, direct and indirect, legal and questionable; from the

District Attorney, from the sheriff's department, from his boss, and then, later, others, too, including one person he would have never guessed.

Thomas's certainty had not been easily arrived at, nor Pollyannaish, nor a product of laziness. His capacity to read others and predict how they'd react was hard-earned and came (not only) from spending the second half of his life so far observing children and their parents. He'd spent the first half feeling, when in his most natural state, like a complete outsider. His defensive strategy to assess and ward off any potential homophobic danger had, up until now, worked. His certainty—that this would be no big deal—resulted because facts had been gathered and cross-checked, experi-ences measured, behavior observed. Also, logic: Why would a pedophile molest a victim in a room of witnesses? And math: After five days a week in a classroom for twenty years (twelve at Country Day) with zero signs—recorded or rumored—of grooming or predatory behavior? And demographics: Country Day's per capita PhD ratio among parents could beat Boulder's and Marin County's and Berkeley's. In another school? Yes. In another place? Yes. But this was not a school nor a town that conflated an identity marker like gay with a criminal mental illness. The Jays and the other parents at Country Day liked science, liked facts.

His ability to observe then predict people and places, even the small stuff, like what you ate, where you lived, were frequently right. Thomas had built his life on his excellent judgement. Sprinkle or downpour? Knuckle sandwich or tongue-kiss? Vegan or meat-lover? Northeast or Northwest? When wrong, he was often close. He could easily clock the differences between gray skies and storm clouds; an ad exec who worked in the Pearl and a banker who commuted downtown; after meeting parents for the first time each fall, he could guess which of them would fill a lunch box with an apple and avocado slices on gluten-free bread and those who'd slip a turkey and cheese on whole wheat into a plastic bag.

No, he did not believe he had perfect judgement. There were exceptions. He had a hard time reading other gay men—this even

7

after spending his entire adult life living in liberal cities. This fact sometimes made it difficult to pick up on cues when traveling to conservative places like Colorado Springs, where his younger brother and mother lived. But he believed in his process.

When his hypotheses about others proved incorrect, he quickly saw his blind spots, and added those to the rest of his data, ensuring that he wouldn't quite misjudge two similar situations twice. He accounted for variables like sleep (or lack thereof) and hunger, drugs (those deemed criminal and those prescribed), religion and cultural influences, mood and personality, age and mental health, character. For Thomas, there was no umbrella broad enough to sufficiently arch over race, social status, gender, sexual orientation. Each was so full of individual experiences, there was only sky.

Still, he paid attention to how each of those and their various combinations could alter a current. Thomas didn't pretend to know it all, not even some, perhaps not even a little. Aware of how narrow (and in the grander scheme, infinitesimal) was his personal area of expertise, he'd trained himself to listen. To cooperate with experts. This was why, up until today, he'd kept his cool and remained sure. And up until today, he had maintained the belief that things would be fine, that his personal and professional life would return to normal. How myopic he'd been. Willfully naive.

Jerome said, "First we need to keep you out of prison. If we do that, and if the press reports on the case it could be good in the long run for the settlement." He meant for the defamation suit that Thomas didn't want. To get back into the classroom had been, up until today, up until this morning's headline, Thomas's only goal.

The DA's report took nearly an hour. When the arbiter called a break, Thomas walked to the men's room. Inside, there was one stall and two urinals. Someone made it to the stall first. Without dividers between the urinals, Thomas pivoted, attempted to angle his body for privacy, but Drew Ackerman came in, stood next to him and stared down—not like in gay clubs, where glances were born of curiosity or lust. Suddenly it seemed to Thomas as if Ackerman were accessing the enemy's weaponry.

Thomas wished he hadn't drunk so much tea because the surge of his urine sounded so (he hesitated, tried not to think it)—virile—splashing against the deodorized piss trap. He even wished his anatomy looked less ready, as Manny, his ex, used to say. Upon initial examination, Manny, a scientist raised in Germany, had made a verbal comparison and assessment of each of the two men's anatomy. "The before-and-after-arousal difference in your penis is almost entirely about density. It's all textural. Mine is both size and texture." Thomas flushed, had said, "In America, we say: I'm a show-er you're a grow-er."

Thomas finished, washed his hands, and walked, as quickly as he could, to retrace his steps behind the row of chairs so he could get back up the aisle to Jerome. In his haste, he tripped on a jogging stroller one of the mothers hadn't quite tucked away under the table by the door, with a trophy on it. A screw—something—on the stroller scraped a line of skin off his ankle. On his way down, he reached for the table to gain balance, but it collapsed a bit, and the trophy slid over. Out of its cup, four golf balls rolled to the floor and clicked as they bounced. Thomas maneuvered around the parents to collect the balls. After he returned them to the trophy's cup, he reassembled the folding table to flat, and then put the trophy back in its place. Not even Kenneth Cue, one of Jacob's two dads, budged to help.

When Kenneth and Ryan came in, Thomas assumed they had showed up for moral support. The three had season tickets to the Pops Series at the symphony on the same night. They'd run into each other a couple weeks ago at beer bust on the patio of The Eagle, where Thomas accepted a pint refill from their pitcher, all proceeds going to some marriage equality org. It had been an unusually warm April day when the trio sat together and laughed, watched a drag queen perform a lip-sync number to an old Madonna track as a shirtless barback circled the patio picking up empties. The day smelled of beer and cigarettes and the first bloom of jasmine. He'd only been to the bar a couple of times in all his years in Portland. The buzz of booze and springtime, the angle of the sun, the beat of the song, and the headiness of body odor and jasmine all combined into one of those halcyon moments that made sharing the experience with Kenneth and Ryan seem like so much more than it had been. Thomas had left the bar more than hopeful, he left feeling whole. Now, as Thomas smiled at them, they too looked down at their phones.

Jerome, sitting next to him, touched his arm as the final participants made their way back into the room. Mrs. Jay looked directly at Thomas for the first time since the town hall began. Her skin appeared slightly swollen. A youthful, vulnerable look that verged on sexual. She didn't get the attention she deserved. All eyes—the mothers' and Kenneth's and Ryan's—seemed to land on Conrad because of his goofy good looks and rugby-player's body. The other dads commented on his luck—rock-climbing and golfing and trekking while his rich wife worked, and his only kid went to school.

Thomas imagined Mrs. Jay naked under her shirtdress and remembered himself a kid at the library with his brother James. The two holed up in a corner studying the bodies of the women in the medical texts. Women who were underweight or overweight or suffering with crooked spines and bowed legs; lactating women, women with two very differently sized breasts—how entirely unanimated they were, standing there, captioned with case study numbers beneath them—and how different his reaction was from his brother's, who tore out the torsos with large round breasts, and tucked the images into his wallet.

Mrs. Jay maintained eye contact with Thomas until her expression shifted, deflated. He imagined her with that same look hunching down next to her son, pointing to his penis and asking, *Are you sure he didn't touch you here?* Repeating it until his *no* turned *I don't know* turned maybe turned *yes.*

10

As they summarized and recapped the earlier details of the investigations' findings, their talk sounded like a television playing in a room next door. It should've been comforting, because they iterated and reiterated Thomas's innocence—or, as they put it, lack of evidence sufficient to press criminal charges—and provided the community access to the adult witness. They brought copies of transcripts of the police interviews and the DA's investigation and used the word *transparency* a lot.

Country Day had hired child psychologists to interview Toby's classmates. Printouts of their summarized findings had been circulated and both psychologists answered questions. Because of this, because of the facts, he hadn't, until today, quite grasped what was happening here, even though Jerome had told him. Up until this morning's headline, Thomas had said, "No. You don't know the parents at Country Day. This isn't the school we attended as kids. Students at my school have two dads or two moms. You're worried about the wrong thing."

Thomas thought Jerome should focus on getting him back in the classroom, because he worried about the effect the misunderstanding would have on his kids' learning. He reached down, fingered the raw skin on his ankle, and as Jerome talked, everything was off, a bit blurry and difficult to follow. Thomas started to see it: Jerome wanted Thomas's presence to push Country Day-ers into saying things he could gather for his civil case.

From across their divide, Mercy listened, took notes, nodded; and Thomas remembered the day he'd met her, the day of his interview, summer of 2001. Her office sparkled. All glass and wood, surrounded by Country Day's near-choking foliage, wet and green, the drops on the glass and the glass itself created tiny prisms that fractured light from the early morning sun.

She'd looked much younger in person than in the photograph on the website. In person, she wore glasses, and her hair looked natural with caramel-tinted highlights along the top and ends, which added even more dimension to her face with its soft angles and rounded lines except for the sharpness of her cheekbones. Her gestures, like using the muscles around her nose to move her glasses higher on its bridge so she could continue to use both hands for papers, revealed a nerdiness that endeared Thomas to her because he recognized them in himself and other teachers. On the website's photo, she'd worn contacts and sported a wig, the same one she wore now, a style Thomas associated with Diahann Carroll, perhaps because, in person, Mercy's features had also reminded Thomas of the actress, even if her body language did not. Both had arched brows and wide brown eyes.

"So," she'd said, the day of his interview, interrupting after listening to Thomas lament about worksheets and teaching-to-testing and his ideas for the project-based learning model he dreamed of bringing to Country Day, "I was a scholarship student at Country Day. One of fewer than ten African American students, and the only Black person with a scholarship during the decade of my course of study. Back then they gave one scholarship per year. There were no openly LGBT students or faculty then."

Thomas had let that sink in. He thought of the brilliant kids in his crowded classrooms in San Francisco, especially those labeled as difficult or exhibiting behavior issues. Every year he'd receive a profile on each kid before meeting them. Thomas looked out the window at the wilderness surrounding this school and realized he'd never met a kid who wouldn't thrive in such a setting.

"If you hire me," Thomas said, leaning in, "I will gladly help raise scholarship cash and I will happily be your gay poster boy."

When the call came in, Mercy congratulated Thomas on being their first pick. After relocating, keeping up with his best friend Dana who stayed in San Francisco, his scattered family, his students and their parents, homework, cooking, and the gym—especially when Manny, his ex, was still around—proved difficult. Thomas didn't have time for a best friend in Portland. With Mercy, he hadn't needed one. Their professional relationship included friendship from the get-go.

Unlike most others who worked at Country Day, neither Thomas nor Mercy had their own children. For those eight hours,

Thomas felt like he and Mercy were the dad and mom at a big mansion in the forest. In a way, he'd found in Mercy what his brothers found with their partners—a person he loved who he could debrief and laugh with at the end of a day's hard work. Together, in the hours after the sun went down, they'd commiserate over the ongoing chore of convincing the board and PFA to move away from the school's traditions. They'd brainstormed strategies to leverage the fundraiser to significantly increase the number of students served by scholarships. When it came to the kitty, the board tended toward new buildings or upgrades and repairs on the property, and the PFA consistently voted in favor of additional opportunities for the tuition-paying students. Every major decision or change in policy needed a majority. As Head of School, Mercy represented the entire staff, but still needed to convince at least one of the other two governing bodies to vote with her. "That's where you come in," Mercy had repeated each year. This year they shared a chuckle about the steep inclines Obama must've faced post-Bush to get moderates and conservatives to hike over the hill toward something new. "If he can do it, so can we," they agreed, and together, Thomas and Mercy worked hard and had finally convinced the PFA to remove the scholarship cap.

And then the town hall ended. All the authorities: the sheriff, the District Attorney and her assistant, the psychologist and social worker had given their reports, which exonerated Thomas.

Mercy stood, waited for a moment, and crossed the room, barely nodding at Thomas but smiling at the parents. It was the same smile she had worn a couple months back when one of the moms, in the middle of a discussion at a PFA meeting, interrupted Mercy, and, apropos of nothing, said, "Oh my god, I love Janelle Monáe. I'd totally be gay for her." After, Thomas had asked Mercy why she didn't tell the mom off. "You're the one who should've done that," she said, and Thomas, after he thought about it, agreed. True to her name, she tried joking, perhaps to alleviate the truth's sting, a habit of hers he'd witnessed many times. "At least when I reported the number of scholarship students—one hundred and one—none of the parents suggested we call them Dalmatians," Mercy had said. She laughed. Thomas had remained silent, ashamed.

As the rest of the room shifted toward the exit, Thomas waited to see Mr. and Mrs. Jay's faces, but they did not look over. Everyone else spoke in hushed tones, as if exiting a theater just after the end of a good film.

Jerome whispered words of encouragement. The rest of the parents moved quickly, like a pack of rats. One parent said something almost audible. Something that Thomas first heard as, "Thank god. I knew he didn't do it." But then they did not stop.

As they passed through the door, the phrase replayed in Thomas's mind as, "Dear god, they couldn't prove it."

Thomas couldn't feel his skin, his face. A mom with a toddler grabbed the expensive jogging stroller that had tripped Thomas, and he imagined her starting her jog behind it, pushing and gaining speed. He envisioned the front wheels, their screws loosening as she pumped her sinewy legs, pushing the stroller faster and faster as the wheels reached the end of the bolts and finally fell off, forcing the buggy to an abrupt stop, sending the toddler flying up and up toward the sun starting to set behind the oaken skyline.

Thomas silently repeated, *I'll get through this, I'll get through this, everything will be all right.* He tried to believe the words. After all, he'd been through worse, right? The breakup with Manny. His brother's health issues. Weren't they worse than this? Weren't they?

Thomas shook as they waited for Mercy and the Jays to exit. Jerome grabbed Thomas, hugged him. Thomas rested his chin on Jerome's shoulder and watched.

Chapter Two

A Year Earlier
April 2012

Two weeks had passed since Thomas's breakup. Before the calls, before the wind had cleared the sky of its clouds, the storm had awoken him, and Thomas laid on his back, eyes open in the dark, imagining his bed a tent in the middle of the woods; the top sheet a roof to house his funk. He knew he'd have to return to Country Day the next morning to teach, but that day he'd wanted to stay at Camp Misery, punish himself with his own stink. The black s's and c's of Manny's body hair still peppered the fitted sheet, and without him there, Thomas's mattress felt vast and lonely. Like failure.

He'd been squeezing, wondering how much longer he could keep the liquid in his bladder when his phone rang for a second time. His nieces and nephew only texted, and none of the parents at Country Day would call that early on Sunday. It had to be a robot; a telephone solicitor. He needed to add his number to the "Do Not Call" list. He needed to do a lot of things. A cantaloupe he could smell from his bedroom sat in a fruit bowl on the counter; a pot of black beans in the fridge had long since fermented into something unholy; a pile of mail and tax documents on the desk had yet to be opened or filed. Through the thunder and rain, he imagined the weeds along his walkway laughing like cartoon villains, planning their takeover.

It kept ringing. He got up, grabbed his khakis from the floor on his way to the bathroom, and fiddled his phone out of the front pocket, hoping it was Manny.

Manny, whose full name was Emmanuel Koroma—his dad, a Sierra Leonian doctor who met his mom, a German artist, in Germany during his residency—had been stubborn (a characteristic Manny attributed to his mom), stoic (something he learned from his dad who'd endured all sorts of racism in Germany), and almost psychotically practical (something Thomas ascribed to Manny being a German and a scientist). Thomas didn't do depression, didn't believe in self-pity as a solution to anything. His disgust in himself for his inactivity deepened the depression that caused the inactivity and made him feel like a snake eating his own tail. He managed to hold it together all day all week, but since the breakup, he spent evenings and weekends in a vortex of crunchy Cheetos, sleep, and bad TV.

In front of the mirror, he paused. Studied his pale face, his salt-swollen eyes, the uneven arc where his forehead met hairline. Your furrows cut deep enough to plant corn, Manny had occasionally teased whenever Thomas worried. Placing his head under the faucet, he gulped as the water poured into and around the sides of his mouth. When he finished, he numbered in the phone's passcode.

Manny had not called. His younger brother's wife, Sheree, and his older brother, James, were the names that appeared on the display under Missed Calls. Thomas felt a sharp jab, a prick of pain in his right side after reading James's text from an hour before. *Call me now. Emergency.*

James picked up before the end of the first ring. "It's Junkels," he said, using their younger brother's nickname. "Neck cancer."

Jake, the youngest of the three McGurrin brothers, had just turned thirty-seven. He and his wife, Sheree, and son, Max, lived in a small, impeccably kept two-bedroom house nine miles from the Colorado Springs airport, toward the base of Pike's Peak.

After referring to Jake, tenderly, as *The Junkie* and *Junk* for years, Thomas and his family now called Jake *Junkels*.

Jake's nickname hadn't always been endearing. Jake's overdoses and months gone missing had kept Thomas and James and their parents on high alert for all of the 1990s. Thirteen years ago Jake had cleaned up, found the twelve steps and God, then married his rehab sweetheart. Eleven years ago, he had become dad to Max. Ten years ago, Jake had tattooed the names of his wife and son on the skin on the outside of his neck. Five years ago, he had moved into his first house. Two days ago, Jake had gone to the doctor after the brothers' mother, Maddy, noticed the odd way Jake strained when swallowing. That morning, James told Thomas that Jake had received a call—from a doctor on a Sunday at dawn—that the cancer cells had multiplied and spread into the tissue at the base of his tongue and on the inside of his tattooed neck.

"You need to prepare yourself for Jake to be dead in three months," James, the doctor, the pragmatist, the straight shooter, said. Always the unmediated knee-jerk speaker, compelled to deliver the most direct, least censored version of what he was thinking, as if doing so meant avoiding the complexities of human emotion.

Thomas hung up. He thought he'd call Jake immediately, but found himself back in the bedroom stripping his bed of its sheets, picking up the clothes strewn across the dark wood floor. "No," he said, after pressing start on the washing machine, again after opening the window shades, after hollowing the seedy guts from the center of the cantaloupe he'd sliced in two. He added the cut-up rind and black beans to the compost, then went outside to yank weeds. When finished, he attacked the pile of two weeks' worth of mail until he'd recycled or filed every piece. "No," Thomas said afterward, still sitting at his desk, as he turned on his laptop and finally called Jake. As the phone rang, pain radiated from his side upward through his scapula and neck to the crown of his head. Then a moment of relief. It could be their game. Their April Fools.

Sheree picked up. "Tommy?" she said. "Did you hear about Jake?"

"Yes," Thomas said.

"I can't," she said, and Thomas immediately knew this was no joke. "I can't. I can't. I can't," reminding Thomas of the last time he'd heard her speak those words to him on the phone. "I can't," Sheree had said, that time too. "It's too much, Tommy," she'd repeated, three months after Trayvon Martin had been murdered after buying a bag of Skittles at 7-Eleven. "Another boy. It's videoed, again," she'd said, fury traveling from her whisper to his ear. It spread through Thomas, like the gasoline that had spilled into the puddle on the blacktop near the end of his driveway, a prism of color. The low, raw tones of Sheree's voice, grief and rage, then and now.

Chapter Three

April 2012

"Homo!"

James's voice ricocheted off the metal conveyer set along the wall decorated with a pastel painting of the Rocky Mountains. But Thomas didn't hear his older brother correctly, even when he yelled it again, the second time like a question: "Homo?"

Thomas recognized the timbre of James's voice as he looked in the direction of the sound: a rich, smooth baritone. He'd thought his brother was calling, "Hello?" So Thomas called back. "Over here!" he said, waving. "I'm here," he repeated, scanning the people by the car rental desks and the airport's Visitor Information Center.

The two older McGurrin brothers were in Colorado Springs for the first time since Jake's diagnosis. James, with his medical contacts, his ability to analyze and galvanize; Thomas, with his capacity to listen, and execute on a plan. The two would now join forces, relieve Sheree and Jake and Max of some of the worry.

Thomas hefted his backpack higher onto his shoulders and looked through the small airport crowd. With the constant addition and subtraction of states offering marriage to same-sex couples, since they'd ruled Prop 8 unconstitutional, and especially since his and Manny's breakup, Thomas had, for the first time, become hyperaware of left hands. Ring fingers, sporting every sort of precious metal and stone, gathered light and sent sparks. Wedding rings were suddenly everywhere: on the mom holding an infant's head; a dad hefting, then tossing, then catching his daughter as she laughed.

As he made his way between the airport entrance and where Thomas stood at the baggage claim, James's smile seemed to float in front of the rest of him. It wasn't a squeal; more of a clear, high-pitched note that erupted from a space somewhere in between Thomas's chest and throat, a primal excitement, delight at seeing his big brother. And not just excitement, but also relief. The news of Jake's cancer had wound Thomas up, wrung out the loneliness from the breakup, and invigorated him out of depression with a panicky edge he hadn't felt in years: The kind of manic dread that had started in childhood, continued in high school, then enveloped him completely during Jake's active-addict years, which coincided with the AIDS years and Thomas's coming out.

"Give me a real hug, you faggot," James said, too loudly, keeping Thomas squeezed to him. James's phone rang, and he released Thomas to answer. Thomas looked back to the carousel; saw his luggage, walked the few feet and lunged, but missed it. A man in an Air Force uniform grabbed the bag, handed it to Thomas. "You and your boyfriend," he said. "Watch the antics around my kids."

"That's my brother," Thomas said, feeling his face heat up. "Not my boyfriend."

The breast of the man's jacket was decorated with colorful pins and patches that Thomas suddenly wanted to rip off. Not today, Thomas thought. He sized the guy up and felt certain that he could hold his own in a brawl—but the guy's kid stood there smiling at him like Thomas was holding out a balloon, and before Thomas could throw a punch or tell him off, the man had already turned around and plucked a hard-sided suitcase from the center of a bundle of duffels. As he made toward the exit, his wife and kids followed. His kid turned back to wave at Thomas as she hopped along the blue and brown geometric patterned carpet. James finished his call, put his phone in his jacket pocket. "Jake refused to have any part of his tongue or jaw removed, and the doctors have six weeks to agree on the exact combination of radiation and chemotherapy. He needs us to get him into shape."

Zombiesque images of Jake's face without a jaw and tongue developed in Thomas's imagination. He tried to repack them, zip them away and replace them with the Jake-face he always thought of first. The pre-dental work, still freckle-faced Jake with a swoosh of bangs, hair sun-bleached a dark golden blond.

"What did that guy say to you?" James asked, motioning toward the door.

"He thought we were lovers," Thomas said. James's skin had a strange yellowish-pink hue, like it had been stained with saffron, then scrubbed with a brush. "He was afraid we might have sex in front of his kids."

"Seriously? Fucking redneck," James said. "Should we go after him?"

Thomas looked up to the blue-painted ceiling, then back at his brother. "No. And just for the record, the look-at-me-I-have-a-gay-brother bit has gotten old. People around here carry guns," Thomas said. "Assault rifles."

James took Thomas's face into his hands. "I'm sorry," he said. "You and Jake. Always so paranoid."

"Well," Thomas said, pulling away. "Jake's wife and kid are Black. Have you turned on the TV?"

"Yes," James smiled. "And I see the Black president and gay men on every channel. Ready?" he said, and James took Thomas's suitcase. "What's in the huge backpack?"

"Next time you pull a stunt like that in public, you'll find out. I'll knock you in the head with it."

The rolling wheels on the suitcase suddenly stopped. Thomas looked at his and James's reflection in the glass. As kids, they'd looked nothing alike. James resembled Stuart, their dad; and Thomas was a near replica of Maddy, their mom. James was still shorter and broader than Thomas, but now, at forty-three and forty-five, the men could pass as twins. "Are you serious?" James asked.

"Don't you get it?" Thomas said. "What always happens after progress? Backlash and revenge."

Chapter Four

Mid–February 2013

Every five years or so it snowed enough to turn Portland from green to white. While visitors loved the city's flora, it could assert itself on its inhabitants like a bully, reminding everyone who ruled. Douglas and silver firs ganged up with western hemlocks. The forest provided cover, but also cast shadows.

Thomas's flight from Colorado had landed safely that afternoon, but Mercy's too-careful driving through the snow from the airport had made Thomas carsick. Once home, he used a Jake-trick: ate an entire sleeve of Saltines, washing them down with mineral water infused with floating slices cut from a knuckle of fresh ginger. Now, with evening upon him, Thomas imagined himself a winter bird looking down from above as he watched out of the kitchen window as a cross-country skier left a pair of parallel lines in his snowy wake. He cooked a ground turkey chili, lunch for the upcoming school week, and willed the snow to stop because if it kept up, Mercy would call a snow day. Desperate for distraction, Thomas wanted to get back to work. He ladled the chili into containers to cool on the counter, cranked up the heat, and plopped himself on the couch. He listened as the snow turned to rain, and the rain to ice. Then the frozen needles of the evergreen tapped the glass of his living room window.

By the time the phone rang, it had gone too dark in Thomas's house to see. He reached over the coffee table and turned on the lamp. The room glowed a reddish gold, a color similar to his best friend's thick hair. Dana and Thomas caught up by phone most Sunday evenings, and after the usual hellos and how are yous, Thomas admitted that every time he returned from Colorado Springs, he missed Manny like nuts. She said into the phone, "Of course. Cancer is grueling and Manny made you laugh. It's been a long time. Have you even called? Told him about Jake?"

"I'm not using the brother-with-cancer card to get the ex's sympathy," Thomas said. The tone Dana used when speaking Manny's name—one of tenderness—caused Thomas's cheeks to go hot. Odd. Other than Mercy, he'd told no one at Country Day about the breakup with Manny, nor of Jake's cancer. Not one of his fourth graders, and certainly none of their parents. Mercy finally agreed to "professional development" as the white lie to account for the occasional Friday or Monday he'd taken off to go to Colorado in the nine months since Jake's diagnosis. Mercy had said, "You could tell them. Openness is a C-Day core value." She tried to convince him to discuss Jake's cancer with his students. "And you can always mention that you're sad because you miss someone you love. Appropriately," she'd added.

No way.

Before and after work and on weekends he dealt with cancer and the fact of being single again. But he didn't want to contend with his students' or their parents' reactions. He needed their neediness for problems he could solve.

Thomas had first called Dana a week after the initial diagnosis, when James's medical school buddy in Head and Neck Oncology at Memorial Sloan Kettering helped the team in Colorado Springs finalize the diagnosis and treatment plan. Jake's cancer turned out to be HPV-related. Originally, the slides had made it look like another, less treatable strain. James revised his original, grim prediction to, "if the treatments don't kill him, he'll survive."

"Are you sure I can't join you for Easter?" Dana asked.

"I'm positive. If the PET scans are bad, it'll be a shit show," Thomas said.

Thomas looked out the window. He'd been fine earlier, but now, talking about Manny and his family, his little house in Portland felt as empty and sprawling as the desert plains he'd left behind when he returned from Colorado. Across the street, his neighbors, the Jurakas, had a walnut tree in front of the spotlight above the garage. The wind made the bare branches cast shadows. He felt his evening dread creeping in.

"I'd never be able to work under your circumstances," Dana said. "What are you going to do tonight? Please don't say stay home and grade papers."

"You're just allergic to work," Thomas said into his phone. "For some of us, it's a relief."

Thomas had cried only once since the breakup and Jake's diagnosis. The two events had become intertwined in his psyche. Like the sides that made up his brain, each had its own set of characteristics and caused its own set of reactions, but they'd also merged into a big blob, affecting everything. A month or so after Manny left, just a couple weeks after his brother's diagnosis, one of Thomas's students, Toby Jay—while attempting a complex series of folds to create an origami frog—reminded Thomas of Jake as a boy. He'd remembered Jake with the other neighborhood kids his age. They'd lined up little toads—a half a dozen or so that they'd gathered from the stream running through the backyard—under the McGurrin's garage door. Cheered on by the other kids, who'd squatted down and tried to keep them from jumping out of line, Jake pressed the garage door button, and before Thomas had realized what they were up to, they'd squashed them all, leaving their skins emptied of their little yellow and white gut sacks.

Jake had reveled in the other boys' attention as he bragged about his dad's electric door opener, but later, he wept after Maddy smacked his face and made him scrub the dried entrails from the pavement with bucket and brush. That memory opened up to a feeling so intense and distant, Thomas couldn't recognize it as his own. He went mute in front of his class in the middle of a sentence. In that pause, he imagined it evening already, at home next to Manny, recalling both stories, the one of Toby with the origami frog and the one with little Jake with the squished toads. When he realized Manny wouldn't be there, Thomas motioned to his aide to take over, locked himself in the bathroom and sobbed. When it had finally passed, he could smell his own body's odor under his woodsy, citrusy cologne.

Now a pile of his fourth graders' papers sat next to him on the couch. He swallowed, said, "I'm behind. Besides, I can't go out. I'm all dried up."

"Bullshit," Dana said. "The forties are the new thirties. You're in great shape."

"I meant my sinuses," Thomas said. "Colorado? The airplane?"

They laughed. He felt something rigid in the pocket of his hoodie. Thomas and his nephew Max had worked on a thousand-piece jigsaw over the last visit, an image of an elephant walking toward the photographer's camera, Kilimanjaro in the background like a camel's hump on the elephant's back.

He pulled the small jagged piece of shellacked cardboard from his sweatshirt pocket and stared at it for a long time. Finally, he rotated it forty-five degrees so blue was on top. Under it, dabs of white over brown. A smidge of snow on the tip of the mountain. A tiny piece of sky.

"I've got a date," Dana said, with a slight tremolo.

"Another bored housewife?" Thomas asked, picturing Dana on her couch with Otto, the purring Himalayan, circling her lap.

"Um, no, and fuck you very much," she said. "That was a phase, not a habit. This one is butch. Like out-and-in-the-WNBA butch. But that's all you're getting. I don't want to jinx it."

"She sounds cute," Thomas said.

"She is. And she's got a huge cock," Dana said. "A whole collection of them."

The image of his best friend shifted from couch and cat and herbal tea to bed and box of dildos. "Charming," Thomas said, and they laughed again. Dana kept him from going morbid. As much now as when the two had met nearly twenty years ago in Berkeley, at Cal, during grad school.

"Speaking of cute and butch, how's our Max?" Dana asked. "Is your nephew gay yet?"

"Not yet, but there's progress," Thomas said, making his way back to the kitchen, turning on the light. "He's the public defender of same-sex marriage in Colorado Springs. Quite the little activist."

"Good," Dana said. "We need him."

"It makes me nervous. He's dealing with classmates whose parents are involved with those weird megachurches and he's the only Black kid in his class." Thomas lidded the plastic containers of chili, now just a bit warmer than room temperature.

"They should move to Portland. Max should go to Country Day," Dana said.

"Totally," Thomas said. Even with Mercy's recruiting efforts, Country Day had a smaller percentage of Black students than Max's school. He closed the refrigerator door and headed to his office. "Jake and Sheree worry. And who could blame them?"

"No one. Aren't the Springs the headquarters for Focus on the Family or whatever it's called? And don't they have an active chapter of the KKK there?" Dana asked.

"Yes on the first. Not sure on the second," Thomas said, but he remembered the first time he'd taken Max to the Cheyenne Mountain Zoo. A mom feeding the giraffes looked at Thomas holding four-year-old Max. She called him a n-lover. Actually used the n-word. The giraffe's giant black tongue grabbed the cracker the woman had balanced on her open palm. Then her pink-faced daughter said the word again, pointing at Max, before mother and daughter joined hands, turned and walked toward the elephants, leaving Max and Thomas and the giraffe silent, blinking. By the time he'd collected his wits and recovered from shock, it was too late. His fury turned to guilt for not defending his nephew—too stunned to talk back to the woman. When he returned home, he immediately reported it to Jake, who said, "What kind of bubble do you live in that you're so shocked? Shit like that happens all the time." Sheree looked at Jake and laughed at Thomas's naivete. "This here," Sheree said, grabbing Max, pointing at Thomas and Jake. "It's whiteness. We don't have that," she said.

Sitting at his desk, phone pressed to his ear, Thomas pulled an envelope from the drawer and put the puzzle piece inside.

"My date just texted. She's waiting outside," Dana said. "Send Max my love."

"Do everything I wouldn't do," Thomas said, lingering on his best friend's phrase, imagining love an object one could send. He thought of wrapping the puzzle piece in a sheet of tissue paper, the kind they use at fancy stores. He licked the glue, sealed the envelope. The two hung up.

Thomas went and turned on the outside flood light to check on the snow and rain from the living room window. A pair of eyes reflected the light and startled him. Whose dog had gotten into his yard on this too-cold night? After locking gazes, Thomas realized that it wasn't a dog, but a coyote, with a rabbit or squirrel in its long snout. The animal's lean body was covered in thick gray-brown fur, gorgeous against the surrounding white. Its long, bushy tail waved once from side to side.

"Hello," Thomas said, and tapped his finger on the window.

Last year, in a unit on local Native American mythology, a storyteller from the Wasco tribe had come to Country Day for a mini assembly. "Sometimes," the man said, "the coyote is a hero; in other stories, he's greedy, reckless, and arrogant. In still others, he is a comic trickster. Lack of wisdom gets him into trouble, cleverness gets him out."

"Then is he a hero or a fool?" one of the kids asked.

"He's both," the storyteller said, looking weary. Later, Thomas heard the man in the hallway on his phone, soon after shaking Thomas's hand and graciously receiving the praise of the other teachers, as he said, "I'm tired of bullshit one-hour gigs that take an hour to get to. They're not really interested in us. They're just checking a box."

Now the real coyote put the squirrel on the snow and looked up to Thomas.

"It's not mine," Thomas said. "Take it."

As if the animal could hear through the glass, the coyote picked up its meal, turned around, crossed the street and pranced into the Juraka's yard before disappearing into the woods.

Chapter Five

Saturday
March 30th, 2013

The McGurrins were desperate to hear the word *clean*.

When he lived in San Francisco, Thomas had celebrated his birthday every year at the airport with Dana. Pre-9/11, the two would pass through security without a boarding pass to imitate the runway struts of '90s supermodels on the moving walkways. They'd pack luggage with stupid costumes: bad wigs and boas, fake mustaches and Foster Grant tinted eyeglasses. They'd change in the bathroom then head for the bars, Dana first. Soon, Thomas would come in and ask the cocktail server to send her a second drink. "I'm married," she'd say. "I don't mind," Thomas would respond, loud enough for others to hear. Once everyone was listening, Dana would add, "Neither will my husband."

Now it was hard to believe that was once shocking. Harder to believe that airports were once fun. Now they were bearable if you had the cash for upgrades, VIP lines and lounges. Everyone else, Thomas thought, better prepare to be humiliated. After nine months of Jake's cancer, Thomas had become as bitter and efficient as the flight crews whose members seemed programmed to switch from kind to downright sadistic, depending on how they deemed your tone when asking for a tinfoil bag that held five nuts.

James and his family had flown to Colorado from New York a day ahead of Thomas. Thomas texted him his location, and five minutes later James pulled up alone in a luxury SUV, the same model owned by all the Country Day moms who didn't have a Prius. The mega-mobile had enough room not only for James, his wife, three girls and all their ski and snowboarding equipment, but also for an additional family. A Mormon one, Thomas thought, getting in.

The brothers talked about flights, food, and their mom's mood. James told Thomas about the New Jersey lottery winner who'd received over three hundred million. "Turns out the guy owes over twenty grand in child support," James said, arguing that good things rarely happened to good people.

"You're a pessimist because you like the attention it gets you," Thomas said. "Karma is real."

"No, it's not. If it were, teachers would be rewarded before they go to heaven."

"Teachers are rewarded," Thomas said. "With job satisfaction and summers off."

"Neither of those gets you a car like this."

"Who would want one?" Thomas said, only to banter. Truth be told, he loved the heated seats. "When do Jake's results come in?"

"This afternoon," James said. "He'll go to his NA meeting, then get the results alone."

"Of course," Thomas said. "Our Junkels. The Lone Ranger."

The six-week and six-month scans had both showed hotspots. While troublesome, the oncologists said it was normal. "Clear on the year is what we want to hear," James kept saying.

As the GPS directed James, the visit seemed more and more to Thomas like a setup for disaster, everyone gathering without knowing the result. Thomas had tried to talk them out of the party, to postpone, but Sheree insisted on timing it with Easter. "If Jesus could rise from the dead your brother can survive cancer. Shit," she'd said, "with everything else he's survived?" James pulled the SUV onto the highway, and Thomas thought of the

African elephants at The Cheyenne Mountain Zoo, the engine's deep rumble like the mammoth animals gulping their water. Max loved those elephants and Thomas knew he would also get a kick out of his Uncle James's fancy car rental, with its touch screens built into the backs of the headrests.

"This for me?" Thomas asked, taking one of the two water bottles from the center console.

"Have both. I'm too nervous to swallow."

"I'm worried, too," Thomas said, and grabbed his brother's hand. He held it until James squeezed back, then let it go. His profile resembled their dad's, and it reminded Thomas of when he and James were kids, before Jake was born. Drowsy, Thomas closed his eyes and watched his memories of sharing the back seat, driving the coast from California to Oregon, the TripTik maps Maddy procured at the AAA office. The only screen the McGurrin boys used back then prevented sunburn. For entertainment, Thomas and James thumb wrestled, made hand puppets from empty potato chip bags, picked and flung their dried snot or their scabs, whichever they had. They competed for finding license plates from the highest number of states; or they sang "one hundred bottles of beer on the wall" all the way down to one.

Thomas woke up in Colorado Springs. Remnants of dirty snow and ice still lingered on the corners of the embankments and center divides of Route 21; bright green dotted the crabapples' and dogwoods' branches as the first buds unfurled their leaves. He pulled down his sun visor and looked in the mirror. Thomas pressed his water bottle to the dark circles under his eyes.

"If they didn't get all of it, there's nothing more they can do," James said, his words coming out fast, as if he'd been waiting a long time for Thomas to wake up. "His liver can't take any more chemo. Radiation will turn his teeth to dust. His immune system is already shot and he's susceptible to opportunistic infections."

Thomas shivered. He hated his associations with those two words—opportunistic infections—hated having to add the image

31

of his younger brother to those he held from college in California, when he'd first cared for someone who'd gotten sick because of AIDS. "Fingers crossed they got it all," Thomas said, trying, lamely, to comfort his brother.

"The poor kid," James said, frothing with worry.

James's relationship with Jake seemed so different from his own. Paternal. Made sense, given their seven-year age difference. Thomas used to think that James hated Jake, hated anyone who showed signs of weakness. After their dad had left, Maddy, their mom, had spells that sent her to bed for weeks. The Dark Place, the McGurrin boys called it, and talked about it like it was an actual place—a block without streetlights where bullies lurked— one that could be avoided by careful maneuvering. Once James realized that no alternative route could prevent Maddy's trips to The Dark Place, he avoided her, throwing himself into extracurricular activities: girlfriends and soccer and biology club and National Honor Society.

Jake's drug problem—which he called his dirty dance with downers—hit its peak when Thomas started teaching, and James started his residency. Both brothers showed up during the rehab days, but Thomas guessed that James felt as guilty as Thomas did about the years that had preceded them, when they'd each gone their separate ways: Thomas to Berkeley and James to New York, leaving Jake alone with Maddy, now divorced from their dad, in The Dark Place.

The sky and the pavement and the dead grass on front yards all shared a similar shade of gray as the afternoon whittled down to dusk. The SUV glided past houses with front-yard porches sporting limp American flags. Thomas decided he'd been wrong about his brother. James didn't hate weakness. He feared vulnerability, and Thomas didn't know what to say to comfort him.

"What are your students up to this time of year?" James asked.

"A vegan chef just taught them how to make a terrine from mushrooms they'd foraged," Thomas said.

"Foraged from where?" James asked. A smile appeared more in his eyes than his mouth. "Whole Foods?"

"The school grounds," Thomas said, relieved that he could distract James.

"I can't remember," James said, and asked Thomas how long he'd been in Portland.

"Twelve years," Thomas said, and slammed the visor back into place.

"Wow," James said, digging in the pocket of his down jacket. "Time effing flies. Can't you open a Country Day in Manhattan? For the girls? The one good thing about the cancer is seeing you and Jake. I miss you guys."

Thomas attempted a smile, but James's compliment didn't land; he'd invited James to visit Portland a dozen times over the years. He'd always imagined his brother presenting on career day, James showing the students the tiny camera he used for his hip surgeries. He imagined taking James on his trail runs in the morning and treating him to Portland's best restaurants at night.

"How does he look?" Thomas asked.

"The same," James said, handing Thomas a pack of gum. "Awful. A bit better."

The last time Thomas had seen Jake, he'd been at his lowest adult weight, including the heroin years. He'd shed fifty pounds during chemo and radiation. Jake's sunken eyes and the impossible-seeming leanness of his face, his legs, and butt made Thomas recall his first boyfriend, Tony, after he'd gotten sick, and the too-many men who wandered San Francisco's Castro district during Thomas's college days, the worst of the AIDS years in America.

"There's still enough snow to ski?" Thomas asked, taking two pieces of the minty gum out of their little plastic shells. "In March?"

"Yes," James said, then pointed to his open mouth.

Thomas put one of the little gum squares onto his brother's tongue, thinking again about Tony Tempesta, his alliterative last name which meant "storm" in Italian. Thomas wondered if he'd be able to find Tony's family in Florida. What with social media and the internet. If he did, what might he say, now?

James chewed and told Thomas, "We'll only ski if it's good news. If it's not, the girls will go home, and I'll stick around. Fingers crossed. Nothing better than a suntan on a ski slope."

Thomas grabbed his water bottle, raised it. "Here's hoping for a good scan."

The SUV was too big for the pebble path that led to the parking spaces behind Jake and Sheree's house, so James parked at the curb, and when Thomas pulled his small suitcase from the back seat, he braced himself for the crowd. Thomas liked small groups best. He'd max out at four or five before it became stressful. On the plane, he'd counted: three nieces, a nephew, two brothers, two sisters-in-law, his mom, his dad, Stuart's wife. Jake's house like a cardboard egg carton with an unfilled vacancy in one of the cups. As he walked toward the door, he imagined the McGurrins a bunch of Easter eggs. He'd complete the dozen.

The front door opened. Their stepmom Dot stood on the top of the landing, her palm flat on the frame. "Jimmy's back with Tommy," she announced to the people inside. Thomas kissed her cheek. Clear and green, his stepmother's eyes held the light like malachite, a crystal one of his kids had written about earlier in the week. She barely wore makeup, save a smidge of lipstick. Stylishly cut, she colored her short hair a believable shade of light brown.

Thomas followed James into the house's biggest room. "Hi Dad," Thomas said to Stuart, who stood up from the recliner. Old Nesta, the rescue mutt, was resting on a pillow under the TV. He lifted his head and let out a couple of barks, then lowered it back down and closed his eyes. James sat down on the couch in front of the basketball game.

As they hugged, Thomas could smell Dot's brand of fabric softener on his dad's shirt. On the coffee table, the elephant puzzle, which Max had completed, lay under the envelope Thomas had used to send the last piece.

Stuart stepped back, looked at Thomas. "So glad you're here."

Jake's wife Sheree came in, wearing an apron with "You're Doing the Dishes" printed on it. Thomas kissed her. Sheree stood shorter than usual. In the house and at her salon she almost always wore those clogs that chefs wear, but now her feet were swaddled in the thick knitted socks Dot had given everyone for Christmas. She looked good. The entire time Thomas had known her, Sheree prioritized her physical and mental health, and gave all the McGurrins something to aspire to: whether exercise, diet, support groups, volunteering. She talked about HIV often, and Thomas hated to admit how uncomfortable it made him. He saw her life as an utter success, and worried about her tendency to keep the past so present. Sheree expressed definite opinions about how gay white men erased others when talking about their own losses and struggles because of HIV, particularly Black women. But Thomas was negative, informed of the statistics, didn't argue, didn't talk about his painful past because of his proximity to HIV or AIDS. Until recently, Sheree's insistence on talking about it seemed to Thomas less of a worry or true concern and more part of her activism. Like others he'd met who'd seroconverted in the late nineties, she took antiretrovirals, stayed healthy. When his mom told him—Sheree had just recovered from two recent HIV-related scares: pneumonia and shingles, one right after the other—it startled Thomas into a new reality. He told his mother in those exact words. "Not new. New for you," Maddy had replied back.

"Where are the kids?" Thomas asked.

"Max took the girls to the skateboard park," she said. "God help them."

"Jake? Joyce? Maddy?" Thomas asked.

"Your mom and Joyce went to buy a cord for Joyce's phone, then to fetch fresh tortillas. Jake'll be home with the news in an hour. That is, if the doctors have it. He texted me that they're still waiting, too."

"Isn't it a bit much?" Thomas said to his sister-in-law. "All of this anticipation? How are you holding up?"

"Now that I got Reggie out of here for a while, I'm better. He decided to drop by, unannounced," she said, "My hair looks good, right?"

Reginald was Sheree's older brother, and her only living family. He'd always been kind to Thomas, engaging. Opinionated about politics (he liked what Obama represented more than Obama's policies: "I already love him, but I want to love him more. He's too moderate, too careful.") charming with Maddy ("You're like my mom, God rest her. You say more with your eyes than with your mouth. That side-eye could torch sugar into caramel.") and funny in a way that Sheree deemed inappropriate.

It seemed to Thomas that Sheree criticized him for the normal stuff of being a brother. James was also a tad rough around certain edges with a tendency to blurt out inappropriate things—but, in this family, that didn't make him stand out.

And Sheree's hair always looked good. Jake used a phrase of endearment many times a day when addressing Sheree, "I love every single inch of you." It was clear to Thomas why. Today she wore a wavy bob, braided close to her scalp over one ear. Curls spiraled down to her shoulders. "How are you really?" Thomas asked.

Sheree took off her apron, put it over the back of a chair and ran her finger over the lip of a plastic spoon. "I just want to know the result. Everyone's on best behavior, but the tension around here? Thick as my chili. Turn off your phone, okay? Every time I hear one ring, I lose it."

As if parenting, owning a business, tending to a husband with cancer, and dealing with her own health scares weren't enough, Sheree drove to Denver once a week to lead a coalition called "WOCE!" Pronounced "woke," it stood for "Women of Color Earn." Business owners mentored young women who were just out of school or college. Or, what Sheree called her alma mater, rehab, even after the university degrees she'd earned. The women visited grade and middle and high schools and connected with people to mentor one-on-one. Sheree also served on a separate citizens' committee that developed programming to train law enforcement to avoid racial bias. She'd convinced Thomas that the only new development in the violence against Blacks in the country was the reporting of it; and that only because of video phones.

"Go make yourself comfortable," she said. A slight hoarseness could be heard at the edge of Sheree's voice, and Thomas could see the weariness in the thin streaks of red and slight tinge of yellow in the white around her brown eyes. Without the makeup she usually wore, a scattering of freckles appeared on and around her nose. Each one a perfect circle.

Two of James's three daughters, Silvia and Teresa, came through the front door, chewing and laughing. They'd adorned their skinny limbs with colorful anklets and bracelets and watches, all things popular among the older Country Day students. Max and Barbara followed. They smelled like grape bubblegum. So unlike Thomas when he was their ages, so self-conscious about how his body moved, how he sounded, the places his gaze landed.

He'd spent his childhood, especially after his family moved from California to Massachusetts, feeling more like an indentured servant in a factory—head down with a focus on productivity until his release date—than a kid. In contrast, his brothers' children seemed, if not carefree, at least free in the broader sense, even though each of them was a bit of an oddball.

Barbara and Max were definitely worriers. Barbara was the perfectionist. Max always had an eye on others to see if he could predict and prevent disasters. Silvia could retreat into herself, sulk when she didn't get her way, and Teresa had an immediate allergic reaction to anyone telling her what to do. But they all moved in their bodies with ease and held their heads high and laughed.

Thomas contributed to each subsequent generation, both as a teacher and an uncle, and was proud of that fact. Kids needed two things to have the kind of freedom he saw both in his classroom and bounding in Jake and Sheree's living room: critical thinking skills so they could sort through the BS, and an environment where arguing is both civil and celebrated by the adults around them. Having made a positive contribution, Thomas stopped wishing his past had been different.

"Fluffiano," Silvia said, as Teresa ran and tackled Thomas where he'd just knelt to scratch Nesta's tummy. Silvia followed her younger sister. Now twelve, Silvia was the only one of James's three daughters to have inherited their father's light complexion and hair. The other two girls had dark hair and eyes like their mother. Silvia pulled Thomas down to the floor, flat on his back, where he squirmed as Teresa straddled his tummy, tickling him. Silvia joined in. "Pig pile on Uncle Fluffiano!" she yelled.

A few years ago, Barbara had taken an Italian class. She was in the thick of it when Thomas visited James and his family in New York. The actor on Barbara's audio drills had her repeating phrases starting with "Let's go . . ." First in Italian, then English. First *"Andiamo a gioccare!"* Then, "Let's go play." *"Andiamo a mangiare! Let's go eat; Andiamo al cinema! Let's go to the movies."* Soon, Silvia was adding the suffix-*iamo* to every word. Thomas had just stitched a torn ear on Teresa's stuffed dog, Fluffy. After his repair, Silvia kept repeating the word *Fluffiano* again and again. "Uncle," she'd say, shaking Teresa's dog. "Look at Fluffiano's new ear." Then, "Uncle. Fluffiano. Uncle. Fluffiano."

Now Max and Barbara stood in the doorway. So tall. The backlight blurred them into looking more like adults than children. A young and handsome couple standing there at the threshold, a catalog cover of two people just in from the cold. "What's up, Uncle Fluffs?" Max said. He wore a tee-shirt that read "Black Lives Matter" in bold print under an open jacket.

"I like your tee-shirt," Thomas said.

Max looked down. "Mom gave it to me. I like the font," he said.

"Are your cousins doing Ollies yet?" Thomas asked, hoping he'd correctly pronounced the skateboard trick. Nesta, who stood above his face, lowered his head and licked Thomas inside the mouth.

"Nesta," Max said, "Stop."

But the dog continued on Thomas's lips, now closed tight into a straight line.

Max hit the dog too hard on the nose. Said, "Stop."

Nesta yelped.

"Max," Thomas said, wiping his mouth. "Don't hit the dog like that."

"Uncle Fluff was making out with the dog," Silvia announced to the room. "He's disgusting."

Thomas got up, dusted the dog hair from his pants, felt light-headed.

"Who wants coffee?" Dot called. "I just made a fresh pot."

Thomas regained his balance, made his way to the kitchen, and poured himself a cup.

As the men of March Madness dribbled across the flat screen and Dot chopped and peeled for Sheree in the kitchen, the girls calmed down around a game of Jenga next to the elephant puzzle on the coffee table. Max snuggled next to his uncle on the floor and opened the music concierge app on his laptop.

"How's it been lately?" Thomas asked his nephew.

"Dad's getting better," he said. "Now that he might live, Mom wants to kill him all the time."

"Back to basics?" Thomas asked.

"Yeah," Max said, playing with the equalizer in the app so that the bass intensified. "As things should be."

"Are you nervous about the results?"

"Sure," Max said, clicking on the keyboard. "But I've been over all the possibilities with my shrink."

An only child who'd attended twelve-step meetings from the time he wore diapers, Max grew up discussing everything. He'd always been off the charts in his advanced verbal capacities, but so had Barbara, and she couldn't match his emotional maturity, even though girls in Thomas's classroom were normally much farther along than boys at their age. "When did you get so grown up?" Thomas asked, reaching over to lower the volume on the computer speakers.

"Not sure," Max said. "When I had to?"

In the kitchen, Thomas refilled his coffee. The back door rattled, opened. Everyone froze, but Joyce entered, wearing a tracksuit with the cuffs of her pants tucked into rain boots. "Adjusting to the altitude?" she asked Thomas.

"Not yet. Green chili pork will help, though," he answered.

Each time he had to engage in or listen to small talk about food or wine or coffee or rain boots or ski lift tickets he felt suspended in midair with no ground below, as if he'd let go of the dowel on a trapeze. He'd grown impatient with meaningless chatter after so many years interacting with Country Day parents. His mom, Maddy, followed Joyce, but stopped in the small mudroom off the back door and straightened everyone else's shoes. Once inside, she plopped a bag of corn tortillas on the kitchen island. Little beads of steam held to the plastic. Then she said, "Any word? That coffee smells good."

"None yet. Plenty in the pot, I think," Sheree said from where she stood at the stove. "Everyone, turn off your ringers."

Thomas kissed his mother and after, leaned into Joyce's embrace.

Thomas felt proud of his brothers for the partners they'd chosen, which made him miss Manny.

"Where's James?" Joyce asked.

Dot said something about their husbands being attached to their devices and after Sheree refused any more help prepping, Joyce followed Dot into the living room.

"Cute hair, Mom," Thomas said. What else could he say? They were down to the wire. "I've never seen it so short."

"We went for a white lady version of Mary J Blige, from

'Stronger.'" Sheree said, pulling bits of a tortilla she'd freed from the bag on the island. She used each piece to taste, then season and stir her green chili. Each of her ten nails was perfectly manicured and painted an elegant pale pink.

"It's the best cut you've had in a long time," Thomas said. Maddy had been returning his calls during classroom hours, leaving voicemails when she knew he couldn't pick up. She didn't offend him. Calling showed progress. When broken or depleted, Maddy had always repaired or recharged in solitude.

"Taste this," Sheree said, holding the spoon to his mouth. So different now, Thomas thought, remembering the Sheree he'd first met all those years ago at the rehab. "Yum," he said. Then, a moment later, "Wow. That's spicy."

In the family area of the rehab all those years ago, Sheree's first words to Maddy were: "I'm Black, HIV-positive, and jonesing. I'm also pregnant with your son's baby."

"You're Black?" Maddy had asked.

"Yes. See it and don't forget it," Sheree said, "And don't give me that color-blind bullshit." Her tone seemed serious, but she smiled at Maddy. Then and now.

"What a delight you are to meet," Maddy had said, "I'm the mother."

"Well, The Mother, don't get any ideas in your head. You didn't keep your son off drugs. And I don't need any of your or anyone else's . . . ," she looked over to Thomas, ". . . bullshit during my recovery."

"Noted," Maddy had said.

Now The Mother was pouring out perfectly good coffee. "Do you have a compost bin yet?" she asked, holding a dripping triangle of grounds held together by a soggy paper filter.

"Not since this morning," Sheree said, winking at Thomas. Sheree complained, even acted like she hated Maddy's constant unsolicited advice and reminders, but the whole family sensed how much the two women had grown to love one another. Sheree remembered her own mom as a kind person. Sheree's and Reggie's

41

parents had been in the Navy. Sheree's mom had been killed when Sheree was only five—not in the line of duty, but in a freak accident on the base. Struck by an airborne fire hydrant while walking. A passing car had struck it, and the water pressure caused a deadly force.

Jake's and Sheree's release from rehab had coincided with Maddy's sale of the house the boys had grown up in. She quit her job to move away from Massachusetts, and before deciding whether to go back to California or on to Colorado she called Sheree and said, "I'm cheap daycare." The three had worked it out so Maddy moved to The Springs and rented an apartment less than a mile away from the transitional housing where Jake and Sheree had lived.

The water gurgled in the coffee maker's well. Maddy turned around, steaming mug in hand.

"Is Reginald coming back?" Thomas asked about Sheree's brother. Their family gatherings were always so lopsided, with McGurrins in every square inch of the house.

"For dessert," Sheree said. "He's sent four texts asking what time. High maintenance as usual."

"It's possible he's texting out of concern for his brother-in-law," Thomas said, treading lightly.

Sheree said, "The only thing my brother is concerned about is a free meal."

Her comment made no logical sense. Reggie and his wife were *DINCs*, double-income, no-children, a term Thomas learned from a marketing person on the scholarship committee at Country Day, used to describe some gay couples' donating potential. Reginald, ten years older than Sheree, worked as a property manager, and his wife, a nurse, also earned money. They suffered for nothing. In fact, Thomas knew that Jake had borrowed money from Reggie more than once, and never vice versa. Reggie needed a free meal like the sun needed a plug-in heater.

"Come on," Thomas said. It wasn't the right time to challenge her, but Thomas always encouraged Sheree to let Max spend more time with Reggie. Her preferential treatment of Thomas over Reggie didn't sit well with either uncle. Sheree lauded Thomas with uncle accolades galore. Her reasons for not liking her own brother, as far as Thomas could tell, had less to do with Reggie being bad and Thomas being good, and more to do with the fact that Reggie knew the old Sheree and Thomas hadn't. The loss of their mom and their age difference also recast Reggie from sibling to parental figure. After their dad died, it doubled. And Thomas taught. Sheree and Reggie had moved around a lot as kids. She often described the kindness of her teachers—those who recognized her talents, her smarts—people she met in places where she'd otherwise felt alone. A soft spot formed for those in Thomas's profession.

"Speaking of dessert," Maddy said, "I made a pie from scratch. This fucking scan better come back negative."

When Jake walked in the front door, Thomas dropped a fistful of knives on the dining room table. Jake pulled Max up from where he sat in front of his laptop. "Where's Mom?"

"Here," Sheree said, standing at the doorway separating the kitchen and dining room, her eyes closed. The nine guests looked on from their various places. Holding his son's wrist in one hand and a piece of paper in the other, Jake said, "Zero uptake," and looked around. "You guys, I'm clean."

Until the unwind, Thomas hadn't realized how wound up he'd become from the worry and anticipation, the trip and the small talk. Now, in tiny increments, the muscles in his neck and shoulders and calves loosened around their bones. He remembered sitting with Jake for his last chemo session. Sharing that small space, Thomas felt as close to Jake as he had when they were kids back in Massachusetts. Jake had just finished the melon from the plastic box Thomas had purchased in the hospital cafeteria, then looked at Thomas and said, "Will you ever settle down? Get back with Manny and tie the knot? Have kids? What with gay marriage getting all legal and shit?"

Before Thomas had a chance to answer, Jake said, "If I don't live through this, and Sheree relapses or dies or gets too sick, you get Max."

"Me?" Thomas had said, sucker punched. First, he had to imagine Jake dead which dampened, to say the least, the simultaneous feeling that came with being chosen. Sheree was the picture of sober living and good health. The idea of his beloved sister-in-law dying felt ridiculous in any literal sense, too abstract, out of the realm of possibility. However far-fetched, Thomas felt real fear. Frightened—not only at the thought of losing his brother, but his sister-in-law, too, and selfishly, maybe even his freedom. He could've been a parent. He'd chosen to be a teacher.

Jake cut the silence. "Come on, Thomas. James and Joyce already have three, and Max wouldn't go for the Catholic stuff. We just wrote the will. It's signed and notarized and in a safety deposit box. Mom has a key, and I have a copy for you. You have permission to open it if Sheree, for whatever reason, can't."

"What about Reginald and Charlotte?" Thomas had asked.

"Reggie's a great guy. Charlotte's cool, too, but Reggie and Sheree's history is too fucked up. They're older than us, too, and Max requires a lot of energy. They're like old school, old school. They watch Jeopardy and Wheel of Fortune and shit. Max would go nuts over there. They have doilies on their tables."

Thomas interrupted. "I love Jeopardy. So does Sheree. You don't choose parents based on what they watch on TV. Reggie has more of what Max might need."

Jake stopped him. "Shut up, I know what you're saying and you're not wrong. If you ever tell her I said this, I'll deny it, but I think Sheree's madder at herself than Reggie. I'm not her sponsor. It is what it is, and we agree. You're our first pick, Thomas. Deal with it."

"There are only two reasons I'm not insisting," Thomas said. "Sheree's health and your recovery."

Now, Thomas stood rotating his neck in the dining room. After his wife and son let go of Jake, Thomas kissed the spot tattooed with the word *Max* on his brother's neck, then got out of the way so his parents could hug him, too. Thomas looked over to James, still on the couch, wiping snot from his upper lip with the back of his hand. He looked at Thomas. Mouthed the words *thank fucking god,* then yelled, "Let's eat!"

Chapter Six

Saturday
April 6th, 2013

Equip all young people, especially the most vulnerable,
with a compass and a flexible and expandable set of ques-
tions, to direct and dissect, help them get back on course as
they sway with the noise coming through their televisions
and phones and the mouths of adults, including their
parents, teachers, and church preachers.

Thomas closed his old notebook after updating his motto. He'd
kept a diary of mission statements since grad school when his
favorite professor suggested it to the class. "You're all fired up
now, but teaching can be a greased slide into bitterness," she'd
said. "And alcoholism," she added. Then, "just kidding;" then, "not
really;" then she laughed; then her face darkened from a flush of
blood under the skin; and finally she regained composure so she
could finish her lecture on the probability of losing one's purpose.
"Update it every year," she said, "and look at it often."

Forever the good student, Thomas carried that same notebook
to his internship, his first classroom, each year's summer adventure, and conferences. And like today, he opened it every year the
morning of the fundraiser, when he also remembered finding
Mercy and clicking the link to Country Day.

He'd grappled with leaving public schools to teach privileged kids. Remembering his own public-school years, witnessing not only the chumless and mentorless kids wilting under ridicule, but also those, like himself, who were ignored. He wanted to offer protection, or at least an understanding ear to those less likely to find it elsewhere. Older versions of his motto revealed that Thomas held zero ambition to use his talents to give to those who, materially, already had everything. He explicitly stated *those in underfunded public schools.* Eventually, he axed out underfunded, and public, too. His earliest statements were less a motto and more a pages-long manifesto, and revealed not only his naïveté and optimism, but a kind of arrogance. Experience had taught him humility. No matter how well-intentioned, Thomas inevitably failed to shield, and managed to ignore. Learning about Country Day, meeting Mercy and participating in the scholarship fund tipped the scale so he could justify working at a place like Country Day. He didn't become a teacher to be what Sheree always called "another wannabe white savior."

Thank god Mercy chose me, Thomas thought, reminding himself of his first couple years' classes at Country Day. Now, twelve years later, those young people were off at University, eager to make change. His first students had already gone on to make huge differences: one boy wrote and illustrated a children's book with a smart, capable protagonist adventuring in a wheelchair; a girl figured out how to pair with local sneaker companies to get unsold stock donated to shelters; two students started a beach cleanup that, over the years, raised awareness and led to a decrease in single-use plastic.

For the first time since Jake's diagnosis, Thomas felt relieved for his brother and excited about the fundraiser as he faced the weekend. He walked to Hawthorne in a Country Day hoodie, wearing his weekend pants and flip-flops to buy a coffee and breakfast. The hem of each leg, if you could call it a hem, fell above his ankle, and the once-red cotton had faded over the years to that shade of pink usually caused by bleaching accidents. The pants had been washed and treated with fabric softener so many times that the drawstring couldn't hold for too long, so he was always pulling them up. After he had paid for his mocha and two old-fashioned buttermilk doughnuts, he stood, wax-lined bag in hand, grateful to be among his fellow Portlanders in a city where people were more apt to stare at someone wearing a suit than a pair of old pajamas.

Thomas called Mercy.

"I bought you a donut. Will you be my date?"

"I'll pick you up at five so we can grab a drink before we get to the Jays."

"Plan," Thomas said, and hung up.

Fuck the poor kids. I say focus on the children who will end the poverty cycle!

That had been the pair of sentences that came along with the job announcement for a fourth-grade teacher thirteen years ago, when Thomas lived in San Francisco in a one-room efficiency, *complete with a kitchenette*, as the apartment listing had reported, across the street from Dana in San Francisco's Noe Valley. The email had been sent by a former colleague who also wrote, *If I were to teach again, it would be here,* and included a link to Country Day's website.

The day he received the email, he'd just returned from work after his lesson plans got hijacked by the usual: a false fire alarm, a kid with his dad's knife in the elastic of his joggers, a no-show by the part-time reading specialist, and a sensitivity training after a dead bird turned up in a shoebox on the librarian's desk.

The colleague who'd sent the email had been Thomas's closest work friend during his first semester of teaching. A person who described her childhood self as "poor" and the place she grew up as "the inner city." When their principal called a faculty meeting, said there was no money in the budget to replace the broken overhead projectors, and presented a new set of teaching imperatives toward standardized tests, she stood up, said, "Enough," and sauntered out of the meeting, the school, and public education—right into a high-paying job in tech. The steady beep of the microwave (where the second half of his leftover burrito rested on a plate like a gray log) had kept time as Thomas gripped the edge of a peeling square of linoleum with his toes, sipped the beer he'd bought with a Safeway coupon, and clicked on the link. Just outside of downtown Portland, nestled in a gulch of evergreens, maximum ten children to a classroom. *Ten?* Thomas thought, getting up to stop the beep. In Oakland, Thomas had twenty-seven students. In San Francisco, thirty-four. Country Day's student/adult ratio in the classroom? 5:1. 5:1? Ten students? Two adults? A full-time teacher's aide? When he sat down, he had discovered his burrito was less a warm meal and more of a tube containing the temperature equivalent of calico: spots of cold next to pockets of nuclear hot.

First place, Thomas thought, when he and Mercy arrived at the Jays' house—all pine wood and glass—for the fundraiser. They'd edged their way into first place, his most beloved parents of his current class. Not easy. The demographic he served favored helicoptering, but because of testimonials from previous years' parents, Thomas eventually (usually by winter break) earned his autonomy, and the Jays let Thomas teach their son without interference.

He and Mercy arrived early. Mr. Jay offered him a drink and Thomas refused. "I'm a lightweight, so I'll wait," Thomas said, but Mrs. Jay insisted.

"Come on, Mr. McGurrin. Take it from me, all work no play is no way to live." She and her husband shared a glance as she tipped the vodka bottle over a glass of ice, then added some soda and a slice of orange, handed it to him.

Sipping, Thomas watched the couple as they prepared for the onslaught. Thomas could see that Toby, who'd gone to his grandmother's before Thomas arrived, had inherited his father's olive skin and his mother's head of loose curls.

At the bar, where Mercy and Thomas had huddled before

coming over, Mercy confided her worry about the Jays. "I thought they might cancel," she said, and explained that Lisa Jay's new boss had screwed with the accommodations her former boss had put into place to make parenting easier.

"Since when?" Thomas asked. The two had grabbed a table at the end of the bench in the Sapphire Hotel bar, and each ordered a glass of sparkling wine. Mercy looked around. "January," she said. "And, between us," she took a sip from her crystal coupe, "there's also the marriage."

Until today, Thomas hadn't known about any issues. Once Mrs. Jay signed on to chair the fundraiser, Thomas left Mercy and Lisa to work their magic. He did what they told him to do, subtly hint to the powerful PFA members about the advantages of having more and more students who represent the country's demographics—not only in terms of racial identities, but income. He also rallied donors by calling the parents he'd had in his classroom throughout the years. The only difference he'd noticed in Toby's behavior in class could've easily been attributed to his age. He hadn't been acting out as much as turning inward. In the fall weeks, he'd been a kid who raised his hand for every question asked. Soon after the winter months, maybe after everyone came back from the long MLK, Jr. weekend, Toby seemed a tad spacey and distracted.

"I didn't know. He's the one picking up and dropping Toby off. He's always so friendly."

Thomas knew that Conrad had gone back to school in his thirties to become a doctor. He mentioned it every time he and Thomas spoke—he'd only finished his third year when Lisa had gotten pregnant on some fluke, and they were so surprised and delighted, they decided they didn't want nannies. They'd share the parenting, but Conrad agreed to the heavy lifting in Toby's younger years, then he planned to complete his last year of med school and start his residency after Toby finished eighth grade.

Mercy pursed her lips, arched an eyebrow. "Off the record," she said, "the new boss insists she attend everything. Apparently, Conrad isn't happy, and Toby's rebelling. He's parroting Conrad, saying she's always gone. She told me that if she confronts any of them—her boss or husband or son—or tells them off, or even asks for what she needs, they respond to her as if she's too needy, or worse . . ."

"A bitch?" Thomas said.

"Exactly."

"Doesn't she have any women in her life?" he asked.

Mercy said, "No. Besides me, only men. At home and work. Can you imagine?"

Nearly all Thomas's colleagues and mentors had been women and he loved it. Once he left the McGurrin houseful of boys, he never went back. Even gay bars felt lopsided to Thomas, who, unless horny, always preferred coed spots, clubs like *The Box* back in San Francisco where he and Dana danced together with their other grad-school party-friends—not just gay guys, but lesbians and straight women.

"You know what else?" Mercy asked.

"No," Thomas said.

"She never wanted to be a mother."

Sipping his drink, Thomas thought of his own mother, who he suspected had ambivalent feelings about family life, and wasn't surprised that neither confided in him. Mothers who regretted having kids? Villains. Lisa probably revealed a crack in her façade by confiding some sort of envy. Mercy could leave the kids after work to go home to a gloriously empty and man-less house.

Looking at the Jays now, he would have never known their troubles or doubts, with the graceful manner in which they welcomed pairs of people into their home, exchanged strategies with the caterers, and introduced one person to another. Back in September, Thomas had asked her if she'd chair the year's fundraiser, think about getting donations from her contacts. Mrs. Jay had gotten her MBA from the GSB at Stanford, and told Thomas and Mercy that she'd been the only person in her class to have worked during her MBA, the only state school grad, and one of two women, so the idea of scholarships meant a lot to her. Now she worked for a consulting company that brokered deals between the buyers and sellers of all things sports. Teams. Fitness companies. Endorsement deals.

Production companies that wanted a certain shoe or team or team's player, past or present, in a film or TV show.

"I'd be honored," she'd said. She immediately committed herself to the project with a take-no-prisoners gusto. Her yes didn't surprise Thomas, but thrilled Mercy, who saw Lisa not only as a conduit for donations, but a person with inroads to the particular type of scholarship student the PFA favored. Lisa's work involved relationships with university coaches, so she also had access to recruiters who started scouting in Portland and the surrounding areas as early as middle school. Lisa could help Mercy find top-notch athletes to be added to the musical and academic prodigies the PFA always pushed into the applicant pool. Mercy's long-term plan included serving kids from underrepresented demographics at Country Day whether or not they possessed prodigy-level aptitudes.

Thinking about what Mercy had said at the bar, he remembered the beginning of the year. Thomas knew that Mrs. Jay worked in New York and Los Angeles frequently, but at the start of the academic year she'd still managed to prioritize her volunteer slot in the classroom once a month. September through the holidays, she had showed up on time or early, without fail. She did seek Toby's approval more than Toby sought hers, but that was a common weakness of the Country Day parents, nothing that made her stand out. While easily embarrassed at times, and sensitive to criticism, Toby was an affectionate, hardworking kid. A good listener. Toby even liked to share. Thomas knew from Toby that she read to him every night at the same time, even when traveling.

"Not anymore," Mercy said.

Come to think of it, Mr. Jay had been showing up for his wife's volunteer slots since the kids returned from winter break. Sitting on a stool at the counter that divided the kitchen from the dining and living rooms, Thomas listened to Mrs. Jay tell Mercy of her many career twists after business school and a stint in wealth management. "I finally landed in sales," she said, sipping.

"Thank god," Mr. Jay said, as he refilled his wife's glass. "She could convince anyone of anything. Right honey?"

Their couple's shtick reminded Thomas of how his older brother and sister-in-law performed their relationship in public. Mrs. Jay played a role similar to that of his brother James's, the confident and competent one whose burden to provide excused her from the daily grind. "What's a vacuum cleaner?" she'd asked earlier, when Conrad told her he needed to put it away. Mr. Jay took on a similar role as Thomas's sister-in-law Joyce, the modest and fumbling character, dedicated to the less glamorous tasks of laundry and packed lunches and attending to guests. "Never mind, honey," he said. "No need to trouble yourself with domestic machinery. You keep making money."

Knowing what he knew of his sister-in-law, it made Thomas wonder what else Mr. Jay might be hiding. Thomas didn't buy his attempts to deflect his own sexiness with the agreeable goofball routine in the same way he didn't buy Joyce's humility when she introduced herself as a "stay at home mom." Once she'd dropped a glass jar of couscous and it shattered on the floor when the housekeeper wasn't there. Seeing Joyce try to maneuver a vacuum was like imagining her a ballerina on stage attempting a pas de deux with the dogwalker holding a bag of shit in each hand. In fact, Thomas burst into laughter when he saw her ruining her Miele by sucking up shards of glass.

Joyce never mentioned her master's degree from Harvard Divinity, and she let James take credit for their art collection, even though she had spotted and acquired their now-most-famous artists' earliest and valuable works. She also homeschooled Thomas's three nieces, and, in half the time per day, those girls out-performed even Country Day students on standardized tests every single year.

Thomas suspected that, like Joyce, Mr. Jay knew his power, and that containing it was part of how he used it. Whether or not Thomas's theory was right, one thing was inarguable, Toby worshipped his dad the way kids normally worship a ball player or television star. Who, including Mrs. Jay, could compete with that, even if she provided all this?

Thomas surveyed their bright space, the spectacular view of the setting sun behind Oregon's coast range, all the custom wood and glass work, the marble and brass surfaces and modern lighting fixtures. This house, the West Hills, wasn't exactly his Portland, but he did have a slice, however thin in comparison. He thought again to that day in his apartment in San Francisco when he first looked at the Country Day website; he had kept clicking, strategically combining his bites from various parts of the burrito's anatomy so as not to freeze or burn his tongue.

Thomas squeezed the orange slice into his cocktail. Both Mr. and Mrs. Jay were buzzing in circles, welcoming and greeting people. Now he was among them. He'd made something of his life. "Yes, try it," had replaced, "No, it's not in the budget." "Let's get parents involved" had replaced, "We'll never get permission slips." When the job announcement listed the salary range, he wondered if they'd accidently added an extra zero. And he'd earned a substantial raise every year since. Before he applied, he could picture his nieces and Max and his brothers sleeping in a guest room in a home he owned. Now he had it. A guest room? Owned? He hadn't even allowed himself to imagine that in San Francisco. Art-house movie theaters? Check. Farmers markets? Gyms? Trails for long-distance runs? Check, check, check. Thomas felt so lucky to be a part of this.

Watching Mercy, he remembered her composure during that interview. She barely let out her impatience when listening to him describe his pedagogical theories, but he sensed it, as if she'd already decided his curriculum would work, and also sensed that she seemed far more interested in his—how would he say it?— his being.

"You'll love our community," she'd said. "And our community would love you."

Other than the title of his master's dissertation on his CV, he didn't remember mentioning his gayness to her. When Mercy called and offered him the job, he remembered the phrasing she read from the board and PFA approval report: *We unanimously agree that Thomas McGurrin is not only the most qualified choice, but it is high time we welcomed an openly gay educator.*

Mercy couched a comment in a polite but slightly biting phrase about how she would've worded their statement a bit differently.

"How?" Thomas had asked.

In a very friendly tone, she said, "Most qualified choice was all they needed."

Years later, the two embarked on a rigorous Mount Hood hike. On the trail from Hidden Lake to Zigzag Overlook, they made it nearly six thousand feet up. Along the way, Mercy spotted a snake, and used her walking stick to get under it and fling it fifty feet, elegantly, calmly, as if the animal were a ball and her stick a croquet mallet. At the hike's highest peak, Mercy stopped, looked at Thomas, said, "If they knew how tough we were, none of them would think what they do."

"Who? What?" Thomas asked, high on altitude.

"The board. The PFA. They think we're non-threatening," Mercy had said, and kept walking.

He didn't ask questions, but never forgot it. And now? He wished Manny were here with him. God, he missed Manny. He surveyed the parents and wondered if they'd think him threatening if he'd brought Manny. Thomas suddenly realized that he'd never brought a date to a Country Day event, and Manny was younger than Thomas, so he wondered about that too. But look at the hosts of this party. Their arrangement and age difference could seem, to some, unusual. They weren't here now, but Country Day even had gay parents.

Thomas had been asked to co-lead the biggest event of the year with his Head of School whose name was at the top of his speed dial. Neither Mrs. Jay nor Mercy had grown up in this kind of privilege. They'd worked hard to prove themselves, and for what they had—like this house. Neither spoke to teachers like hired help.

Still, Thomas made a mental note to ask Mercy, also now mingling, what, exactly, she'd meant by that—by "not threatening."

Immediately after Mercy made the offer, she mentioned the salary and the relocation fee. He immediately said yes. It was so good, such a relief, he didn't negotiate. By the year 2000, Thomas wanted out of San Francisco. His last five years there had been as adventurous as they were stressful.

In 1995, during his last year of graduate school, AIDS deaths in the U.S. reached an all-time high. The New York Times reported that AIDS had become the leading cause of death among all Americans ages twenty-five to forty-four.

Every week since he'd come out, he read the Bay Area Reporter, which printed, alongside their obituaries, so many faces of young gay San Franciscans. Many of them looked like Thomas. *AIDS*, they reported. *AIDS AIDS AIDS AIDS AIDS.*

At the end of 1999, 733,374 cases of AIDS had been reported in the United States. 429,825 were dead. As gorgeous as Thomas found the city, San Francisco had become a gay graveyard, and since his schedule and salary rarely allowed him to enjoy the city's physical beauty or many of its cultural attractions, Thomas wanted out. He was afraid of becoming a statistic. Thomas had always been horny, and after a single beer and a kiss from any of the creative, handsome, articulate, fit, funny and equally terrified men he met when out with friends—with a margarita while watching videos at the Midnight Sun; lounging with Dana on a Sunday at Café San Marcos talking to LJ, their favorite cocktail slinger; dancing with his friend M. Wayne on Monday nights to hip-hop by the fan in the back corner of The Stud; or in the disco room with his friends Lil E and Leona at Colossus—he could not say no.

If the guys he met agreed, Thomas had to have sex. He mostly wore condoms and mostly avoided bottoming, but he just didn't have the willpower to stop if the kissing was good. He'd waited too damn long for it. Sex made him feel, well, as corny as it sounded to him, alive, but at the same time, he knew he'd been dodging bullets. He wanted, finally, to be himself and to be adored. The only people who made Thomas feel as adored as the gay men who flirted with and flattered him were the children he taught. And since sex, in his mind, equaled death, and children were safe, Thomas knew what he needed to do, where he needed to go.

Thirteen years later and Thomas was still HIV-negative. Still fit, articulate, confident. And now there were antiretroviral cocktails so that even if he slept with someone positive, they'd have a full set of T cells and no viral load. He'd sacrificed one thing to gain something else, and now, especially after meeting Manny, he felt like he could have it all, even if—Thomas sighed—Manny was gone. "Cheers," Thomas said, and finally got up from the stool to join the other guests.

As the evening went on, Thomas shared laughs with Country Day's parents. Madeline's dad made him blush. "She quotes you, invites us to make better behavior choices. Corrects our English."

They introduced Thomas to the parents of his future classes: parents whose kids were still in preschool and already had their minds set on Country Day, parents in kindergarten through third, and even one couple whose IVF twins were still in utero.

As Mrs. Jay got tipsier, she became more and more effusive. "My boys are my best things," she kept repeating. "And Thomas, you're one of my boys." She carried herself with a reserved elegance that layered itself, thrillingly, over her intensity. Perhaps it was that intensity that made her so attractive.

Back in the kitchen where the Jays and Mercy and Thomas had started the evening, Thomas refused Mr. Jay's offer of another drink, even though they served his favorite cocktail with a delicious slice of blood orange. Instead, he rested on the counter's stool and reached into the sleek silver bowl and grabbed a handful of cashews. Mr. Jay annoyed the bartender by insisting on making his own drinks. He handed one to Thomas and said, "Just take it. You don't have to drink it."

Earlier that evening, another mom, Gail Samuelsson, had given Thomas half her truffle, whispered that she knew a woman with whom Conrad had an affair. She'd stood so close Thomas could smell the damp bitterness of chocolate and wine in her mouth. He didn't believe Gail that Mr. Jay was a womanizer. He loved her, but Gail seemed lonely and bored, which made her a troublemaker.

Thomas finished chewing the nuts, got up from the stool and headed to the bathroom just down the kitchen's hallway. Mr. Jay trailed behind. "That one's occupied," he said, slurring just a bit, holding his drink with one hand and a stained kitchen towel in the other. "I'm heading upstairs to grab Lisa a sweater. There's a bathroom up there."

Following Mr. Jay, Thomas watched the cool way he sauntered, and could certainly see his charm. And his physique. He had the large legs and ample ass of an athlete, and tonight his tight khakis emphasized both. Thomas wasn't stirred by his brand of sexiness. Sure, he could appreciate Mr. Jay's considerable looks (he looked like he could be Jeff Goldblum's more rugged brother) and fit body, but the way he engaged people, while magnetic, seemed slightly false, inauthentic. Mr. Jay and Manny shared the same body type, but the thing that Thomas missed most about Manny wasn't his looks nor his beefcake, but his directness, his authenticity.

Once through the crowd, up the stairs, down the hallway, past the room where Thomas saw Toby's backpack leaned against a desk, Conrad pointed to the Jays' master bathroom. Thomas crossed their bedroom, recalling all of what Mercy had said earlier at the bar. Once in the bathroom, he could feel the heated tiles on the balls of his feet, where the soles of his oxfords were thinnest. He put down his cocktail and turned on the sink in case Mr. Jay hadn't yet grabbed the sweater and gone downstairs. Curious, Thomas opened their medicine cabinet, perhaps to find scurrilous prescriptions. But what nowadays would qualify? Anyway, he found nothing for depression or pain or erectile dysfunction; instead it looked like a La Mer department store display. Mr. Jay, like Manny, used an electric shaver. Thomas picked it up and touched one of the three circular blade screens, felt moisture, thought of the way Manny's close-cropped beard framed his face, and placed it back, gently closing the mirrored door. When he finished peeing, he flushed the toilet, ran the faucet for a second time, took one last sip of his drink. He caught his thoughts circling back to Manny. Since he already felt quite buzzed, and didn't want to go morbid, he poured out the rest of the cocktail before lathering his hands with a liquid soap that made the air smell of lemon verbena. The plush cotton hand towel was the same gunmetal gray as Mrs. Jay's eye makeup, which had been left open by one of the two sinks. The applicator pad still held a dark sparkle.

Thomas stepped out, heard the din of voices downstairs, and looked around at what he thought was an empty bedroom. He rounded their bed to peek into the enormous closet he'd seen in the architecture magazine.

"Shit," Thomas said. "You startled me."

"Sorry," Mr. Jay said, standing right past the threshold of the closet's door, looking out into the bedroom. "I remembered that I needed something, and now I forgot what. Does that ever happen to you?"

"Mrs. Jay's sweater, and all the time," Thomas said and smiled, suddenly aware of Mr. Jay's cologne. A pine scent that smelled more like a disinfectant in a mop bucket than the neck of a rugged and outdoorsy man. "My brothers and I call it, 'The Walgreens' Effect,'" Thomas said. "The second you pass through the doors you have no idea what you came to buy. Sorry for being nosey. The architecture. I was curious."

Mr. Jay walked deeper into the closet, halfway toward the shelves of shoes that covered the room's back wall. "Come here for a sec. You're allowed to be curious," Mr. Jay said. Thomas stepped in. On one side, a wall-hugging row of built-in shelves and drawers held impossibly well-organized clothing under a dowel hung with dry cleaning bags, dress shirts, and suits—mostly Mrs. Jay's. Conrad fingered the sweaters hanging before he turned around. On the other side, a dressing chair in front of an illuminated full-length mirror stood behind him, halfway between Thomas and the shoes. Mr. Jay opened one of the drawers and pulled out what looked like a cashmere cardigan. In the reflection, Thomas noticed that Mr. Jay was not only the same build as Manny, but about the same height, with much larger hands.

He came closer to Thomas, but paused, pointing to a section next to a few sports coats and men's dress shirts. "My birthday present from Toby," he said, pushing a button on a plastic gizmo attached to the dowel. A small motor hummed, and soon, a necktie appeared under the motorized tie rack's light. "Holds seventy ties," Mr. Jay said. "But I only have two."

"Well," Thomas said, standing close enough to Mr. Jay to notice a small spot near his ear where he'd missed his beard with the electric shaver. "Toby can give you a new one for your birthday each year. You two can fill it up."

Mr. Jay stepped even closer. Now the pine seemed tinged by a vinegary smell of nervous sweat. "When will I wear them? To parent-teacher conferences at Country Day?" he asked. He grabbed Thomas by the belt, sliding all four fingers of his right hand between the waist of Thomas's pants and the shirt he'd tucked into them. He pressed his face to Thomas's and kissed him on the mouth. The kiss wasn't pleasant, nor did it arouse him, but Thomas suddenly felt drunk, and full of dread, like this were his fault, as if his subconscious crossed its wires, maybe even conjured the whole bizarre scene, not out of desire for Mr. Jay, but for Manny. Thomas gently pulled Mr. Jay's hand out of his pants, and in a daze, walked backward out of the closet. He had almost formed a sentence in his head. Something like, *I think you've misunderstood.* Or, *You've had too much to drink,* but when he opened his mouth, he said, "I'm sorry."

Then, Mrs. Jay. Her voice. She said, gently, "You two are missing the party."

Thomas turned around. The light coming in from the hallway silhouetted her in the doorway. She'd recently reapplied her lip gloss, and the glow surrounding her shone as shiny as her lips.

"Indeed," Thomas said.

As he approached the door, Mrs. Jay made just enough room for him to pass.

Chapter Seven

Sunday
April 7th, 2013

Thomas woke while dreaming of the party and Manny. The part he remembered most vividly: Manny making out with Thomas's high school classmate, a kid named Chad, on the Jays' huge sectional, Conrad Jay watching, while Thomas, working for the caterer, pushed a cart around the house and collected empty glasses.

He'd barely slept, his face and neck muscles still sore from all of the smiling at the Jays'. As soon as the alarm sounded, he flashed on Mrs. Jay standing in the door of her bedroom. He shuddered, equally convinced of two opposite things: that Mrs. Jay had seen the kiss and that Mrs. Jay had not. Lying awake in the dim light of dusk, he kept reminding himself that he'd done nothing wrong.

Now, just before dawn, Thomas grabbed his phone from the nightstand, already lit up with reminders. *Silvia's Birthday*, it read. And: *Make Soup*. He pulled on a tank top, a sweatshirt, and his weekend pants. He hung his suit back on the wooden hanger and threw his dress shirt and tie in the dry-cleaning pile. On his way to the kitchen, Thomas quickly texted his niece in New York. *Happy Birthday from the co-founder of the Middle Children Club of America.*

A message from Mercy had also arrived sometime in the night, a picture of the two of them with their arms around each other's waists, Mercy in profile, showing off the green backless dress she'd worn; Thomas facing the camera head-on in his black suit and skinny tie. They'd left separately. As Mercy held court with the highest donors, Thomas called a cab. In it, he thought about the Jays and other parents at Country Day. He vacillated. Some days, some weeks and months and academic years, most, in fact; when thinking of the students, their parents, his colleagues, the commute, the pay, and his life, he found more to love than tolerate. The kids: their curiosity, their openness, seeing them thrive and realize their potential, watching them continue on to middle then high school, usually at Country Day, then, finally, leave for college.

The alumni who twelve years ago had been Thomas's first ten Country Day students were now drinking age. Those who kept in touch majored in journalism and philosophy and biology and sculpture and creative writing. Twenty-two former students were in college. He knew because he and Mercy worked together each year on the update for the website's "Where Are They Now?" page. They were pre-med and pre-law. Three had come out to him. One wrote an email saying: *I told my dad I'm gay expecting him to yell (he's such a homophobe), instead, he said,* Be like McGurrin. Live your life, be happy, but don't rub our faces in it. *So, thanks, I guess?*

At the time, it flattered Thomas. Now it reminded Thomas of Mercy's statement on their hike. *Non-threatening.* How would a young person even manage to rub their sexuality in a parent's face? Thomas counted—literally counted—his blessings, a tool he borrowed from Sheree, who, when anxious, texted him gratitude lists. One: Most people's jobs fit squarely in the more to tolerate than love category. Two: Summers off and a paycheck that afforded him a month in Italy with Dana every July. Three: The classroom—the place he'd felt most at home, most in control, most certain of what he had to offer, more than any of the places he lived growing up, more than in the dorms, more than at any gay bar or sports field or restaurant or church he'd ever entered, house he'd slept in, table where he'd eaten, turf he'd played on, or pew he'd prayed in. Like James in his surgical room, Jake as he designed and planted someone's yard, Thomas had found his domain. Four: living in a city with a decent symphony and an accessible airport so he could easily visit his brothers' families whenever he wanted.

Sure. He had to put up with bullshit. James had to deal with malpractice threats, his patients' unrealistic recovery timelines and their lies about their commitment to PT. Jake had to haul a lot of rocks, throw down a few tons of bark mulch every spring to pay the bills in between the residences or businesses that let him do his real thing, his art. Everyone who worked endured, tolerated. But hadn't Conrad taken it too far? Asked Thomas to tolerate just a bit too much? The kiss shook him. Not in itself. Under regular circumstances, who would care? The old joke: What's the difference between a gay guy and a straight guy? A six-pack and a backrub. Crucial difference: no backrub. Not one of Thomas's actions could've been classified as flirtation. It bothered Thomas for what it represented. Can't have your cake and eat it, too.

In the closet, no less! The symbolism required zero imagination. The metaphor was too spot-on. The Jays weren't in an open marriage. How did he know? The fact that he didn't know. Had it been true, he would've heard by Toby's second week of kindergarten or, if a recent development, Thomas would've known twenty minutes after. That's just how it worked at Country Day, and Thomas, more than any of the other teachers, had one ear to Mercy's mouth and another to the moms'.

Had Thomas been assaulted? Harmed in any way? Abused? No. He hadn't been a victim in that sense. But who in the fuck did that asshole think he was, putting Thomas in that kind of position? With everything clearly in his favor? Any idiot could tell you who held the power and how, from the outside, the situation would be perceived. Country Day didn't pay Thomas for committee work. He volunteered in order to give the kids of those parents some semblance, some hint, however tiny, of the world where kids grew up in small apartments with single parents who worked service jobs.

Thomas picked up his phone. An email from Mercy read, *Scholarships? Check! Double what we'd hoped. The Jays are my personal heroes!*

Victory! Thomas wrote back, a moment of relief. *Let's debrief tomorrow.*

He'd left the beans soaking yesterday before heading to the party, and now, thinking of the word *hero,* he placed the cast iron crock on the burner, then doused the pot's base with a healthy cover of olive oil. Despite this one anomaly, he, too, loved the Jays, appreciated the work they'd put into the event, not to mention the money they spent on the catering and booze. Next time he'd do better to keep his distance, not get too close. He pulled the pork knuckle from the fridge. He'd lost too much weight since the breakup, and Sheree had told Joyce at Easter that it was her personal mission to get Thomas to eat proteins other than grilled chicken breast. As he pulled together his ingredients, he recalled one scholarship committee meeting where, waving the dossiers in hand, Mercy had said, "What about an average smart kid? Like, someone who isn't already stellar? What about using part of the money to invite someone who might be better off because of us rather than vice versa?" She looked around the room at the others on the committee and Lisa laughed. Not out of rudeness, but because she'd misunderstood. She thought Mercy had been joking.

Thomas turned on public radio. As he reviewed Sheree's recipe, he listened to a touching segment on Roger Ebert, the film critic who'd just died; and then a report of the lengths the Chinese government went through in an attempt to contain the deadly bird flu outbreak, including disturbing details about destroying profitable inventory at a poultry factory. The longer segment highlighted the story of a high school sports coach, a transgender man, who'd come out to his small Rhode Island town. Listening, a series of memories seized Thomas, bringing back his college days at Cal, at Berkeley. He remembered standing in front of the Shattuck Theater as the autumn sun abandoned the sky. Berkeley's afternoon light, golden amber, made everyone, even the sickliest of folk cruising the avenue, glow. Thomas remembered feeling like he did now: slightly nauseous, not from a hangover back then, but from the fistfuls of popcorn he'd eaten, along with a pound box of Red Vines and a huge diet soda. He could see himself, eighteen, standing still in front of the ticket booth, greasy napkins in hand, trapped in the moment between day and night, lunch and dinner, fantasy and reality.

Now, as the onions caramelized, in a segment about his high school basketball career, the coach talked about how sports saved him. Soon after, the school had hung a banner, listing his old name, commemorating players who'd scored more than a thousand points. He talked about his desire for the school to update the banner so it could make him proud instead of soiling the accomplishment with the reminder of the suffering he endured when trying to conform to expectations associated with the dead name. Thomas cut the tie from the paper around the ham hocks, dropped them in, and added chicken broth. While his peers at Berkeley were pledging fraternities and playing drinking games at the dorms, Thomas had preferred to sneak away to the gym, or to go for a walk along College Avenue.

He recalled his pre-coming-out days so clearly, his two-hour Friday afternoon class usually morphed into Friday evening plans for the rest of his classmates. Coffee right after class felt safe, especially when the conversation focused on the professor instead of the students. He avoided the boozy events after hearing his classmates' flirty personal questions and jokes about gay people.

His favorite shop on College Avenue sold portable music players, the latest headphones, calculators, and watches. A couple months into his first year at Berkeley, Thomas bought a bunch of Christmas gifts to send to his family: an electric kitchen timer for Maddy that could be set to go off twice, an alien-themed hand-held video game for Jake, and sports cartridges for the game console James took to the dorms. A salesperson named Tony had helped him. Thomas pushed open the door, setting off a string of bells that hung from its handle. Dozens of earphones rested on wall hooks behind Tony.

"Tom," he said. "Does he like it?"

"Does who like what?" Thomas remembered asking.

"Your brother? Ultimate Basketball?"

Tony, with his delicate walk and muscular physique. Dark, curly hair and thick eyebrows. Brown eyes with long lashes set in from a protruding forehead. He reminded Thomas of an actor on a soap opera Maddy watched when she ironed in front of the TV. The director often shot the daytime star showering. "Beefcake for ratings," Maddy would say, spraying starch. Thomas came close to coming out to Maddy during that show, more than once, as he did homework and she ironed, both peeking at the actor's swollen pecs. Maddy would've cared, but only in the true sense of the word. In the small universe that only Thomas and Maddy shared, Thomas had been the one not ready for the declaration.

Tony spent twenty minutes helping Thomas choose a pair of headphones and offered him his employee discount. "Ulterior motives," Tony said, exposing a mouth of bright teeth.

The delicious smell of onion in pork fat now enveloped Thomas's kitchen as he poured a second cup of coffee into his travel mug. His phone buzzed on the island. A new message: *Love you, Uncle Fluff. OMG my new boots! Thank you! XO, Silvia.*

Love you, too, Thomas wrote. *Dana helped me pick them out.*

How lonely he'd felt in California that first year of college, before Dana, before he'd come out to his family, before James met Joyce, before Jake met Sheree, before the birth of nieces and nephew. He would not have traded it. The loneliness, like his whetstone, dull and gray, sharpened what he pressed against it: freedom, excitement, hope, and lust.

He'd found himself in the electronics store a third time, the very next afternoon; that time, to thank Tony, and tell him how great the headphones sounded. Tony smiled, said, "Follow me," and led Thomas to a room with thick foam rubber-lined walls and ceiling. A small window allowed Tony to keep an eye on the counter and register.

"You think the earphones sound good?" he said, grabbing a remote control. Tony sat down first and then patted the space next to him on the small couch, a love seat really. Their legs touched, as Tony told Thomas about something called surround sound. That small charge, that tiny bit of heat that migrated through the fabric of Tony's khakis and Thomas's jeans while Roxy Music blared from all sides, opened a yearning he'd never experienced before.

A customer disrupted the moment, cruelly, mercifully. Cruelly because of the wait. Boys like Thomas waited years for that moment to arrive. Mercifully, because the warmth of Tony's palm on Thomas's thigh had almost made him come. Thomas, flushed, composed himself, used his backpack to cover his erection while he exited. He resisted the urge to leave the store altogether, and steeled himself to stay, buy the same batteries he could've gotten cheaper at the drug store.

"Don't just use me for my discount." Tony smiled.

"I'd never," Thomas said. "Never," he repeated, as Tony pressed his change and a receipt into his damp palm.

"Relax," Tony said, grabbing Thomas's shoulder from the other side of the glass counter. "I'm just kidding," he said, squeezing Thomas. "But you can do me a favor."

"Sure," Thomas said, embarrassed, putting the coins into his pocket.

"Buy me a cup of coffee? I left my wallet at home, and I'm about to clock out."

As the radio show continued, the coach told his story of the townsfolk's attitudes shifting, however slowly, toward acceptance. "Winning games didn't hurt my cause," he laughed, and Thomas's memory of the foam-padded stereo room morphed into Tony's apartment on Martin Luther King, Jr. Drive. Thomas remembered how ginkgo trees grew from dirt plots on the sidewalks, and their leaves shaded the mix of houses and stucco-faced apartment buildings.

James Baldwin and Rita Mae Brown and Edmund White and Larry Kramer lived on Tony's bookshelves, sharing space with

Ayn Rand, Hemingway and the Bible. A glass mannequin head sporting a long black wig rested on his coffee table next to scattered mail, which revealed his last name, *Tempesta*. A macrobiotic recipe was taped to Tony's crock-pot. Thomas asked him if he followed that diet.

"Not yet," Tony said. "But it interests me. I'm trying it out."

Tony's simple response triggered what he felt standing in the closet with Mr. Jay. Anxiety rushed through his body, leaving him light-headed.

"I don't get it," Thomas said, in Tony's kitchen, the light too bright coming in from the sliding glass doors.

"Get what?" Tony asked, looking through his record collection for something to put on the turntable.

"What are you?"

Tony smiled. "What do you mean?" he asked, slipping a record from a dark blue album sleeve. On it, a woman in a blue dress sat in a blue room with the word *Dummy* printed under her.

Thomas tried to match Tony's kind, quiet tone. "Your books. This place. Are you a socialist or a Republican? Drag queen or redneck?"

"Wow," Tony said and laughed. "Let me guess. You haven't come out yet."

Thomas still listened to that Portishead album. In fact, he had bought a digital copy for his oldest niece. Hip-hop beats played along with the kind of otherworldly sounds of sci-fi soundtracks. Tony had turned up the stereo, then walked to Thomas, and placed one hand on Thomas's waist, and the other in his hair. Tony's cupped palm captured the warmth from the crown of Thomas's head and sent it radiating back into his body. Then he kissed Thomas, slowly, multiplying the warmth, before unzipping Thomas's sweatshirt, and pulling at the hem of his tee, lifting it off.

Tony's bed took up nearly half of the studio, but it wasn't the bed that seemed so big. For the first time in Thomas's life, the whole universe seemed contained in the form of Tony's body. Just seeing Tony's muscled arms, his long legs, his cock, as hard as his own, the purple nipples surrounded by soft, dark hair, his butt

68

crack, his lips, his tongue. He expected the sheets to smell more like Tony—like the woodsy-scented bar in his bathroom's soap dish and the slightly sour tinge of the nearby hamper. Instead, Thomas inhaled something close to a memory, of delivering the Sunday paper in summer in Massachusetts: morning air, moisture on grass, earth, pancake syrup. By now, the only thing left on Thomas's body were his white briefs, the brand Maddy bought him for Christmas every year. Thomas's cock hurt, first from pressure. Dizzy and a bit nauseous, Thomas kissed and grabbed, grabbed and kissed, lost in a frenzy of sensation and memory of every boy he liked but couldn't touch, even after he saw them naked, drying themselves in the locker room to the almost inaudible sound of high school-issued towels sopping the water from wet pubic hair.

He'd wanted to slow down, but as he groped Tony's forearms, his chest, as he ran his fingers through Tony's armpits, Thomas could not control his memory or himself. Tony, once and for all, released Thomas's dick, while saying something stupid like, "He's a big boy and needs to come out and play." Thomas came immediately. Thomas would've chastised himself, would've been embarrassed, would've apologized, lied and said he could last forever, but Tony didn't stop, didn't let up, which left Thomas, what? Not quiet—he'd been that so many times, countless times—but languageless. Thomas did not have access to words, not even to say *slow down*, or *not yet*, or *that hurts* or even *no*.

Tony wiped the stripes and dots of liquid decorating Thomas's stomach with the sheet and then immediately put Thomas into his mouth. Thomas writhed. He hadn't imagined it going this way. He imagined the opposite. As Tony's mouth released Thomas and moved to his balls, then asshole, then back, Thomas imagined himself Tony, and Tony himself. When that image clarified in his imagination, Thomas came the second time, and Tony moved from facing Thomas to lying on his back. Then Thomas didn't stop. A hunger overcame him, insatiable. Still dripping, he twisted, repositioned himself and took Tony, repeating the series of acts he'd just been shown.

Finally, Thomas finished, joined Tony at the head of the bed, the two next to each other, shoulder to shoulder, looking up at the ceiling. Thomas cried a bit, so quietly as to be indistinguishable from their breathing. He watched the triangle of light on the wall, listened to the argument on the street below Tony's window—two people speaking Spanish—while he ran his tongue over his teeth.

Tony got up. The time he spent showering seemed equal to the duration of Thomas's whole life up until that moment. Bright light busted through the fern fronds hanging from the ceiling near the sliding glass doors.

"Nobody loves me," the singer sang, "it's true, not like you do."

Tony plopped down smelling of the same shampoo Thomas's father used. Tony moved first, from his back to his side, one hand holding his chin, the other gliding over Thomas's stomach. He pressed just hard enough to make shallow impressions, then pulled away, and watched his disappearing fingerprints.

"Do you worry?" Thomas asked, finally able to speak. "About the future?"

"No," he said. "I have all I need right now."

Thomas opened the refrigerator, saw the carrots and celery, and pulled them out. The story on the radio had ended, as did the arousal he always felt when remembering Tony and the electronics store. Thomas sharpened his knife on the whetstone, chopped the veggies, and wondered if he should call the Jays. Talk to them. But what would he say? He did not know how to read the men who found him attractive. Look at what had happened with Manny. Look what had happened with Tony.

Six months in, Thomas had been staying at Tony's more nights than not and mentioned that he'd started applying for grad school. "Good," Tony said, untangling himself from Thomas and the sheets. He leaned to his side of the bed, grabbed his sketchpad and pencil box from the floor. "You should go."

"It's not that kind of news," Thomas said, snuggling up to Tony's neck. "I'm re-applying to Cal. I'm not leaving."

"Doesn't matter," Tony said, shrugging Thomas off.

For a full minute, the only sound between them was the scratching of Tony's sharp pencil along the thick paper.

"I'm confused," Thomas finally said. "I thought you'd be happy."

"I am," Tony said. His gaze rested on Thomas's face, then away, to his window. "It's not you," he said.

"Really?" Thomas said, suddenly afraid. "That line?"

Jasmine green tea, sex and sweat, graphite and wood. Thomas remembered the smells of that apartment and Tony faltering.

"I hate this," he said. "No matter what I say I'm an asshole."

"Why?" Thomas had said. "Why not just be kind? And tell me the truth?"

"I can't," Tony said. "Except to say it's time."

"Time for what?" Thomas had asked.

"To call it quits," Tony said.

That day, as Thomas got dressed, Tony continued sketching the dying fern without looking up. Thomas waited at the apartment door thinking of the contents of Tony's sketchpad. All objects. Weeks' worth of them. An avocado in a glass bowl. A rosary draped over a thumbtack stuck into crown molding. A baseball in the palm of a worn leather mitt. A ceramic ashtray overflowing with empty candy wrappers. Then the dozens of drawings of Thomas.

Now Thomas used the just-sharpened knife's edge to scrape the celery and carrot from the cutting board into a pan. Once they were soft, he'd add them to the rest of the soup he'd take to school tomorrow. Yes, tomorrow. He comforted himself by thinking of tomorrow: of school, of his classroom, where everything would be in order.

Chapter Eight

Thursday
April 11th, 2013

When the phone rang, Thomas answered, but put Mercy on speaker so he could fold his newspaper and organize his backpack at the kitchen table. According to the article he'd finished reading, Obama had become the first Democratic president in history to target Social Security in his budget. His plan also cut over $350 billion from Medicare, $19 billion from Medicaid, and tens of millions from the government's heating assistance program for low-income Americans.

"There's a problem," Mercy said, her voice echoing in Thomas's kitchen.

"I know," Thomas said. "He probably had to cave to the Republicans. Who knows how they're forcing his hand."

"No," Mercy said. "An accusation. It's about Toby. The Jays."

"Toby? Is he okay? You sound nervous." Thomas put the Tupperware full of stew into his backpack, poured coffee into his thermos. "Who's being accused?"

"Jesus, Thomas," Mercy said. "You. They're accusing you." Her strained tone carried concern.

"Me? Accused by who?" Thomas asked, as he tried to get his laptop to fit in the backpack's sleeve. This wasn't the type of thing Mercy joked about.

"The Jays," Mercy said. "Toby said something, and they contacted me. It's serious."

"Toby or Conrad?" Thomas asked.

"What?" she said. "Toby."

Mercy reminded him of the mandatory reporter rules, how she'd already contacted the sheriff's office. "I have to put you on leave, immediately. You might want a lawyer." She let out a series of quick, successive coughs.

"What? How serious can it be?" Thomas worked to organize his thoughts and the timeline around anything related to the Jays. Their fundraiser, the farmers' market; then Toby had come to school Monday, but nothing unusual had happened. In fact, they'd barely been in the room together because of enrichments. He was out Tuesday and Wednesday, but the office informed him that Toby was sick, and Thomas had sent the Jays his schoolwork, even received thank you emails in return. It hadn't even been a week since the fundraiser. Mandatory reporter? That's when a kid alleged abuse.

"I just saw the Jays Sunday at the farmers' market," Thomas said to Mercy. "And immediate leave? What are you talking about? It's culminating projects time, Merce. I can't stay home. We have to finalize the selections for the anthology, get the manuscript to the printer. I've already lost so much time flying back and forth to Colorado."

"You're not getting it, Thomas," Mercy said, too loudly for the telephone. "This is bad. I've had to report you for an accusation of intentionally touching Toby's genitals."

The phrase "he was beside himself" occurred to him in the same moment it took form. As if there were a second Thomas sitting next to him at the kitchen table. As if while on the phone with Mercy he'd been cloned.

"I emailed you Country Day's protocol for dealing with these kinds of accusations. It's in the handbook. You'll want to review it." She started to say something else, but Thomas hung up, pulled his laptop out of his backpack and walked from the kitchen to the family room. He stumbled on the coffee table's leg. The bottoms of his feet had gone numb. He had to stop and lean against the wall. He looked down, wiggled his toes in his running shoes, and remembered Mrs. Jay standing in her bedroom door as Thomas stepped out of her closet saying "I'm sorry." When he looked up, his vision was blurred.

Thomas lifted his arms and said, "The quick brown fox jumped over the lazy dog." His vision slowly cleared. Not a stroke. He blinked, looked in the mirror. His face held the sheen and color of a waxed apple, but there was no drooping. *You're fine,* he told himself. Now he sat at his desk, tee-shirt now stuck to his armpits, his back. He opened his laptop, waited for it to boot, then touched the mouse sensor, found Mercy's email with the little paperclip icon. He clicked on it, and the Country Day handbook downloaded into his PDF reader. Then he remembered the name of that lawyer, and called. An hour later, Jerome Carter, Esquire, called him back. Thomas answered Jerome's questions one by one.

"I'll take the case," Jerome said. "For a percentage of the settlement."

"There won't be a settlement," Thomas said, then read what he'd just written in his notebook: *I want to resolve a misunderstanding and return to work.*

In the pause, Thomas felt plastic, hollow. Not like he was sitting at his desk in his house in his town, but as if he were watching a blow-up version of himself, part of a set in a play on a stage. And cold. The damp cotton of his tee-shirt left him shivering.

"I didn't do it," Thomas said, suddenly, through a constricted throat, his voice weaker than he'd ever heard it.

"I already knew that," Jerome said, and transferred Thomas to his secretary to schedule a meeting for the following day, Friday, April 12th.

"Hello, Mr. McGurrin," Jerome said, placing both his laptop and a coffee mug on the mahogany desk before sitting down. He looked better now than he had twelve years ago. Then, he seemed rough at the edges, splintery. Now his slick appearance matched his office, where everything was sanded, stained, shellacked.

Thomas looked at the clock on the wall behind Jerome. It was 1:40, and Thomas wondered what his kids in the classroom were up to after returning from lunch.

"First," Jerome said, opening his laptop, "I'm so sorry about all this. Mercy sent me copies of your employment files. Impressive."

Thomas could smell the gel strip that greened the pink center of Jerome's tongue. He tried to smile again, but his anxiety had doubled. He eyed the degrees and awards and articles framed and hung on the wall.

"I remember meeting you. You were new to Portland and the school. Do you remember?" Jerome asked, smiling.

They had met on a sex site. Or, rather, a dating site that evoked sex because a dozen years ago gay internet pages made do with advertising from porn outfits since no one else would buy.

Jerome had suggested a coffee house near Thomas's place for the date. Thomas walked along Hawthorne, his soundtrack a symphony of birds: chattering kingfishers, tchewing blackbirds, and the caws of crows that shared the complex grid of phone and electrical wires above the avenue. As he passed the funky shops and wood-sided bungalows and four-square homes, the wires felt to him like a kind of protective web, the boning of an otherwise invisible force. The first thing he had noticed after moving to Portland was that people said, "Good morning."

"I remember," Thomas said now, to Jerome.

He'd arrived first and ordered an iced coffee that the barista served in a pint glass. After sitting in the slouchy mustard-colored couch, he thought better of it, and chose a table against the wall and waited. Once he walked in, Thomas first noticed the hands. Then as now, Jerome's hands reminded him of Jake's. As neighborhood shoppers came in with their skateboards and Baby Bjorns and ordered dirty chai teas and decaf lattes, Jerome had talked about civil rights law for a half hour before finally asking Thomas what he did for work. By then, a tiny pile of coffee grounds rested at the bottom of his pint glass. Above it, a layer of water where the ice had melted.

"I'm a fourth-grade teacher," Thomas had said, and expected Jerome to be impressed when he told him where.

"Why not a public school?" Jerome had asked.

"Why private practice and not HRC or Southern Poverty Law?" Thomas said, annoyed by Jerome's insinuation.

Jerome smiled, said, *"Touché,"* and asked Thomas to join him for a beer.

Despite Jerome's personality, Thomas found himself rushing back home to grab his car. He felt anxious at the red lights as he drove west on Hawthorne; relief when the lit-up Morrison Bridge remained undrawn. They reconvened at the gay bar on Stark Street, where music blasted out of enormous speakers near the place's tiny wooden floor. Talking was impossible, so they drank and danced. Well, Jerome danced. He held both hands to his heart, tilted his neck back and spun, face up to the strobe light. Thomas watched, mesmerized, as the soulful vocalist sang, "Finally it's happening to me right in front of my face, and I just cannot hide it."

Now Jerome combined various questionnaires and began bundling them under a clipboard with a clamp massive enough to decapitate a cat. Thomas remembered being at the bar and reaching the bottom of his beer, the song ending, and Jerome standing in front of him.

"You looked good out there," Thomas had said, and handed Jerome a small stack of cocktail napkins. Jerome wiped his forehead, leaving a tiny wet triangle of paper stuck to his face. Thomas reached for it, gently removed it, and then leaned in. Jerome put his hand on Thomas's chest. "Not sure it's a love connection, buddy," he'd said.

The night of their date, back home in his bathroom, Thomas had splashed water in his face, and took a long look in the mirror. *Buddy?* Thomas thought. *Buddy?* Confusion plus desire. Or better: desire plus confusion. That's how Thomas had always felt about gay men. Hadn't Jerome invited him to the bar? Basked in the audience Thomas provided?

A couple of days later, Jerome's profile appeared on Thomas's computer screen, and Thomas's pulse quickened as he clicked on it. Jerome's shirtless pictures had been locked back into their private folder. Not the six-pack nor ripped style of muscular physique, but the strong, bulky kind Thomas preferred: gym? Sure, sometimes, but also a second hearty slice of lasagna. Thomas messaged him: *I'm curious why it wasn't a love connection. Any insights?*

The cursor blinked for a long time. Then, *None that I want to share.*

Thomas waited for Jerome to look through the clipboard of papers and missed his kids, his classroom. He wanted to go there, slice apples, sprinkle them with cinnamon, listen to them crunch.

"I've read Lisa Jay's accusation," Jerome now said. "Let's talk."

Thomas nodded, suddenly reassured by Jerome's tone and confidence. Yes, Jerome seemed gay, whatever that meant, and absolutely unapologetically so. Thomas noted the same set of mannerisms he remembered Jerome showcasing on the dancefloor—the flair in his gestures, the slight theatricality of how he'd positioned himself in his chair—less like a person doing a job and more like an actor in a tableau. But he also had an air of—Thomas hesitated to call it straightness, but what? How would he describe Jerome to Dana? Cocksureness? A sanguine quality, even in this circumstance. Bold, for sure. And undaunted, too.

"Absolutely zero contact with the genital area?" he asked, looking up from his clipboard.

"Zero," Thomas said. "Not even close."

Last night, just before sleep, when the cold dampness of Oregon, even in April, seeped into the wooden planks of his house so it cracked and creaked, he thought of words that rhymed with pants. First, the single syllables: dance, chants, ants, plants, France. Then, others, not so on-the-nose: romance, at first glance, cash advance, game of chance. Because he did not want to give up his certainty, he hoped sleep would come before the suspicion that, perhaps, any sentence containing the words *Thomas* and *touched* and *pants* coming from a little boy would have caused all this. Could it be, even after all he'd done to be good, that *Thomas* and *touched* and *pants* together in a sentence could unravel a whole life?

No.

"In an email my boss told me that Toby told his parents, 'Thomas touched my pants.' Other than one email giving Mercy the home number of my teaching assistant, who witnessed everything, and telling her that Toby's classmates saw what happened, I've said nothing."

"That's good," Jerome said. "We still need to be vigilant. This happens all the time and it ruins lives."

"In 2013?" Thomas asked.

Jerome's eyes looked sad, but he forced his face into a small smile. "Yes. And in Portland and San Francisco and New York, and all of the rest of the places we'd call progressive."

"There's something else," Thomas said, and recounted the encounter with Mr. Jay along with Mrs. Jay's reaction. "I'm not even sure she saw. And I know this couple. They're good people. They wouldn't concoct this out of pettiness, I just feel it in my gut, but I worry."

"That she's made some sort of weird transference?" Jerome said.

"Exactly. Because the stupid thing with Toby's pants happened before the party, not after. How and why would it have come up days later?"

"The report says he told them the day it happened. They maintain it took until the next week to sink in."

"See?" Thomas said.

"Yes," Jerome said, making notes.

The next two and a half hours, he grilled Thomas about his relationship and sex history. "I need every detail," he said, his sleek silver pen poised on the clipboard with its inch of paper.

When the questionnaire was done, Jerome coached Thomas on how to phrase things during the remaining investigations. "We'll end here. Before you go, remember: Do not contact any of your students' parents. Especially the Jays. Not by phone, nor email. If they reach out to you, don't respond. Let any calls go to voicemail. Forward everything to me. If you see them, politely avoid them." He stood up, shook Thomas's hand, and said, "I have another client waiting." He collected his materials and said, "Come on, I'll show you out."

Almost as hungry as nauseous, exhausted as wired, Thomas stayed busy for the rest of the day and evening, and went to bed at eight thirty, but couldn't sleep. He couldn't stop thinking about Mercy, about the Jays that day at the farmers' market.

He picked up his phone at least once or twice an hour, but no one texted or called. Finally, when darkness took cover, he decided to get back out of bed, go for a drive. It was just after nine thirty. Weary, but wide-awake, he crossed Hawthorne Bridge, thinking he could stop at a restaurant in The Pearl for dessert, or a gay bar downtown for a drink, or both.

Mouth dry, he opened his glove compartment to grab his box of Altoids. Before he could get them, his bird-watching binoculars fell out. He hadn't used them since his last long hike with Mercy. He forgot about them again even as he drove by the bars and restaurants, and kept driving toward the West Hills; didn't pick them up from the passenger floor until he found himself parked on the street below the Jays' house, where he had a perfect view of the floor-to-ceiling glass on the downtown-facing side of their home. He grabbed the binoculars when looking up into the Jays' family room, only able to see the outline of her standing in the spot she had occupied during most of the fundraiser.

His phone buzzed. Suddenly and loudly from the passenger seat, startling him. *Jerome Carter.* Thomas silenced the phone and picked up his binoculars. He quickly adjusted the focus to bring her into high definition.

Joyce and the girls had sent the package insured. The binoculars and his new watch in their boxes on top of the sweater, all so expensive. The card had read, *Happy Birthday, Uncle Fluff! Hope you spot a Solitary Sandpiper or a Ruddy Turnstone!*

Thomas located Mrs. Jay, where she stood in front of the coffee table. As he adjusted the focus, she looked in the direction of the three mountains behind the city skyline. He didn't see Toby or Mr. Jay. It was almost ten, by then, so Toby was likely in bed. The binoculars magnified her image so sharply it was as if she stood three feet in front of him. She cupped her ear with a phone, and after looking straight out for the first few seconds, her eyes lowered, and she appeared to be staring directly at Thomas.

Thomas held it: the image of her, their incredible home, the life that the Jays shared, mother and father and kid. *How lucky they are,* he thought. To live there. To have such a healthy son. To have each other, however imperfectly. He usually didn't covet, but watching her, Thomas felt loneliness, as if it were a handful of ice pressed into his bare chest.

Mrs. Jay turned around and began walking away from the family room toward the kitchen, when, suddenly, a *tap tap tap* on Thomas's car's passenger window. The sound of metal on glass. Mr. Jay stood outside, leaning close to the window, a key between his knuckles. Again, Mr. Jay *tap tap tapped*. "Thomas?" he said, his face so close to the window his breath formed tiny beads of condensation.

"Thomas?" Mr. Jay repeated, louder that time, as Thomas sped away.

Chapter Nine

Wednesday—May Day
May 1st, 2013

Thomas held his phone in one hand and pulled the hood of his rain jacket with the other, ending his call just as his brother James said, *I love you*. The yellow flowers of the dwarf jasmine hugging the rocks along the walkway gave off their sweet perfume. When had they bloomed? What else had he missed? He'd endured nearly a month of days and nights pretending business as usual before finally mentioning his situation to James. The mere mention of a problem at work created almost as much tension as it relieved, like shaking a soda can and opening it. Thomas locked the door behind him. A zingy charge enveloped him as he approached Jerome's car, a slip of something electric, the buzz of being watched. Absurd, it seemed, that he, Thomas McGurrin, a fourth-grade teacher, would be walking toward a luxury sedan owned by a lawyer who'd been on TV. Ruth Juraka stood across the street under the ancient walnut tree near the manzanita growing by her mailbox. She waved.

Thomas waved back. She hadn't seen the headline yet. He opened the door to Jerome's car, and got in. Before he greeted Thomas with a hello or handshake, Jerome said, "I'll remind you again. Your one and only job is to stay composed; and in the meetings, let me do or direct all the talking." His umpteenth reminder that Thomas defending himself could only deepen suspicion and have an adverse effect on the settlement.

Two men on the talk radio station discussed a recent think-piece. Not only had Thomas listened to the original airing of the show, he recalled seeing the article, a few months ago in *The New Yorker*. One of the show's hosts agreed with the journalist's findings. He reported on Obama's predicament as the Nation's first Black president, and criticism from a small but substantial percentage of Black voters who thought Obama should have been doing much more for Black people—and to fight racism in particular and conservatism in general. The other guest disagreed with those who criticized him, said, "The writer gets it right. What could he do in a racist nation? Where people question whether or not he was even born in this country? He's done the most, by far, and is the most qualified person who has ever taken that office." The host read a quote from the article, something about Obama conducting an affair with Black people, meaning intimacy doesn't happen in public, but behind closed doors.

"Sounds like a description of Conrad Jay in a gay bar," Jerome said, and switched the station to classical. Thomas's neck and chest pulsed. He hadn't slept the night before, except in fits. The accusation switched the lens through which Thomas had experienced life. Reversed. Instead of seeing others, it reflected the eye of the viewer. Back in Colorado, during the final part of his chemotherapy, Jake had talked about the "Detached Witness," a strategy he'd started practicing when he kicked heroin without methadone. "You try to experience your body in its circumstances as objectively as possible," Jake had said. "As if you're incapable of reacting emotionally."

Thomas tried. It didn't work. Just that morning he had typed *how to survive terror* into his search engine. Denial and terror—his two states. Terror less because he feared being found guilty, and more that he'd been wrong. But wrong about what? Country Day? Mercy? His whole life? *Listen to music and pick out various instrumental parts. Hear them individually.* And: *Count to seven as you breathe in, hold it for six, let it out for five.* And: *Concentrate on what you love.*

Thomas loved his brothers. For a month he'd ached for his family. Jake's cancer had united them, they'd become a team again. Too much an agnostic to believe that their rallying saved Jake, Thomas felt good that they'd ushered him through the medical process. Now Thomas wanted help but couldn't ask. Telling them might make it real. They'd just spent a whole year with nothing but worry. Thomas couldn't lie to anybody's face—at least not convincingly—but conceal and compartmentalize? Yes and yes. He'd already sent too many texts like the one he wrote yesterday, *All good with me, but I'm swamped. Let's check in when things settle down a bit.*

"Who was that?" Jerome asked, indicating the phone.

Thomas clicked the male part of the buckle into its slot. "My brother," he said. "Can they really do this? Publish my name?" Thomas held out the screen showing the photograph with the black bars across his students' eyes.

Jerome looked at the photo and said, "So long as they say allegation. Did you tell your brother?" Jerome asked.

"Sort of. Not yet, I will," Thomas said, sick to his stomach. That headline, the photograph, would exist online forever. Forever like the rain as the sky continued its pour on Portland. Thomas tried to separate the parts of the song playing quietly from the car's speakers from the rain on glass, listen to one instrument at a time: the bass, the violins, the drum, the clarinets; but he couldn't concentrate. Instead, the rain reminded Thomas of his last time in a gay club, because Mercy had said, "Water, water everywhere nor any drop to drink." He remembered her face, dewy, smiling. She'd convinced Thomas to go to a tea dance one Sunday afternoon, right from the airport. Thomas had watched Mercy as she tossed her twisted hair. Her white tank top glowed under the black light on her golden skin as she danced. Not solo, like when Jerome had taken to that same dance floor after coffee on their first date. Mercy danced with the boys she'd met through a friend from her orchestra, the guy who'd invited her. Thomas remembered feeling impressed, almost awed by Mercy's smile, her genuine capacity to draw others to her, how she looked at each of them, reached out to join hands for a twirl. He remembered the young men's openness in welcoming her—an interloper, a newbie—into their circle. He wondered why something so easy for her felt impossible for him.

"Are you close?" Jerome asked. He pressed a button that made the wipers double their speed. "With your brother?"

Thomas nodded, turned the radio off. "You?"

"No," Jerome said. "Have barely spoken to my family in twenty years. I've seen them once. Two years ago, at my sister's funeral."

"I'm sorry," Thomas said.

"Don't be." Jerome braked suddenly at a yellow light. "My parents are bigots. Leaving me alone is the one good thing they've done for me. If your siblings have children, be prepared, they might . . ." Jerome started to say.

"Don't," Thomas said, looking at Jerome's hands as they moved around the ribbed circle of the sedan's steering wheel. Thomas pitied him for whatever he'd suffered. "My family. They're not like yours." Jerome had worked around homophobes for decades. He earned the right to issue warnings. Still, Thomas knew—that in this one thing—Jerome was wrong.

As kids, Thomas and James had shared a small room. One day, with an idea to create more play space, Maddy traded their separate beds for bunks, and James claimed the top bunk, no discussion. Before sleep, Maddy would come in and kiss each of them. James first, then Thomas. Three kisses: both cheeks and the forehead. "Sleep tight. Love you," they all said to each other. Every night.

The city outside Jerome's windshield looked like a study in grayscale, except for the red of brake and traffic lights, which reminded Thomas that he and Mercy had argued about the final scene of *Schindler's List*. Thomas had hated Spielberg's choice to colorize the little girl's coat, thought it ruined the film. Mercy loved it. Now the window disappeared into the car door as Thomas pressed the button. He put his hand outside and promised himself,

84

right then, with the cool, damp Portland air racing through his fingers, that he would tell James everything that very evening; then ask James's help in rolling out the information to the rest of his family.

Thomas put up his window and Jerome kept the course, winding toward Country Day through Portland's forest, its saturation of green and slick black on the damp roads. The woody and musty scents of evergreens and mushrooms. Thomas's childhood room had always smelled of James: of his older brother's soccer socks and sweaty shin pads, his breath, the plates of hot food he ate in bed while reading or listening to records. It never felt like their room. Instead, it was as if Thomas had been allowed to sleep in James's room. And Thomas liked it. He wanted James hovering over him at night. When Thomas found himself alone in the room, he studied his brother's belongings, training himself on the objects of boyhood. Soon after Jake was born, the family moved from Northern California to Massachusetts, and Thomas was given his own room, three times the size. He sat on the floor with Maddy, rug and wallpaper samples stacked high. "What shall we do?" she'd asked. Once he and his mother had executed the plan, he found it odd to be surrounded by everything he'd chosen for himself. There was too much freedom. Too much privacy.

Jerome held his hands at ten and two. "The consequences of being an innocent gay man accused of touching a boy are often worse than the punishments given to convicted male child molesters who're married to women."

"Well my brothers don't think that way," Thomas said. "Let's focus on today. I just want you to show the parents everything they need to be convinced to let me come back."

Jerome looked from the road to Thomas's face for the first time. "You're not hearing me, Thomas. I'll say it again. Country Day will never allow you near children. You'll likely never teach again."

Yes. He'd said it. More than once. But no, Thomas thought. He's wrong. The parents would insist on reinstatement. Soon. The parents venerated him, recommended him, sent invitations to parties and graduations and recitals and performances, years after their kids left his classroom. They needed him.

"What if I don't want to?" Thomas said. "Resign?"

"That's where we have leverage for the civil suit. But if you insist," Jerome said, "parents will crawl out of the woodwork with made-up stories. Everything you've ever done or said will be revised. They will portray you as a predator."

Thomas pulled the seatbelt from where it cut across his chest. "Isn't that a bit paranoid? My students' parents trust me more," he said, "not less, because I'm gay."

"They do until they don't," Jerome said. "Folks want to believe the monster lives in the woods."

Thomas looked out the window at Forest Park and remembered how curious he'd been on every side trail when he first moved to Portland. Mesmerized on too-long runs, Thomas forgot about food, about water. Disoriented, he'd start to panic about finding his way back to the main path. Lately, he'd been taking hikes with Mercy, the two of them swapping the fancy binoculars Joyce and the girls had gotten him for his birthday so they could spot rare birds. A month ago, when Thomas had bragged to Sheree about his and Mercy's four-hour hike, she said, "Better you than me. You two alone in the woods? To me, that's a nightmare waiting to happen." At the time, Thomas reassured Sheree, suspected he knew why she'd said it, but also felt she needed to get out of The Springs. He told her those types of hate crimes didn't happen in Portland.

The view of the woods started to blur as Jerome continued talking.

"You're lucky, in a way, that the parents insisted the sheriff's office turn their investigation over to the district attorney. It works to our advantage that both concluded that there's no basis for a criminal prosecution, but this town hall we're going to? This so-called community forum? It's a sham. Mercy's doing it to show diligence, not to give you a chance to get your job back. She feels badly, and wants you to see the outrage she's fielding from the parents before firing you, or insisting you resign."

Thomas closed his eyes. He couldn't get air into his lungs. He unlocked his seat belt, unable to catch his breath. Jerome pulled over as Thomas's peripheral vision went dark, created a tunnel. Soon, Thomas heard Jerome's door and umbrella open. Soon after, the passenger door. Jerome squatted, leaned in, and took Thomas's knees, led them sideways toward the dirt turnout hugging the forest, and pried them open as drops of rain sounded against the umbrella fabric. "Put your head down here," he said, and patted Thomas's lap with one hand, holding the umbrella with the other. After several minutes, Thomas sat back up. Jerome dabbed his forehead with his handkerchief.

"Sorry," Thomas said.

"That's one word I don't want to hear," Jerome said. "My job is to collect the apologies from them. Not you."

As they pulled into the parking lot, the perfume of cedar trees and ocean spray and honeysuckle came in the cracked window. Up until today, Thomas had spent the last month thinking, *any minute Mercy will call.* Or she'd use her housekey to barge in with a petition signed by the parents to let him teach again. She'd respond to the one and only email he'd sent (after Jerome told him not to) suggesting supervision: Mercy or a parent or an undercover cop or nanny cams—he didn't care—until the sheriff's office finished their paperwork proving it a misunderstanding. He knew she'd need the PFA or the board to agree then vote, but hadn't she, by now, earned their trust? The first week of being home from work, Thomas, when not refreshing his email, executed the craziest housecleaning he'd ever done, down to soaking each of his refrigerator's Plexiglas shelves in a sink of suds and diluted bleach.

Each day of waiting proved harder than the last. Some days he couldn't get out of bed. Some days he became frenzied. One night, a week ago, he had arrived home from the gym with nothing to do. He had no papers to grade, no lessons to prepare, no parent emails to return, no phone chats with Mercy or his colleagues. He couldn't bring himself to call Dana or his brothers or his parents. Not yet. He worried how his situation might plant a seed of doubt in the minds of his nieces and nephew. Better to suffer alone. Of course, they would have comforted him. Dana would be on the next flight to Portland. But he didn't want to answer any more questions, and he especially did not want to manage her outrage. He could have confided in his parents, too, especially Maddy; but Jake's cancer scare had left her fragile. So, he stopped at Krugers, where he bought oranges and asparagus; and at Pastaworks for homemade noodles and a bottle of wine. When the police returned his laptop, he backed up his files to an external disk. He re-vacuumed the throw rugs and wrote a thank you note to Joyce, who'd sent him the care package for his birthday with the fancy watch and the expensive binoculars along with a Scottish cashmere sweater. This past Saturday, he streamed four of the movies he'd been too busy to watch over the past twelve years. Sunday, he spent the day web-searching random stuff like the value of property in his neighborhood, the prices of condos in San Francisco, the amount of donations each of his students' parents had given to recent campaigns. Monday and Tuesday, Jerome prepped him for today. After each of the calls, Thomas swallowed Valiums from a prescription he'd saved after a minor oral surgery. He stayed in bed, rarely getting up except to drink or pee.

Thomas asked Jerome, "Must we? A public forum?"

"Yes," Jerome had said. "These parents need to hear from the experts that you're guilty of nothing except being an exceptional teacher."

The men exited the car, and as Thomas grabbed his raincoat from the back of his seat, Gail Samuelson pulled up, and broke the rules by using the faculty lot. She stepped out of her SUV. She wore her usual workout clothes, but also a face full of makeup. "Good morning, Gail," Thomas said, as he shut the car door, the words already out before he remembered the rules.

Jerome placed a finger to his lips. Gail pretended not to hear.

She pressed the button on her key fob, which made her car chirp, then walked to the hatchback and opened it, rummaging around until Thomas followed Jerome from the lot under a canopy of ancient eucalyptus trees toward Mercy's office. He'd been to lunch with Gail Samuelson a half dozen times over the last year. He remembered what she'd said about Mr. Jay at the party, the smell of her breath: red wine and chocolate.

In the twelve years he taught at Country Day, Thomas rarely forgot to notice how beautiful the surroundings were. *Lucky,* he'd often think, walking from his car to the faculty lounge where he'd greet his colleagues, place his packed lunch in the refrigerator, and top off his travel mug with fresh coffee before heading to his classroom. Now, still shaking from the chill he'd caught at the side of the road, Thomas listened to the clicking of Jerome's oxfords against the path's tightly packed stones.

"Don't worry," Jerome said, placing his hand on Thomas's shoulder. "Today is the day when it all ends."

The warmth of Jerome's hand, however slight through the rubber of his raincoat, nearly made Thomas cry. Thomas had been forced to dwell alone, outside of Country Day, his camp. He'd read about a quarantine forced upon the Byzantine Empire. The king dumped bodies into the sea. Other times in history, isolating oneself ensured safety—flu epidemics and whatnot. He wondered how those in history stayed home for such long periods. The hours on end with no job to do.

Still woozy, Thomas couldn't feel the bottoms of his feet, and hoped he wouldn't slip on the narrow stretch of hardwood planks. His face felt numb, too, save his eyes, which itched. When Jerome opened the door to the administration building, Thomas's knees buckled at the familiar scent of glass cleaner and damp old wood. He wanted his life back.

Thomas and Jerome sat in two of the three chairs opposite Mercy's large glass desk. When Thomas had interviewed for the job, her desk, then made of wood, faced the window. A set of parents had recently donated the services of their interior designer, who convinced her to paint the walls. They'd been white and now were a rich, dark blue-gray. The desk was moved to face the door. The walls' dark color contrasted and highlighted the natural light from the room's huge window. Mercy's degrees, the school's awards, and the signed headshots of famous alumni had been identically framed and artfully arranged on the walls.

Once Thomas and Jerome settled, she said, "All parties have agreed to a town hall-style open forum. This is a fact-reporting mission. As you know, no legal charges will be filed. This process is to answer parents' questions. The board of trustees and the parent-faculty association will gather parents' reactions and use today's findings to vote on next steps."

Thomas noted her leg shaking. Her old desk covered her legs, so he wondered if she'd always been a leg shaker or if it were the circumstances. Odd that he didn't know. She'd removed the framed picture of the two of them—with last year's class at Tillamook Air Museum—from the landscape of her desk. She'd joined him on the field trip, and they'd posed with his students in front of the Aero Spacelines Mini Guppy. He couldn't believe it when he found a frame made out of the salvaged parts of a Boeing 377 online. Now, a tiny potted succulent sat squat in its place. Moisture from the rain clung to the window behind her, making it difficult for Thomas to differentiate between the droplets clinging to the allspice and hydrangea just outside, and those against the glass.

"Toby came in from the bathroom," Jerome said, as if repeating it one last time would make Mercy call off the town hall and give Thomas his classroom back. "His pants fell down. The other kids started laughing. Thomas went to Toby, and pulled them up," Jerome said. "The kid was flustered. Thomas helped the boy. In a room full of witnesses."

"I know," Mercy said. "But from the parents' point of view, Toby's hesitation, his getting flustered. Shit. You both know it would seem odd even for a kid half Toby's age to stand there with his pants around his ankles. And Toby's mature."

"Everyone witnessed it, Mercy," Jerome said. "Odd shit happens all the time. Exactly why I suspect Toby was manipulated. That he's complicit."

"You think they set him up to drop his pants?"

"No, but once it all happened, they may've influenced him to believe that what Thomas did was wrong. Add that to Mr. Jay's unwanted advance?" Jerome said. "An advance Mrs. Jay may've seen? I have a witness ready to testify that he's had sex with Mr. Jay. I can sue for slander."

"I'm not the one who needs convincing," Mercy told him, trying to get a pen to write in a notebook. "You know we wouldn't be here if it were up to me."

"Bullshit. Did you see the paper this morning? Who sent in that photo and leaked the investigation? The sheriff's office and the DA stripped Thomas of his privacy and attempted to humiliate him."

The leaves clung to the window behind Mercy, so green and wet they looked black. Jerome leaned forward in his chair, tried to straighten his sports jacket so it rested more squarely across his shoulders. "By 2025, it's estimated that up to 10 percent of lower grade pupils in Portland will be the kids of same-sex parents. That's up to one in ten applicants. These are people who, if not deterred from bringing their children to a homophobic school, will give disproportionately to your scholarship fund. You boast about Thomas's sexuality when it's good marketing. To maneuver progressive parents into paying this school's outrageous tuition, but the minute a question is asked you pull him out of the classroom? Off the website? What does that say about your loyalty? And what about the boys and girls who're actually getting molested? These theatrics are why people don't believe real victims."

Mercy gathered herself, shuffled papers, moved a letter opener from a rectangular tray holding various sizes and shapes of paperclips into the copper cup placed next to the potted plant. Up until the newspaper headline, Thomas, no matter how hard Jerome pushed, couldn't see Mercy as vindictive, certainly not homophobic. How could she be? She'd hired him, coached him, been his best friend in Portland. They knew the names of every member of the other's family. They'd taken trips to attend conferences, gotten drunk, laughed, danced, hiked, biked, strategized, purchased each other birthday and Christmas gifts. They picked each other up from the airport. She'd met and laughed with and hugged and got to know Manny. She confided her worries to Thomas. She owned a key to his house. She watered and tended to his plants, inside and out, when he'd take off for winter and summer breaks—and he hers.

And not just Thomas and Manny, she kept in touch with several long-standing and close gay friends from college. Considered the other members of her community orchestra, several gay, her Portland family. A lesbian minister led the Episcopal church where she sang and attended services.

So no, he did not agree with Jerome, even though he saw the logic of his argument. Mercy had earned a flawless record as an administrator—beyond reproach—more capable and nuanced than any he'd worked with or known. Her reputation among Portland's elite had not come easily. Not often, but from time to time, her desire to maintain it overshadowed her judgment. Perhaps as a woman, a Black woman, she shared a sliver of the predicament the journalist described in that think-piece about Obama. To Thomas, her blind spot wasn't homophobia, but— how, exactly, would he describe it?—she too easily traded her authority for approval. She doled out too many yesses. She'd buffed her veneer of control into a smooth, bright surface. Its shine mesmerized them all, convinced them it couldn't crack.

Jerome would never convince Thomas of Mercy's hidden homophobia, so what caused the sudden fury that made him want to pick up that letter opener and stab someone—who? Mercy? Jerome? The Jays? Himself? The whole lot? It came from knowing her as utterly committed, completely loyal, supremely focused, and bitingly strategic. Even with all that abundance of skill and intelligence, she chose the board; the PFA; the Jays, their money, their prestige in the community; and the optics of the school over him, Thomas, her friend, a decent, hard-working fourth-grade teacher.

Clear, hot and calm, that's how Thomas suddenly felt. Hotter and hotter: his hands, his forehead, his chest. His body heat made the air around him hot with his own fury. He hadn't recognized it as such. Not until hearing Jerome's outrage and seeing Mercy's impatience on full display. Inside and outside, under his ribs, around his body, hotter and hotter as he was made to listen to Jerome's argument about the Jays. Did Thomas believe that Lisa had fabricated this accusation out of some kind of petty revenge? A marital version of kicking the cat or killing the messenger? He did not, and he didn't think Jerome did, either. Thomas had witnessed the distortions born of loneliness and ambition, of maintaining appearances at all costs. He'd suffered himself because of those very things. Everyone had, and it wasn't until this moment that he realized that the fury he felt was for himself. For every minute he'd enacted some version of the same thing Lisa and Mercy and the police and the board had done to him.

"You're off," Mercy said to Jerome. "Under my leadership, Country Day was one of the first schools in the country," she said, explaining their zero tolerance for bullying LGBT kids and families and allies. "My school has always been hospitable."

"She's telling the truth," Thomas said, his voice thin, his throat dry.

Her expression shifted, just for a moment, from the unflappable businessperson, the defender of the kingdom, to his friend. She looked at Thomas, and that's where he saw his Mercy, in her eyes.

He broke the eye contact. His head pounded. Every part of his body touching the chair: back, butt and legs, felt impossibly hot, stuck to the thin layer of wool separating his skin from the leather upholstery. Thomas expected to be admonished by Jerome for speaking. Instead, he placed his hand on Thomas's forearm, but did not look away from Mercy. Jerome defending him so unsparingly both frightened Thomas, and, in some way, turned him on, gave him what he wished—who? His mother? James? Jake? His dad? Manny? Mercy?—had given him. Hadn't they all been good enough? Supportive enough? Compared to so many others, Thomas received an unfair portion of support.

Perhaps. But perhaps not.

Jerome defended Thomas not only against the accusation and treatment by those conducting the investigation, but also against Thomas's own warped sense of what he did and did not deserve. It wasn't until hearing Jerome accuse Mercy and the Jays that Thomas felt the first tinge of vindication. In his fury, he not only questioned the loyalty of Mercy and Country Day, but his whole family. Was that why he'd avoided them? Had any of them worked to accommodate Thomas? Or had Thomas done the work to make them comfortable?

"How many openly queer people do you employ here, Mercy? As far as I can see, there are three: Thomas, a librarian, and a gardener. I've interviewed a trans woman who applied for a tech position in your science lab. You told her the school found someone with more experience, but the position remained open, and you continued to run the job announcement for months after you turned her down. The person you finally hired published his resume online, with considerably less experience than my client. She's willing to file a complaint. Putting up a rainbow flag and a poster about bullying doesn't undo the fact that you gave Thomas's laptop to the sheriff without a warrant."

Mercy's voice remained calm, her gaze steady, but when she lifted her fingers from where she'd placed her hands flat on the desk, Thomas saw a slight trembling, and under her palm, a circle of perspiration. People said "poker face," but Thomas imagined a pilot's—if the pilot had been highly trained, and needed to make an emergency landing in a huge airplane on a tiny strip. Thomas had never seen this particular set of Mercy's expressions.

"You're conflating issues that are much more nuanced than you're presenting them, Jerome. The computer is school property, the scientist had zero experience with children, the person we hired is highly qualified and represented a demographic we serve in our school, and we do double what most schools do to unpack the meaning behind symbols like the rainbow flag," she said, and then, to all their surprise, slammed her hand on her desk. "This whole thing could be way worse," she said. "Imagine if Thomas were Black?"

Thomas sat still, looked in the pen cup as Mercy quickly re-gained her composure, and imagined all three of them lunging, taking turns with the letter opener to jab the tender parts of the other. Jerome had pushed Mercy, and she broke the character of Head of School. They both knew, in some way, she was right. And instead of joining forces and fighting the bigger thing causing all this, they'd turned against each other. Imagine if Thomas hadn't been Thomas, but another person accused of doing the same thing somewhere else. Someone Black or brown. What if he'd spoken with an accent? How often had he heard the Country Day mothers speculate about theft by the housekeepers who cared for their homes and the nannies who raised their children? What if he were without money, lawyer, a family he could fall back on, an education? What if he'd been the trans coach he'd heard interviewed on NPR? His injustice wasn't even special. The true jab, Thomas thought, isn't that this had happened, but the understanding that it hadn't happened sooner.

"Sorry, Thomas," Mercy said. Thomas knew her well enough to understand she meant it, even if her words seemed insincere and lacking tenderness. Mercy had always struggled when her job forced her to ignore her gut. The result? She doubled down on the script, on playing the part. He'd seen her in hundreds of in-teractions with parents, mitigating when one parent made threats, reacting to their child's mistreatment. The more ridiculous she thought the perceived injustice, the more robotic she came across, and the more she relied on protocols. "There's nothing I can do to change what's in the minds of those parents. That's not up to me. That's up to you."

"Let's make something very clear," Jerome said. "We will not walk out of here quietly—no matter how convinced you are of your own integrity. We don't buy what you're selling us. You and your board better insist Thomas be reinstated on Monday. If that doesn't happen, you can say goodbye to your scholarship fund."

Mercy stood, flattened her jacket to her stomach and slacks. "You don't need to threaten me, Mr. Carter. I invited you here out of courtesy so you'd both know whose side I'm on. I'm the one who told Mr. McGurrin to get a lawyer. I'll let you two use my office to prepare for a few moments. I have to meet the folks who'll be reporting today. You can join us when you're ready. We'll see you in the assistant principal's office as you requested, then head to the recreation building in a half hour."

When the door shut behind Mercy, Thomas closed his eyes, and listened not to Jerome, but to a branch brushing against the glass.

Jerome insisted on negotiating the terms for the town hall, and everyone, except the Jays, met in the assistant principal's office. Jerome's terms? No past students. No press. If, after the morning's headline, any press showed up, they'd be told this simple statement: *After exhaustive investigations, no criminal charges have been made against Mr. McGurrin, which proves the falsehood of the allegation. This is a town hall for the Country Day community to gather information for next steps. The logical next step after reviewing the facts of the investigations would be an offer to return to work.*

Thomas and Jerome had taken their places to the left of the podium just before the Jays came in. Mercy and the colleague who'd witnessed the event in Thomas's classroom arrived soon after. They greeted him with nods.

He didn't respond. Thomas had entered a vortex, where time seemed to swirl in on itself, the same minute circling back again and again. He looked up as frequently as he felt he could without appearing to stare at Mrs. and Mr. Jay. Thomas flip-flopped between magnanimous magical thinking and rage. First, he wanted them to meet him face to face and ask him questions, including whatever questions they had about the night of the party, and he would answer them. He'd remain calm and objective, so his answers would force them to admit they'd gotten confused. He knew them well enough. They possessed the capacity to admit mistakes. Who among us hasn't allowed a mix of family struggles,

96

fear, social pressure, and doubt to mix us up? Had they fucked up? Yes. But it wasn't too late. Thomas could still catch up with his students and their culminating projects. Mrs. Jay could still work a full day. Mr. Jay could go home, hang his tie on the rack Toby had given him. Eventually, all of the adults who cared about Toby could sit down and talk it out.

Then, the DA's assistant would tilt his head to a certain angle, and it would spark a memory of the insinuating questions he'd asked Thomas, about the color and style of Toby's underwear, illustrating Jerome's point about statistics, the fact that openly gay men's sexual violence against children existed only in one place, the imagination of straight people.

And Mercy? One moment Thomas wondered if she'd come around, decide to blow the whole thing up. *I'm your best friend,* he kept thinking. You want to trade me for their approval? What will this indulgence bring you? A ride on a private jet? An invitation to use some ranch house in Sonoma? The insults fell flat, deflated; he couldn't get legs under a rage directed at Mercy. Personal ambition and gain weren't her motivators. Still, he couldn't decide which rage was more dangerous: the unjust, displaced kind aimed at scapegoats? Or the justified rage innocent people felt at evils so pervasive, so enormous that no amount of aiming or shooting at anything but oneself would provide relief?

Mr. Jay didn't look over. Thomas had planned on telling Jerome about the night with the binoculars but had not. He didn't want to be chastised. Did not want to explain something he could not have explained to himself. He thought again of the encounter he'd had with the Jays at the farmers' market the morning after the fundraiser. Before they all went on their way, Mrs. Jay had smiled at Thomas like one might smile at a child, convincing Thomas that she hadn't seen him in the closet with her husband.

After the bathroom, after the golf balls, when Thomas returned to his seat, before they were dismissed, the DA said, "Country Day and the Washington County Sheriff's Department, along with the excellent investigators in our office, have done their jobs in responding to a concern that a child in our community may have been touched improperly." She said the investigations dug deep into Mr. McGurrin's entire career. "No evidence exists that any child has ever been subjected to any form of mistreatment in Mr. McGurrin's classroom." The small woman put down her paper and then used both hands to adjust the band keeping her bangs from her forehead.

Tadd Harrison stood up. Asked, "How are we supposed to trust him with our kid in his classroom? Even if there's no evidence?"

"You'd trust Mr. McGurrin the same way you'd trust any other adult," she answered.

"But he's not a father," Mr. Harrison said. "In emails, he referred to our kids as *his.*"

Jerome interjected. "We can try and help clarify the facts of the investigations, sir, but Mr. McGurrin has been cleared of any suspicion. You agreed to the parameters set forth for this meeting."

"If you have a specific question about the investigation . . . ," the DA said, sternly, to Mr. Harrison.

Drew Ackerman stood up as Tadd sat down. Drew's daughter, Brianna, had been Thomas's student a decade ago. His wife sent Thomas a Christmas card every year with a family photo, this last year in front of the Bridal Veil Falls. Thomas now winced, imagining the recent conversations at their family's dinner table.

"People do bad things and leave no evidence," he said.

"In cases involving child sexual molestation, it is our department's experience that it's easy to find indicators and often not too difficult to find evidence of something that indicates that the accused is a perpetrator. Remember, in this country, one is innocent until proven guilty," the district attorney said. "All evidence clearly points to Mr. McGurrin's innocence."

As a kid, Thomas felt in possession of an extra organ hiding in his chest, something small behind his lungs. After Maddy read him the story of Rumpelstiltskin for the first time, Thomas decided it looked like a tiny dollhouse-sized loom. In the story, the miller lied, but Thomas didn't care; his imagination lit up with the idea of a magic loom that spun straw into gold. Whenever his parents fought, whenever the evening had turned dark, and James still hadn't come home, Thomas believed he could inhale—like adults inhaled the smoke from a cigarette—and the little loom in his chest could transform the scary stuff. When he exhaled, the loom turned the smoke like straw into a vapor like gold. Anger or fear into peace and reassurance. When the DA said the word *innocence*, sorrow took hold of Thomas from the inside, and roamed the empty space where that loom had once lived.

Mrs. Jay stood up, straightened the belt built into her shirtdress. She looked at the District Attorney. With her palm turned up, she extended the pointer finger of her left hand toward the DA, as if pointing to a stack of peaches at the farmers' market. "You said he had pictures of children in a drawer. Lots of them."

The DA stepped back; one of her investigators went to the microphone. As tall and skinny and pale as a white birch tree, the investigator put on his glasses. "They're his nieces. His nephew. Nothing less innocent than the photos in the Country Day yearbook. The photos were mentioned not by way of comparing but contrasting those hidden by perpetrators."

Her elbow stayed at her hipbone, but her body and finger turned to the investigator from the sheriff's office. She said, "How did you get a search warrant if there wasn't . . . ?"

"Again, we didn't have a warrant," the officer said. "We had no probable cause. Mr. McGurrin gave us full access to his place. He let our investigator take his computer off premises."

"I thought you said they had a warrant?" She turned to Janet Williams and said, "You told me on the phone that he let the kids feel his muscles."

Each time she spoke, her voice seemed thinner.

Janet Williams's neck reddened at the slightest confrontation. Now his aide's skin looked like the kind of rash that required a shot of Benadryl. She'd gone on record as saying she once witnessed a kid make a comment about Thomas's big muscles before grabbing his biceps. Now she shrugged, unable to look up at Mrs. Jay.

"Why?" Lisa asked. "Why did Toby say it if it wasn't true?"

Trying to sleep each night after the start of the investigation, after each interrogation, each humiliation, he tried to hang on to his faith in his own good judgement. Each night, the memory circled and circled, the scene replayed. First, he saw it as it had happened; then how he might have imaged the same story if it hadn't been about him, but someone else; then he imagined the story as if told through the filter of the imaginations of people like . . .

No. He couldn't, wouldn't allow himself to imagine this as a result of that.

What was *that?*

It started with apple juice and parmesan. Colette, who shared a table with Toby, gave her classmate her juice box, which Toby drank, along with his own. Add that to the extra refill and drain of his stainless-steel water bottle. He always drank two between snack and reading time when his father packed the dice-shaped squares of cheese for snack. Thomas insisted all the kids take a bathroom break afterward. But Toby had drank too much. And reading time was Toby's favorite, the only one of the day's activities when he wouldn't gladly take the opportunity for an extra trip to the toilet.

Janet had been reading passages, discussing a book with the kids, whose bodies formed a semicircle by the window when Thomas, looking up from the paperwork at his desk, noticed. Thomas often looked up at them during story discussion, to see how their features would reshape their faces as they listened to Janet's expert voice modulation and followed along in their own copies. That day, Toby Jay didn't seem transported by curiosity or wonder. His expression showed a kid in physical pain. He rocked back and forth.

"Toby," Thomas had interrupted. "Up. Go. We'll wait." Always compliant, Toby jumped up, ran-walked out the door, and a couple minutes later, came back. In his haste to rejoin the circle, he tripped. He immediately regained his balance, but let out a bit of a screech, then knocked a chair over, and everyone turned around. Toby apparently hadn't fastened his snap and belt. One classmate pointed; then the rest started laughing. Toby froze, just like he had during the applause at his group report. Toby could be a practical joker from time to time, but it quickly became clear to Thomas that he'd again entered a mild shock state. Janis stood to go help him. "I've got it," Thomas said, as the other kids kept laughing at Toby. Thomas went to Toby, pulled his pants to his waist, snapped them shut, and told him to join the group. That was that.

This? A call from Mrs. Jay who said she worried that Toby had been touched inappropriately. Mercy, a mandatory reporter, called the sheriff's office, and then Thomas. She didn't have to explain because he too was trained as a mandatory reporter. The sheriff's office sent two male detectives to investigate. They issued a Miranda warning and asked him, sometimes demanded, again and again, to recount *that*. He cooperated, even when they purposely tried to get him to contradict himself, when they said, "Are you sick of hiding, Tommy? Tired of pretending? Ready to give up?" Thomas cooperated even when, on their way to search his garage, his car, he heard one officer say to the other, "Are we going to find a buncha fruit roll-ups in his glove compartment?" They also requested and he agreed to allow them to search his home, workspace, and personal and work computers. Questions like, "Did you angle your hand so it would touch his penis? His scrotum? Did you rub against his crotch in any way? If not your hand, would you say one finger brushed against his genital area? Two? Your forearm?"

"No," Thomas had said, and remained calm. "There wasn't even a zipper on the pants, only a snap. I touched the waist. I went nowhere near his crotch."

"How far away was your hand from his genitals?" they'd asked, and Thomas didn't know, tried to picture it in those terms, then guessed at least six or eight inches. The officer then said, "That's pretty precise. Sounds like you know what you're talking about. No zipper? That's detailed."

This activated the parents' phone tree, and Thomas didn't be-lieve Jerome when he said the parents would be more excited by the possibility of Thomas's guilt than relieved by the facts of his innocence, even after the board and PFA pressed the DA to con-duct a separate investigation. One of the DA's investigators stood in Thomas's living room, drinking a mineral water from a bottle Thomas had poured in a glass pulled from his shelf, then shut off the recorder and said, "Guys like you like to hide in plain sight. Is this a game? A dare?" His partner added, "Is that why you have that big-ass Costco thing of lotion on your work desk? I can just see you with a fistful as you kick back and watch your kids."

Forty-four hours of meetings and phone calls and writing nar-ratives and answering questions. Forty-four hours not including the time Thomas spent one-on-one with Jerome preparing to an-swer their questions. Each time Mercy asked him for something, he thought, *This is it. Do this, and it'll be done. Then I can get back to teaching, lesson planning, making dinner, cleaning house, doing my laundry with the windows open to the sound of the rain.*

One hour to review defensive strategies one last time with Jerome. Three hours of initial interviews. Four for the investiga-tors who scoured his laptop. Six to review the transcript before signing it. Thomas sat through every one of those minutes. His fourth graders could've easily deduced the investigators' strategy. Thomas remembered something Toby told Colette when his classmate cried because she hadn't mastered a tongue-twister: "The point is to help us, not to get us to mess up."

What was the point here?

After meeting with Mercy, Thomas felt awful. And that awful kind of lucky that came from knowing that you'd survived some-thing unjust. Yes, it could have been worse for someone else, somewhere else. The internet teemed with stories of gay men in similar circumstances who'd been arrested without evidence, taken to jail, denied bail.

Now, having just sat down after the break, the DA said that both investigations showed that Thomas did not fit the profile of a molester; there was no evidence to suggest wrongdoing. The incident in question was witnessed by several of the children and a classroom aide, all of whom were interviewed by a social worker and a specialist. The newspaper had erroneously printed that a child said a teacher pulled down his pants (not up), a mistake a child (but not a newspaper) might make. "Mr. McGurrin has been advised not to assist students with their clothing in the future. We have also compiled a list of training resources for the entire staff at Country Day with suggestions on how to handle situations such as the one Mr. McGurrin faced with Toby. Now it's up to the administration, the board, the Parent Faculty Association and Mr. McGurrin's peers to decide how to proceed. I'll state it one last time for you: there is not one single piece of evidence to suggest that Mr. McGurrin is a danger to your community."

"That doesn't mean he's innocent," one of the parents said.

"No. But he is now meticulously screened," she countered. "Few other teachers will ever be scrutinized as closely as Mr. McGurrin," she said, before telling Thomas she'd never seen a person remain so calm under the circumstances. "I hope," she said, "that this investigation will not have a negative impact on your continued success."

A din of chatter erupted. On TV it would've been the moment before a judge pounded a gavel against a sound block, yelled for order. Jerome grabbed Thomas, hugged him, held him up in his chair. Thomas couldn't tell if it were relief or panic that forced him to stifle the cry. Suddenly dizzy, he leaned his face into Jerome's chest, coughed into his jacket, then looked up over his shoulder as the parents filed out. Most of them, including the Jays, avoided eye contact. How odd he must have looked, there in his lawyer's arms. Childish? Lascivious? He could no longer imagine, because those who held his gaze, people whose expressions he thought he once knew, were suddenly and utterly unreadable.

He didn't feel exonerated—he felt, if anything, more accused. The parents gathered their things, paused for a moment on their way out to toss beverage containers into the proper bins. Disappointed. That's the closest he could come to assigning a word for how they looked. As if they'd come to watch a bomb and witnessed a dud. As if they would've been happier, more satisfied, had they learned Thomas had, in fact, molested a child. As they passed, Jerome said, "This utopia can't exist with an occasional pariah."

Thomas didn't understand and didn't ask Jerome to clarify. He'd caught a chill and wanted Jerome's warmth, so he held on until he could contain himself, get up from his chair and stand in the strange and electric combination of relief, seething anger and dread. He'd grown accustomed to anger and dread. Relief was welcome, but its powers proved limited. It didn't eliminate the other two feelings, only shifted them.

After he and Jerome had reached the faculty lot, Thomas refused Jerome's offer for a ride home.

"I need to walk," Thomas said. The rain had stopped, but the sun played shy behind a cover of clouds. Thomas wanted the chill of the fresh air, the smell of pine and eucalyptus. "At least to the bus stop."

Jerome drove away just a few moments before Gail Samuelson arrived, alone, at her car in the faculty lot. When she saw Thomas, she dug her right fist into the leather bag that hung from the crook of her left arm.

"Gail," he said, approaching her.

"No, Thomas," she said. "Don't." Her voice shook.

"Don't what?" he asked, moving closer to her.

"Get away," she warned.

"I wanted to ask why," he said.

"Leave me alone," she interrupted. "Or I'll call the police."

"And tell them what?" Thomas asked. "That I wouldn't come to your fucking house for wine and hors d'oeuvres?"

She got in her car. He heard the electric click of the door's lock. As she drove off, Thomas noticed, for the first time, her vanity license plate. There, in the middle of two Obama 2012 bumper stickers it read, *NUM1MOM*.

As Gail drove off, Mercy came out of the back door. She called his name—her inflection a pleading one—one he'd noted only a handful of times, saved for the rare moments she found herself caught in the middle, playing both sides, in an attempt to appear, what? Thomas hesitated. Clean? No, not clean. Not innocent. More like untouchable. Yes. That was it. An inflection of someone who wanted to appear concerned when watching someone else fall from where she stood on the top of a mountain.

Mercy kept calling. Thomas turned, faced her. "Fuck you," he yelled, both his middle fingers up, "Fuck you, Mercy and your fucking bullshit rainbow-flag-unpacking school." He then turned again, walking swiftly away from Country Day.

Thomas replayed the nights and weekends and winter breaks he'd spent with Mercy, planning. And Gail Samuelson? Gail had begged Thomas for his cell number. Thomas tried to tell her, as he told all the parents, to contact the office manager. He reassured Gail that the office would forward her calls to his classroom. But Gail charmed. Insisted. After she had it, Thomas feared she'd give his number to all the parents. But she didn't. She kept it for herself, often texting him during the last hour of school. *Running late but on my way.*

He thought of Amber, Gail's daughter, and the hours he'd spent with her so she could keep up with her peers. Often the two sat at a table in the afternoon light under the tawny wooden beams of the library, reading while the librarian helped the middle and high school students find the reference books the internet hadn't made obsolete. Most recently, Thomas had helped Amber with figurative language. "It creates a picture in your mind—to give the reader a better understanding of your ideas. Like, it's so hot in here I'm roasting!"

"Why not just say it's too warm?" Amber would ask. "Or turn down the heat?" He'd committed his whole life to education. Walking, he didn't understand exactly what he'd hoped to gain in return for his contributions. Up until the accusation, Thomas would've said meaning, or a kind of legacy. Jerome-types may've judged him, thought him not queer enough, too assimilating, accused him of seeking redemption or approval. Dana and Mercy would've both said something more generic, less pointed, like you don't choose your profession. Your profession chooses you.

He remembered only two male teachers in his whole student career before college, both in high school. One, a married guy who taught a couple of algebra classes and coached girls' field hockey. His own daughter played on the team. He looked like Tom Selleck, and a lot of the girls talked about their crushes on him. The other was Mr. Whittaker, a tall, quiet, elegant, handsome man who reminded Thomas of an East Coast prep school version of Anthony Perkins. In two years of social studies, Thomas never learned a single personal detail about Mr. Whittaker, but listened to him, mesmerized, as he eloquently dramatized the details of soldiers fighting on fields, dynasties lost and conquered, the first airplane taking flight. He wore a wedding band, but never mentioned a wife; and while the other teachers covered their desks in personal knickknacks, including family photos, Whittaker's, apart from one bizarre item, contained only pens and books. The item? An old-fashioned steel and glass gumball machine filled with little shiny, bright globes that looked mouthwateringly real, but were, in fact, painted wood.

Those gumballs! He'd always wondered if Mr. Whittaker were gay, too. He had to be. His flair seemed both evident and covered, like a tuxedo under a raincoat. Evident perhaps only to those looking in the gaps between buttons. Covered so as not to be spotted. Sure, there were whispers, but no screams. Were the wooden gumballs a reminder to look and not touch? Was the classroom for Thomas a place to hide? Or had he wanted to trailblaze? Take what he'd learned and admired from Whittaker and add to it, show that you could also decorate a desk with a framed picture of a lover? Thomas never wanted to go into business or sales, like his father, who golfed and ate and met and had drinks with other men. As corny as it sounded, he wanted to make a difference. Mr. Whittaker used a one-line refrain after each chapter in the history textbook: "Now that you know what they say, your job is to look for and find what they didn't. The truth of history isn't in the book. Not yet." Students had started the year dreading social studies and graduated with acceptances to major universities where they went on to study history or political science.

Gail's brake lights had disappeared around the bend, and Thomas kept walking away from the parking lot, wondering if Mercy followed behind him—he wouldn't look—or if Jerome would circle back for him. He took out his phone and scrolled through his text history with Gail Samuelson. Cell reception was bad in parts of the woods. He pressed *Load Earlier Messages* again and again until finally, they appeared: *Hey, you. Lonely here on the ranch. Come over for a glass of chardonnay? Saul is gone again, and Amber's at a sleepover. #feelingsingle.* Ten minutes later, another had come in. *Don't ignore me! PS. Just sent the housekeeper to pick up a whole pig's worth of charcuterie from Olympic Provisions, and I have an unopened bottle of Domaine Serene Monogram Pinot Noir. 2006!*

Thomas turned ten the year his father received a promotion that included the family move from California to Massachusetts. There, everyone was Mister and Missus. Growing up, he'd even heard his friends call aunts and uncles by their last names. It created space. He'd let the last name drop once the kid left his classroom; but until then, he tried his best to remain formal, which was tough in a place like Portland, where kids called adults, including Thomas, by their first names. He'd managed to do so with Toby's parents, but not Gail. She'd insisted on "firsties."

Gail, Thomas had written back, strategically, *It's Thomas, Amber's teacher. I think you confused my number with that of a friend's.*

OMG, she wrote. *URsoSQAURE! We aren't friends?! Can't I invite my daughter's teacher over for snack and juice? LOL. Besides, it's not like you're ordering what's on my menu, so we might as well be girlfriends.*

Thomas shoved his phone into his rain jacket pocket, furious with himself for not telling her to go fuck herself, and while she was at it, hire a babysitter if she didn't want to parent. *And NUM1MOM?* he thought. *My ass.*

The ivy walls of Cedar Hills along Barnes Road angled in on him, brushed his face, occasionally forced him off the sidewalk into the street. As he passed the entrance to The Oregon College of Art and Craft, he recalled his last visit there. He'd gone with Mercy for a juried exhibition of high school artworks. The college had chosen six Country Day students' work, but Thomas couldn't recall their pieces as he walked by the school's entrance. Instead, he remembered meeting one of the jurors, a sculptor named Malia who'd grown up in the wooded foothills of rural Oregon. One of the students asked her how she'd become an artist. She said her dad left an issue of Esquire magazine laying around. "A little fact," she'd said, "I found in my dad's magazine stuck with me." And that fact made her become an artist. What did it say? they asked. "Earthworms," she said, "feel pain."

At the time, Thomas judged her Save-the-Worms stance as downright corny, in line with a regional earnestness that would've made a New York art fan like James roll his eyes. But her sculptures mesmerized Thomas. She said, "I use the weird art of taxidermy," to describe how she constructed them. She'd wall-mounted the bust of a deer made out of shiny black rubber. Protruding nubs replaced antlers. The object conjured both the power of the wild beast along with a human need to dominate. The rubber looked downright fetishy, the nubs suggested an amputation. Bambi-delicate, but bound and flayed. Violence disguised as cuteness? Vice versa?

Thomas walked for five miles before catching the 20 bus. He rode it until he had to transfer to the 75. He looked out the window, imagining all the blind worms in the forest, their thin pink skin, the dirt they ate, the trees above them, and saw Portland in a way he never had before.

Chapter Ten

Wednesday
May 29th, 2013

Thomas reached down his running shorts and released his genitals from the tangle of liner at his inner thigh. Even at his gym, far from work, up until the day he was asked to resign, Thomas would've taken this concern to a private stall in the men's locker room. Or at the very least, he would've tried to camouflage the action by tucking in his tank top. Today he thought: *Fuck it.* The treadmill's motor had warmed up, and now it pulled the rotating rubber mat faster and faster beneath his feet. Finally, his balls could bounce gently and freely in the contained space of his underwear's pouch.

He'd been forcing himself to the gym every day. After lifting, he'd run an hour on the treadmill, where he'd "2-1-2-1": alternate two minutes low-speed high-incline with one-minute high-speed flat run. Late morning on a Wednesday, the gym looked open and spacious compared to the prime times on weekends and before and after work. Other than the small scattering of college students and telecommuters, it was empty.

A relief. Thomas had started to feel uneasy around too many people. He'd been circling his house twice a day since his photo appeared in the paper. He pretended to check on the shrubs, his peonies and dahlias while scanning the property for words like *faggot* or *queer* spray-painted on the side of his garage or car.

Even now, Thomas hated the word *queer*. He'd been vocal in the Zero Tolerance meetings leading to Country Day outlawing its use in any negative context because he held the unpopular opinion of wanting the word banned altogether. On decision day, the straight people on the panel, including Mercy, thought the kids in the upper grades should certainly be able to identify as queer and talk about the political movement. Mercy passed bound dossiers of well-researched supporting materials illuminating the righteous arguments for the success of the reclamation of the word.

On that last day, Thomas said little, knowing the upper-grade kids would still hurl the slur as a dig then claim it as an identity marker to avoid punishment. Thomas remembered that girl at the giraffe park, with her plastic pink barrettes and pink eyeglass rims or her pink eyelids and her pink tongue calling his four-year-old nephew the n-word. He wondered if next year he'd be asked to pass around a dossier of scholars and entertainers who reappropriated that word, so that white kids who "identified" with the "movement" could refer to themselves and each other as such and go unpunished.

When the new rule was entered into the next year's student handbook under Codes of Conduct, Mercy listed the names on the panel, citing Thomas's first, out of alphabetical order. Initially, he questioned this decision, felt like confronting the PFA's secretary, but like so many other times, he sidestepped his instincts to accommodate their demands.

Now he wanted a redo of every last meeting he'd ever attended and kept his mouth shut or chose to smile instead of letting it rip. When he remembered those faculty and PFA and board of trustees meetings, Thomas didn't picture his friends and colleagues sitting around a conference room trying to provide any real or lasting policies to offer opportunities for students. Instead, he pictured a big circle-jerk, a bunch of lube-fisted liberals pleasuring themselves while reciting the rhetoric that allowed them

110

to think of each other as models of enlightenment in Portland's post-racial, pro-queer, Obama-bumper-sticker bubble of wealth. And no one was more to blame than he: for buying it all, for absorbing all of their attention and accolades.

He pressed the display's buttons to increase his speed to a sprint.

His was another era: no gay characters written into TV sitcoms, no marriage equality act, no hate crime legislation, and certainly, no Gay/Straight Alliance existed. In high school, Thomas used sports and books to secure the barricade between his public and private selves.

Maddy had tried over the years. In California, his mother would drive Thomas to the beach, talk vaguely about the importance of being true to oneself. In Massachusetts, she arranged field trips out of the suburbs into the city, to museum shows featuring openly gay artists, and to art-house movie theaters in Cambridge to see movies like *Parting Glances* and *Longtime Companion*.

Instead of comforting Thomas, the art of the era quadrupled his anxieties by drawing a straight line from sex to death. Then, everything gay equaled AIDS, so he contained his eccentricities, learned James's and his friends' modes of physicality. His strategy to use soccer as camouflage went according to plan, at least at first. After tryouts, Thomas played halfback for the junior varsity team. Not center. Not forward. He led in assists, not goals. Even in practice, he made sure to come in third or fourth in drills. Mercifully, the locker room had separate, private stalls, and most guys brought their underwear to the shower, got dressed behind the curtain.

Stuart attended all but one of the championship games and even joined the other dads to throw a celebratory spaghetti dinner when they won. Thomas remembered his dad's lips: thin and gleaming with the butter of a piece of greasy garlic toast. "I'm proud of you, son."

It worked. Thomas finished freshman year as a division champion with a 4.0 GPA. One down, three to go, Thomas had thought, until he'd return to California. He planned a year-two repeat, but the coach promoted him to the varsity team. The first game of his sophomore year, Thomas's opponents assaulted him with their lean muscularity, their thighs. He felt like a pink flamingo. Bearded dudes with chest hair curling up from the necks of their jerseys replaced the bare-faced skinny boys who'd been his opponents the year before. Thomas's performance on the field morphed from steady and predictable to erratic and occasionally fierce.

Sweat dripped onto the treadmill's display. "Do not succumb to bitterness," Thomas said aloud, panting. His new earphones, their buds made of a moldable gel-like rubber that filled his entire concha, made his voice sound like someone else's. The voice of someone wiser, someone who knew what a waste of time it was to focus on the faults of others. "They're good people," he whispered again, thinking of how the parents at Country Day could rarely end a PFA meeting without discussing the crucial need to increase diversity among the faculty and student body.

But were they? And Thomas circled back, catching a peek into his own mind's obsessive habit: like his 2-1-2-1 walk run walk run, the parents switched from saints to sinners back to saints again. He'd always hated ambiguity.

Once on the varsity team, Thomas met Damien, a senior, two years older than Thomas, the child of the owners of the town's bakery. Damien wanted to hold Thomas's feet at practice during sit-ups, partner with him during passing drills, share a bus seat when traveling to away games. He apologized to Thomas for his job because it prevented him from hanging out after practice. Damien did not trigger the flow of blood to Thomas's groin, but his affection made Thomas crave it from others. The physically mature boys on the opposing teams from nearby mill towns sparked Thomas's lust, and the only scheme he'd concocted to contend with it was to put himself in harm's way. He'd propel his body in front of guys twice his size, like tossing a mattress on the tracks of an oncoming train. He had once lost consciousness for a full minute and woke up at the center of a huddle of his teammate's faces, Damien at center. During one game, the forward broke into a dribbling sprint down the field. Thomas outran him, blocked his body while staying on his feet, but the center forward's forearm pressed into Thomas's ribs while the two fought for the ball. The physicality of it sent blood to Thomas's extremities, leaving him with an erection in his silky uniform shorts.

Certain someone noticed, Thomas tried bracing himself for the consequences, but they never came. That afternoon, once home, Thomas took a shower and nap, then went into the woods behind his house and hiked until he found a stone the size of a football. He took off his shoe and sock, and raised the stone to his chest, then dropped it on his left foot. His wail echoed in the valley. He put his shoe back on and limped home, told Maddy that he'd been goofing off in the woods, trying to fix a hole in a stone wall. "Look," he said, taking off the shoe, showing her the swelling and blood.

Maddy grabbed her purse, two Frescas, a bag of frozen peas and her car keys. Thomas obeyed her when she told him to gently tape the peas to his foot with the duct tape in the glove box, then elevate his leg out the window. She sped him to the emergency room where the doctor wrote a note excusing him from gym class and physical activity for the rest of the year.

Thomas never played soccer again.

His pinky toenail grew back a year later. During that time, Thomas often used the band room door as a shortcut from study hall to the cafeteria line. The door led to the backstage of the auditorium. A thick curtain separated backstage from the cafeteria. "Fucking queer," he heard one day, crossing the threshold, then stood still, sure the day for his punishment had arrived. On the other side of the stage, two boys had cornered a kid named Chad.

Thomas had admired Chad almost as intensely as he avoided him. At the time, he found Chad's combination of overt gayness and natural beauty alluring, threatening, and obscene. A head taller than most of the other boys, and reed-thin, his body rested at angles that brought to mind a collapsed marionette. His eyes were a blue so dark and bright they seemed a consequence of some disaster. The blue you might find in the center of one in a million gray rocks at the base of a volcano.

Before the day in the band room, there had been the time Thomas sat a row above Chad on the bleachers in the gymnasium with a few other students with their books and notebooks, studying, while others socialized or shot hoops. Normally, Thomas and Chad weren't in the same class, but the gym teacher and the study hall teacher had both been out sick, and the school only found one substitute, so students could either study or play. A group of cheerleaders had been rehearsing for a rally. When they finally stopped, they talked in a circle of five or six. One of the captains smiled and waved at Chad.

He pointed to himself. "Me?" he mouthed.

She nodded. She'd made her thin lips look thicker by using a pencil to trace outside her lip line before she filled them with gloss that looked like pink cake frosting. She broke off from her pack of friends and approached Chad. "Yes you," she said. "Chad, right?"

Thomas tried to mind his business, to look at his book, but her voice sounded deep and hoarse, a contrast to her small frame, delicate features, and thin hair so blond he could see her scalp. She wasn't at all pretty in the way one might think of a cheerleader. Nor was she vapid. Thomas had been in several classes with her, and she was as intelligent as she was ambitious, which is how he assumed she had made it to captain of a team of tall beauties.

"Yes, I'm Chad," he said and smiled. "Hi."

She came closer, climbed onto the first row of bleachers so she stood within arm's distance of him. "Come here," she said, smiling. "Lean in."

"I don't understand," Chad said.

"Lean over to me." She smiled.

Chad didn't move. And neither did Thomas; transfixed with curiosity, perhaps even jealousy, he couldn't take his eyes off of the two, both delicate in such different ways. Two rare birds sharing the same branch, each exhibiting a kind of power Thomas knew he possessed, but had never expressed, only contained. "Lean your face toward me," she said. Without asking why, Chad scooted to the edge of his bench and bent at the waist to lean down to where she stood. She took his chin into her left hand and then gently wiped her right thumb over his lips, then eyes. First, she looked at her thumb, then turned to her friends and said, "Nope."

"Harder," one of the girls said, in a playful tone. The others giggled.

Chad stayed still, his chin resting in that girl's palm. Then she did it again. She dragged her thumb down his face starting at the lid of his right eye and then across his cheek and over his lips. She'd pressed so hard a thumb-thick red line appeared on his skin where his blood had rushed to its surface. He looked like a warrior.

After, the cheerleader did something that Thomas never forgot. She smelled her thumb then touched her tongue to it. Finally, she let go of Chad's chin, turned the pad of her thumb to the circle of girls. "I won," she said. "No lipstick. No mascara. Natural."

Pink had bloomed where white had been in Chad's eye before he cupped one of his slender hands over it.

"I should fucking kill you for being so pretty," the girl said, and her friends laughed, then she walked into the center of the circle.

That's when he got the first glimpse of the consequences. Now Thomas's legs moved swiftly, efficiently, beneath him. The parents at Country Day rallied, whispered in their honeyed tones, attended galas to support the ballet and opera, funded the women's shelter and gave blankets to the abandoned babies. Now, even the sprinkling of students whose parents Thomas once admired, those who'd adopted their kids from countries in Asia and Africa, seemed part of a larger Country Day show: white parents performing multiculturalism, straight parents performing how much they wanted gays to marry, the gays performing their assimilation on altars and in fertility clinics. And all the children, his students, those who Thomas had believed to be the future, the ones who'd end the poverty cycle, suddenly seemed nothing more than props the

Country Day parents used to manufacture the image they had of themselves, guaranteeing another generation of entitled narcissists.

Or not?

Arguably, Thomas's brother James and his wife Joyce pushed their image of success and privilege even harder than most Country Day parents, because, well, they were New Yorkers. The privileged Portlander preferred the humble brag to the outright boast, the Craftsman to the high-rise, the flat sole to the spike heel. After the town hall meetings had ended, Thomas called his big brother every day, and it never felt like he'd gone to the priest to complain about a pastor.

James took every one of Thomas's calls—even stepped out of surgery to do so—and listened to Thomas's rants. "It's bad enough how they act with their nannies and housecleaners and dog walkers and gardeners. But their kids' teachers, too?"

Except for the occasional "that cuts too close, bro," James never argued. James and Joyce had burned through several nannies and housekeepers and dog walkers and gardeners over the years. Not to mention tutors and caterers and private chefs and manicurists and massage therapists who made house calls. Not once did James attempt to reframe Thomas's complaints, put a single thing in perspective. Instead, he listened.

Casual acquaintances of both brothers were surprised by the two oldest McGurrins' closeness. What do a single gay Portland schoolteacher and a married-with-children New York City surgeon have in common? It sounded like the setup line for a stupid joke. Ambition twinned the brothers. Each needed to be the best in their chosen field and catered to the same demographic. Every time James operated, he made himself vulnerable to litigation. Wealth allowed him to pad himself with outrageous amounts of insurance, but in the beginning, one disgruntled client could've robbed James of his practice. Thomas either refused or hadn't been able to see the equivalent in his line of work. James had joined the demographic he served. Thomas had convinced himself that he had, too. But he'd been wrong. How else had he been wrong?

With more confusion than contempt, Thomas had rejected the idea of living his life within the confines of a gay ghetto—as people used to call the Castro in San Francisco—bordered by a few bars and jobs like cutting hair or working in retail. He'd always loved the neighborhood but wondered about the people who'd relegated themselves to provincial enclaves. Had he wanted his cake and to eat it, too? To be an out gay man who could also pass? Could he even claim being openly gay as a badge of honor when he did nothing to correct people's assumptions of his straightness unless it served him?

People like Chad sacrificed for him. People whose reaction to conventions—like rigid notions of femininity and masculinity, for starters—was to reject or abandon or ignore them altogether. They faced double rejection: first from those unlike them, again from those who wouldn't or couldn't muster the courage to be themselves. Thomas hadn't looked hard enough. Mostly he didn't think about it. He didn't have to.

The truth? He hadn't seen the people who worked in the salons and stores and banks in the Castro. Ten city blocks or the whole wide world. Thomas's idea of freedom had become so warped by the small world he inhabited, that of Portland, of Country Day. He bought the schoolbook version of history without challenging the stories contained in the pages. He'd mistaken his distant admiration and affinity with the fighters and nonconformists as some sort of open-mindedness. What had he done to earn his place in the community? What had he sacrificed?

How had he ever mistaken himself for brave?

The line of treadmills faced the weight room, where benches, free weights, and Nautilus machines sprawled across a floor. Thomas threw around the weights in a halfhearted attempt to be muscular, because he bought the same batch of body-perfect bullshit sold to so many gay men of his age, but truthfully he hated weights as much as he loved running, which he loved almost as much as anything else, including teaching. Both disciplines proved impossible to master and both could send a rush that produced a high as intense as it was elusive. In that high, Thomas could use the body to transcend itself. The bag of blood and bones seemed to disappear. Thomas ran on the treadmill closest to the wall, which had the best view.

The screen on his phone lit up after it registered a voicemail from Jake.

Thomas knew he couldn't avoid Jake or the rest of his family much longer. He hated lying to his family, and he'd lied when he wrote them that he was okay. Typically, reading and cooking to the sound and smell of rain brought him so much pleasure. That morning, he had started with the newspaper, but found himself enraged that they never followed up on their initial story about the accusation, never reported on his innocence, never published Jerome's comments about the case.

He had alternated between wanting to call Mercy and the Jays as he paced between coffee pot and his reading chair. But to say what? Tell them off? Tell Lisa that Toby and Conrad preferred his company to hers? Out of spite? *It's no wonder that spite is just spit with an e*, he thought, *worth no more than his own drool.*

Thomas's shirt was now soaked, though the treadmill's timer showed that he'd only been at it twenty minutes. He took a sip of water. When his two-minute walk ended, he cranked his speed to twelve miles per hour. He looked at the safety clip hanging over the heart rate sensors on the treadmill's handrail. He should've clipped it to the tail of his tank top. So rapid the pace, he couldn't look down, but felt his shoe loosening and wondered if it had come untied. He kept pumping, imagining himself plummeting, and the force of the mat's movement spitting him into the aisle. The minute ended without injury. Thomas grabbed his towel, dabbed his face, thought again about Chad. There'd been many witnesses, even the substitute teacher who caught the end of the ordeal. No one intervened. He hated the Country Day parents for their silence, for not defending him, but hadn't he done the same to Chad? More than once?

That time with the girls was the one he remembered most often, but it was the time with the boys that made Thomas hate the word *queer*. Thomas had hidden behind the stacked stage platforms by the band room door. The boys had shoved Chad between each other and into the band lockers. Faggot, yes. Cocksucker, too. But *queer* was the word they kept repeating, their plan to cage him in one of the empty lockers built big enough for a tuba. "Fuck," one boy had said as the other held Chad in a headlock. "I can't get it open." They pushed him between each other, and into the locker, calling him queer up until and including when they shoved Chad so hard into the percussion cage his head split open on the padlock. One of the two boys lived on Thomas's block and played tag football with James. The second? Damien. He was the one who yelled, "AIDS-blood!" before they took off.

Thomas had crouched, terrified of Chad discovering him there. He was Chad's only witness. "Oh no, oh no, oh no, oh no," Chad said in a strained, panicked pitch, his long bangs wet, stuck with blood to his forehead. Soon Chad had moved toward the band room door, and as he got closer, Thomas could see the blood on Chad's palms. "Why?" Chad said. "Why?" Thomas backed up a step and pulled at the door, wanting it to look like he'd just come in. Chad looked straight at Thomas. "Move," he said, and Thomas stepped forward, and Chad flinched as if Thomas were about to strike him. He wanted to walk Chad to the nurse's office. Or, he wanted to want to. When he couldn't find the words, he thought, *I should go with him. Or at least follow.* Instead, Thomas froze, the drops of Chad's blood trailing from the instrument lockers to the band room door. It disgusted Thomas almost as much as it frightened him.

What a set of mistakes. But before regret, it had been relief. That the bullies had chosen Chad instead. Thomas had been so convincing in his imitation of them, that even with an erection on a soccer field, he'd managed to remain undetectable. With that knowledge came a rich, smug satisfaction, so intense it caused an internal physical collapsing of energy. Like a plug had been pulled. From adrenaline rush to a complete deflation where he felt better than Chad, for passing. For his ability to imitate his brothers' mannerisms. His ability to contain his eccentricities. *I'm more and less,* Thomas had thought, shaking. *More of a man and less of a faggot. I will not let them win.*

He never saw Chad again.

Thomas stopped the treadmill, unaware of how long since his last sprint. Panting and soaking wet, he picked up his towel and wiped his face and arms. Chad may've paid with blood, but he won, Thomas realized, suddenly.

Thomas walked across the gym with his phone and empty water bottle in hand. He stopped at the drinking fountain, re-filled, then entered the locker room where a man stood naked, facing the wall. The skin at his midsection and around his butt sagged. As the man toweled off, Thomas noticed the ring on his left hand. Thomas moved closer, sat down on the bench, pulled on his sweatpants. The man turned around. First Thomas looked up at the man's face, but felt his gaze travel downward, where he took a long look at the loose skin at the man's chest and waist. Then the flaccid penis in a mound of hair.

"What are you looking at?" the man said.

An intense urge took over, as Thomas stared at the bright doughy flesh of the man taking up so much space: in the locker room, at the bench dominated by his oversized gym bag, on the sink with the contents of his shaving kit spread across the entire countertop. Thomas wanted to punch his face. "Your ring," Thomas finally said. "I was looking at your wedding ring."

The man looked down to his left hand.

Thomas got up, waiting, hoping the man would say something to justify a fight. *Just say it,* Thomas thought, *and I will do to you what you did to Chad.*

When the stranger said nothing, Thomas left him to dress, scrolled through the numbers on his phone, found his lawyer's, and pressed *Call.*

"Thomas?" Jerome said, like a question.

"I've changed my mind," Thomas said, getting into his car. "Forget what I said before about depleting the scholarship fund. I want as much as you can get."

"Done," Jerome said.

"Press hard," Thomas said, thinking of the mark left by the cheerleader's thumb after she'd dragged it down Chad's face.

"No need to say it twice," Jerome said. "I have so much shit on the Jays and that school, I'll file a case against both, and all the named parents on the petition, people who said they'd pull their kids if you returned to the classroom. My guess is that they will settle. Just in case, I've got LAMBDA Legal and the ACLU Gay Rights Project ready to help. My friend runs the place and just confirmed he could easily get folks from the LGBTQ Center to help us stage protests in front of Country Day."

Chapter Eleven

Early June 2013

Thomas took the carton of cherry tomatoes out of his arm basket. Put them back in. Took them out again.

"Do you want me to come kill her?" Dana said into the phone. "My dad owns guns. I know how to use them."

Telephone to his ear, Thomas stared down at the tiny orange and red and yellow orbs, their skins as bright and taut as the undersides of a baby's toes. The pyramid of cartons glowed under a chalkboard sign that read "Season's First Batch!" The sign-maker had used red chalk for the *O* in *Season* and topped it with green sepal leaves.

He couldn't remember if Dana's murder offer applied to Mrs. Jay or Gail Samuelson or the PFA or the board or all of the above. She'd been voicing her outrage on his behalf toward all of them since he left his house for the organic grocery store.

"No," Thomas said. "But if your homicidal itch needs scratching, you should come here. They're charging four dollars and fifty cents—per pint—for cherry tomatoes."

"You guys have cherry tomatoes already in Portland? Are they dry-farmed?" Dana asked, deadpan.

Thomas smiled. Dana deserved more than his avoidance during his ordeal, but he'd felt as tentative toward her after his ordeal with Mercy, as with his brothers and their families since the accusation. He'd finally sent her a text, *Guess what? I'm moving back to San Francisco. No longer working at Country Day. More details soon.*

She responded, *WTF?* And *Yay!*

Organic vegetables, a pending move, chalk-written signs. It all reminded him of the 1990s, of Berkeley. A week after his breakup with Tony, Thomas received his acceptance letter to graduate school, just before he met Dana, when he decided he'd celebrate by moving out of the dorms. *Small duplex, clean and bright*, was written with blue ink in perfect cursive on an index card pinned to the corkboard outside the College of Education office. Thomas made an appointment to see the place on the corner of Etna and Parker. He'd parked his scooter at the curb near the walkway that divided the small front yard in half. From where she stood at her door, Thomas had guessed the landlady to be in her early sixties.

"Ms. Edna Park," she'd said, extending a long, thin arm, half covered in thick bracelets so black they looked like real ebony. "I answer to my name and my cross streets."

Other than his own mom, Edna had been Thomas's first real confidant, and if he knew anything at all about deep friendship, he'd learned it from her. The two had shared a wall that divided their living rooms and kitchens. Her radio and TV came through as white noise, and Thomas missed her when she wasn't home. Soon, he started inviting her for dinner. Her company filled some of the space Tony's departure had created. She helped him turn the breakup into the useful kind of trauma. Thomas gained the reputation of a true academic because of his laser focus. In reality, he was as horny as he was scared of AIDS, but Edna encouraged Thomas to redirect his lust and fear into his studies. On weekends, they ate liverwurst or tuna salad on thin slices of toasted pumpernickel. Most evenings, they drank wine to the drone of the honeybees collecting their nectar from Edna's lavender garden.

Thomas made his way back to the tomatoes and put one carton into the arm basket, grabbed a second carton, and walked to the aisle of nuts. He missed Edna, wondered what she'd think. Once Dana had heard the details of what happened at Country

Day, her rage on his behalf helped Thomas get out from under the weight of his own. Today that meant groceries. He'd rarely had an appetite since the accusation, so he set his phone with reminders to eat. Last night he had watched as a TV chef quick-seared a bunch of cherry tomatoes in garlic-infused olive oil before tossing them in a big bowl already filled with cooked rigatoni, toasted pine nuts, lemon zest, goat cheese and fresh herbs. His mouth watered.

Other than his brothers, Thomas's closest relationships had always been with women. Dana, Mercy, Sheree, and Joyce: his four closest. Thomas wondered why. Perhaps his attraction to men would have been deeper had he found the courage to reveal more of himself, like he could within the safe bubble of platonic friendship with women. He held bunches of mint, then cilantro, then oregano to his face and inhaled, thinking, no, the struggle to be close with people you wanted to fuck was hardly a market cornered by gay people. Everyone he knew suffered those challenges. Maybe it was that straight line connecting sex with AIDS? But Jake knew Sheree's HIV-status from day one and those two could teach workshops on emotional intimacy. In fact, they probably had. Thomas didn't like awkwardness. Who did? But he *really* didn't like it, and for someone as horny as he'd been in his teen years and twenties, he now found sexual tension exhausting; and negotiating whose bits with what wrappers are going into the other's holes in which order? "No," he said, aloud, gently tossing all the herbs into his basket.

When they first talked, he'd asked Dana if he could capitalize on her sympathy by sending her a couple of websites with apartment listings for her to peruse on his behalf.

She'd asked, "Isn't it too soon to move?"

Thomas listened to her describe the apartments she'd seen so far. Variations of too much rent, not enough light, no on-site laundry. "Keep sending links," she said. "You can stay with me until we find something good." Thomas fingered the bags of almonds, pistachios, cashews, pecans, walnuts, Brazil nuts, and finally peanuts.

A young white person with matted hair (did she think them dreadlocks?) stood next to him. She wore an apron with a name badge that read *Hello My Name Is Sin-dee. How Can I Help?*

He asked Dana to hang on a sec. "Do you know where I can find pine nuts, by chance?" Thomas asked.

The woman didn't respond.

"Sin-dee?" Thomas said, like Cindy.

She looked up. "It's pronounced with the emphasis on the Dee."

He smiled, said, "I'm sorry."

"You might want to think about your assumptions," she said, her voice infuriatingly sing-songy.

What a gift, Thomas thought. He'd been collecting reasons to leave Portland.

"Look," Thomas said. "I can't find the pine nuts."

"That's because they're seeds. They're by the chia and hemp on aisle four."

Thomas started walking, put the phone back to his ear.

"Oh. My. God," Dana said. "I just heard every word. Send more apartment links."

"Love you," Thomas said, and hung up.

The last time Thomas moved to San Francisco to be near Dana, he'd signed a lease on the apartment across the street from where Dana still lived on Douglass. The morning after, he slid his thirty-day notice under Edna's door, and stared at the London plane tree in her back yard. It had already dropped its flowers and a few of its leaves. Thomas ached, knowing how much he'd miss his friend, miss watching the thick, gnarled branches shed to bare. The same day he gave his notice, Tony called, insisted they reunite.

Thomas had called Dana then, too. She said she wanted to meet the man whose powers had left him celibate. Not funny, he'd said, and asked what to wear. Thomas went to Edna's and rang her doorbell. When she answered, he said, "I'm going to meet Tony. Dana told me to wear this."

He stood with his arms out showing off his tee-shirt sporting a life-sized print of Grace Jones's face.

"Come in," Edna said, and he followed her down the hall.

"I have to be there in ten minutes," he said. Pale blue and white hydrangeas bobbed their heads above a squat vase at the center of the table next to the card with his thirty-day notice. He watched Edna as she gathered a tray from a cabinet, her long string of pearls clicking quietly over a black tee-shirt as she filled the base of two snifters from a decanter.

"Drink this," she said, handing him a glass.

Edna had heard the long version of the Tony breakup story and matched his heartbreak with stories of her own. She told him she'd miss him when he left. Then added, "But it's probably good you get out of here. Maybe that way we'll both find a new man."

Light-headed from the brandy, Thomas pulled up to the same café where he and Tony had gone for their first date.

"Fancy meeting you here," Tony said, standing outside the café's glass door. "Buy me a cup of coffee?"

He sounded rehearsed. "Sure," Thomas said. As they walked in, Thomas bumped a book off a table. When Tony turned around, Thomas had just placed it back on the table, and Tony knocked it over again.

They started with small talk. "She's been like a second mom to me," Thomas had told Tony about Edna. "But I've been dividing ninety percent of my free time between a lesbian and a grandma. I need to get out more. Leave Berkeley. If one more vegan pedestrian flips me off for not stopping my scooter at a crosswalk they're approaching, I might explode."

Tony's hair had thinned, and Thomas wondered if his gums had always receded so far up his teeth. Had Tony lost weight? He kept looking out the window. "I have some stuff I need to tell you," he finally said, and took a sip of his tea. When he placed it down, light reflected in the thin sheen of bergamot oil on the surface of the steaming water.

৩ ৩ ৩

126

That June marked his last month in Berkeley. It had started off hot, the scent of honeysuckle always competing with jasmine, but the weather turned cold around the same time Tony's AIDS symptoms appeared as KS lesions. First on his neck. Shaped like a child would draw a mouth or a canoe. By the time the one on his cheek grew to the size of a plum, Tony had lost forty pounds and told Thomas to stop coming around.

In the beginning, Thomas didn't listen, and showed up with containers of hot and sour soup. Plastic-lidded paper cups of decaffeinated Earl Grey. But Tony stopped answering the door. The building manager found Thomas knocking and calling, said Tony had moved back to Florida. Thomas left that day's soup and tea at the door like the Thai ladies left offerings at the Buddhist temple on Russell Street. He'd read that Buddha didn't need food, but such offerings temporarily relieved the suffering for those who made them. Walking away from Tony's apartment, Thomas couldn't feel his own feet or hands. Putting on his helmet, he closed his eyes. *Please God,* he said, tightening the chin strap. *Do not give me AIDS. And I will do your bidding.*

As he grabbed the tiny Mason jar with *Organic Pignoli* printed on its label, Thomas remembered 1990, when he'd been a freshman at Cal, and the local newspapers reported that Ronald Reagan apologized for his neglect of the AIDS epidemic when he was president—but only after Ryan White, a young white kid with hemophilia from Indiana who'd contracted the virus in 1984, had died. Turned out, he hadn't apologized. He'd only attended a fundraiser for an organization started by someone who'd contracted the virus from a blood transfusion. Then he made a public service announcement for the Pediatric AIDS Foundation. That same year there were more than 18,000 other reported deaths that went unmentioned in the former president's speech. Lunatics on TV were still calling AIDS a punishment from God.

Four years later, he met Dana. She encouraged him to write his master's thesis on the importance of LGBT teachers being out in the classroom. "You're tall and white, and people think you're butch," Dana told Thomas. "You're palatable. The kind of person parents might not fear."

"Ouch." Thomas had said. "Palatable? Fuck you. Thanks."

Dana explained, "People who look and sound radical struggle to change minds. You could be our Trojan horse."

At the time, Dana's assessment gelled with Thomas's own desires to merge the various parts of himself that seemed so different from one another. He figured he'd inherited his personality from his parents—polar opposites. He never felt super close to Stuart, his father, who seemed too compartmentalized, robotic, his PR-machine always running. His mom? She mistook her emotions and opinions as fact, and that leaked over into her professional life. Always snapping back or rolling her eyes at the doctors; her fellow nurse friends loved retelling their juicy Maddy-at-the-hospital stories, and Maddy and Stuart argued about the write-ups and warnings she received for insubordination.

Thomas didn't want to be exactly like either. Who did he dream of becoming? He could've never admitted it to another soul at the time, but to himself? He wanted to be like Oprah Winfrey. He tried each semester to schedule his classes so he could have a break at four p.m.; that way he could crack a diet soda and watch the wonder woman of daytime TV, who seemed the living embodiment of where the Venn diagram intersected between the two circles of personality and professionalism.

Thomas eyed the organic lip balms and fair-trade chocolate bars and the celebrity's face on the cover of the Buddhist magazine that shared space on a wall of racks, and was tempted, just for a moment, to blame Dana for the fiasco at Country Day.

For his final semester of grad school, Thomas, who'd never been out, let Dana talk him into the gay-teacher-spokesperson role. Two panels at UC Berkeley led to a keynote student talk at a national conference in Atlanta. After his lecture, Dana led the half of the room who stood for an ovation. The naysayers called him egomaniacal, "The classroom is about the students, not who you sleep with," and agenda-driven: "using kids to further a political cause?"

One woman told the room that she was the only Asian American in a Catholic school with mostly white students. "Add dyke to that?" she said, looking around the room, as if for hidden cameras. "Suicide."

A man in his third year of teaching had come up to Thomas and told him he was out, and that parents never stopped watching him around their kids. He said his sister even hawk-eyed him as he held his nephew. "I regret it."

Thomas asked him where he taught. "The Bronx," the man said.

Thomas walked toward the front of the store remembering the other teachers at the conference who had donned name badges similar to Sin-dee's, with taglines like *Christian Educators*. The conference agenda listed lectures like *Walk with Jesus in the Classroom* and *Bringing Christian Values into Secular Systems*. More than one person had commented that gay teachers put kids at risk. One high school teacher said, "Yeah, for the AIDS."

"The AIDS?" Thomas had said from the podium, and a sudden rage shot through him. He leaned down into the mic. "It's an acronym, you fucking idiot. There's no definitive article."

The moderator had ended the Q and A and chastised Thomas for his reaction, but Thomas's paper was published at the same time he passed his credential exam. After finishing two years apprenticing in Oakland without ever being asked about his sexuality, Thomas started his first solo teaching job in San Francisco's Unified School District under the leadership of a gay principal. His emboldened remark at the conference turned out to be less of a preamble to Thomas's courage and more of an opportunity to seem badass in front of a bunch of people he'd never see again. Sure, he'd planned on coming out in his first week of classes, but as soon as he heard a group of single young moms talking about how hard it was to find a man who didn't "suck dick like some white faggot"—he revised. When push came to shove, he reverted.

He heard how the kids mocked the principal's speech patterns, laughed at his attempts at sternness. The part of himself he'd discovered behind the cafeteria curtain with Chad reemerged. He started avoiding the gay principal when his kids were around, didn't call them out when they made fun of his boss for being effeminate. When the most insistent and curious students asked if Thomas were married, he'd say, "Yes. My wife's name is Dana." When they bought it, he'd feel that keen, peppery, illusive sensation of thrill and shame.

Thomas got in line. Sin-dee and the cashier were talking about something called pulling. The cashier did it twice a day, and Sin-dee said she'd just started. They agreed that the organic coconut oil the store sold was "amazing for popcorn and pulling." Waiting, Thomas envisioned a mule in front of a cart and wondered how coconut oil could be used to help pull anything. By the time they acknowledged him, his basket's metal handle had cut off the circulation between his forearm and hand. Maddy would have slapped his face for paying what he did for those few groceries. "May I have a bag, please?" Thomas asked, and the cashier slowly reached toward a shelf below the register while rolling her eyes. "Sorry," she said, opening the sack. "People here usually bring their own."

Thomas scooped what little was left of the goat cheese and herbs and tomatoes into a small bowl, then covered it with a plate and put it in the fridge. He washed the pasta pot and the sauté pan and picked up the garlic bulb's paper-thin skin that had somehow gotten everywhere. After, he sat down at his desk, turned on his computer, opened his San Francisco bookmark folder and clicked. One by one, he sent apartments to Dana.

Full of pasta, Thomas now sat on his sofa and grabbed the notebook he'd abandoned two nights before. It rested face down on the coffee table, and Thomas turned it over to the splayed-open page where he'd drawn a line of circles on top of triangles, little ice cream cones, with teardrops of cream dripping down like rain onto the second cluster of circles, each enclosing a set of angled lines. A childlike rendering of a mob of angry faces. He turned the page and saw *I want a partner* written in black ink on the top line next to the word *vanilla*. He had no memory of writing either.

Shortly before Thomas had decided to leave San Francisco for this job in Portland, Dana had encouraged him to place a personal ad. She'd been trying to help him get over the shock of Tony. The investigators found what they'd written in one of his computer files. It said, *Nerd who goes to the gym seeks nerd who goes to the gym.* They hadn't read the ad to the parents during the town hall. He had hoped they would report on his lesson plans. The number of them. The detail they each contained. His word processing program tracked the hours of revisions made to each document. Instead, the sheriff's investigator reported on his porn. If it hadn't been his own life, Thomas would've thought it comedic, their faces, as the officer made the report. "Some scenarios dramatize a seduction of quote straight men unquote, but most depict what's referred to as quote vanilla unquote gay sex."

Vanilla.

When the investigator said straight men, Mrs. Jay looked back toward Thomas but did not let her gaze rest. She looked beyond him as if the hallway contained the future in which Thomas would never work again. That's when Thomas entered that strange, real-time amnesia, when he started drawing the cones. Cum cones, he imagined, dripping over the faces of hungry spectators.

Before the town hall, Jerome had grilled Thomas about past sexual relationships. "Tell me everything about anyone more than five years younger."

"I've always been attracted to older guys. At least until I hit my thirties. Then I started dating guys my own age." Thomas told Jerome about Manny, the only younger person he'd ever hooked up with or dated.

"That's it?" he'd asked. "No one under twenty-five?"

131

When Jerome then wondered how long since the breakup, Thomas realized the effect Jake's cancer had had on how he'd experienced time. "Jesus," he'd said. "Almost a year."

Jerome asked if there'd been anyone since. Thomas said no, and that he still missed Manny.

"You need to get out more, my friend," Jerome had said. "I thought I was bad."

Had Jerome been flirting? Imagine that. Thomas had forgotten about himself as a sexual person. What would a new personal read? *40-something/yo SWM Jobless but Proven Not Guilty of Child Molestation Seeks Love.*

For the first time since the investigation, Thomas let out a tiny chuckle. He turned the notebook's pages. By the time he reached the end, his heart was pounding, thinking of this past year. Breakup. Jake's cancer. Accusation and public humiliation. Joblessness. He'd always thought of himself as a person wary of nostalgia. Someone who embraced the motto better to look forward than look back. But these circumstances were like someone shoving his face into a viewfinder with a slideshow called Look At Your Life! Turned out, he needed to rewind, find the knowledge living in that femme kid's head before his family left California. He should probably find a shrink to help him unravel some of the terror he endured during the first fifteen years of the AIDS pandemic. He needed to stop pretending. He needed to stop living his life for them—whoever they were. He needed to get in touch with Manny and apologize. He needed to get out of Portland. He needed to go live the life he should have lived in San Francisco. He went to the kitchen, dumped the notebook into the trash.

Chapter Twelve

Thursday
July 25th, 2013

What to wear to dinner with Dad after being accused of sexually molesting a nine-year-old? Thomas spun around and around on the chair in front of his desk. He had learned from the dance teacher at Country Day that a focal point kept the twirling dancer from getting dizzy. He chose the latch on the window in front of his desk, kept his eye returning to it as he spun, and decided that the latch represented San Francisco—the new focal point of his days. Before he bought this chair, he'd read his students' homework in bed and at tables in damp coffee shops that smelled of alfalfa sprouts and the burnt onion bits on bagels. He'd planned his lessons on the couch and used his phone to correspond with parents and colleagues while at the gym.

Sporadic quests to mid-century antique shops had led to the acquisition of this perfect piece of furniture, and it still delighted him all these years later. Form, yes. Function, too. Style without being flashy. His chair, its pleasing lines, the perfect way its armrests nestled under the glass top of his desk. All of these were qualities his father taught him to look for, and he owed it to his dad, who'd flown to Portland and rented a car and made a reservation, to be on time.

His neighbors, the Jurakas, Ruth and Bernie, parked their minivan in front of the curb as their teenager, Buzz, played hoops in the driveway. The giant black walnut tree at the end of the yard made it impossible to see the hoop, but Thomas heard the familiar sound of rubber bouncing on the pavement and the ricochet of backboard and rim.

After his family had found out about the accusation, when his father had finally got hold of Thomas, he'd said, "The plane and place are booked. This isn't negotiable." The next morning, Thomas had a confirmation email for the restaurant reservation in his inbox. *I've read about this place in one of Dot's cooking magazines. It sounds like a winner. See you Thursday at six.* Buzz went inside and sounds of basketball were replaced by the calling of a crow and a commercial truck beeping a warning that it was moving in reverse. Thomas had sixteen minutes before Stuart would arrive at a restaurant fifteen minutes away. He still had not brushed his hair. He needed to add the newspapers to the recycling and bring the pile out to the garage. The phone on the desk startled him with its vibrating buzz. A text from his father, *Got here early. Solo with a nice table. Dot's sick. C U soon.*

On my way, Thomas wrote.

Anything other than the weekend pants, he thought, getting dressed: a red checkered oxford-style dress shirt, a pair of flat front wool slacks, a blue sweater vest, socks with thin alternating pinstripes of navy and heather gray.

Looking in the mirror, Thomas could find no visual or physical cue to express what he'd been through. No scar. Even the once dark circles under his eyes had lightened up, at least when compared to the Manny-breakup period and Jake-treatment phase. After an overdue trip to the barbershop and a shave, he now looked, well, normal. Like what? Like a teacher? Like James? Like his father? The investigation had taken the time and mental energy he used to spend on the kids. He woke up every day at five thirty, often ready to start the coffee for a school day. For the first few seconds of consciousness, he'd forget. Then, he'd remember.

In the weeks since the investigation, the intense fear of bricked windows and spray-painted epithets morphed into something worse: silence. Jerome had moved on to the next case, and Mercy and Thomas's colleagues and all their former students and families got on with their summer vacations. At this time of year, Thomas's feed had always been flush with pictures taken in Cannon Beach or Lincoln City: close-ups of kids' faces smiling wide in front of frothy waves or frowning while pointing to the lighthouse at Cape Disappointment. Most of the parents had already unfriended him before Jerome instructed him to immediately abandon all social media and to hire a tech geek to scrub Thomas McGurrin from the internet.

Parking in The Pearl proved easier than he expected. He snagged a spot on NW 13th and rushed to Flanders Street where the restaurant operated out of an old warehouse. From the outside, the place was exactly what Thomas preferred. Stylish and unpretentious, filled with the evening's natural light. He opened the heavy wrought iron door. Edison-style filament bulbs hung from the ceiling by jute rope, and canvas slips covered the backs of chairs. The place smelled of garlic cooking in butter, of crisped sage. Thomas scanned the bar and the booths again but couldn't locate his father. Most of the tables were visible from where Thomas stood at the entrance. A young woman holding an electronic tablet greeted him.

"I'm a few minutes late for a reservation under Stuart McGurrin," he said, hoping not to see parents from Country Day.

"Thomas?" she asked.

"Yes," he said. "How did you know?"

She pressed various places on her touch screen, then looked up at his face, and paused.

He hoped she was too young to read newspapers.

"Magic," she said, and smiled. "This way." Then, when they arrived at the table, "I saw Stuart head toward the restroom. He should be right back."

135

A nearly empty Pellegrino bottle sat next to an orchid blossom, its stem snaking its way from a narrow vase. Thomas took his chair, poured the rest of the water into his glass, and reached across the table to the crumpled cloth napkin. As he folded it, he caught a musky whiff of Pinaud Clubman, an aftershave Stuart had used for Thomas's entire life. He pictured that gold and green bottle, the decal decorated with a drawing of a man sporting a top hat while leaning on a cane.

The server greeted him. "Shall I give you menu notes," she asked, "while you wait? Your dining partner has already heard them."

"Thanks, but no," Thomas answered, putting away his phone. "My father will be right back. I'd love a glass of white wine. Something crisp?" Thomas leaned forward and pulled his wallet from his back pocket and took out his credit card. He asked the server to add twenty percent to the bill and charge it to his account instead of presenting a check. "That way my dad won't argue."

She took his bank card. Her smile tightened. "Your dining partner," she said, removing the wine list from where it sat in the middle of the table, "was waiting just in case you wanted to order a full bottle."

"Just the glass for now, please." And then, "He's my dad," Thomas said, his jaw tight. "Just my dad. Not my partner," Thomas said, thinking of the Jays and so many of the married straight parents at Country Day who used the word partner instead of husband or wife.

The server pushed her futuristic-looking eyewear to the top of the bridge of her nose and tucked a small notebook and pen into the pocket of her apron before walking off. Thomas watched as she stepped into the ordering station. Another server stood next to her.

"Are you okay?" Thomas heard the other server ask.

"Totally," she said. "Just a bitchy queen. Fuck him."

The server's face, her mouth, the shape of her lips when she said the word *fuck*, made Thomas recall his mother. "You know your dad doesn't like it when I swear," Maddy had said to five-year-old

Thomas. "So never tell him again." Their secret, her love of profanity. Two Mondays a month Thomas's kindergarten had half days, and he and Maddy would go for a drive. One such Monday, her face was swollen like she'd been crying. Thomas noticed it when she picked him up, and they'd just exited onto Route 17 from 101, heading south from San Jose to the beach in Santa Cruz. "I need the ocean," she'd said, "to keep from jumping off a cliff."

"Asshole," she'd said, as if the tailgating driver could hear her. She grabbed her Seven Eleven cup by a coat of dampened napkins and used her teeth to remove the lid and straw so she could get to the ice, then tossed Thomas a pack of black licorice. All during his childhood, Thomas clawed for the front seat on rides that included James, but when he and his mother were a duo, Thomas preferred the back. In the back seat, he could spread out, study Maddy's face in the rearview mirror, listen as she crunched her ice and sang so softly with the songs playing on the R&B station. But that wasn't the real reason.

The real reason was what happened when he closed his eyes. Little Thomas believed the car would de-materialize, go invisible, he and his mom, bound by an energy field, a warm bubble. In it, Thomas could deliver her from traffic, from other people, and float far from the curve of cliff, above those California clouds. It only worked if they were alone and never talked about it. Once, Thomas had said, "I know where we go when I'm back here with my eyes closed. I can feel it."

"You're my sensitive one," she'd said. "You feel everything."

"But we're not allowed to talk about it," Thomas said.

"Thems the rules?" she asked, a fingernail tapping on the wheel.

"Thems the rules," Thomas said.

Around that same time, Thomas had told Stuart about Maddy's cussing. Nothing prompted it. Thomas wasn't angry with her. Waiting for his father to come back from the restroom, he recalled the scene. All three stood in the kitchen, his mom trimming her fingernails, letting the little slivers fall into the sink. Thomas had been playing with the sofa cushions from the living room, trying

137

to make a fort in the kitchen like James could, but he couldn't get them to stay and grew bored. He'd stared at his dad who had been on the phone since returning from work. Thomas watched Stuart's expressions freeze for a few seconds then change. First a smile, then a look of surprise, then a smile again.

"Daddy, guess what?" Thomas asked him. "Mom swore today. Said the f-word." By then, Thomas had placed a small couch pillow under his tee-shirt.

"What?" Stuart said. "Why would you say that?" He picked up the phone again. Looked into an address book, found a number.

"Mom's a swearer," Thomas said.

Hanging up, he asked his wife the same question.

Maddy smiled at her husband from the sink. "You know his imagination. Look at him. He's pretending he's a pregnant woman, for God's sake."

Most of all, Thomas recalled the emphasis Maddy put on the word *woman*. It confused Thomas at the time because he knew his mother loved it when Thomas wore her hats or shoes, used his bathrobe as pretend long hair to play Rapunzel over the back of the couch. That night, Maddy sent Thomas to bed soon after he finished dinner. Said it was for lying. Later, when she came to tuck him in, she got into the lower bunk and under the covers with him and kissed him three times. "I understand why you did it, honey," she said, taking him into her arms. "Don't do it again, though. You and me. We're the team." Thomas apologized, eventually understanding that unless the two were alone, he needed to act more like James. "I'm not angry," Maddy said. "I just pretend I am sometimes when your dad's around."

In the car that half-day Monday on the way to the beach, with his eyes closed, Thomas felt the car lift up and up. No more traffic noise or "fucking idiots" running yellow lights. Proud of himself for his discipline—he knew James couldn't keep his eyes or mouth shut even for a minute. "I packed us some corn chips and sandwiches," she'd said after a while.

"7Ups?" Thomas had asked, opening his eyes slowly so that the car could make a smooth landing.

"Two each," she said.

Soon after they'd parked, Thomas had his back pressed against a cartoon sign of Popeye with his hand hovering four feet above the ground. *You must be this tall if yer gonna ride,* the sign read. Thomas cleared it by at least two inches, and Maddy hugged him, said, "You're my big boy," and bought two tickets to The Giant Dipper. "What would I do with three kids?" Maddy said as the roller coaster car clicked to the top. Then, "You might be getting another brother. Or maybe a sister." She took his hand and put it on the small but firm curve above her waist. Maddy's smile looked worried, uncertain to little Thomas. "Don't tell James or Dad," she said. "Sometimes babies change their mind. Sometimes they stick around. Sometimes they don't."

Thomas hadn't closed his eyes when the roller coaster plummeted down the steep decline. He stared at the waves and ocean as they zipped around the curves.

"Son!" Stuart said, standing over him at the table.

Thomas's chair got caught in a groove in the poured cement floor. He tried again to get it to release him, but it wouldn't. By the time Thomas managed to get up, the waitress had returned and positioned herself between the two men. She said, "You two found each other." Then, "Reunited at long last."

She stepped back, her rear end almost touching the next table, leaving no room, so Thomas and his dad shook hands instead of hugging before sitting down. Stuart waited for her to position the globe of wine in the midst of the other objects, and then he attempted to grab Thomas, maybe by the shoulder, but couldn't. Instead, he leaned to the side and reached under the table. The squeeze to his leg sent a shock to Thomas's spine, and he jerked back.

"You're looking great, Dad," Thomas said, trying to recover. His father's face seemed sun-kissed, relaxed. "How's Dot?"

"Caught somewhere between jet lag and sinus infection," Stuart said, pulling a roll from the breadbasket.

"Shouldn't you be with her?" Thomas studied his dad's eyes, an even lighter blue in the restaurant's abundant light.

Stuart said, "I'm suspicious that Dot bowed out to give us father-son time. Sinus infection is her go-to when she wants a spa treatment. How's Dana?" Stuart asked. "Bet she's happy you're moving back to San Francisco."

Thomas told him about Dana's new girlfriend, how she'd been helping with the apartment search.

"You know," Stuart said, "you two once talked about starting a family."

"Dad," Thomas said. "I told you that anecdote so many years ago. Dana didn't want to have a family with me. She wanted me to give her my sperm and take the kid half the time so she could go fuck women. Did you even hear me say that she has a new girlfriend?"

The intensity of Thomas's response took them both by surprise. Stuart's mouth took the shape of an *O*. The server arrived to puncture the moment, and they ordered. When the server left, Thomas hesitated, and then said, "Look, Dad. I know it's awkward, but I just want to say——"

"Tommy," his father interrupted. "I know you didn't do it. Dot and I have never suspected it to be true."

A bus person at a nearby table shook open a white tablecloth. The tiny white fibers slowly fell toward the floor. A sharp, bitter taste rose in Thomas's throat: regurgitated pinot grigio. Thomas recalled the Country Day parents' faces, hungry-looking—but what for? Salacious details? —in that ridiculous town hall. Now he easily imagined his father's and Dot's faces among them.

His father said, "We love you very much." After a pause, he added, "Very much."

Thomas swallowed a sip of the cold, carbonated water, waited for it to settle his stomach. The same week as Thomas's undergraduate graduation from Cal, he had taken his dad out to a restaurant in Berkeley, and like a jack released from a box, he'd said, "Happy Birthday, Dad. I'm gay."

Stuart had remained silent for a good long minute before he said, "Are you sure you want to complicate your life?" As if Thomas had just told his dad that he had decided to live on a houseboat.

"This whole thing is awful," Stuart now said. "I was once accused. Not of little kiddie stuff, but . . ." He tore a dinner roll in two. "It was a nightmare." He placed the two halves of the roll on his bread plate, and then used the pad of his finger to pick up each crumb that had fallen on their tablecloth.

Thomas took another sip of the mineral water. His father's face was impossible to read. *That thing about knowing something by a look in someone's eyes is complete bullshit,* Thomas thought, remembering having to return to Mercy's office one last time with Jerome. She had showed them a petition—parents who threatened to pull their children out of the school if Thomas returned—and asked him to resign his position at Country Day. Even after everything, he still thought that she'd come to her senses, argue. Insist they find a way he could stay.

Outside the restaurant's windows, Portland's sky had turned from light to blue to a dusty purple, like a plum covered in gray mold. A color he associated with Oregon. The sun wasn't due to set for a couple of hours, but the dense clouds could snuff sunlight like no other place he'd been.

The server brought the first course.

"Some pepper, honey?" she asked Thomas.

"Sure," Thomas said. Then, as she cranked the peppermill over his tomatoes, he felt a sudden welling. He said, "Just curious. Why do you call my father 'sir' and me 'hon' or 'honey'? Is it because I'm a bitchy queen?" Her face reddened. She opened her mouth, but Thomas jumped in, said, "Save it. I'm a teacher, which makes me a black belt in reading lips." The server left, and Stuart wiped half of his roll across the plate, sopping up the oil and vinegar.

"Jesus," he said, before putting it into his mouth.

"I'm sick of it," Thomas said. "Now hurry up and finish your story because I've got my own to tell."

"It's not important," Stuart said.

Thomas picked up his knife. "Finish your story, Dad." He sliced his tomato in half.

"It happened before Jake was born. It's why we moved from California to Massachusetts. It was also the last straw with your mother."

The tomatoes had released their seeds onto the plate, clustered in pockets of five or six, like little wet sacks. Thomas forced himself to eat. "What were you accused of?" he asked his father.

"A woman was convinced I harassed her. Sexually." He explained that the woman had been friendly and eager during the interview, had won his sympathy as a single mom.

"You did nothing?" Thomas said, tearing at his bread. "You were completely innocent, like me?"

"She didn't know her ass from her elbow," Stuart said, telling Thomas he'd used that exact phrase after she screwed up spreadsheets that made him look bad.

"They relocated you across the country for that?" Thomas said.

His father broke eye contact and looked over to where the server was placing her wine on a tray. "Once, in the copy room, I was trying to move around a machine so I could grab a stack of papers. She backed up just as I was coming by, and her backside touched my front side."

Thomas nodded.

"Her friend, another secretary, said she'd witnessed it, supported her story." Stuart said she quit less than a month after she got her money. "By then, your mom and I had already sold the house."

The bus person took the plates from the first course.

"I never dealt with it," Stuart said, wiping his mouth with the corner of his napkin. "Your mother had her reasons to suspect it was true. I tell James to work less. Thank God Jake gets it. He works hard, but Max is his priority, and that kid knows it. I thought I was the one who'd gotten ripped off. But when you didn't call me during your tough time, I realized, no. You and your brothers and your mother were the ones who got ripped off. And now you're getting ripped off again."

142

Soon after Stuart's and Maddy's separation, teenaged Thomas arrived home after his final period one afternoon to discover Jake's weedy limbs jutting from under the afghan, his baby brother sleeping on the couch next to twin bags of potato chips, empty on the shag rug like a pair of lungs. Thomas usually met Jake at the bus stop after school. That day, when no Jake jumped from the bus's bottom step, Thomas imagined his mother had kidnapped her youngest, making a run for California, where she'd been happy or, at least, happier.

Once through the storm door and kitchen, it turned out Jake hadn't made it to school. Maddy hadn't managed to get him there. As she slept upstairs, Jake watched TV, fed himself from the junk food cabinet. After Thomas cleaned up the crumbs and trashed the empty bags, he scrambled some eggs. James came home while Thomas cooked. He shook Jake awake, and the three brothers ate while the hostess on the TV spun the Wheel of Fortune.

As Stuart continued, Thomas remembered something else, even earlier, during Maddy's pregnancy. James had gone off to soccer camp, and Thomas had helped his mother prepare the meal by shucking corn and pulling off the fine hairs still clinging to the kernels. He'd never had a family dinner alone with his parents. They ate each night at six thirty, and Thomas sat down at his seat five minutes early, eager to have his parents to himself. Maddy stood over a big pot of boiling water. His father came in late, apologized for his tardiness; said there had been an accident on 495.

"Really?" Maddy asked. Then, quietly, she said, "About a half hour ago I was at Nancy's."

She'd lied. Maddy hadn't left the house. She told Stuart that she had needed a stick of butter, and said, "Vito came in from work while I was there." She paused. "Said 495 was a breeze from Marlborough." They ate in near silence. After dinner, Stuart said he left something at the office. That night, Thomas got up from bed to use the bathroom. On his way down the darkened hallway, he heard the television on downstairs, so he was surprised to see

143

his mother in the lit-up bedroom. Thomas stood near the doorway as she undressed. He marveled at the giant roundness of her middle. After she'd changed into her nightgown, she sat on the bed with a tube of body lotion and a jar of night cream. Thomas watched as she smoothed the moisturizer into her legs, how the oil caught the lamplight and reflected on her shins. Then she stopped, hands on her belly, and started crying.

He didn't go to her. He wanted to comfort her, to tell her it would be okay, but he couldn't move. Adults, Thomas discovered, lied. They lived two lives at once. In one, a woman does dishes at the sink looking out a window, telling her children to wash their faces and change into their pajamas. When she's done cleaning up, she serves them pie. In the other, she's a woman whose hands are shaking so much she's unable to put cream on her face. She's curled into the shape of the letter *C,* sobbing.

By the time Thomas finished telling his father every detail about the party, Toby's pants, the investigations and the town hall, the grease had separated from the cherry sauce covering the lineup of pork medallions. The pile of quinoa, no matter how many bites he took, never ended. Finally, the server cleared their plates.

During coffee, Stuart said, "I'm so sorry, Tommy. I remember how my shipmates talked about gay people when I was in the Navy. They seemed to believe you all prowled playgrounds and preschools for recruits." Stuart didn't look up from his coffee. He kept circling the cup with the spoon. "I can't even imagine how much your students miss you."

"Thanks, Dad," Thomas said. "My lawyer negotiated a huge settlement by threatening them in a hundred different ways. San Francisco and selling the house isn't a reaction. It's a plan."

"That doesn't mean it's fair," his father said. "You could find a reporter at *The Oregonian.* Or *The New York Times.* Take a stand like I should've. Maybe if I had, I'd still be married to your mom."

"I have no regrets," Thomas lied. "And you shouldn't either. We all know Dot's a better match. My lawyer made sure they'll think better next time. Now I'm free. I can do anything."

The server presented the already-paid check on a small tray. Thomas picked up the pen to sign the receipt.

"No," Stuart said. "Let me get this."

She said, "House rule. First one who offers, pays."

"Listen, young lady," Stuart said, with a tone that Thomas imagined his father had used with his disgruntled secretary. "Void that. Charge mine. Right now."

"Dad," Thomas said. "You flew to Portland. Let me get dinner."

Stuart's complexion deepened to a flush of red that spread downward from his cheeks along his neck. "No."

Stuart extended both his arms. One with his credit card, the other toward Thomas's. "Please," he said. "Please. I am his father. He is my son."

Chapter Thirteen

Wednesday
September 18th, 2013

His ninety-minute run left his tank top and running shorts spongy, wet. He stretched his calves by angling the tops of his jogging shoes against the pod at the end of his driveway. At his request, the real estate agent had never put a sign in the yard. She called ahead, only showed the place while Thomas was out, and didn't insist on a staging. Standing in front of the house he'd just sold, he pictured the graph and the stages of grief he'd been visiting and revisiting. The experts said selling a house and moving ranked up there with losing a job or death. Thomas thought, *Fuck Kübler-Ross. I'm skipping depression by doubling down on the two-stage T. McGurrin plan: experiment and take action, a fast track to integration.*

His newfound confidence had come when, a few days after the first viewing, the real estate agent called to say, "We have a buyer with cash who's making an offer above asking. You want to go ahead?"

Thomas had been standing in the master suite's bathroom when the call came in. The mirror allowed him to see all the way through his bedroom, the living room, the entryway, and out the wall of windows to the street. "Definitely," Thomas told the real estate agent, as if he'd been offered whipped cream on a slice of pie. Elated, he expected some other, darker emotion to emerge later, but so far, knock wood, it hadn't come calling.

For the first couple of months after the breakup and Jake's diagnosis, it felt like he'd been ping-ponging between denial and bargaining; then, after the accusation, denial and anger. He'd hit every one of the substages, too, but not for this. Even after all he'd done to this place, he felt almost euphoric to leave it behind. Without Manny, without the promise of his family, his house felt like an airport hotel. The agent said it could take forty-five days to sell the Portland house, but in three weeks it was a done deal. Once the paperwork was signed, he called a moving company that dropped off the rectangular pod. Now Thomas walked slowly across the small front yard. The chilly autumn air hurt his throat and lungs. He stopped, stood for a moment, letting the sun's slanted rays rest on his shoulders, then walked toward the house that would soon be owned by someone new. From the time he accepted the settlement, a thread of fervent, childlike joy had emerged from the shithole of other feelings, and morphed into obsessions with two things: the first, moving to San Francisco by Thanksgiving. The second?

Manny had never officially moved in, but in their twenty months together, he'd probably spent the night at least five hundred times, maybe more. He'd travelled with Thomas, met every single one of his family members, developed relationships with each of them individually. "Are you a cat person?" Thomas said aloud, in his best German accent, imitating what Manny had asked Thomas on their first date. The two had met on the same site where Thomas had met Jerome, leading to coffee, but with Manny it turned into dinner. "I don't have pets," Thomas had said. "I work a lot, live alone and wouldn't want to leave them."

"But do you like cats?" Manny insisted. Every seemingly innocuous question felt to Thomas like he'd been asked to cross the length of a minefield because of the intensity of Thomas's attraction. "I let the cat decide. I like some individual cats. But am neutral about the species."

Manny smiled. His lips and jaw, the slender opening of his

eyes made his whole face delicate, despite the dense shadow of his beard. "Your relationships with cats," he'd said, "sound like mine with people."

The university had provided Manny with a studio in a building for visiting researchers, and he used it occasionally after tending to his experiments in the middle of the night; but by the end of their first month together, he'd left most of his clothing at Thomas's. A few days after Manny moved out, one of Thomas's students brought in a picture to show the class. A giant turtle separated from its shell. The children giggled, but the animal looked human at first glance, with its surprisingly long withered limbs, its familiar fetal pose—like a person might look, if she or he had been born with a shrunken trunk and an open, elongated mouth. The image made Thomas gasp. "That's how I feel," Thomas had said, suddenly.

He never told his students about Manny, never introduced him to their parents, and now he wondered why. After all, he'd insisted on introducing him to his whole family, Dana, and Mercy. They'd all gotten to know Manny despite the reality of a soon-to-expire J-1 visa and Manny's plans to live permanently in Germany. Thomas had cringed after his sudden and compulsive shell-less turtle disclosure.

A casserole dish now sat on his doorstep next to the fake rock where he hid the spare house key. He peeled off the folded note taped to the foil. *We're sorry to see you're moving. We'll miss you. Good luck! —The Jurakas.* Refolding the note, an upwelling of stinging heat radiated from his chest. He thought about the word tender, and how Sheree's recipe for sautéed veal called for tenderizing the meat, which meant pounding it with a cleated mallet. The Jurakas' kind note had been one to add to another half dozen. Two from former students, another two from co-workers, a final pair from parents. All expressed some sort of regret—for the circumstances, for the not showing up, for not knowing what to say during and after the investigation. *I believed you,* they all wrote, which allowed Thomas to move toward something resembling tenderness.

Thomas remembered the day he first saw this house, soon after he'd settled into his second year at Country Day, when he'd realized he lived in a city and worked at a place where he made enough money doing what he loved to afford a home of his own. Definitely a fixer-upper, he thought, but worth it. Before making an offer, he wanted to see the house at night.

So he'd parked along the curb and watched through the windows as the small family went about their lives. The young mother had stood at the sink. Thomas could see her husband in the living room watching television; colors from the screen flickered across his chest and face. Their kid sat on the floor and slid one foot at a time into a pair of red wellies. He'd imagined his own brothers and their children running around in the small yard, chasing each other up and down the length of the driveway to the side of the house.

Watching them roused images of his first job, delivering newspapers to the doorsteps on the unlit streets of suburban Massachusetts, and also of driving to the Jays and spying on them through his binoculars. His whole life Thomas had longed to see an image resembling what he might want to work for, realize, earn.

He had made an offer the next morning. Once his, he toiled before picking the paint for the wood exterior and its trim. He ripped up carpeting to reveal, then repair, parquet floors. He spent full weekends scouring shops and estate sales for the fine wool rugs he'd use to cover them up again. Stripping then staining the built-ins after years of previous owners layering paint. Scoring sixteen identical beveled glass and brass doorknobs for the eight doors. Then landscaping. Lighting. Thomas had carried a measuring tape and used it in every store. He required a lot of space around each piece of furniture. The rugs, upholstery, sheets, shower curtains, dishtowels, all had to be of a superior quality: cashmere, fine wool, Pima cotton, linen. They could not call attention to themselves. Neutral colors and basic patterns. But luxurious.

His mother helped. She'd buy him the thing he hesitated to buy for himself when, on his visits, the two took trips to Boulder to shop. When he tried to refuse, she'd say, "Do you know how expensive grandchildren are? And a pair of recovering junkies? You're cheap. Let me at least buy you an overpriced blanket and a fancy sauté pan. If you play your cards right, I might even get you a couch."

His nieces and nephew were all so small when he first bought the home, but he'd imagined them growing older, wanting to come to Portland during summer. He installed a bike rack in the garage that could hold five bicycles. He hung hooks for four little helmets. He had his cabinet guy build bunk beds in the guest room. James and Jake and his parents offered their spouses and their children to the world. Their spouses and children shed sideways light on who they were, and who they'd become. This house would be his offering, he thought.

But it hadn't happened. Except for his father, each member of his family had come to visit exactly once, spread out over the first five years he owned the place. In subsequent years, Jake and James found it too hard to book flights for spouses and kids. Everyone agreed it was easier for one person (two, during his pair of Manny years) to see four. Stuart had come a total of three times, including the recent trip, but didn't stay in Thomas's home. Dot insisted that it was Thomas who needed his privacy and preferred to get a hotel.

What a mistake. Embarrassed to admit how badly he wanted them to stay with him, he put on the poker face, unable to express excitement or disappointment. His inability to be honest about his desire bit his backside again and again. He should've said something to Dot; argued, told her that she'd been the one to inspire the baskets full of fancy toiletries he had waiting for them under the guest bathroom sink.

He brought the casserole to the kitchen and placed it down, then opened the fridge, grabbed his protein shake, and got to work.

Thomas slit the tape sealing the box marked *MEMORIES* and put down the knife. He'd pulled the box from the garage with the intention of filling the recycling bag he placed at its side, but he couldn't toss the stuff. His avoidance of accumulating junk had reached the neurotic level years ago, but he'd somehow held on to everything that reminded him of Manny: boarding passes; theater, dance, movie, opera, symphony tickets; birthday cards; show programs; museum exhibition pamphlets. He opened one of the museum brochures to a bunch of photos: a bowl made of dyed goose feathers, copper wire, and glass beads; an amulet made of bone; a mask made of human hair, paint, cedar bark, and wood. Thomas had watched as Manny walked from wall to Plexiglas cube meditating on these objects in the Native American art display at Portland Museum. Manny had read every word on every placard, his lips moving, head nodding gently. Every so often he'd ask about an English word. "What's basalt?" "What is an awl?"

Thomas, blissed out about being in a museum with a person who took his time at each station, waited, but instead of studying the art, he studied Manny. With others he'd become accustomed to having to rush, get through the exhibit only to graduate to the café or gift shop, but Manny stood in front of each object like a child might stand under the sky to watch his first rain or snowfall.

A thick envelope fell out from between the thank you cards, and Thomas opened it and unfolded the letter.

Dear Thomas,

I'm embarrassed at my behavior. I am not normally storming off in the middle of a conversation, but because my mind was so full, I didn't know the alternative.

It is now nearly two years that we are seeing each other, as I get ready to finish this phase of my research here in the States, I must express my doubts. I will try and get to the point as quickly as possible. I love you. There. I did it. German, right? To be so direct?

The announcement that my lab's funding was cut, and I therefore must return to Germany, came as two surprises. While I'm not always the best (like Dana) at decoding your signals, I'm not always the worst either. You know my work won't relax before I leave. Nor will yours. Night and day, you work for those goddamn children.

You were so irritable, checking your phone obsessively. I didn't say anything. When you told me that you didn't want to hear my story about work, I stopped talking and tried to be affectionate. When you asked me if I'd eaten garlic for lunch I went to the bathroom to brush. When I returned, you'd moved to your office. On the phone with Dana.

I am thinking, fuck you. When I left—and you didn't try to stop me—I hated you for the first time. If you're pissed I'm leaving, and you hate me I can handle it. But you never tell me anything.

Because my boss is unable to renew my visa, I must leave before the expiration. I want to finish writing my dissertation and then see what happens. I want you to consider moving to Germany, but it's not the only option. You think Portland is full of opportunities in biosciences. It's not. Many of the best opportunities are in California. You've talked about wanting to live in Europe. You've talked about moving to San Francisco. Starting a family. Was this a lie?

Manny

Thomas put the letter next to his knife. He looked up and out his window to the tree in his yard just as a flock of blackbirds burst from the leaves.

It hadn't been his nieces or nephew or brothers or parents. His house finally became a home when Manny moved in. How had that not made sense to Thomas? Didn't membership as an out homosexual get you a free pass from the bullshit of convention? Of being around kids all the time? Of being a parent? Of taking distance from the traditional notions of brother and uncle and son? Now, he opened the door, and the pod blocked his sight of the Jurakas' kitchen window. He'd go over and thank Ruth after he showered and changed. She'd always been so sweet. Manny had talked with her more often than Thomas, as Ruth had learned some German while living in Bavaria after college.

He pushed the stack of boxes in the center of his living room to the wall, then picked up the phone from the table. He searched his archived mail for the name *Emmanuel Koroma*. There it was:

Manny,

I've read and reread your letter. I'm so taken by your humor and humanity and handsomeness, I overlooked the larger issues: our significant age difference, the fact that you eventually want to move back to Germany, and I want to stay here. Yes, I've fantasized about living in San Francisco or Europe someday, and yes, I've mentioned starting a family, but I thought I'd been clear, it's a fantasy. At least for now. I love my job at Country Day. San Francisco has become so expensive, and I'm too busy for children of my own.

It might be difficult for you to understand, but it's not just teaching that drives me. It's teaching at Country Day. I'm part of something larger than myself. These children go on to make significant contributions to society.

Perhaps it's time to bid each other farewell and best wishes. This way our experience together can be logged as a joyous memory. I've always had wonderful times with you and wish you every happiness.

Sincerely,

Thomas.

The moment Thomas had finished typing, he remembered, he had pressed send. Closing the email, Thomas thought, *why didn't I tell him how much joy he brought me? Selfishness? Control? Doubt?* He'd traded a chance for a relationship for Country Day.

One small mercy that kept him from teetering back in the direction of utter shame and regret: the email had bounced back to him a couple hours later. Manny's university's policy was to strip their researchers of their affiliated addresses the moment they left. *Thank god,* Thomas thought, as he closed his horrible and unfeeling email, which now seemed to him as if it were written by a bot. He could still apologize, respond like an adult if Manny would allow it. What a fool he'd been, what misplaced loyalty. He'd panicked, written it on impulse, and tried applying logic where logic didn't work. Thomas redialed Manny's number dozens of times that day, but Manny had owned one of those awful prepaid cellular phones, and once they ran out, they didn't ring. And even when they rang, there was no voicemail, so Thomas drove to Manny's apartment, but he'd moved out. When Thomas went to Manny's lab, one of his colleagues said he'd scored a cheap last-minute flight. Thomas had thought of calling Manny's mom's in Cologne, but even if he could get Manny on the phone, what would he have said?

What would he say now?

After the accusation, it was easy to see, but at the time none of it seemed so cold-hearted, nor had Country Day been the only factor. With all the back and forth to Colorado Springs for Jake's cancer treatment, a week had turned into a month, a month turned into three. Manny didn't use social media when they were together, and not since, Thomas knew, because he'd been searching for him regularly. So, they'd never officially broken up. He'd tried so hard to justify the no-breakup breakup. He cataloged Manny's immaturities. Once, an argument even turned physical. Thomas tried to wrestle with Manny as he changed the sheets on their bed, and Manny told him to leave him alone. Thomas refused, and Manny elbowed Thomas, hard, in the arm. Without thinking, Thomas slapped Manny on the shoulder. Manny said, "If you ever do that again, I'll punch your face."

Thomas said, "You punch me, and I'll call the police, have you deported back to Germany."

The whole scene had frightened Thomas. His own threat disgusted him. Proof that they brought out the worst in each other. The truth? The men had burst out laughing, shook the fight off quickly that day, forgave each other, and went to the farmers' market, the same market where Thomas had run into the Jays. There, shopping with Manny, Thomas felt less doom for their relationship and more of a back-door kind of joy. He relished the fact that he was part of a couple who had a fight that had gone too far. They hadn't fallen for the pervasive and destructive trap that seemed to be gaining popularity all around them, on TV, in the news, at work: the tendency to take a single mistake outside its context and use it to destroy. As they shopped, a woman yelled at her husband to get off his phone. A man scolded his girlfriend for her failure to save him the last bite of the apple. He and Manny had fights, just like his parents' fights and James's fights with Joyce and Jake's fights with Sheree. He'd finally joined the mix. When they got home, they'd talked about all the ways their particular altercation proved problematic and promised not to make the same mistakes twice.

One recent night, after coming home from Jerome's office, while making dinner Thomas was scraping julienned mint from his cutting board into the summer squash when he cried. Suddenly and audibly. By the time Thomas realized what his body was doing, the tears stopped. As did the noise and the sudden grip of emotion he felt when he realized that Manny wasn't, in fact, there. *I'm afraid,* Thomas thought. *To be honest about who and what I love.* Like everyone else in his family, except Jake, Thomas visited his own emotional life like someone visits the theater, infrequently. On rare occasions, you went, you sat, you watched, you felt, you experienced catharsis. Once purged, you left the theater, handed your ticket to the valet, drove home and the next morning, up and back to business. True to form, Thomas laid out the placemats, but only one plate, napkin, and set of flatware. He ate summer squash and mint, enough for two, alone.

Thomas, shivering, walked across the empty TV room to the thermostat. The phone rang. Its face read *Mom.* He turned up the heat, took the call. "For a sec, I thought you'd be Manny," Thomas said.

"Disappointed?" Maddy asked.

"No. Thrilled to have you break up my no-breakup breakup reverie. I just said breakup three times."

"Four," she said. "I miss him, too. You should call him."

Maddy neither worshiped nor coddled Thomas. Instead, she

treated him less like a strange object and more like a friend, a confidant who shared her struggles to accept the other boys in the house and in the world. She'd always used Thomas to lament her ex-husband's and his brothers' shortcomings. She seemed shocked each time they fell short of perfection. When Thomas screwed up, his mother rarely reacted with surprise or frustration. She seemed to think him more like her, human.

"What's up?" Thomas asked.

"How you holdin' up?" Maddy asked.

"This experience will go down in history as an inconvenience," Thomas said. "I didn't spend one night in jail."

"You sound psychologically centered, son, and I don't believe it for one second. You don't know it, but you're a mess. I'd be crashing the PTA meetings, screaming. I never liked Portland anyway," she said. "Nor did I like that school. Those rich brats."

"You don't know Portland. You only visited once. And it wasn't my students' fault. And I was a mess but now I'm busy. And at Country Day it's called the PFA, not the PTA."

"F for fucked?"

"Faculty," Thomas said. When he was a kid, Maddy had chosen Thomas to take to Santa Cruz, to ride the roller coaster, and the two had been getting on and off it ever since. He never knew how strongly she felt about Country Day and Portland, would have never guessed, and it made him wonder what else she thought.

"How precious. Thirty thousand dollars for grade school tuition? And they have to audition? Meet intelligence requirements? Isn't that a bit Nazi-like? Makes me sick. There are kids in the public schools that need you in San Francisco," she said. "They'll love you there."

Something caved in him as he decided now was not the time to tell her he'd never teach again, but he promised himself that eventually he'd confide in her all the reasons he knew this to be true. "Gotta go, Mom," he said, his voice breaking a bit. He rested his palm to his chest, took a breath. "I need to get out of my running clothes before I start growing mold."

"Love you," she said.

"Love you back," Thomas replied, scarcely audible, and the two hung up.

Thomas quickly changed into yesterday's jeans and tee-shirt, and then filled his plastic cup with water from the kitchen sink's tap. He looked out the window. The pod would be picked up in a week. He'd load the boxes that had been packed in his living room in the morning. He peeled back the foil covering Ruth's casserole dish. Tuna. With pasta in the shape of small shells. And zucchini and yellow summer squash. Cheese and garlic and onion. Little basil leaves. Thyme. Maybe marjoram.

The doorbell rang.

Thomas looked through the peephole at Jerome's face. "Hey," he said, opening the door.

"I called earlier," Jerome said, coming in. "You didn't answer."

"I was on a run," he said, walking to his desk and leaving Jerome in the doorway. "Be right back."

Jerome stayed put but took off his jacket.

"Here," Thomas said, returning, holding paperwork with bank information for the eventual wire transfer that Jerome's secretary had mailed. "Thank you."

"Send that to my office," Jerome said, reaching toward Thomas. "I would've been happier had you gotten double."

Thomas reluctantly received the hug, surprised by how warm Jerome felt in his thin sweater. "Why are you here?" Thomas asked.

"To keep a friend company," Jerome said, tucking the tail of his tee-shirt back into his pants as he walked deeper into the house.

"Don't you have to work?" Thomas asked.

"Another case settled out of court. Afternoon off," Jerome said. His jeans looked less like a designer brand and more like something he bought at Costco. The tee-shirt under his sweater was likely an XL from a six-pack of BVDs. Out of his suit, he looked

157

more like a member of the NRA than the HRC. Jerome followed as Thomas walked back to his desk and put the paperwork next to the envelope.

"Want some casserole?" Thomas asked, and grabbed Manny's letter to put back into the box.

"Just ate," he said. "No thanks."

"I'll send that stuff this afternoon," Thomas said, drawing the blinds. The room went darker than he expected.

"Whenever," Jerome said, pouring himself some coffee from the carafe in the kitchen. He picked up the newspaper, the picture of the Pope, a headline: *Pope Francis Lifts Liberals' Hearts*.

"Progress, right?" Thomas said.

"Ya think?" Jerome asked, then took a sip of coffee from Thomas's #1 Teacher mug.

"Sure," Thomas said. "From Catholics?"

"Rhetoric isn't a step in the right direction unless it's met with action," Jerome said, before a speech about how the Catholics should use the church's money to fund reproductive health clinics. Free up the opportunity to all genders and sexualities to enter the priesthood. Hire a team to immediately stop putting children in the crossfire of actual sexual predators.

"Oh god, Jerome. Do you ever hang it up?" Thomas said, noticing Jerome leaning against the counter, tightening the top of the coffee carafe, totally at home.

Jerome took a sip of his coffee. "You just nailed my ex's number one complaint. I asked him to tell me when it got annoying. He'd say 'PTC!'"

"Politics timeout chime?" Thomas guessed. "Please talk casually?"

"Preaching to the choir." Jerome smiled, grabbing the newspaper, looking at the picture of the Pope. "I guess you're right; I guess it is progress. For the Catholics. But your reaction to my anger is a projection. You haven't gotten angry enough."

"And you can't get past it," Thomas said, and smiled. "And as your client I thank you." He thought about the truth in what Maddy had just said, his tendency to, at all costs, appear psychologically centered. "And you're probably right about me. Speaking

158

of Catholics," Thomas said, desperate to pivot. "Do you know the famous story about Tallulah Bankhead?"

"Which one?" Jerome asked.

"One Easter she was in Chicago for a role at one of the downtown theaters. Her publicist thought it would be wise if she made an appearance at Cardinal Cody's High Easter Mass. The processional began and, decked out in full Catholic regalia, Cody started down the aisle with all his acolytes. Cody swung the incense-burning thingie, and as he approached Miss Bankhead, she said ..."

Jerome interrupted, "Darling, I love your dress, but your purse is on fire."

The two laughed, and Thomas wondered what Jerome must be like in a real courtroom. So self-confident and assured, passionate. "I'll be right back," Thomas said. Once in his bathroom, he locked the door and turned the water to hot. While it warmed, he looked at himself in the mirror. The pieces all formed: He remembered Jerome saying that he needed to let go of Manny, get out more. Here to say hello to a friend? Now, talk of exes? Not here to collect the paperwork? Casual clothing? An impulse led Thomas to grab the mouthwash, take a pull. He kept it in his mouth as he brushed his teeth, then spit, brushed his tongue and then rinsed with hot water. With his pants around his ankles and his shirt on the basin, he washed his crotch and armpits with a sudsy washcloth before tossing it into the hamper. He toweled himself off and got dressed again, then crossed the hall into the bedroom and quickly picked up the dirty clothes and empty potato chip bag he'd left by the bed. Finally, he brushed the crumbs from his sheets and straightened the comforter before returning to the kitchen.

"You smell good," Jerome said.

"Grapefruit basil, I think," Thomas said. "My sister-in-law sells fancy soaps."

"Yum," Jerome said. "When do the movers come?"

"There are none. I just put stuff into that thing at the end the driveway," Thomas said, explaining how it would go into storage until one of Dana's apartment leads panned out.

"Can I help you pack the pod?" Jerome asked. A small brown dot rested under his bottom lip, a tiny drop of coffee that dried into a stain.

"You'll do that?" Thomas asked, noting the innuendo. He cocked his head to the side, narrowed his eyes, said, "Without billing me at your hourly rate?"

Jerome's eyes nearly disappeared when he smiled.

Thomas felt his throat tighten as he walked to Jerome, then took his forearms in his hands, backed him against the counter, and kissed his neck. The salt of his skin penetrated the minty medicine flavor in Thomas's mouth. Jerome placed his hands over Thomas's ears and gently forced his head away. He looked into Thomas's eyes, and Thomas pushed his mouth toward Jerome's.

"Thomas," Jerome said, quietly. His voice as soft as the palms pressing into Thomas's cheeks.

Thomas planted his feet squarely, used his strength to lean into Jerome, pressing his erection to Jerome's groin while reaching to kiss him. Jerome moved his hands from Thomas's skull to his shoulders. Thomas braced himself, maintained eye contact. "Was it a test? That night at the bar? To see if I'd fight for you? Is that what you wanted? Someone to fight for you just like you fight for everyone else?" Thomas pushed harder into Jerome. The two men stumbled from the kitchen to the dining room, barely missing a stack of boxes, as Thomas moved Jerome toward the bedroom.

"I'm your lawyer, Thomas," Jerome said.

"Not anymore," Thomas said, digging into the density of Jerome's shoulders.

Jerome lowered into a squat, grabbed Thomas by the waist.

Thomas fell to the floor. Pinned under Jerome, Thomas could smell the coffee on his breath and suddenly realized what was happening. He tried to squirm out from underneath but could barely budge. "Let me out," he finally said.

Jerome released him.

"What the fuck are you doing here?" Thomas yelled.

"I'm here to help you," Jerome said, getting up. Then he offered Thomas his hand.

Thomas refused. His body had gone slack, his mouth dry.

The night before the final hearing, Thomas had had a dream. In it, a ticking sound distracted him from work. Like a coin being tapped against glass. He walked from his desk toward his bedroom where the tapping was met with sounds of air bubbling to the surface of water. He opened an immense set of curtains that revealed a glass pool the size of the shark tank at the Portland Aquarium, where he'd gone every year with his fourth graders, where he'd stood with Toby. A figure was huddled up against the opposite wall of the tank. Everywhere, fish of all sizes and colors darted around each other at various speeds. Thomas played with the panel of light switches along the wall. They brightened different areas of the tank, highlighting and darkening various corners of the underwater world. The dark mass was motionless except for a single finger with a long nail, which he tapped against the glass. It started swimming, jutting itself toward the top of the pool, but could not break the surface, and it kept cascading down, eventually sinking to a place on the aquarium floor directly in front of Thomas. Seaweed covered the face except for his mouth. *Help*, it said, as little bubbles rose from his nose and lips. When Thomas woke up, he thought the figure in the dream was Mr. Jay. Now he wondered. Perhaps he'd been the one trapped under all that water, held behind that glass.

"Take it," Jerome said.

Finally, Thomas grabbed Jerome's hand. He helped Thomas to his feet. "Too soon?"

"For now. Come here," Jerome said and pulled Thomas to him. "I'm here," he said. "To help you pack." Then he pulled away from Thomas and looked at his face. "Not pack fudge, you dork."

While wrapping the objects of his home into old newspaper, Thomas told Jerome about his college years with Dana, his affair with Tony. They listened to Thomas's old CDs—The Psychedelic Furs, Echo and the Bunnymen, Blondie, and The Jesus and Mary Chain. Thomas even admitted to cutting the toes off his soccer socks in grade school to make legwarmers. "I also cut the neck out of a sweatshirt and wore it over one shoulder. I wanted to be Jennifer Beals in *Flashdance* so badly," Thomas said. "Locked up in my bedroom, I danced nonstop to that soundtrack."

"I thought the lyrics were *Flashdance!* Take your pants off and make it happen!" Jerome said. "Imagine how disappointed I was years later when I went to karaoke and read the actual lyrics."

"You turned 'take your passion' into 'take your pants off?'" Thomas said. "Tells me a lot about you."

The two laughed.

Finally, they'd rolled up and stacked all of the rugs.

Jerome used a dry mop to dust the floor in the nearly empty living room. The last of the sun, copper and gold, came in from the west-facing window and warmed a three-foot wide section of the birch floor.

"I'm sorry for all this, my friend," Jerome said, pushing the broom to a corner where he let it rest.

"No need to be sorry," Thomas said, and meant it. His voice echoed a bit now that nearly all of the boxes and much of the furniture had been moved.

Looking around, Thomas recalled that Sheree had made a comment after she first saw the place, "You pink-skinned people are practically invisible against all this beige and gray."

He didn't tell her that he'd planned it that way. His brothers and their families and his parents and their spouses were meant to provide the color. He left space around the furniture because he wanted room for the kids to run around. Play charades, assemble a giant puzzle on the floor, make blanket tents. He chose the kitchen countertops because they were impossible to stain, the best place in the Pacific Northwest to sit and make art projects. He'd imagined the creation of elaborate Easter eggs and Halloween masks from aluminum foil and paper-mâché.

Jerome stepped into the kitchen to take a call. Thomas stood still on the threshold between the bedroom and the living room where he watched the light slowly travel across his floor.

Jerome walked back in. "Call me when you get settled in San Francisco? Keep in touch?" Jerome asked.

"Of course. Sorry again about before. And thanks so much for everything. Really, Jerome. You're incredibly talented."

Jerome smiled. "Country Day's and Portland's loss will most definitely be San Francisco's gain." He touched Thomas's face, hugged him, and walked out.

Thomas returned to the kitchen, tossed the #1 Teacher mug into the trashcan, and grabbed a beer. In the shower, the liquid warmed his insides as the water spread over his skin. When it was almost gone, he poured the rest into his hair. He lathered it in, felt his scalp tingle while imagining his airplane touching down at SFO.

Chapter Fourteen

Late October 2013

Dana stood waiting, backlit, just beyond security, at the top of the escalators that led down to SFO's baggage claim. He spotted her, waving. Up until this trip, he'd always lifted his roller carry-on because one of the little wheels was partially stuck and wouldn't spin fast enough to keep up as he ran toward her. This time, not sure why, he walked, until Dana's face finally came into clear view. She grabbed him, held him in her warmth. A puffy coat softened her lean, athletic body. Her damp hair smelled like sweat, or sex—as if she'd just fucked or worked out—then jumped into the car without showering. It had grown long enough to hit her shoulders. Gone were the days of spikes and buzz cuts and one-side-shaved asymmetry. Waiting for the elevator, she unzipped the shiny black coat. Underneath, she wore two more layers, a tank top under a fuzzy hooded sweatshirt, and a pair of snug jeans tucked into leather boots.

In the car, soft lights from 101's traffic lit her face. "I'd totally given up on the idea of monogamy. Never mind relationships," she said. "Honestly I didn't even like Mel at first."

Thomas relaxed into the heated seat. The Bay hugged the highway for a couple of miles before they came upon Candlestick Park.

"She never asks me for money," Dana bragged about Mel's work producing animated blockbusters.

"Finally. A sugar momma," Thomas said, already exhausted by the banter. "Just what a trust fund baby needs." Thomas had finally admitted to himself that he probably—and mostly unconsciously—didn't tell Dana anything at first because she had so much in common with the parents at Country Day—at least financially. A motorcycle whizzed between Dana's and a second car. "Does she get to go to Hollywood movie premieres? Hobnob with the voice-over celebrities?"

"Yes. But she won't bring me," Dana said while adjusting the temperature of the car. "She thinks actors are too horny and I'm too impressed by fame."

Thomas smirked.

"See?" Dana smiled. "She knows me. Have you heard back from Manny?"

"I finally called his parents' landline, but the number didn't work," Thomas said. "The second I get settled I'm going to continue the search."

"He'll turn up," she said.

Thomas smiled even though her reassurance didn't quite quiet the turmoil he felt about not yet finding Manny. "Will I get to meet Mel at dinner?"

"She's in Los Angeles. It's just you and me."

Thomas and Dana had met in the queue for Cal's graduate school orientation in August and were best friends by Halloween. She talked him into going to a frat party as Sonny and Cher. Afterward, at Thomas's apartment, Dana had taken off her high heels, one at a time, and tossed them at Thomas. "Next year," she said, rubbing her feet, "You're Cher, and I'm Sonny."

Dana finished her Master of Architecture a year before Thomas finished his Master of Education. She moved to San Francisco first. That year, the two were always crossing the bridge. Thomas on his motor scooter. Dana in her old VW Bug.

"Do you ever go to Berkeley anymore?" Thomas asked.

She clicked on the wipers to clear the cleaning solution she'd just squirted on the dusty windshield. "I went to see a show at Berkeley Rep with Mel," she said, and steered right onto Bryant. "Every time I go over there it's like Memoryville."

"Speaking of memories. Can we go to Taquería Vallarta?" Thomas asked.

After securing dinner, they pulled into Dana's garage on Douglass Street, and then bounded up the stairs. Thomas followed her into the small hallway at the top. He'd forgotten how cold she kept her place. He pulled his suitcase into the dining room, opened it and took out his jacket. She turned on the oven and threw their foil-wrapped burritos inside, then led him outside to the garden. The fog came in thick and early from Twin Peaks. Dana loved carnivorous plants and had cultivated a garden with dozens of varietals. The Venus Flytrap, with its leaves that looked like little-toothed envelopes, had been the only carnivorous plant Thomas knew. Most of Dana's were tuberous and bulbous, super bright.

"It looks like a Tim Burton film out here," Thomas said, and followed her up the terraced steps of her garden toward the greenhouse that she had built near the fence. Looking closely at the plants, Thomas said, "What's the adjective when something is like a vagina? Everything in your garden is either phallic or vagina-like."

"I say *vulvic*," Dana said, pulling weeds, then tossing them near the fence. "Others say *yonic*. I can't say *yoni* without laughing."

Thomas let out a giggle.

"See?" Dana said.

The last moments of sun left little light through the fog, so the two went inside, and Thomas was glad for the heat of the oven. He sat down on a stool at the kitchen's island. "I've been saying that word for years, in front of the children, when I get tired. When I yawn, I say I'm yawny."

"You are yoni," Dana said, taking the burritos out of the oven and putting them on plates. She passed one to him. "Now eat your phallus."

Thomas took a bite. He'd been waiting a long time—since the day he decided to move back to San Francisco—to eat this exact meal with his best friend—but he couldn't quite settle into it, not yet. Dana's sink's backsplash extended across the entire wall. Bright, autumn-colored, hand-blown glass tile. Yellow-orange. Orange-red. Red-yellow. Yellow-green. Dana's pale skin, her freckled chest and arms, the heather gray hoodie on the back of her stool, her auburn hair—all of it made her look a bit too perfect, like a creature evolution sculpted to blend into her environment.

"Wine, beer or water?" she said.

"I'm finally here, and I would like a Dana-cocktail with which to toast."

"You have no idea what I'm about to do for you," Dana said, got up, and kissed him on the top of his head.

She pulled a skull-shaped bottle from one of the up-lit shelves in the TV room and returned to retrieve her blender from one of the island's cabinets. She filled the blender's jar with enough tequila to tranquilize a lion, then added ice and took a tube of limeade from the door of her freezer, spooned a glob of the syrupy concentrate, then grabbed a mandarin from the wide shallow bowl between them. She peeled it almost bald and then added it to the mix before fetching a saucer and a big jar of salt.

She turned on the blender and took another bite of her burrito. Thomas stared at her face, watching the workings of the muscle and bone of her jaw. He loved the angles of her head resting on her slender neck as she moved her gaze from her plate to the salt to the blender—all of it so subtle, so familiar.

"I'm nervous for you to see your place," Dana said, cutting a lime, and then used a wedge to dampen the glasses' rims before twisting them on a salt covered plate.

"You picked it," Thomas said, in an effort to quell his own

doubts. "I'll love it so long as it's not that shithole across the street you picked for me last time."

This time, Dana had called on a Saturday morning at the end of September telling Thomas that her neighbor's daughter was about to leave an apartment. He remembered sitting down at his desk that morning, opening his laptop, and running a search on the address. On Green Street near Van Ness, the center of a cross where Cow Hollow and the Marina and Russian Hill and Pacific Heights all converged. He could walk to Ft. Mason Park and the Marina Green, but it was still far enough south not to go down with the landfill that had split open during the last big earthquake.

An hour later, his text tone woke him up from a nap. Dana wrote, *It's fantastic.* She followed it with a half dozen pictures. He had never imagined himself living in that neighborhood, but he wanted it over with, one less decision he had to make on his own. By the end of the afternoon, Thomas had a credit check, letters of reference, and bank statements sent to the property manager. He printed out a pdf of the lease, signed it, scanned it and sent it back. Then he searched plane tickets. *ONE WAY*, he had clicked, then entered his credit card numbers in the field above *PAY* and below *ALL SALES ARE FINAL.*

Dana transferred the icy slush with a spatula, careful not to remove the salt from the rims of the glasses, and then added lime squeezes and an extra splash of the tequila to the top of each. She handed Thomas his drink.

"Here's to you," Thomas said, hoping the booze would help him relax.

"And to finding Manny."

Thomas let out a sigh. "And to Mel." The two touched glasses, and Thomas took a sip. "Wow," he said. "You don't fuck around."

"The margarita or bringing up Manny?"

He took another big sip. "Yes," Thomas said. "Twice."

"For what it's worth, your eyes look gorgeous when you're frail." Dana pulled her stool closer to his. She took a bite and then rested her head on his shoulder.

"Thanks," he said, even though something about the comment irritated him. Too wiped to get into it, he changed the subject. "Speaking of frail, I wonder if Edna is still around."

"I saw her once at the Alameda Flea Market buying some old step stool. She looked strong. Seeing her made me excited to get old," Dana said. "We have to call her, throw some sandwiches into a cooler and take her to Lake Merritt. Or maybe we should bring her to The Exploratorium. I haven't been since it moved, and she liked that place, right?"

"Loved it. And she'd love this drink," Thomas said, looking to the wall of windows dividing the sunken living room from the back yard. The floodlights failed the garden, illuminated only fog. He thought of Edna and Tony and the places they all inhabited. He thought too of all of the other places he'd never forget: the woods behind the house where he'd moved, from California to Massachusetts. The places in Italy he'd visited with Dana: Umbria, Venice, Rome, the islands off Naples where they served olives in paper cones. Santa Cruz, Muir Woods, all of the California Coast, up Highway One, north to Mendocino or south to Pescadero with its artichoke bread and cheap avocados. So lucky he'd been to go to so many places. So lucky not to have returned to others. So lucky.

"Another?" Dana asked, holding the pitcher of margaritas.

He said yes.

Dana filled his glass and excused herself to the bathroom. Her steampunk kitchen chandelier reminded Thomas of a family intervention when Jake was in one of his rehabs, where they believed in craftsmanship as a tool to keep the addict from relapsing. Clients had made the room's lamps from pipes and pipe joints screwed to wooden bases. They'd placed the lamps around every fourth chair or so, and the counselor who led the intervention talked passionately about the healing powers of welding.

When it was Thomas's turn, he had to remind Jake of his visit to Berkeley, the time Thomas had given him the keys to his scooter, his ATM card and password. Jake was supposed to get some groceries and a pizza while Thomas finished his homework, but Jake had stolen all the money in Thomas's checking account, wrecked the scooter someplace near San Jose, and never came home. Thomas's plea had lacked the passion in his father's and brother's tough love approach and also the weepy desperation of Maddy's. Thomas thought it was weird. Wasn't an intervention supposed to convince someone to go to rehab? Jake was already there. Still, he cooperated.

According to the outrage expressed by the others, it seemed Thomas should've taken Jake's robbery personally, should've been infuriated. He had no extra money, could not replace the scooter, but he felt less victimized than vindicated. The experience allowed an almost-buried doubt to surface about the place he held in his loved ones' lives. *Of course, Jake chose drugs over me,* it whispered. He tried to sound convincing when following the script and suggestions, but what he really wanted, seeing his brother, was to take Jake's hand. Say, *Yes. We are a family. But we suffer alone.*

A sudden rush of sensation sloshed around his gut, leaving him queasy with a panicky dread. Thomas opened his eyes. Said softly, "This is now. I'm here." He and Jake would have a second chance to experience The City. The cancer was gone. They could make new memories to layer over the others. He'd take his little brother, this time with his wife and son, to all the places Thomas loved: Café Flore, La Palma, Fort Mason Park, The Lyon Street Steps. "I am here," Thomas said again. The toilet flushed. The sink ran. Metal hardware that held the hand towel clanked into the wall. Dana came out. She crunched her used napkins into the burrito's foil, the foil into the paper bag, the bag into the garbage pail under the sink. "Excited?" she asked, pushing her stool to the island.

"Yes," Thomas said. "And drunk. And tired."

Her phone buzzed on the counter. She picked up the call as Otto emerged from the dining room. Soon Dana held the fluffy white Himalayan to her chest. "Go shower if you want. It's Mel. We'll be on for a while."

Upstairs, Thomas looked out the guest room window onto Douglass Street, into the apartment where he'd lived all those years ago, the first time Dana helped him find a place in the city. Waiting. That's what he remembered of life in that apartment. The two weeks in between the drawn blood and the HIV test result. Distracted amidst his students' worksheets, sitting at the Formica kitchen table he inherited from a guy, dead of AIDS, who had lived and died in that apartment. Until the accusation, it had been the longest two weeks of his life. Every single second of intimacy with Tony, including removing a bee's stinger from his cheek, played and replayed. A wild shot, Tony's ejaculations had landed in all sorts of places, including, once, smack dab on top of Thomas's uncovered eyeball.

Thomas now sat on the chest at the foot of Dana's guest bed, untied his high-tops, and kicked them into the corner. He found the music channel on the television, turned up hits from the 90s while he unzipped his bag. His phone beeped. A text from James. *According to my calculations, you've already had two hours to adjust. Now Joyce and the girls and I want to know, are you coming to New York for Thanksgiving or what?*

Yes, Thomas wrote, too tired to argue, and put down his phone. He'd gotten used to being alone in these last months. He'd buy his tickets in the morning.

He showered, brushed his teeth, and got into bed. When "Creep" by Radiohead ended, Thomas found the remote, turned off the TV and texted Dana *Goodnight.* Tequila spun the room, but the sheets felt so soft and cool that Thomas decided to enjoy the ride.

"Ten," Thomas said, relieved. Dana, like the Country Day parents, would never consider living in an apartment as small as this one, but got caught up in how cute she thought stuff could be. She often used words like *cozy* and *quaint* while concentrating on one tiny detail, like original wainscoting or a built-in ironing board closet.

Not this time. Dana stood next to him in the empty and echoing family room of the Green Street apartment, surrounded by hardwood floors and postmeridian light. She'd just hooked her arm into his, leaned into his shoulder and said, "Be honest. On a scale of one to ten, how much do you like it?"

He meant it. The new neighborhood seemed like a different city. Dana's house on Douglass Street straddled the dividing line between the Castro with its gay bars; the even-more-gentrified Mission, with tech brats entering and exiting busses to and from the peninsula; and Noe Valley, with lesbian mothers pushing strollers to and from Whole Foods. On Green Street, women in yoga pants bellowed into cell phones. A bottle of juice from a pop-up shop cost the same as an actual meal in a restaurant. Dry cleaners were "green." A leaky pipe under the kitchen sink had caused water to get under the linoleum and David, the apartment manager, wanted to strip and resurface the hardwood floors. "They're original. From 1904," he said, and asked if Thomas could delay his move in until the first of December.

"Sure." Thomas smiled. "I'm heading to New York for Thanksgiving anyway."

"Perfect," David said, and handed him the keys.

Practically inseparable since he'd arrived, Dana and Thomas shared meals and saw movies and shopped at farmers' markets and bought soil from the garden store and browsed mid-century modern shops as far north as Sonoma. He couldn't pinpoint it but felt a slight and constant tentativeness around her. In recent years he'd spent tenfold the time with Mercy, and even on his and Dana's jaunts abroad, Thomas was always emailing and texting Mercy. Perhaps the time with Dana made him miss Mercy. Still, he tried. At the Presidio, he and Dana jumped for an hour at the trampoline park (loved it) and struggled to get to the top of a rock-climbing wall (hated it). They squeezed delicious bites of *wat* and *tibs* with the *injera* bread at Dana's favorite Ethiopian café in Oakland; ate at all the restaurants Dana loved and Mel refused to go.

"She won't go to In and Out?" Thomas asked, eating his fries. "Seriously? What about Pho?"

"She'll eat any cuisine so long as there's candlelight, cloth napkins, and tablecloths. She requires all three. And a wine list with at least one old-world pinot noir."

"Ew, sounds like my kids' parents," Thomas said. It came out more harshly than he intended. Then, "Glad to be the stopgap in your relationship."

While hauling weeds, lugging a love seat she had finally reupholstered, and pulling the compost and recycling and garbage bins to the curb, Thomas told her the whole story in five and six and seven-minute installments. Every detail, starting with the party and ending with the final meeting with Mercy and Jerome.

Dana listened. She remained even and steady. "I'd be much more pissed," she said, "if it wasn't the thing that got you to move back."

The two had been sitting together on a blanket. Seventy-something degree second-summer day at Dolores Park. Known as Gay Beach, they planted themselves on a flat shelf of grass dotted with beautiful men in bikinis who shaved their legs and armpits and handsome women in board shorts and tank tops who did not. Their piece of the park divided two steep declines near the intersection of Church and 20th, overlooking a row of giant palms and San Francisco's skyline. Thomas lugged a cooler bag with a picnic of Dana's favorites. She removed an olive pit from her mouth. "I know a gay nanny, and he's booked. There's a huge waiting list of people who want him to take care of their kids. What the fuck is wrong with Portland?"

"Maybe it's not Portland," Thomas said. "Maybe it's not personal."

"Ok, but why didn't you tell the parents what happened at the party?" she asked, crunching on a piece of fennel. "I mean, his wife accused you of doing what her husband did to you. It's classic."

"Jerome really wanted to. I kept thinking I wouldn't have to. I entered some weird optimistic denial realm. I thought any minute the whole thing would be over, and I'd be back in the classroom. I liked the Jays. Mr. Jay loves his wife and certainly loves Toby.

He's a good dad. They'd been so kind to me. I wanted to show them my loyalty."

"That's fucked," Dana said, ripping apart the baguette that Thomas had sliced down the middle and filled with a thick layer of sweet butter. "It's one thing to be out and proud and bisexual in an open marriage, but it's another to be on the down-low and then ruin someone else's life. What's that thing called when the kidnapped person turns all loyal and melty toward the kidnapper? Or when the tortured person protects the torturer?"

"I wasn't kidnapped or tortured," Thomas said. "Come on."

"Not physically," she said. "And for the record, I'm not criticizing as much as I'm, I don't know . . ." Dana looked around at the others in the park. "Sympathizing? Queers have been protecting the people who kill them from the beginning of time."

A woman with a basket on her arm weaved in and out of the crowd that had gathered. Soon she stood over the two. "Magic brownies?" she asked. "Space cookies?"

"Yes," Thomas said, and bought one, split it with Dana, and the pair spent the next two hours laughing. They were shivering before they realized the fog had come in and it was time to go home.

That night, in Dana's guest room bed, no longer high, wide awake on his back, Thomas returned to what she'd said at the park. The darkness provided by wooden shutters became the darkness in between what he believed then and what had been revealed since. Perhaps he'd known all along what the Jays and Country Day would do.

He kept thinking of high-school Chad. His giant scarves. His elaborate hair. His arm of rubber bracelets. His pointy patent leather shoes. The blood that had been transferred from his body to the floor; from the floor into the thick cords of cotton at the end of the custodian's mop; from the mop to the lukewarm water mixed with Pine-Sol in a bucket; from the bucket to the gutter outside the cafeteria, down the drain. Soon after the incident in the band room, the principal forced the teachers to interrogate the students. She'd demanded that anyone with any information about what had happened to Chad come forward.

Thomas had sat still as his teacher threatened expulsion not only for those involved but also witnesses, anyone found to be withholding information about Chad's attackers. Thomas's neighbor, Joey Demopoulos—one of the guys who'd attacked Chad—stared at Thomas. Joey wiped his forehead every few seconds with a yellowing handkerchief that probably belonged to his hairy dad.

Had Joey seen Thomas that day? Was his stare-down a threat?

Thomas had written the list of four names, including Joey's and Damien's, under *CHAD'S ATTACKERS* on a piece of notebook paper, which he'd folded into a square and hid in the inner pocket of his jean jacket with a plan to leave it in the principal's mailbox during lunch. He'd done so immediately after hearing Chad had detailed the attack before he dropped out without naming his perpetrators. Thomas reached inside his jacket and fingered the corner of the paper as Joey continued to stare. Joey had gone through puberty early, started shaving in sixth grade. He worked out on a weight bench in his basement, bragged about how much he could press. Thomas became aroused. It happened every time he thought of or looked at Joey for too long.

In Dana's guest room, Thomas's memory jumped to an article he'd read. Where? In *The New Yorker*? A profile of Roy Cohn, the attorney who worked for McCarthy to hunt down supposed communists, many gay. Cohn had defended that idiot, what was his name? Who'd been brought up on countless real estate discrimination cases? The guy who put his name on everything. The beauty pageant judge. Thomas couldn't recall, but he absolutely could remember how Cohn also opposed gay rights initiatives during the height of the pandemic. As he withered away from an AIDS-related infection—known for keeping young, blond male lovers—he framed then hung the get-well-soon letters written by Ronald Reagan on his wall. Thomas remembered a quote from the profile, *Roy was not gay. He was a man who liked having sex with men. Gays were weak, effeminate.*

As their homeroom teacher had segued from threats to announcements, Joey smiled at Thomas. After the first-period bell had rung, Thomas skipped class, walked to the scene of the crime, behind the stage curtain, where he tore his paper with the list of names into tiny pieces. He tossed half the confetti into the tuba's cage and sprinkled the rest along the trail to the band room door where he had kept himself hidden.

Chapter Fifteen

Tuesday and Wednesday
November 25th and 26th, 2013

Mornings started slowly in the north part of San Francisco. The thick mist hid the sun until noon. Early mornings were for bankers and partiers. One set headed out, the other arrived home from someone else's. Through the window, there he was. A man at a desk with a laptop and printer. Cords dangled. Around him, a scattering of photos. Swatches of color set against white walls. The photo-printer's cardboard box sat empty next to his right foot. Thomas waited for the image on his laptop screen to transform into an object he could hold.

The tiny colored lines stacked up on one another, eventually revealing his nephew Max's hat, then hair, then neck, then knee. Air-bound, mid-kickflip, floating above his skateboard. One of many snapshots Thomas had printed before entering a vortex of repeat-scrolling through a Manny photo-loop: Manny hugging Max in front of those giraffes at the Cheyenne Mountain Zoo, laughing during a game of Jenga with Jake and Sheree, staring at Van Gogh's "Sunflowers" at The Met with James and Joyce. Eating mac and cheese with Maddy. Unwrapping a set of old-school headphones in front of Stuart and Dot's Christmas tree.

Thomas ran Manny's full name through the engine one more time. When nothing came up, he closed his computer and pulled on running shorts and shirt after smoothing a layer of waterproof sunscreen into his face, arms and neck. He remembered to slip a ten-dollar bill and his ID in his phone's case. After he had locked his door, he cranked his music.

The sun finally pierced the fog as he ran west on Green Street. His legs started to warm up, his jaw relaxed, his shoulders began moving down, away from his neck in small intervals as he turned left on Gough. Soon he faced what had to be a 40 percent grade. Blood filled his legs' muscles, sweat started to break through the film of sunscreen, and his hair began to dampen. Since his arrival in San Francisco, Thomas's thoughts, when alone, switched regularly and rapidly from future to the past. Future meant fear. *What will I do once I'm settled? Will I ever work again?*

Past meant Manny.

By now, Thomas had reached the last part of Divisadero, which gave way to streets with Terrace names: Alpine Terrace, Buena Vista Terrace, Upper Terrace. The sky, a menacing blue, contrasted with lush green palms and honeysuckle, bottlebrush trees, rooftop gardens. Thomas decided that the second he got back to Green Street, he'd go to the web page and finally email the people still on staff at the lab in Portland where Manny had conducted his research, ask if any of them had new contact information.

Finally, he arrived at Dana's house, rang the doorbell, turned off his music. Dana didn't answer. He pressed it again before walking to the garage to key in the code. Inside, he grabbed a bottle of water from the case near the recycling container. Drinking it, he knew he was too tired to run back to the apartment. He'd take a cab back to Green Street, where the hardwood floors had been refinished, and the building manager said he could stay overnight now if he kept clear of the kitchen until his guys finished the new pipes and linoleum. He'd print out his boarding pass for New York, grab a bite in the neighborhood and then get to bed early. He threw his clothes into Dana's washing machine, and walked, nude, upstairs to the guest bathroom.

The built-in rain-shower produced a breadth of water so warm and wide that Thomas stood under it for a full five minutes before reaching for soap.

As the steam faded, his reflection in the mirror developed like a photo from his new printer. He wrapped the towel around his waist.

"Freeze," a man clutching a gun in two hands yelled when Thomas opened the door.

Thomas's towel fell to the floor as the gunman pulled the trigger. The two stood, the gun pointed straight at Thomas's cock.

"Thomas?" Mel said. Then, "Oh my goodness. Get dressed."

Mel's gun turned out to be a realistic-looking toy, a prop used as a model for the illustrators in the animation room at her job. She'd borrowed it for a costume she'd worn to a cowboy-themed wedding. She didn't apologize or blush. She walked toward Dana's bedroom at the west end of the hallway, clicking the toy gun as she took a work call on her mobile. After he had fetched his clothes from the dryer, Mel offered Thomas a lift home. Their conversation was brief, as phone calls kept interrupting, but Thomas liked Mel much more than he suspected she liked him.

He studied her face as she drove. Before meeting Mel, he'd imagined her dark-featured. Dana, while at Berkeley, dated brunettes. Later, after graduation, she'd started attending Michfest every summer, and she'd come home with a row of lovers. An Iranian carpenter. An Indigenous-Brazilian *capoeirista*. A first-generation Sicilian American artist who worked in metal. A Black American poet. Mel's eyebrows were as translucent as her colorless lips and hair which she'd styled to look like the crown of a pineapple. Her skin looked so delicate, so white, it held a cast of blue: sky blue, like skim milk, or a thin roux. As she drove and talked into the invisible microphone buried somewhere in the ceiling or dash of the luxury SUV, her whole face morphed into various shapes, like an aerial view of a water ballet troupe, its members clad in beige suits in pale water. That, and she wore the coolest patent leather shoes Thomas had seen since Chad.

When they arrived at Green Street, Mel stopped next to the courtyard and put on her hazards. Thomas got out, and she pressed the button that made the passenger window go down. "Next time," she said, "wear pants." She leaned over from the driver seat, reached out her arm, and shook his hand.

Newark seemed nicer than he remembered. He wasn't sure what they'd changed. Maybe everything? Nothing? Still groggy from the red-eye, Thomas walked directly to the bus stop.

Why Newark? James had texted after Thomas forwarded his itinerary. And, *Next time call first. I have a million miles, and my office manager can book you in first class, hook you up with a car service.*

Thomas ignored James's offers. A bus to Newark Penn Station. A train to Journal Square. A subway to the western part of the East Village where James lived in a three thousand-square-foot loft apartment. He enjoyed the commute from Newark to downtown Manhattan on public transportation. Not like in Portland, where diversity felt more like an intellectual idea rather than a reality. Here, necessity forced the Hasidic to ride with Muslims, Pakistanis with Dominicans, Laotians with Filipinos, European Americans with Africans, Puerto Ricans with Indians. Each ignoring the other while busy on their books or phones or rocking prayers. Today, a pair of women wearing hijabs sat across from a couple of lesbians holding hands. A pregnant woman fanned herself with a newspaper in her left hand while holding a toddler with the right.

Three men, too. One wore a striped tee-shirt and a jacket tied around his waist. He stood toward the back of the train car, earphones in, his pale skin contrasting his violently red lips and dark stubble. The second guy sat across from Thomas, the left side of his body angled to the window. He pressed a cell phone to his right ear while repeating the word *no*. His large, brown hands were the dark caramel color of a worn baseball mitt and almost the same size. They looked as if they'd been dipped in paraffin, wrapped in cotton, then manicured for a photo shoot; perhaps an ad to sell a watch worth twenty grand. The third wore eyewear that looked more like safety goggles than glasses and held his computer tablet within an inch of his face. He kept adjusting himself in his pants.

Thomas looked away and did not look back until he reached his stop. He'd emailed Manny's lab just yesterday. One of Manny's colleagues wrote back immediately, said she'd forwarded Thomas's info to the address Manny had given her.

Now, he wanted to see his brother, his sister-in-law, and his nieces. Use a bathroom. Rehydrate. Shower. Eat. Give them the gifts he had managed to fit into his bag: a notebook-sized journal he bought at SF MOMA's gift shop, and a set of Japanese ink pens with tips so fine Barbara could write a hundred words on a single line. He had found handmade enamel barrettes for Silvia while shopping in his new neighborhood with Dana. Silvia loved anything bright and handmade. Teresa was tougher than the other two. She wanted the same trappings as many other nine-year-old girls but grew bored unless the gift engaged her intellect. He had settled on a sophisticated coloring book with descriptions of various types of butterflies and moths. On their last video call, Teresa had said, "Ever since I was little, I've loved butterflies. Now I'm obsessed with centipedes. So basically, you can call me an arthropod-phile."

When the PATH train stopped at World Trade Center, Thomas, weary, opted to skip the walk past Ground Zero to Cortland Street where he'd usually take the subway. The taxi stopped in front of his brother's building which shared space on a block with an upscale health club and a Japanese retailer of minimally packaged goods. Thomas got out and walked toward their building's slowly opening front door.

"Mr. Fluffiano," the doorman said, taking his bag.

"Stoyan," Thomas said. "You look well."

He handed Thomas a key. "Mrs. McGurrin stepped out, but the girls are expecting you."

The elevator opened onto the fourth floor. The hallway leading to each of the floor's three apartments looked more designed than the interior of most people's homes, with its lush, dark carpet that absorbed the sound of footfall and the squeak of his suitcase wheels. Thomas looked tanner and healthier in the reflection of the hallway's mirrored walls than he did in daylight. He heard Teresa and Silvia laughing or arguing on the other side of the door. The silver keyring held a placard engraved with *Country Day*, a gift Mercy had sent James and Joyce for their donation to the scholarship fund. Thomas fiddled with the fancy key, trying to remember how the damn thing worked.

These last few months, as Thomas interacted with the sensual world, he'd become accustomed to sudden rushes of intense emotion. The sensation hit hard, as if delivered through a needle—slipped, without consent or knowledge—into one of his veins. The frayed cuff of Stoyan's sports jacket, the smell of dog fur in the elevator, the damp socks in his shoes clinging to his toes, the memory of the man on the train's ruby lips. The mix of such things could uncoil unquantifiable amounts of gratitude or alarm or both as he pulled his suitcase across a hallway. Seeing that keyring, Thomas felt nothing other than, perhaps, a slight smugness in the symbolic appropriateness of his gift, mostly housed in a dusty drawer, being used to hold an occasional guest key.

He kept jiggling. Finally, the door opened. The dogs barked, then jumped, then crotch dived, then kissed. Teresa and Silvia grabbed him by the waist and pulled him into the guest room. Soon Barbara appeared in the doorway. Thomas got up and approached her. She reached out and lightly hugged his neck.

"I hate to say it," she said. "But we're off to a birthday party. I just got a text that our friend's nanny is downstairs waiting for us. Mom said you'd probably want to lie down anyway."

"Go," Thomas said. "Have fun."

After the girls left, the echoing taps of the dogs' toenails clicked on the hardwood all the way back to James and Joyce's bedroom.

A vase of still-closed autumn lilies sat on the table, and the Murphy bed had been pulled down from the custom nook that helped the room double as an art gallery when there weren't guests. A homemade card rested on the desk. The girls had written *Welcome, Uncle* in four languages on the front and *See you around 6* on the flip side.

Thomas imagined his fourth graders, construction paper spread across their desks, waxed crayons, magazines, magic markers, and glitter glue. He remembered the valentine Toby had given him. He'd drawn a heart on the cover. And not just the lone diagonal arrow like most of the other kids, but several arrows piercing the center of his heart from every direction. *Be My Valentine?* it read. And, on the inside, *Love, Toby Jay.*

Thomas, unzipping his suitcase, felt a sudden uneasiness, the anxiety that might come from a pleading question remaining unanswered. He took out the gifts he'd brought everyone, including the coffee beans for Joyce and the saltwater taffy for James. He'd walked to Fisherman's Wharf to get the sweets his brother loved, only to find out that the taffy shops he'd remembered from childhood, with the machines that pulled the candy in the window, were extinct. Now they sold prepackaged assortments.

Without the hallway's flattering light, he looked worn out in the mirror above the bathroom sink. He rinsed his face with cool water, then lined up all of his toiletries, took a half-hour shower, remembering the man on the bus, his large hands. He tried not to think of Manny. People called it self-pleasure, but the accusation had robbed masturbation of its satisfaction. He wasn't quite dead from the waist down but broken. The men of New York used to trigger his libido at full force. Now sexual stimuli pinged him, like tiny drips into a bucket. When the drops in the bucket reached the tipping point, Thomas would empty it. But afterward, he'd stand there, full of dread.

The turbo blow drier dissipated the steam that had turned the small room into a sauna. Opening the door, a rush of air raised goose bumps on Thomas's arms as he wrapped his towel around his waist and headed out for a tour of his brother and Joyce's recent art purchases.

"Hey, bro," James called. "Welcome," he said, standing between two of the twelve chairs surrounding the dining room table.

"Jesus," Thomas said, tightening the towel around his waist before crossing the room. "You scared the shit out of me."

He'd barely recovered from the naked drip-fest with Mel, and now James was grabbing him, holding Thomas tight. When they pulled away, Thomas could see that water had transferred from his chest and shoulders into the fabric of his brother's beautifully tailored suit.

"Holy ripped buffness, Batman," James said.

"Why aren't you at work?" Thomas asked, backing up.

"A patient canceled last minute, so I thought I'd come greet you. Are you up for the gym?"

At first, it seemed James had developed some nervous jaw tick, but he was chewing. The taffy bag sat half empty on the table. "Hope you don't mind," he said. "I saw it on your bed."

In the cab, James couldn't put down his phone. After he had finished one email, he started another. "After this one, I'm all yours."

James explained that his lawyers had come up with a patent for a new procedure, and he needed to get the paperwork done before the long weekend. He'd sold the training and the permissions to hospitals and clinics, and he was working on a device.

"Impressive," Thomas said, and he meant it.

Thomas asked James if he ever thought of slowing down.

"Now?" James smiled. "No way. A man's most productive work years are from forty to fifty. Got to take advantage, right?"

As the cab staggered up 3rd Avenue, Thomas watched out the window as giant leaves fell slowly from their trees.

A Renaissance-style building with arched porticos in Midtown on Park Avenue housed James's Racquet and Tennis Club.

James said, "Have I taken you to the pool? You'd like it. Everyone swims naked."

"Oh yeah," Thomas said. "Love droopy nut bags on old white guys."

"Don't lie," James said, grinning. "I know you like 'em young." Then, before Thomas could respond, he added, "I meant Manny," and his face turned red. "Remember?"

At the gym, James chose the two treadmills in the far corner, and Thomas soon found a good pace for his warm-up. They talked about Jake, sad that he couldn't join them, how next year they'd all run a turkey trot together.

"Motivation for Jake and me," James said. "So we can be like you, Tommy."

"Unemployment," Thomas said. "The number one way to meet your fitness goals."

In fact, Thomas, who'd ditched the weights for more running, had probably lost muscle, at least on his torso, since the last time the two were together, but James never stopped flattering Thomas. Ever since they were kids, James had bragged to his friends about Thomas's most mundane accomplishments. It felt so damn good.

"Congratulations on the new patents," Thomas blurted. "Your success is such testimony."

James's face flushed. "That was cute," he said. "Tommy tried returning a compliment."

They laughed.

"Sorry," Thomas said. "Not my specialty."

That was a lie.

Thomas had always been generous with compliments. An expert at finding the tiniest of things to notice, point out, validate in others. But not with his brothers, and he didn't know why. James avoided direct inquiry about Country Day but asked about the move from Portland, the new apartment in San Francisco, how much Thomas had made on the sale of his house. "Let me know if you decide to buy something. San Francisco's nuts," James said. "I can help."

The two continued in silence for a long time before James slowed down the speed on his treadmill and asked, "Did you do it, Thomas? Did you touch that kid?" His face was shiny with sweat. "Did you do it?"

Thomas pressed *STOP*. As the treadmill slowed, Thomas lowered from a steep incline to flat before it finally came to a standstill. He stood, chilly in the gym's air conditioning, looking at a man who'd been kissed and fed and tucked in by the same mom, the same dad, taken to the same doctor and same dentist. He and his brother had eaten the same foods by opening the same refrigerator door and brought it to the same table with the same view out of a pair of sliding glass doors.

Did you do it?

Why would James's patient cancel on a weekday? Thomas thought, and started to panic.

I would have preferred a nap, Thomas had wanted to say back at the apartment, now wishing he could reverse time, to before his brother asked him the question. Instead, he had agreed to the gym. To witness and acknowledge his brother's success. His private club with its mahogany bar lounge, its changing room's marble sinks, its rooftop tennis courts.

Again. Again and again and again and again he stepped into his brothers' lives.

He had worn the unflattering suit James told him to wear at his wedding and wrote the best man speech within the boundaries of what James had deemed charming and appropriate in front of his Catholic and Republican in-laws and colleagues and friends.

Thomas stopped. Opened his mouth to say something. It wasn't that he couldn't find the words. There were too many. *I waited for hours in and outside the birthing rooms where all three of your children were born, Thomas thought. I walked into the boutiques where your wife bought their baptism and christening gowns. Endured sermons by priests who preached the sanctity of marriage as exclusive to a man with a woman. I've gathered around your table, your Christmas tree, sang your songs, ate your food, laughed at your jokes. All of it was worth it. Not one second was too much. I'd do it all again. I'd show up early. Do dishes. Change diapers. Chop onions. Wash sheets. And it has been the absolute least I could do in return for what you have given me since the time I was a big enough boy to understand—on whatever level— the incredible gift of being one of more. Of belonging to something. Of having an ally.*

He still couldn't speak. James's hands moved from the treadmill's display to the top of his head to the air in front of his mouth, then the choreography reversed: mouth, head, display. *Together we endured our parents' bitter rants*, Thomas thought. *Their slammed doors, their charges in and out of rooms and cars. Together we were guinea pigs for Maddy's unorthodox pie phase. Her gluten-free phase. Her depressions, when she stayed in bed for weeks at a time as Stuart traveled on business and left you*, Thomas thought, looking at James, *to make lunches and dinners for me and Jake. When she'd resurface, we rode in Maddy's Toyota station wagon to school, to soccer, to every movie we ever wanted to see. How many*, he wanted to say. *How many? Pairs of paper cups sitting side by side on who knows how many rickety tables separating their two chairs in hospital waiting rooms after Jake's ODs. You are my hero. My compass. My very favorite person.*

Now, the two men stood still on twin treadmills. Months after Thomas was found innocent by two separate investigations of what had started as an unlikely accusation. Thomas stared at James. He'd grown old. What had been a solid jaw and a firm neck had already, at forty-five, softened. But he also looked so very young. The expression on James's face looked childlike, one of complete confusion.

"I'm here to help," James finally said, filling the silence between them, "not judge."

Thomas's temples pounded. "You didn't have a cancellation, did you?"

James said nothing, alternating his gaze between the monitor on the treadmill and Thomas's face.

187

"And the girls didn't have a birthday party. Who invites a four-teen-, a twelve-, and a ten-year-old to the same party?" Thomas said, quietly now, as if to himself.

"Of course, I had a cancellation," James said. "Of course, they had a party."

"Really? Or did you want to interrogate me first, get them out? Inspect my luggage? Is that what you were doing when you saw the taffy? Scouring for kiddie porn? Seeing if they're safe in your absence? Did Joyce tell you to do it?"

By now, Thomas had stepped off his machine, moved to the threshold that divided the cardio room from the hallway leading to the locker room.

"No," James said. "We were never worried about the girls."

"What about Max? Were you ever worried about our nephew? About other little boys? Fuck you, James," Thomas said. "And your bullshit men-only club. And your prime working years. And your not judging. And your obnoxious plane ticket and house-buying offers."

Before his brother could answer, Thomas walked the length of the hall. He used the key card to release the locker's magnet. He grabbed his clothes from his brother's bag and got dressed. He exited the locker room, then the club. Once outside, he breathed in the crisp fall Manhattan air. He stopped for a moment when he realized he'd been walking uptown instead of downtown. A guy in a wheelchair ran into the back of his legs. "Hey," he said. "Watch it, man."

As the guy backed up to go around him, Thomas said, "What did you call me?"

"I said, watch it." He sped away, twice the pace as the foot traffic.

"No. What did you call me? Say it," Thomas called after him. "Say it again."

As Thomas dropped the keys at the desk, Stoyan looked surprised, but his training forbade questions. Luckily, the girls hadn't made it back from the party and Joyce still wasn't home.

At the ticket counter, Thomas didn't ask the price. Instead, he offered his phone to the handsome man behind the counter, showing the itinerary with the unused leg of his round-trip ticket. Thomas said, "I have this return flight and an emergency. I'd be most grateful if you could switch it to the next flight to SFO."

"We have a 6 a.m.," the man said, pointing to his screen. "But you should decide fast. It's nearly booked. The day before Thanksgiving and all."

"That's fine," Thomas said.

"Can you provide proof?" he asked. "Of an emergency? A doctor's note?"

"My brother is a physician," Thomas said, trying to come up with a convincing on-the-spot fib. "To be honest, my brother was the emergency."

The man looked back and forth from Thomas to the screen while typing on a keyboard. He finally said, "A brother doctor is good enough for me. Best I can do is charge you the difference," he said.

"So kind," Thomas said.

"Ulterior motives," the stranger said, smiling.

"Let me give you my number," Thomas said, planning to jot a fake one.

"Already got it," he said, pointing to the computer screen.

Thomas gave him the credit card.

"I'm Russ," he said, handing Thomas his new boarding pass.

Thomas smiled and stepped out of line.

Chapter Sixteen

Wednesday November 28th
Thursday—Thanksgiving Day—November 29th, 2013

Thomas felt the phone as it vibrated against the hardwood floor at the end of its charge cord. A snake with an enormous rattle. It had started an hour ago and wouldn't quit. He plucked out his earplugs, picked up the phone, swiped the screen and said, "Hi, Junkels."

"Tommy?" Jake said. "Finally. We were worried, you weirdo. Since when do you storm off?"

His voice had regained almost all of its former strength. Either that or Thomas had gotten used to the new, thinner sound.

"Max couldn't believe you bailed on Thanksgiving."

"I didn't," Thomas said. The fitted sheet had come off one of the corners of the mattress. "How would Max even know?"

"Bro. Do you need me to put him on the line? He texts with Silvia. And James keeps calling."

"I'm fine," Thomas lied. "And James will be too," he said, failing with the sheet's gathered elastic. "I'll call him soon," Thomas said.

"James feels awful," Jake said.

"He should. I will never do another thing to make a straight guy feel better after he fucks up. I am done."

"You sound like Sheree," Jake said.

"She's been right all along. In fact, you should put her on the phone. I need to tell her I'm sorry for every second I've spent engaging in or justifying the bad behavior of douchebag white men."

Thomas found a pair of sweatpants and a tee-shirt, pulled them on. He grabbed his phone and made his way into the family room, where the bay window opened to the courtyard. He'd turned off the steam radiator before leaving for New York and hadn't thought to put it back on until now.

"How's Max doing in school?" Thomas said.

"He wrote a poem. We'd hoped it would be a trend, but it was a fluke. A crush," Jake said, telling Thomas that Max did okay in math and science, but needed to work on his writing.

An engine revved and roared. Thomas looked onto Green Street from the small dining room window. A guy wearing full leather gear sat on an enormous souped-up motorcycle.

"A crush?" Thomas asked, watching the man on the bike. The chrome suspension, roll bars, and exhaust pipes glinted and shone from the street even through the morning fog.

"No," Jake said. "A visiting poet. Some white chick that says her name is Charna. She teaches Gwendolyn Brooks and Gil Scott-Heron. Max says she tries to speak Black when she reads their work. You should hear him imitate her. It's hard not to encourage."

"I bet," Thomas said, struggling to stay engaged as he watched the man on the motorcycle polish the bike's side-view mirrors with a cloth he'd pulled from between the dashboard and wind-shield.

Jake went on about the poetry teacher's English degree from Harvard. "Now she teaches poetry in the public schools. In Colorado Springs," he said. "Her parents must be shitting their pants."

"I taught poetry. I have a liberal arts education from a good school," Thomas said, louder, as the motorcyclist warmed up his engine.

"Exactly why I know her parents are shitting their pants," Jake said and laughed.

"So were you, when you were a junkie," Thomas said, as the man mounted his motorcycle.

"Not quite, Bud," Jake said. "Opiates cause constipation."

"Gross," Thomas said, as the motorcycle sped off. He asked Jake about Max's poem.

Jake told him to hang on while he looked through another stack of school papers. Thomas listened to the heavy exhales his brother breathed into the phone. Thomas remembered when he and Jake were boys, the nights after his parents separated, when Maddy worked the eleven-to-seven graveyard shift at the hospital, and James spent most nights at his best friend's house in New Hampshire, near the private school he attended. Jake would stand for a minute in the hallway outside Thomas's bedroom door before asking if he could sleep with Thomas, who always said yes. They'd wrap their arms tight around each other's torsos; entwine their legs to stay warm.

Thomas scooped the ground beans from the bag as Jake described Max's ode to his collection of Air Jordans. After, Thomas told him about a DVD of a bunch of socially conscious slam poets he could send. "It might encourage him to go a bit deeper."

"He doesn't want a DVD, Tommy. He wants his uncle."

"You can pour it on thick, Jake," Thomas said. As the coffee warmed and woke up his body, a feeling started to swarm up to his chest, his throat. Thomas put down his mug.

"Sheree and I miss you, too. Do I need to come out of remission to get you here?"

"I appreciate your concern," Thomas said. Other than anger, he could not access what he was feeling after New York.

"You okay?" Jake asked.

"I'll tell you more about it next time we talk."

"Mom told me not to bug you, but she wants you here, too."

"I'll come," Thomas said.

"You sure, bro? That you're fine?"

"They did me a favor. I was too comfortable there and probably would've never left."

"New York?" Jake said. "At James's?"

"No. Country Day. I'd convinced myself of something that wasn't true about those people, those parents, that place."

Was it betrayal? He regretted trusting James so thoroughly during and after the hearings. Regretting his assumption that James believed him to be innocent. "You can do me a favor, Jake. Get everyone off my back. Stop being so concerned. It's exhausting, managing everyone else's anxiety over me. I have enough of my own to manage."

"Ten-four. I know exactly what you mean," Jake said.

"Let me get through this long weekend," Thomas said. "Tell Max and Mom I'll come for Christmas."

"Sweet. We'll expect you. Meanwhile," he said, "happy Thanksgiving."

The weather app said San Francisco was serving sunny seventy-degree days for Thanksgiving weekend. After he had finished his coffee, Thomas decided there was only one thing to do: buy a motorcycle.

He'd ridden a scooter around the streets of Berkeley during college. In Portland, weather ruled. No one wanted to be on a motorcycle in the rain. He opened his computer. There were calls he still needed to make. To his tax person. To his credit union. He needed to cancel his gym membership in Portland and join one in San Francisco. He still had to deal with his car and cancel the insurance. Call Ruth. The Jurakas had agreed to keep it in their garage while he decided whether or not to fly out and drive it back or just sell it. Instead, he searched for motorcycle dealerships. The one closest to his apartment had good ratings. He closed the computer and then showered.

As he applied the sunscreen that Sheree had given him, the same one Mercy loved, Thomas remembered his worry about Jerome's initial number, the amount he insisted Country Day and the parents on the petition pay in exchange for a resignation and non-disclosure agreement: five million. It seemed ridiculous, outrageous enough to undermine their credibility, Thomas thought, but when Jerome had finished tallying ten years' salary, cost of relocation, loss of reputation, the amount of Country Day's endowment, the net worth and salaries of the parents on the petition?

Mercy didn't blink. She listened. Then said, "My guess is that with very few exceptions, the parents, especially the Jays, who circulated the petition threatening to pull their kids, will want to make this go away."

When the whole thing was signed and done, and the monies sent, she called and left a voicemail. "If Jerome would've asked for ten million, I, personally, would not have argued," she said. "You were put through it, and it was not fair. I'm so sorry, Thomas. I'll miss you terribly."

He didn't return her call. He, too, now wished he would've asked for ten million so he could have donated it to an org fighting gentrification in his brother's supposed edgy Manhattan neighborhood. Fund or open a center catering to queer runaways and dropouts. Thomas had left that meeting—the thing he'd spent so much energy anticipating—feeling enraged and empowered. They settled on two million. Thomas ended up with $1.2 and Jerome and his firm $800K. He knew he'd start his own scholarship fund. Other than that, he knew nothing. With the sale of his house, that meant he could pay himself his current salary for at least ten years, which sounded more comforting than it felt.

Jerome said, "I've read of cases like this where the school settled for fifty thousand. Or less. We showed them that we are not disposable."

"Did we?" Thomas said now, leaning in close to the mirror. "Or did we just prove that with money they can do whatever they want?" *Motorcycle,* Thomas thought, flossing.

A Japanese upright. Metallic silver. A few years old, but low mileage. A 650. Big enough for a passenger and to take it on the highway. Small enough to lane split and manage in the city. Used. In case he dinged it or the whole thing turned out to be a whim, the object of a mid-life crisis. Thomas also bought helmets. Two of them, one hinged to the hook under the seat, the other on his head. And a walkie-talkie system. Thomas stalled three times within fifteen feet of where the salesperson had parked it at the curb.

Turning right from Pine onto Franklin, Thomas stalled again, and a Lexus almost rear-ended him in front of Whole Foods. The rest of the way home, he worried a cop would pull him over, cite him for driving without license and insurance, then charge him, justifiably, with reckless endangerment. Another thing to put on his Monday list: Apply for California driver's license. He parked the motorcycle on Green Street against a spread of curb too small for a car. Standing on the street, he called Dana. She asked about the Big Apple, wondered if he'd take the girls to the parade tomorrow. Thomas hesitated. In the background, he could hear pots and pans and muffled voices. Dana's parents were in town from Chicago for the holiday.

"I flew back," Thomas said. "Long story. I'm just too wiped out for Thanksgiving this year."

"Wait. You're in San Francisco?"

"Yeah. I wanted to let you know because you might see me buzzing around town. I'm sending you a pic of my new motor-cycle."

"Hang on," Dana said, and asked her mom to keep an eye on the stove. Soon, the sound of a sliding door. "What happened?"

"I'll catch you up when you're not juggling your parents and a turkey."

"I would've picked you up," Dana said. "Don't even try to hang up before I insist that you come over tomorrow. My parents will be thrilled. Mel, too." Dana paused. "Well, she's curious to see what you look like with clothes on."

He looked at the motorcycle. The Beautiful Silver Bullet, un-registered, uninsured, that Thomas didn't have the experience nor license to drive. How quickly it had been dampened, his fantasy of riding south on Highway One tomorrow while others stuffed themselves with turkey.

"It's just too awkward," he said to Dana. "Seeing people. Explaining why I left Country Day."

"Earth to Thomas. Come in, Thomas. My parents? 'The Polites'? The people who've never made anyone feel uncomfortable?" she said. "They'll never mention it. They're from the Midwest."

He asked if she'd told them.

"I told them how fucked the whole thing is," Dana said. "And how excited I am to get my best friend back to the Bay after all these years."

"Did you tell them it was a sexual accusation? Me touching a boy?"

"Yes," she said. "No. I didn't go into detail."

"Dana," Thomas said, wary. "I'm in charge of who gets told. Not you."

"Fair enough," she said. "Sorry."

Thomas walked to Van Ness and stood still as pedestrians, cars, and buses passed him.

"My dad is, right now, mouthing for me to tell you hello," Dana said. "They were disappointed when they thought they wouldn't see you."

Thomas pictured Dana's mom. Her dimples and stylish bobbed haircut. Then Dana's dad, Larry, a direct descendant of one of the country's first captains of industry. Great-great-grandson of a man who started an iron mill. Now a lumber and sawdust and salt and glass company magnate. Leading retailer and owner of some of Chicago's most prime real estate. Thomas resisted. But Larry could kick some serious butt at both Scrabble and Risk, and he loved to talk about nature and travel.

"What can I bring if I come?" Thomas said. "No promises."

"Don't promise or bring anything," she said. "But see you at two. I need you to keep Larry out of the kitchen."

"What about my motorcycle?" Thomas said. "No reaction?"

"Congratulations? Since when do you know how to ride a motorcycle? Please tell me you signed up for that safety class and that you bought a helmet."

196

Thomas heard Dana open the sliding glass door. She said, "Thomas is coming."

Thomas shelled out more for a pie at The Real Food Company on Polk Street than he had at the farmers' market in Portland. And it looked halfway composted. Still, he wouldn't show up empty-handed at Dana's family gathering. He'd taken a long shower. Scraping his face free of stubble, he wanted to look innocent. He resisted the temptation to ride the motorcycle because he didn't want to wear the pie or a body cast. The cab driver kept the needle at twenty-five, which allowed him to catch the synchronized green lights on Gough without having to brake until they finally caught a red light at Haight Street. Two men walked by holding hands. One of them seemed to be laughing. Or crying. And the other's face looked dead serious. He held a red leash attached to an old mutt's collar.

For years, Thomas had suspected Dana of wanting a monogamous relationship. He wouldn't have, had she not spent so much time talking about not wanting one. Just before Mel, Dana had been dating a few people, but fell for a married woman with a husband in declining health. He'd encouraged his wife to have an affair with Dana and report back the details. Dana said she loved it. "It inspires me to test my performance limits."

Thomas never bought it. No matter how Dana tried to spin it, it sounded like another straight woman reaping all the benefits of lesbian sex without sacrificing a thing for the cause. His friend's love or skills or both were too valuable to use to titillate a wealthy man.

The cab turned left on Dolores and sped up the hill. The sun on the palm trees and park made it impossible to miss Portland, as did the couple on Haight Street who held hands so casually. When they arrived on Douglass, Thomas gave the driver a big tip and gathered his pie. He rang the bell, thinking about how long it had been since he'd dated. Once, Manny had accused

Thomas of having intimacy issues, but with Manny's German accent, and his matter-of-fact tone, the words *intimacy* and *issues* sounded more like: You have mints in your shoes.

Where the hell was Dana? He rang the doorbell a third time. Finally, the door opened.

The place smelled of Restaurant Zuni's panzanella recipe, what Dana made instead of stuffing. "The TV is way too loud. You should've let yourself in."

"No. Learned a lesson. It's better to ring."

Dana smiled, took the pie in one hand and Thomas's wrist in the other. She led him down the narrow hallway to the kitchen, put down the dessert and went to the stove. She wore her hair up when she cooked, stirring and fussing at the pots. "Mel is upstairs, and my parents are still out back. I'll hug you in a minute," she said.

The living and dining rooms were both impeccable, filled with flower arrangements and light. Beyond the family room, Thomas could see Dana's parents in the garden. They both had one ear to the same cell phone.

The dull fluttering of missing Manny lingered. He watched the huddled pair, their shoulders touching, one smiling as the other spoke.

Dana bent at ninety degrees in front of the oven; her long legs were extended by heels. Back to wearing dresses after a twenty-year hiatus, and heels after ten. And make-up? Thomas noted lip gloss and mascara for sure, if not blush.

"You're here," Jean said, as she crossed through the den, closing the gap between the sliding doors and the kitchen. "We were just on the phone with Larry's sister. She never stops talking."

"Pot kettle black, Mom," Dana said, taking off her oven mitts.

"No," Jean said, "I'm chatty. That woman talks like a sports commentator." Her hair looked lighter than when Thomas last saw her. She wore a colorful silk scarf tied elegantly and loosely around her tailored blouse.

Larry walked in soon after Jean. "What did she say about my sister?" he asked Thomas.

"That she's loquacious," Thomas said, as Larry reached toward Thomas's hand.

Dana had inherited the shape of Larry's mouth, his sideways grin. He wore a pale pink button-up, lightly starched, with a pair of polished silver or platinum cufflinks molded into the shape of two identical turkeys. After he let go of Thomas's hand, Jean gave Thomas the kind of hug one would give someone wearing patchouli oil.

"Help me, Mom," Dana said.

Jean went to a wall hook, grabbed an apron and joined Dana at the stove.

Larry talked of weather. Today's menu. Asked Thomas about the new apartment. Thomas tried to concentrate, but the television blared. "I'm surprised you guys aren't watching football," Thomas said.

Larry said he'd been bored with Thanksgiving football since Longley threw that fifty-yard touchdown pass to Staubach. "That was a game," he said, straightening his slacks at the waist, so the pleats realigned down the middle.

"I only meant to see Selena Gomez," Thomas said. "Halftime show?"

Larry attempted a smile, but barely. He had no idea what Thomas was talking about.

"Mel?" Dana yelled toward the stairs. "Thomas is here."

"Have you seen this show?" Larry asked, pointing to the family room. "Speaking of football stars, there's one competing this season. And he's good. It's not enough that they have us in sports. Now ballroom? My bet? He'll win."

"They?" Thomas said.

Larry's face flushed, turned the color of his oxford. "I meant it as a compliment," Larry said.

Thomas stood still a long time before he said, "My dad and his wife love *Dancing with the Stars*."

"You two should take ballroom lessons," Larry said, recalibrating, the pink finally receding from his neck and face.

Just then, Mel walked into the kitchen. "Who should do ball-room?" she asked, combing her fingers through her spiked hair.

"Everyone," Larry said, after a pause. "Everyone should," he repeated, looking toward Jean, now in the sunken family room, as she tried to get the television to go off, but couldn't find the right button on the remote.

Dana, oblivious, grabbed Mel's hand. "You want to do dance lessons?" she asked in a baby voice Thomas had never heard.

Mel kissed her softly on the lips.

"Thomas? Remember Mel?" Dana said. "Mel, this is what my best friend looks like when he's not naked."

"Tom," Mel said, "you can do ballroom with Dana. You have my permission."

For a moment he thought of correcting her, telling her that his name was Thomas, that he didn't go by Tom. Or calling her Melanie, which Thomas guessed was her full name. Instead, he said, "Are you going to write me an actual permission slip? I miss those."

The TV went off. Everyone looked at Thomas, then away, at each other, but no one spoke. Did he break a new rule? Was he to pretend he'd never been a teacher?

Larry smiled so wide and tight Thomas imagined his teeth cracking and turning to dust.

What had happened? When did his best friend become a fifties housewife? And why was Mel impersonating the kind of man who believed his wife an object he owned? And when did an organic turkey stuffed with heirloom panzanella become enough of a reward that Thomas would put up with this kind of bullshit? From his brother first and now his best friend?

"What are you drinking?" Mel asked. "Vodka tonic? I can't remember what Dana said you drink."

"I can make margaritas again," Dana said.

"Mineral water," Thomas answered. Everything reminded him of the night of the fundraiser. "Unless you don't have it. In which case, tap is fine. I'll have wine with dinner."

Larry seemed desperate to get Jean to follow his clown-y cha-cha-cha across the kitchen. Mel asked Thomas if he preferred lemon or lime or orange or berry.

His face grew hot as Mel filled a tall glass to the brim with chips from the refrigerator's automatic ice maker.

"Plain," Thomas said.

"That's the only flavor we didn't buy," Mel said, flatly.

"Sorry," Thomas said about the water and also, for his whole life. "Flavors. Not garnish. My bad."

"Expects fresh-cut fruit for his water," Mel told Dana, who was back at the stove. "You didn't tell me he was so fancy, babe."

Thomas opened his fist to accept the glass, which he put to his forehead.

"Thanks," he said and drank the water down.

"More?" Mel asked.

"I'll get it," he said, his voice louder than he intended. When Thomas opened Dana's refrigerator, he couldn't locate a thing in its right place. As he looked, he felt damp fabric pulling at his armpits. He scanned the contents again: Otto's cat food, a salad bowl topped with a creaseless layer of plastic wrap. A bottle of 2004 Veuve Clicquot La Grande Dame. Pickles.

"Am I nuts?" Thomas asked. "Didn't I just see you pull a bottle of mineral water out of here?"

"In the door," Dana said, as she handed a stack of dinner plates from the cabinet to Mel. "New fridge."

Yes. The door. A gigantic shelf held four liters of mineral water and a box of unsweetened almond milk.

You can do this, Thomas thought. *You can pour some water into the glass and sip. Calm down,* he thought. *This moment will pass, as did the one before it. This year will pass, as did the one before it.* He was not going to walk out on a second Thanksgiving. No. He'd eat the delicious and tender turkey Dana and Jean had cooked. He'd even ask Larry, who would carve, for a drumstick. He'd help himself to lots of Zuni stuffing and sweet potato mash. He'd drink sparkling then white then red wine with everyone else. He'd stay, too, for coffee and a slice of the stupid, sad-looking compost-pie along with a tiny sliver of the rest of the desserts. Then he'd go into the cabinet to the left of the sink and grab himself a twenty-ounce Tupperware and fill it to the brim. Then he'd scratch Otto behind the ears and under his chin, and he'd walk out into the chilly fog of Noe Valley.

Thomas looked up. All eyes had left him. Dana returned from the sink where she'd been pouring the excess liquid out of a sauté pan of green beans. Her dad placed the turkey on the island, and Dana used the basting tube she and Thomas had bought together, joking to make sure it was dishwasher safe in case they decided to reuse it for insemination.

"God that smells good," Thomas finally said. His forehead had cooled. His neck and chest, too.

"Doesn't it?" Dana said, tossing the basting tube into the sink. She walked to Thomas's side of the island, where she put her arms on his shoulders for a moment before going to the table.

Her hair smelled like fennel, like mint.

By now, Dana's mom and dad were back in front of the TV, now set to a low volume. Dana stood at the stove transferring things from pots to bowls. Mel leaned into the small expanse of counter between the refrigerator and the sink clicking away on her phone, occasionally looking up and smiling.

"Work or family?" Thomas asked Mel.

"My family is work," she said, looking up. "My brothers. And my nieces never stop texting me."

"How many brothers do you have?"

"Two."

"Me, too," Thomas said. "Three boys."

"That's what my mom says, too. Tom Boy makes three."

"You're not that butch," Dana said, breadbasket in hand, stopping to kiss Mel on her lips.

"Butcher than you," Mel said.

"I'm butcher than Dana," Jean said from the family room.

"I'm not," Thomas said, and the five made their way to the table.

The pie had been one of the best he'd ever tasted. When Thomas finally left with his bag full of Tupperware and the tang of sour berries on his tongue, he texted James in a moment of drunken optimism. *I'm writing while you're asleep, hoping it'll wake you from your Ambien and red wine stupor and that you'll suffer horrible insomnia. Let's talk soon. Kiss the girls for me. I'm still pissed.*

Thomas walked down the steep hill from Noe Valley into the Castro, stopped in one of the gay bars, and ordered a beer. A scattering of mostly twenty-somethings talked and laughed in small huddles of three or four around the cocktail tables. Thomas scanned for guys his age. Of the three he spotted, two were a couple, or seemed to have found each other, and the third, walking toward him, a cute guy with shapely lips, asked Thomas if he'd enjoyed Thanksgiving.

"Very much," Thomas said. "Once we got through the racism, sexism, and homophobia."

The man looked perplexed. "Exactly why I don't do Thanksgiving. Family?"

"A friend and her family."

The man held his beer toward Thomas's. "Here's to the holidays." They clinked glass and Thomas looked up to the bar's flat screen. Cher straddled a cannon on a naval ship and told the boys in the bar and the sailors in the video what she'd do if she could turn back time.

"Glad you came in. I'd almost given up," the man said, rotating a roll of mints before popping the one he'd freed from foil onto his tongue. "You're lucky you didn't come in here earlier. I felt like the chaperone for all these kids."

Thomas hesitated. "No. You're lucky God gave you those lips," Thomas said. He took another sip of his beer.

The man smiled. "Do you have a car? We could go make out."

"No. I ride a motorcycle," Thomas said, delighted to use that sentence. He held up his beer. "But not tonight. Drinking." On

203

the screen, Cher danced in front of the ship's five giant phalluses before finally laying down, prone, in front of the army of men in naval uniforms.

"Hot," the guy said.

"Think so?" Thomas smiled.

Soon, the two kissed to the throbbing bass line of the next diva's song.

When the bartender shouted, "Last call," Thomas finished his beer, thanked his new friend, and gave him one last long kiss.

Chapter Seventeen

Wednesday
December 4th, 2013

"I nearly divorced James after I heard," Joyce said. "You should've slugged him," then handed her husband the phone.

"I swear to god," James said, "I didn't ask if you'd done it out of suspicion. I asked in case you needed to unburden yourself."

"You're a fucking asshole," Thomas said into his cell. "And Joyce agrees."

"You just seemed so furious when you first told me. The anger seemed misplaced with all your talk of nannies and dog walkers. It seemed like a smoke screen."

"And here I thought you were empathizing. This is a sad set of excuses. We're not done."

"Fine," James said. "But let me ask you one question: why have you spent your whole life trying to be like me? Or getting people like me to like you?"

As Thomas stood in the kitchen of his new home on Green Street, his silence wasn't for a lack of possible things to say, but an abundance. As he looked at his reflection in the microwave's glass, he found the almost invisible diagonal scar leading from his lip to his nostril, narrow as a line drawn from a just-sharpened pencil. When they were kids, James had accidently pushed Thomas down the basement stairs. Thomas kept perfectly still at the base of the stairs while blood ran down his face from whatever had torn it on the way down. His brother called from the top, "Tommy? You okay?"

Thomas held in his stomach and didn't make a sound.

"Thomas?" James called again, halfway down the stairs. He shook Thomas, who faked involuntary slackness. Back upstairs, James called 911. Thomas got up and grabbed a wad of paper towel from Stuart's workbench, exited the basement door, high from the sight of blood. He ran to the woods behind their house. An ambulance came. Thomas watched as they rushed in. James had wept in the driveway after the ambulance pulled away from their house.

"Look," James said on the phone. "I'll say it a million more times: I'm sorry."

"Apology acknowledged," Thomas said. "I'll let you know if and when it moves to accepted," and the brothers hung up.

Thomas silenced his phone and pulled out his new saucepan (the deep one) along with the eggs Dana had brought over yesterday on her way home from the farmers' market. He submerged the entire dozen in cold water, put them over high heat until they boiled; then he covered the pan and cleaned the kitchen for exactly thirteen minutes before grabbing the slotted spoon he'd bought for the sole purpose of transferring eggs to ice water. Once the eggs melted the ice, he dried the little guys on a dishtowel and placed them back into their carton.

He set out to see a documentary about the wild parrots of Telegraph Hill because the Clay—the theater playing the film—offered tiny salt packets the size of data chips. He bought a large popcorn to assuage the guilt of stealing salts from the fishbowl that held them. He counted them. Fourteen. He used two, then put the other twelve into his jacket pocket.

Back home, he placed the carton next to the salts on the kitchen table. The idea to decorate eggs with ladies' faces and salt packets to look like tiny purses had come to him when he was, what? Ten? He recalled the desire every time he came into contact with a tiny salt packet. He had never mustered the courage to ask Maddy, but he remembered the idea every year at Eastertime into adulthood when his students made traditional egg decorations. "Finally," he said after he drew the twelfth clutch flap on the twelfth salt packet, and twelfth face and hairdo on the twelfth egg. It was bright green and orangish red inspired by the parrots in the film. He cleared his desk of his staggering collection of magic markers (notable not only for color variety, but also tip width), and turned on his phone.

Dad said u r coming. Text me proof.

Don't be so demanding, Thomas texted Max.

Max wrote, *According to Mom, that's my specialty. BTW she just asked me if you bought your ticket yet.*

Thomas wrote, *Put down your phone and go outside. Ride your bike or skateboard.*

He put the eggs away and opened his computer and booked the flight to Denver, then texted Max the details.

Thomas scrolled through the history of his phone's voicemail. While he was thinking of plane tickets, he found the 646 number, and listened again to the message from Russ, the flight attendant from Newark. Russ said he'd flown into town and was camped out at the Holiday Inn on Van Ness.

Russ answered on the first ring.

"Sorry I didn't return your call Friday," Thomas said, surprised he picked up. "I . . ."

"I'm in San Francisco again," Russ interrupted. "And bored shitless and fogged in until tomorrow. What are we doing?"

"I'm not sure I can arrange it for today. It's going to get dark soon."

"You can't go out after dark?"

"I can go out. It's just I bought a motorcycle. I need to practice, and my learner's permit doesn't allow me to ride in the dark."

"Swear to god I've ridden motorcycles since I was twelve. I'm an excellent teacher."

Thomas looked at the dishes in the sink, said, "I have an extra helmet."

∾ ∾ ∾

Thomas stood in the bathroom, a few feet from the mirror so he could see more of himself in his new jeans.

"Just go," he told his reflection, then grabbed both helmets. Russ had told Thomas that he'd take a cab to the parking lot off 3rd Street near the baseball park, a location the message boards said was a great place to learn. Thomas bicycle-mapped the flattest route. Right on Van Ness from Green. Left onto Broadway. After two stalls, he managed to get the clutch in third gear and catch the green light at Polk. In the Broadway tunnel, the wind plastered his jeans to his shins. Seventy on the motorcycle felt as smooth as twenty on his college scooter. With the face shield down on his new helmet, he could barely hear traffic over his breathing. He passed the Chinatown shops with ducks and chickens hanging from hooks, then the strip joints in North Beach before he faltered into the right turn onto the Embarcadero. He passed the Bay Bridge and finally made it to 3rd Street and the stadium.

Russ sat on the curb of the parking lot, waving. Thomas remembered his hair gelled-down, but now the breeze lifted his loose curls. Thomas managed to dismount with a small degree of dignity, despite the heft of the machine.

Thomas lifted the visor of his helmet. "Waiting long?"

"No," Russ said, brushing off the back of his pants. "This place is deserted," he said, turning up the Sherpa-lined collar of his jean jacket. "And cold."

Thomas pulled off his helmet.

Russ walked over, took the key from the ignition, and used it under the seat to get the spare helmet. "These beauties are fast," he said, fastening the chin strap. "Do you mind?" he asked, putting the key back into the ignition.

"Go for it," Thomas said, balancing his helmet between his side and arm.

Thomas felt so small in the big open lot, which he'd seen packed with tailgaters and Giants fans and laughing concertgoers. The space sprawled: utterly empty, save Russ and Bull. That's what he'd named his bike. Short for Silver Bullet.

Electric orange California poppies grew through pavement cracks, which made him think of his students. He wondered if Toby Jay had ever seen one. Thomas expected Russ to pop a wheelie. Instead, he circled the lot's perimeter. He returned, flipped up his visor and said, "Get on."

Thomas climbed on, placed his hands over Russ's shoulders.

"No," he said. "Hold at the waist."

What a great story, Thomas thought. *The flight attendant who came to town and taught me how to ride in the twilight fog at Giants Stadium.*

"The best thing you can do is nothing. Relax. Tell future passengers to maintain some space by sitting up straight. If you lean into me, my crotch will get squashed into the tank."

Thomas adjusted.

Soon the time came for Thomas to drive again, and Russ made the sign of the cross on his torso before hopping onto the passenger seat.

"That's hilarious," Thomas said. "Shouldn't I first try it out on my own?"

"No," Russ said. "I'm cold." He snuggled up, threading his fingers together on Thomas's stomach. "Besides, you made it here, right?"

"Going fast isn't the problem. It's all the stops," Thomas said.

Russ coached him to maneuver by leaning, how to engage the clutch and brakes, and to steer not with the bar but by looking at the horizon. Thomas concentrated on going from a stop to five miles per hour, from first to second, from second to third to a quick stop. Eventually, he'd managed to repeat most of the moves several times without stalling. When they stopped, Russ said, "Riding a bike is weird. At first you have to think: right hand, brake, left hand, clutch, left foot, gear shift, right foot, brake. It's exhausting. But one day you'll hop on and get all the way there forgetting it's a motorcycle that brought you. Trust me."

The sky had traded its gold for gray, and Thomas killed the engine. He told Russ, "I'm illegal at night and with passengers on my permit. Mind driving me home?"

Russ smiled. "I thought you'd never ask."

Thomas held tight as Russ sped between cars. They drove up to Washington Street, so Russ could teach Thomas how to do the steep hills. Then he wanted to take California, follow the east-west cable car. Finally, they parked in front of Thomas's building. "If you want a beer, we should go to the corner store. I only have water and coffee."

"Water's good for me," Russ said, pulling off his helmet. He loosened his curls through his fingers. "As long as your place is warm, and it has a bathroom."

On the way through the courtyard, Thomas pulled off his gloves and tucked them into his helmet. The lavender and rosemary bushes fragrant in the fog, he stopped for a moment, fingered each, smelled his hand. He said, "All my stuff is coming after the New Year, and I kind of wish it wouldn't. I think I'm allergic to too much stuff these days."

"Are you turning into one of those San Francisco spiritual people?" Russ asked, imitating how Thomas touched the plants. "All minimalist and shit?"

"Not at all," Thomas said, unlocking the building's door. "But I just moved here from Portland, so I'm warning you, my place is pretty empty. My neighborhood in Portland, Southeast, was maximalist. Folks there didn't know how to get rid of junk. Inside, they called it shabby chic. Outside, they planted succulents in and around objects most people take to the dump." Thomas noticed a small bag on one of his neighbor's doors with a Toblerone chocolate bar sticking out if it and wondered if his new neighbors left each other birthday treats. "I'm thinking of getting rid of my cell phone, though. Getting a journal. I spend too much time looking down and not enough looking up."

"Yeah," Russ said as Thomas opened the apartment door. "Motorcycles will make you notice all sorts of stuff. So will moving. Quitting a job. Starting fresh."

Once inside, Thomas instantly felt the warmth pumping out of the old steam heater. "You sound like you know what you're talking about," Thomas said.

"I did the whole MBA thing," Russ said, handing Thomas his helmet before taking off his shoes.

Thomas loved Russ's socks. He hadn't noticed them on the motorcycle, their fabric a repeating print of Andy Warhol's bananas.

"By thirty, I'd made a little money. I hated being closeted with my family, my clients. I hated my job, my life. And once I'd bought all the stupid things I thought I wanted, I was like, so what? I'd just started up the food chain and my boss pressed me to make the next step and it just looked ugly."

"Why were you closeted?" Thomas asked.

"Let me guess," Russ said. "You grew up on one of the coasts? If you grow up in the South or the Midwest the question is never why."

Thomas showed Russ the bathroom, then went to the kitchen, washed a couple of glasses from the sink and filled them with tap water. When Russ came in, Thomas handed him a glass. Said, "So you gave up a finance career to become an Air Mattress?"

"Air Mattress?" Russ said, and the two laughed. "I prefer Wagon Dragon."

"Latrine Queen?" Thomas said.

"Um, no." When he finished his water, Russ smiled. "I will not answer to that one." Russ's Adam's apple pressed the tiny hairs of his five o'clock shadow straight out. "I applied on a whim. I wanted to travel but was used to working like, twelve hours a day, and I was terrified of getting bored so I thought it would be fun and it is."

"Have you ever had to serve one of your former clients?" Thomas asked, washing the last dishes in the sink.

"Not that I know of," Russ said. "A school friend once boarded my flight. But she sat in first. I work economy. She was like, 'Russ? Is that you?' all loud, then got up to say hi and hug me. I had to tell her that the seatbelt sign was on. Most of my former colleagues pity me," he said, making his way to the sink. He refilled his water glass. "Like instead of leaving a bank I mutilated my face."

"I remember when I worked in public schools, before moving

to Portland, when I lived here the first time," Thomas said, studying Russ. Thomas loved the guy's features, the big open face and broad shoulders; his beautiful body language, like a cross of Midwest cowboy and ballerina. He took up so much room and yet his posture seemed deliberate, arranged. "My days were so long. I had countless students with huge hurdles. Not to mention I was totally broke. I'd go to the taqueria and ask for extra rice in my burritos to make them last two meals. I hate it when people romanticize being underpaid, but my challenges felt real. I thought the job I left behind in Portland made me happy. But it was just easier, until it wasn't."

He kissed Russ, felt the warmth of his soft lips, then maneuvered around him to cross the small space between the kitchen sink and the dining room windows so he could close the shades.

Russ came over and pressed himself into Thomas. "I'm still cold," he said.

Thomas led Russ to his bedroom, to the mattress, and soon interrupted his kisses to strip him of his jacket and sweater. His skin smelled like opening a jar of tea. Dark leaves. And citrus. Thomas inhaled, closed his eyes. How many men, right now, here in this city, were having sex to the sound of foghorns?

Thomas removed Russ's pants. To some, the horns sounded like a dirge, but Thomas was lulled by them, hypnotized by the image of the barges passing safely under the bridge. On his back, Thomas watched Russ, naked and going down. Thomas studied the workings of Russ's shoulders, his forearms, the muscles around his neck. He reveled in the physical strength contained by the length and width of his mattress. Sometimes during sex, he understood the absurd draw of the boxing ring: the dance, the thrusts, the pivots, the spit, the sweat, the occasional blood.

His beautiful gay flight attendant, his motorcycle coach, his latrine queen. Thomas delighted in the rhyme of the nickname, despite the fact that it was probably meant to shame. Thomas thought Russ should reclaim it like people had done with the word *queer*, wear it like a sash. Latrine Queen: for the right guest, the ruler will summon you to his quarters, however cramped, for the royal treatment. How on earth had he let himself become Country Day's token gay? He had practically turned himself into a eunuch to please the parents.

Thomas wrested out from underneath and settled on top of Russ. He balanced on his knees to grab the condom he'd brought home from the bar on Thanksgiving. A plastic square with the circle inside, that, up until today, seemed as out of place on his nightstand as a wedding veil would be in the boxing ring.

"You into it?" Thomas asked.

"Totally," Russ said.

"It's been a while since I . . ." Thomas started, but Russ sat up to kiss Thomas and help him secure the rubber.

Thomas spent a lot of time holding Russ's face while licking and sucking his lips, his neck, his nipples before Russ spit in his hand and transferred it. When Russ wrapped his legs around him, Thomas knocked once, twice before he made a passionate shove then a partial stroke. Russ stared. His eyes, brown and liquid, looked wet. Thomas expected tears each time he blinked.

Russ's repeated "Yes," sounded less like a word than a sound, like the foghorn, meant to signal something approaching. Russ took Thomas's thrusts, convulsing a bit before grabbing Thomas's waist and pulling him. Russ's body twitched, inside and out, his eyes, his lips, his pelvic muscles. Russ let his head fall back, and his body went loose for a moment, before he tensed and readied himself again, tilting to look at Thomas, who stared at this stranger he'd first met the week of Thanksgiving in Newark dressed in a navy-blue airline uniform. Now prone beneath him, his body so strong, his skin so tight.

At some point, Thomas lost himself as if he and Russ switched positions, like he had with Tony all those years back. In this reversal, Thomas always found a strange freedom, a wildness, a feeling that lived inside him from a long time ago, before he knew of sex. It felt like being a child again, with his brothers in the yard running, sweating, swatting bugs, laughing, free.

§ § §

He didn't know how long it lasted. Five minutes? Ten? Half hour? All the tension in his life collected in him like shards of metal. As if, behind his pelvis, there was a magnet that had gathered and reversed their charge. When he came, Thomas yelled loud enough that Russ cupped his palm over Thomas's mouth. Russ came soon after, but Thomas barely noticed, still shivering, laughing. They pressed into one another, closing gaps. Thomas thought of earlier, on Bull with Russ riding home. *Let Go* was sprayed in yellow paint on California Street. Instructions to the cable car's gripman. For the first time in a year, Thomas let go.

"How long have you been in San Francisco?" Russ asked.

"Three weeks," Thomas lied. He wasn't going to say two months.

"Really?" Russ said. "There's mail in the kitchen with an October postmark. Addressed to you."

Thomas turned from his back to his side, faced Russ, brushed his bangs away from his forehead, put a finger through a curl's ring. "I found the place quite a while before I moved in," Thomas said, snuggling closer. "You're observant."

Russ sat up, scooting his back against the headboard, and Thomas rested his cheek on his thigh. "I can't help it. I go all hyper-vigilant right before I sleep with strangers. I also looked at your laptop and noticed an email from your brother with *I'm Sorry* as the subject line."

"How do you know it's my brother?" Thomas asked, looking up.

"You told me at Newark that your brother's a doctor. I knew your name. I saw the *I'm Sorry* email from Dr. J. McGurrin on your laptop screen. My mom did raise me to mind my own business. But since we're naked," he said, massaging Thomas's neck, "I thought I'd just be honest and ask."

"Wow," Thomas said. "Well, you asked. I answered."

"What was your sickness? Why did you leave New York early? You said it was medical. Don't make me regret not asking you before sex," Russ said, smiling.

"Oh. That. It was psychological."

"Should I be nervous?" Russ said, adjusting the pillow so he could make direct eye contact.

"No," Thomas laughed. "It was a preventative measure."

Once they were out of bed and showered and partially dressed, Thomas held out the carton, offered Russ a hard-boiled egg and a purse. "You, my friend, broke the spell." Thomas hadn't thought of Manny once during sex. He leaned in and kissed Russ.

"Wow," Russ said, choosing the redheaded egg. The one with orange lips and green eyes. "She looks like Julianne Moore. I don't want the matching clutch, though. Can I have the blue one?" He fished the blue salt packet out from another egg's space in the carton. Traded it for the orange one. "I shouldn't peel it. These are the faggiest, most fabulous eggs I've ever seen."

"Thanks," Thomas said, and picked the one that looked like Mrs. Jay, cracked it on the sink, threw away the shell, sprinkled it with salt, and popped it into his mouth.

Chapter Eighteen

Thursday
December 5th, 2013

After brewing and pouring his coffee, Thomas opened his email. The first time in weeks he did not go to his inbox hoping for something from Manny, it arrived: *Dear Thomas, I got your message. Coincidentally, I just tried calling you, but your home phone is disconnected, and I deleted your mobile. When your Country Day email didn't work, I called Mercy, who said you moved to San Francisco. She seemed weird. I'm in San Francisco and would love to meet up! Yours, Manny.*

Thomas responded immediately: *Let me buy you a beer. 4:30? What's your number? I'll text you the address.*

Manny confirmed, and Thomas called Dana.

"Don't focus on Mercy. Focus on Manny. Good things come in twos," Dana said, her left knee bent, the top of her foot behind her butt in her palm. After she stretched her quads in Thomas's living room, the two went on a run to the Golden Gate Bridge.

Good things do happen, he thought, relieved to be gaining traction. Max and Jake and Sheree had been sending texts all morning, looking forward to Christmas. Now this.

Thomas had chosen a bar surrounded by windows on the corner of Polk and Vallejo. He'd gone in once before with Dana at night, and everyone looked like the good kind of fake, as in gorgeous and happy, even before drinks. Thomas liked the spot because of its large room of vignettes, variations of love seats and chair-surrounded tables. Dusty ferns and Tiffany-style lamps were set to dim. That evening with Dana, the mood had been set by a packed room, its golden glow, the quieted din of nightlife visible through the glass, a bluesy musical playlist mixed with ambient laughter.

Now, from the street, Thomas immediately spotted Manny on a barstool, back to the window. Thomas felt a rush so intense it blurred his vision. He paused at the entrance to collect himself. Late afternoon on a Thursday, the bar's furniture upholstery couldn't stand up to the scrutiny of daylight. The place was empty, save Manny and three others. One, a woman, sixtyish, reading a thick paperback, sprawling across a love seat, sipping white wine from a glass meant for red. Two, a suspender-wearing bartender, whose ultra-high-waisted trousers and wide-collared print shirt brought to mind old-timey swing dancer. Three, a guy in blue coveralls working on a silenced stereo system. He scanned each of the three, cataloging details in an attempt to restore his vision and balance. Thomas had recognized Manny by his body's shape, the jeans and sneakers and loose-fitting, long-sleeved tee-shirt. He walked over to him, said hello.

Manny got up, hugged Thomas then released him, looked at his face, then hugged him again.

"That's a relief," Thomas said. "I wasn't sure if you'd hug or slap me."

"Me neither," Manny said. "It's been, what? A year?"

The bartender looked over with a raised eyebrow but waited a moment to approach Thomas, who'd become flustered by how well Manny looked, and the familiarity of his smell. Thomas thought he might lose it somehow, turn around and leave, or worse, cry, but he managed to sit at the bar and order a beer by pointing to Manny's. The bartender dropped it off with a cardboard coaster. When he left, Thomas said, "Here's to reuniting."

"Yes," Manny said, and they clicked glasses.

Thomas took a long pull from his pint. Manny's teeth were

whiter than Thomas remembered, and he wondered if Manny mashed up a strawberry and mixed it with some baking powder to make toothpaste. He'd once said the resulting chemical interaction would likely work as well as American teeth-bleaching systems.

Manny continued to smile. "Are you single?"

"Waste no time," Thomas said, relieved that Manny had asked. Constricted by the tense muscles of his neck, Thomas's throat had narrowed, and he expected his voice to crack. It didn't, but his hands shook as he took a sip of his beer, afraid his spine might crumble as he adjusted his butt on the stool. "I am single. You?"

"Seeing a guy. A sports medicine doctor. He's nice. You'd like him. We're engaged."

"Congratulations," Thomas said suddenly, too quickly, too loudly in such an empty room, and leaned back on his stool, balancing on two of the three legs. In that moment he realized that his own grief had convinced him of a lie. *The world will wait,* it had whispered. The world had not waited. Everything continued.

Soon after Russ had left his apartment, Thomas had typed a text to him, *call me next time you're in the city* but hadn't pressed send; instead, he put down his phone and went to the bathroom. Brushing his teeth, he tried to think of a cute way to spice it up, phrase a double-entendre using the word *layover.* When he came back, ready, the email from Manny had come in and Thomas's psyche rearranged. He erased the draft of the text to Russ altogether. Now he lost his balance a bit, had to grab the underside of the bar. He took another swig of his beer, then said, "I'm seeing a finance guy—totally weird for me—an MBA based in New York." Then, after a pause, "Why did I say that? God. I'm turning into my father, my brother. He actually quit banking to be a flight attendant. His name's Russ. It's new."

From happy to happier, that's how Manny's face rearranged its expression. He didn't seem interested in the details. He said, "This is so civilized. I'm never friends with exes. Especially after I send them a love letter and never hear from them again."

"There it is," Thomas said, and then finished his beer. He

motioned for the bartender and asked for another round. "For the record, I wrote to you, but your lab returned the email. It's probably best."

"That bad?" Manny asked. His posture, even on a barstool, looked like that of a soldier.

Thomas nodded. "Not for the reasons you might imagine."

Some children looked as though they'd been born grown. Their faces and bodies made it easy to predict their adult features. To Thomas, Manny was the opposite. Even though he stood just under six feet, easily weighed two hundred pounds, clean-shaved his head, and wore a dark shadow of trimmed beard, every time Thomas looked at Manny he could see the curious expression of a child. He should've pushed harder for Manny to stay in Portland. He would've married Manny, Thomas thought, suddenly, had it been legal. What did it even mean for a gay couple to be engaged if they lived in Oregon or California? Thomas could not have justified asking him to stay on an expired visa. Do what? Hausfrau? Get a job working under the table at a coffee shop?

Manny sipped his second beer, scratched his tiny whiskers, waited for Thomas to talk. The woman with the paperback had gotten up from the love seat, placed her empty glass and a ten-dollar bill on the bar. "See you tomorrow, hon," she said, and made her way to the door.

Once she was out of earshot, Thomas said. "My email was just stupid. Like, unfeeling. Too practical. With the age difference, I always worried that once you got settled, accustomed to your surroundings, the things that I had to offer would become less compelling with each passing year. I could see you finishing your doctorate and post-doc work and getting a job in biotech."

Thomas paused. The man who'd been replacing one set of speakers above the bar's cash register was now standing on the bar taking down a pair hanging from the ceiling. The screwdriver he used looked like a baseball at its base, and as the man loosened the bolt, the ball made the sound of a quacking duck.

When they were a couple, Manny insisted Thomas learn German, insisted he—at the very least—would imagine living in

219

Europe one day. Get to know Manny's family. Spend serious time with Manny's friends, most of whom he had known since first grade.

"Because of our age difference, I worried your friends and parents would look at me as a . . ." Thomas hesitated, took the now-damp cardboard coaster from under his beer and tapped it on the bar.

"What?" Manny asked.

"A predator. A fetishist. An old man." Now that he had said it, Thomas didn't know what to say next because he didn't know what Mercy had told Manny, if he'd seen the newspaper.

Manny smiled. Nodded with a bit of delight.

"What are you thinking?" Thomas asked. Manny had placed his hooded sweater on the barstool.

"From out here," Manny motioned wide with his arms to the space surrounding them, "outside that thick head of yours, that story seems about 20 percent plausible. I appreciate the attempt at vulnerability, but I call BS. Just say it, you loved your job more than you loved me."

"These two are on the house." The bartender stood in front of them with two new beers. "For being such a cute couple." His gaze rested on Manny's upper body.

"We're just friends," Thomas said quickly, hoping it would be less painful to say than hear.

"Wow," the bartender said.

Thomas imagined how his brothers would react if he showed up someplace in the bartender's outfit. He could smell the thrift store or the moth balls and resisted the urge to call him Elvis, or better, Fred Astaire.

"Sorry," he said. "I would've sworn you two are a couple." He sauntered back toward an enormous bag of oranges.

Manny said, "Why even bother correcting him? Why not just say thank you?"

"I like to be accurate," Thomas said. He took a deep breath, tried to loosen up. "What if my next boyfriend comes in here?" In his head, he'd heard the lines like a cheerful melody, but they came out flat. Or perhaps sharp. Or both. His words landed with the lightness and grace of a belly flop.

"If you'd rather flirt with the bartender," Manny said, "be my guest."

"No," Thomas said, grabbing Manny's wrist. "I'm sorry. I'm such a jerk."

"Relax," Manny said. "I'm joking. I can't believe you left your school. What happened? Mercy wouldn't tell me a thing."

Thomas took a sip from the cold glass. The whole time Manny and Thomas had known one another, Manny never once called it Country Day. Always "that school." Or "the school in the forest." Or "Country Way." Or "Humphry Day." Most people in Portland knew the school by name and were impressed by what they'd seen and heard. Manny? The first time he saw it, he'd said, "This is ridiculous. Kids don't need all this excess, and making parents pay for education? How much? Don't your private universities look favorably at private schools? How is that even fair? How many Black kids attend this school?" Now Thomas looked around the empty bar, unable to imagine how to spin the story to a person who had only ever attended public schools in Germany. "I was let go. I mean, I decided to leave, but I was forced." He looked around. Then he said it. "I was accused of touching a kid inappropriately."

"That's ridiculous," Manny said. He reached for his sweater's sleeves and pulled them up from where they hung down from his stool, crossed them on his lap.

"Yes," Thomas said, so quietly he could barely hear himself.

What was it about saying the thing he did not do?

Thomas knew himself capable of wrongdoing. Of greed. Of manipulation. Of revenge. Even violence. He imagined himself an innocent person wrongly accused of embezzlement, fraud, even murder. No one is beyond scrutiny—this Thomas believed wholeheartedly—so from the day James asked him if he'd touched Toby Jay, he had obsessively scanned his life, over and over, for any indication, however slight, of his worthiness of suspicion. He found nothing. Then, after hanging up the phone after

221

talking to Jake at Thanksgiving, Thomas remembered holding Jake when they'd been boys. Boys in underwear, spooned back side to front side or intertwined face to face. James, home early one morning, woke them, their bodies a tangle of limbs and sheets. "What the hell are you doing?" James had asked, standing above them. Thomas had no idea what to say. No idea he'd done anything other than comfort his brother. "Nothing," Thomas had said. "He was scared. You and Mom were gone." James said, "Don't do it again," leaving Thomas the rest of his life to wonder why. Why couldn't he hold his brother?

Manny reached over, warmed the spot he circled on Thomas's back with his palm. Feeling the warmth of Manny's hand through his shirt helped Thomas catch his breath. "I thought of not even telling you," Thomas said. "But you know I'm such a bad liar. I'm glad you got in touch."

"You've changed," Manny said.

"I know," Thomas said. "Changed how?"

"You used to be so brittle. Now you seem tender or something. It's cute."

Thomas turned around. Outside, the golden hour appeared in the sunglasses of pedestrians. He knew if he left now and walked west on Vallejo, he'd see pink and purple in the sky, smeared together with all that orange. Inside, the man in the overalls had moved to what had to be the last set of speakers. When they were a couple, Manny demanded just one thing from Thomas. Honesty. And Manny delivered it. Almost pathologically. Not only in the larger, more philosophical sense of the word, but also in smaller, more mundane things. Do you think I'll get the raise Mercy mentioned? Do you like this tie? Has my chest gotten bigger since I changed my workout regimen? Even the most obtuse of his former lovers would have known what Thomas had really been asking: Am I the one you want to be with? Can't you see how hard I'm working? Do you still find me physically attractive? Manny's answers? You said your kids' test scores were higher last year. Why would they give you a raise for no improvement? And: That tie has never been my favorite. And: Your chest

222

looks the same to me. Why don't you measure it or take a picture if you're curious?

"I wanted to respond to your letter," Thomas said. "In fact, I kept thinking I would. Like those people who join a gym and then never go."

"That's a pretty sad comparison, Thomas," Manny said. "We lived together for almost two years."

Thomas sipped his beer. Put it down, watched Manny play with the cuff on his sweater's sleeve. "I tried to convince myself I was afraid of holding you back. Like letting you go was some grand gesture of love and generosity," Thomas said. "Jake is fine now, but there was a big cancer scare, too, and I was completely distracted. Now it's been a year. I'm embarrassed. And I apologize. You deserved better."

"Thank you for saying that," Manny said. "I agree." He stared at Thomas for what seemed like a long time. "Jake had cancer but he's okay? What kind?"

"Neck. For a minute it was bad. But he's good now. You know Jake. Nine lives."

"Thank god. Sheree okay? Max? How's Reggie? Still driving Sheree nuts?"

"Sheree and Max are better now that Jake is good. Reginald can do no right in Sheree's book, but Sheree worked a lot when Jake was sick, and he spent a lot of time with Max. I should call him. Thank him for being the best of all Max's uncles."

"You should," Manny said, and winked. "Why wait?"

"Did you see me in the paper?" Thomas asked, suddenly. "The accusation."

"Yes. Well, no. Not when it was happening. Or I would've found you. I only saw it later, when I was looking for you," Manny answered, then sipped his beer.

"I could tell you knew. But thanks for pretending you didn't."

Two young women entered the bar, laughing, just as the stereo turned on so the man in the coveralls could test the speakers. The women wore thin cotton dresses that fell to the floor with jean jackets over them. They laughed, one saying something to the other about the salad place on the next block. It certainly wasn't hot in San Francisco but warm enough for cotton dresses, warm compared to December in Portland.

"I didn't come here out of pity, Thomas. I sought you out because—other than disappearing—you were good to me. I was worried," Manny said, just audible above the music.

"Shit," Thomas said, thinking back to high school, his soccer team, Massachusetts, Berkeley, San Francisco. Even Manny. Now Country Day, and Portland. "When afraid I guess I disappear. But you shouldn't worry about the job loss. This guy, Jerome, a lawyer, helped me, so I have a lot of money," Thomas said. "And absolutely no direction. That's the only scary part."

Manny leaned back on his barstool a bit, keeping his balance. "Is that why you've taken up daytime drinking?"

"Yes," Thomas said. "But only on weekdays. And weekends."

Manny laughed. "A lot of money as in house in Spain lots of money? Is your lawyer on TV sometimes? About the Boy Scouts and gay marriage equality?"

"That's him," Thomas said, picturing Jerome's face, always so serious. "It's a lot for me. I don't want a house or stuff. Scholarships is what I'm thinking—to anywhere other than Country Day."

"You could start a trust. I remember seeing that lawyer in person once when you and I were together. I worried, too, you know. That you'd get bored with me, a nerdy scientist from a small German town, and graduate to someone like him. Smarter. American. Your age."

"Smarter than an immunologist getting a Ph.D. in biology?"

The bartender spoke quietly on his phone as he prepared the garnish for the evening crowd. He looked up and his finger made the shape of a circle.

"What is your boyfriend doing?" Manny asked.

"Asking if we want another round," Thomas said. "I don't. Do you?"

Manny shook his head no. Thomas already felt drunk and had barely sipped his third pint.

"What are you going to do?" Manny asked. "You need a plan."

"I've sold the house. Moved here," Thomas said, but wanted to go back and tell Manny that he wasn't seeing Russ. How could Manny already be engaged? When did he meet the new guy? How soon after he left for Germany had he come back to the States? But he couldn't. He said, "When we were younger, Dana and I planned on having a kid. I haven't talked to her about it yet." Thomas said. "Because I have to decide what I want to be when I grow up."

"A kid? I could easily see you as a dad. And about growing up? Welcome to my world," Manny said, holding the base of his pint. "The woman who supervised my research was recruited to start a lab to study HIV and HEP-C. She wants to hire me."

"That's incredible," Thomas said. "Isn't that grown up?"

The chandeliers above the bar suddenly went bright then slowly dimmed back to low. The bartender made adjustments from the switchboard on the wall. "Thorsten can't move," Manny said. "He works for the Trail Blazers and the Timbers and all the university teams. He loves his life."

"And your mentor? She's not in Portland?"

"San Francisco," Manny said.

"Oh," Thomas said, ashamed of the delight he felt. "I'm sure that another opportunity will come your way."

"No," Manny said. "I've decided to take it. In fact, I've already accepted the offer."

"What about your engagement?" Thomas asked, his whole body warm.

"I love Thorsten. He's American, Swedish-American, but studied German, you know. He works a lot, but when he's with me, he's with me. And the minute we became serious he started renting movies in German and using language-learning programs in the car to refresh his memory. Unlike someone else I know," he said, getting up. Manny took the sweater from the barstool and put it on.

"Ouch," Thomas said.

Manny smiled. "I have to get back to my hotel. My mom is expecting me to call and I'm meeting some future colleagues for dinner at eight," Manny said, pulling out his wallet.

"Don't be silly," Thomas said. "I've got this one." Thomas placed a small stack of cash on the bar, enough for the beers and a big tip for the bartender. "And tell your mom I said hello."

Manny smiled, grabbed Thomas's face and left a quick kiss on his lips. "My mother hates your guts," he said. "But I'll tell her."

The two men walked out of the bar. Soon, the 45 bus pulled up to the stop.

"So long," Manny said, passing through the bus's open door.

Yes, Thomas thought. *So, so long.*

Chapter Nineteen

Christmas Week & New Year's Eve
December 2013

In just a few short seconds, he would be pulled into arms: not only Jake's, but also Max's and Sheree's. One of them would, no doubt, have hot tea steaming from some stupid mug, probably in the shape of Santa's head or a reindeer sleigh.

He couldn't wait.

When Thomas had showed up to Jake's two days after the diagnosis, Jake grabbed hold of Thomas and said, "I'm so glad you're here, bud," and began crying. Sheree and Max stood there waiting, barely noticing their husband/dad's outburst, used to his emotion.

Now Thomas rang the doorbell. Knocked. He expected one or two or all three of them to have been waiting at the window, especially since Thomas had called Jake and left a voicemail and texted Sheree to let them know he'd landed, rented the car, and was on his way.

He thought he heard something stir in his brother's house. "Nesta?" Thomas called.

Needing to pee, he rang and knocked again before walking down the steps then past the squat shrubs to look into Max's bedroom window. Other than clothes on the floor and the mess of a twelve-year-old with too much stuff, there was no sign of life. A horn sounded from the street.

Where were they?

He checked his pockets for his phone, rechecked them, and then realized that he had left it in the car. *One more try,* he thought, and just as he was about press the bell again, Max opened the door.

"Hey buddy," Thomas said, reaching toward him.

"Oh my god, Uncle Thomas. Come in. Hurry," Max said, grabbing Thomas by the left wrist. Max's palm fit over Thomas's watch. *Look how much bigger his hands have become since Easter. Bigger and stronger,* Thomas thought, as Max pulled him across the threshold into the house.

"What's wrong?" Thomas asked, as the seemingly disparate threads of the day's anomalies started to weave together. Jake hadn't answered Thomas's call. Sheree hadn't returned his text. They hadn't noticed him struggling to fit in the alley's parking space. *Focus,* Thomas thought, and reached for Max's face, placing it gently into his hands. "Whatever it is, I'm here now."

Perhaps one of their friends from the meetings had relapsed. Something had happened. They never forgot Thomas's arrival time, and rarely left Max alone. God forbid the oncologist had called and said they found uptake, or Sheree had fallen ill with some infection.

"Talk to me," Thomas said with the quiet openness that he used to calm his fourth graders.

"Mom took off," Max said, and started to cry. He nuzzled his head into Thomas's coat, and Thomas leaned his face into the softness of Max's hair. "She's a lesbian."

"A what?" Thomas asked, sure he'd heard wrong.

"A lesbian. She's leaving us for a lady at the salon. She told us this morning." Max sobbed.

"Where's your dad?" Thomas said, growing impatient. His concern started to morph into annoyance.

"Gone," Max said, crying. "Took off after Mom a couple of hours ago. Told me he'd be right back but now he's not answering his phone. Neither is she," he said. "I'm scared."

Thomas let go of Max's face, stood above him, registering now that neither the car nor truck had been parked in the alley. The old feeling of Jake-related dread rushed through his chest, and he fought the impulse to leave Max, hop into the rental car, drive to the airport, buy a ticket back home.

Max collapsed on the carpet, not far from the synthetic Christmas tree in between the couch and love seat. His crying turned to sobs so loud they sounded fake. *The kid has already been through so much,* Thomas thought. Now this?

What did it mean, Sheree is a lesbian? "What the fuck?" he said, walking toward the bathroom to grab tissue or towel or toilet paper to clean Max's face.

He pulled at the doorknob, and it wouldn't turn. The door wouldn't budge.

"What. The. Fuck?" One word for each successive pull.

As he tugged harder and harder, his hunger and fatigue and dehydration and the need to empty his bladder all collected at his center.

"What the fuck?" Thomas said. But not just this. Also, his whole life since May, and the drive in the freezing convertible after the asshole car rental salesman duped him into believing it an upgrade. A convertible? In December? Thomas should've, long ago, given up on thinking he could control anything—but he'd get that door open if he had to grab the ax from his brother's shed. One last pull, Thomas thought, and then:

"Surprise!"

Laughter.

Jake and Sheree squatted on their haunches in the bathroom, cackling.

Then Max jumped onto Thomas's back. Hugging him around his neck.

"April Fools!" Jake said. Then the other two. "April Fools," they yelled on the icy Rocky Mountain afternoon in late December.

"April Fools. April Fools. April Fools!"

Max had stopped hugging him, and Sheree had left lipstick smeared on his cheeks. With his wiseass smile, Jake revealed both a receded gum line and deep grooves around his eyes. Thomas excused himself to the bathroom, vacillating between an impulse to laugh and blow the place up.

In the kitchen, tortilla chips sat alongside Sheree's homemade salsa and guacamole and a crudités of bell pepper and cucumbers. Sheree, leaning against the fridge, pressed her cell phone to her ear, covering the speaker with her second hand, and mouthed *work* to Thomas, while Jake stood at the stove stirring the green chili pork.

Thomas had smelled the pork as soon as Max opened the door. He saw Jake's truck and Sheree's hatchback parked on the same stretch of the curb as his rental, but a half-block away. How had he fallen for such a stupid joke?

When Thomas left Massachusetts for California, Jake was only twelve. Years passed without the brothers seeing much of one another (the occasional Christmas or Thanksgiving), until Stuart and Dot hosted a reunion on the occasion of Thomas finishing his grad degree and Jake graduating high school. James couldn't join, but Thomas and Jake spent a long weekend that summer getting dined and wined and relaxing with their father and stepmother. There, Thomas met a version of his baby brother he'd never imagined: a man. Jake's contradictory nature, his unquenchable desire for something new: at eighteen he'd already worked summers and winters on an Alaskan fishing barge, as a ski-lift attendant, and as a private snowboard instructor. Much later, Thomas would find out that Jake even had a brief stint, while using, as an unlicensed massage therapist and personal trainer. "I even got blown by a dude once while I wore a ski mask," he told Thomas, years later. He admitted it right in front of Sheree. "Back then, I'd do almost anything for fifty bucks."

The world had taught their older brother James to express outrage when he found Jake and Thomas snuggled together to keep warm as children. Thomas hated the world for it but hated himself more for giving in to the outrageous demand. On subsequent nights as children, when Jake, afraid in a huge house with no parents, came to Thomas, Thomas refused him, scolded him, insisted he go to his own bed.

Then, when Thomas came out, the shame of the memory of James chastising them multiplied. Thomas had just turned twenty-four the year they reunited, and Thomas's attraction to Jake, then eighteen, bordered too close to sexual. He'd never repressed nor indulged an incestuous fantasy, the kind gay porn outfits made fortunes from—with their Brazilian triplets and Eastern European twins—but Thomas couldn't help but acknowledge his brother's dark features, strong bone structure, his staggering level of physical fitness, with striations of muscle visible through the fabric of his tight Henley.

Jake and Thomas had spent their days at the condo complex's pool. Thomas hadn't seen his brother without a shirt since they were children. Jake's body hair made the muscles of his tattooed chest, forearms, calves, and abdominals appear at once soft and hard. He laughed often, and easily, gentler than a guffaw, but hearty and contagious. Little did Thomas know that Jake had already smoked heroin (shooting it would come later) in the pool house changing room, but only after he politely excused himself. Then and now, Jake had an all-consuming desire to please and be liked by all: Maddy, James, the waitress, the tollbooth attendant, Reginald, the airport traffic cop, the telephone customer service representative, their father, his wife, his son's teachers, his coworkers, and perhaps more than anyone else, Thomas.

Pretending Sheree left the family for a lesbian lover? It must have been his brother's family's dimwitted attempt of expressing how cool they were with Thomas. An attempt to say we love you, we see you, we feel so free with you—and, we get to fuck with you. Why else would they do something so stupid?

Max said, "May I go with Uncle Tommy to get the tortillas? In the convertible?"

"Sure," Jake said. "So long as Thomas isn't too tired of being in the car."

"You're not, right Fluff?" Max said.

Sheree asked her colleague to hold for a minute, then told Thomas and Max to go to the La Casita on 8th, and to stop by

Circle K to get some butter. "Don't let Max talk you into buying any other crap. Here," she said, handing him a twenty.

Thomas took the money, and he and Max walked to the car. "You're a good actor," Thomas said.

"You should have seen your face," Max said, opening the passenger door.

Thomas paused for a moment once they both sat down, waited for his mind to clear so he could tell his nephew what he thought of their joke. "That joke was a bunch of bullshit," Thomas said. "It hurt my feelings."

Max looked at Thomas. He said, "Sorry, Uncle. Should we call a family meeting later?"

Thomas smiled. He couldn't believe how open his nephew seemed, how willing to listen. So far beyond his years. He'd grown up around recovery groups and a hair salon—the only child of an interracial couple surrounded by the most diverse collection of people Thomas had ever seen. Max's was the opposite of James's, Jake's and his own experience. Everything in their house had needed decoding.

Max's parents talked. They brought their pain to the wider community. They modeled self-inspection, taught him to see what they called "the fourth column," some part of their twelve-step practice where they looked for their own contribution to what pissed them off. "Maybe," Thomas said. "Meanwhile, should we go topless?" Thomas unlocked the hooks at the corners of the windshield that held the roof to the frame.

"Hell yeah," Max said, cranking the heat.

"That doesn't work very well," Thomas said. "So, you may want to pull down your hat."

Max had placed his beanie at the back of his head, so it hovered. He didn't touch his hat. Instead, he gave Thomas directions to the grocery store. "We'll stop there first, so the tortillas stay warm."

Even though Thomas knew the way to the supermarket, he let Max narrate. As a little kid, Max had exhibited superior verbal skills, and Thomas loved listening to him. By the time he was twenty months old, he'd already developed a vocabulary nearly twice that of the average toddler. While the other little ones at daycare could either play or talk, Max could do both simultaneously. At six and a half, he'd already mastered more nuanced verbal skills—variances of pitch, tone, and rate—typical to eight-year-olds. Thomas always bragged about his nephew's gifts, but he was the only one who seemed impressed. "We're just glad he's healthy," Jake would always repeat. "I hope he doesn't grow up to be a junkie," Sheree would say. "Or worse. A Republican," Maddy would add. As Thomas drove, something kept puncturing the moment. Subtle, like a pinprick in a tightly woven fabric. Invisible, unless stretched in front of light. He couldn't put a finger on it beyond the hyper-awareness of being alone with Max. "Your dad said you wrote some poems. One about your shoes?" Thomas said, trying to ignore the feeling.

"Yeah. But it was lame. My poetry teacher made me write an ode. My first drafts were about Dad, but they all came out like he was dead already, and I didn't want to discuss them with Colleen, my shrink, or spend an hour a day with the school counselor who smells like old Band-Aids and seems stoned all the time. The one about my sneakers sucked compared to what I can really do. For charity, they made me read it at the assembly."

"Charity?" Thomas asked.

"You know," Max said, looking at his uncle. "The mixed-race kid with the cancer dad? Mom says they always put people like me at the podium, so they get to feel all supportive and inclusive."

"Sounds like you've got it all figured out," Thomas said, parking. As they walked through the electric glass doors into the supermarket, a Black woman wearing an Olympic Training Village sweatshirt said hello.

"Who's she?" Thomas asked.

"Who knows," Max said. "All us Black folks say hi to one another, don't you know that?" They passed the pyramid of apples into the produce section en route to dairy. Max added, "Maybe she knows my mom from the salon. Ma makes everyone in her chair look at photos of me."

233

"Your mom's proud of you," Thomas said.

"Or," Max said, "maybe that lady likes her men super young?"

A waft of air chilled their space as Max opened the refrigerator door. He laughed as he grabbed a pound of salted butter sticks.

"Don't say stuff like that, Max," Thomas said. The door sealed shut.

The two paid for the butter. After picking up the tortillas, Thomas insisted on putting up the roof.

Maddy screamed when Thomas walked in.

"I didn't scream," she said to Jake, "I let out a joyful cheer."

"Yeah," Jake said. "Deaf Nesta wouldn't stop barking."

Thomas put down the warm bag of tortillas and hugged his mother. When he let go of her torso, he kept his hands on her shoulders. Her sweater felt so soft. She wore a pair of flattering wool slacks, and her hair, bright white, offered a lovely contrast to her monochromatic charcoal-gray outfit. "How much have you lost?" he asked.

"I don't know," she said. "Fifteen pounds? Sheree?"

"I think so," Sheree, who dipped a bell pepper into guacamole, said. "Mom is losing. Jake and Max are gaining. So many pounds are flying in and out of here I can't keep track."

Max pulled a clean kitchen towel from the drawer and tossed it to Maddy, who opened the tortilla bag and grabbed a dozen or more, wrapped them in the towel, and laid them in the basket on the counter. Thomas handed Sheree her change while Jake stirred one last time, then removed the insert from the crock-pot and put it on the table. Jake had gained another fifteen pounds since Easter. His radiation burns had healed, and his beard and sideburns were starting to grow back in.

Sheree looked at Thomas and chuckled.

"What?"

"What what?"

"What's funny?" Thomas asked.

"Did we get you with that April Fools' joke or what?" Sheree said. "I nearly peed my pants listening to Max's fake crying through the bathroom door."

"Totally," Thomas said, stirring food around his plate. Max looked over with raised eyebrows.

"Still not as good as you knocking up a woman," Jake said. "Now that was hilarious."

Before James took off for college, the three McGurrin brothers had come up with rules for their year-'round version of April Fools' Day. Their jokes could be staged and executed on any day other than April 1st. The joker could only stage a joke after he had been the jokee. No one could perform two or more jokes successively. The joker could engage allies. The joke itself must reference—in some inarguable way—the last joke that was played by the now-jokee. At their Eastertime reunion, all before the accusation, Thomas, giddy, made the dinnertime announcement that he'd accidently gotten Dana pregnant, and they'd decided to keep the baby. Maddy didn't fall for it but didn't interfere. Stuart had stood up and proposed a toast before Thomas called April Fools.

The family spooned pork into bowls from the crock-pot.

"Yours was pretty damn good," Thomas said to Jake, who was already on his third taco. "Max had me convinced something was wrong, but, for the record, I was less worried about Sheree's supposed lesbianism than I was my bladder."

"Are you saying I could be gay?" Sheree asked.

"You totally could be," Max said before Thomas could answer. "You and your girlfriends are all over each other."

"Yum," Jake said, eyebrows going up and down. "And I'm not talking about this taco."

"Gross," Max said, then laughed. "Not to mention inappropriate."

"Stop being such a prude," Maddy said to her grandson. "Even though I agree."

"You don't get it, do you?" Thomas looked down at his hands. They were shaking. "I'm all for a good laugh, but at Easter, I wasn't pretending I'd gone straight. I was joking that Dana and I were going to have a baby. It wasn't about sex."

"Don't be so serious," Jake said.

Thomas looked at his brother. "Maybe you're right," Thomas said. "I need to relax. See lesbianism for the true emergency that it is. And recognize the hilarity in the possibility of my being a parent. I'm such a killjoy."

"That wasn't how we meant it," Sheree said.

"Really?" Thomas said.

Everyone at the table looked at each other. Thomas finished dinner without looking up. When his plate was empty, he walked it to the kitchen, put it in the sink. "You done?" he said to Maddy, and when she said yes, the two left.

"I'm so damn glad you're here. I can't tell you how sick I am of my other children," she said.

"After last night's welcome back party, I can finally see your point." He rested his chin on the top of her head. He hadn't slept well.

"They're masters at the art of bad timing," she said, crossing her kitchen to fetch Thomas a coffee. "They did not consult with me about that asinine joke. For the record, I had no part in it. You have enough reasons to resent me without adding that one to the list."

"I know," Thomas said, taking the mug from Maddy. "Otherwise I would've checked into a hotel."

Maddy tucked her hair behind her ear, took a sip of her coffee. "When are the three of you—meaning you and your brothers—going to stop disguising the affection you have for one another with all the adolescent bullshit?"

Thomas nodded, sipped from his own mug.

"I have a proposal." Maddy said she had twenty pounds of frozen veggies from her garden and zero desire to cook. "Will you make stuff with me? It'll kill two birds with one stone. I haven't bought a single Christmas gift."

"Let's get started," Thomas said.

With two glasses of fresh veggie juice, member-supported

public radio in the background, and steamy pots on all four burners, Thomas said, "Dad told me about the woman in California who accused him of something he said he didn't do. What's your take?"

"Oh that," she said. She looked out her kitchen window, waved to the neighbor next door. Behind their house, a spread of the Rockies, including Pike's Peak, sat on the horizon. "I wasn't at your father's office that day, but," she said, "my gut feeling? Your dad never touched her. He may have ignored her. Condescended to her. Belittled her ideas. Called her some stupid nickname . . ."

"Got it, Mom," Thomas said, holding up his wooden spoon.

"My guess is that no matter what did or didn't happen, she probably earned that money. But who knows? The innocent are sometimes made guilty and vice versa. I hate to say it, kid." The microwave let out a series of piercing beeps until she released the door's latch. "You're not the first, and you won't be the last. And you can't let this ruin your life. Bitterness will eat you alive," she said. "Trust me."

She took out a Ziploc of now-thawed zucchini and handed it to Thomas.

"I'm sweet by nature," Thomas said. "My brothers are both jerks, and they make me bitter."

Maddy pulled another bag from the freezer. "Really?" she said. "It's all their fault? Sweet? You're more interesting than that. I'd say calculated."

Thomas touched mushy squash to test its temperature, felt cold crystals, and put it in the microwave again. "I'm embarrassed. I thought if I played by the rules nothing bad would happen. I mean, you know. Not that I'd be impervious. Just . . . ," he couldn't finish the thought. "James and Jake. They've never been careful. And look at everything they have."

Maddy pressed buttons. The turntable in the oven started to spin. "Once I started working for hospice, I got sent to Mass General. There was a patient on the cancer unit. A gay guy. He'd run away from home a few years earlier, made money hustling. The doctors diagnosed him with late-stage leukemia. We finally found his mother's number, and we kept calling, but she didn't have an answering machine and didn't pick up. By the time we got in touch, her son was critical. She flew to Boston from God-knows-where. Kentucky? I'm pretty sure it was Kentucky. But she arrived too late. The doctor took her into the room with her son's body. I remember hearing her wail."

"That's awful," Thomas said.

"Her son thought she'd rejected him, but I'm not sure he had the whole picture. I talked with her in the visitors' lounge. She'd paid for the plane ticket and a hotel and had never been to Massachusetts. I encouraged her to stay, visit the places her son loved: Harvard Square and the North End, Faneuil Hall and Quincy Market. I invented the list because her son never opened up to me. Poor kid was so sick, so angry."

"Did they teach you that in hospice training? To lie?"

"They trained us to withhold judgment. To stay present with people experiencing grief."

"I don't know how you did it," Thomas said.

"Dying people are often much easier to deal with than the living," Maddy said. "The next day, she came back and asked if she could sit with men on the AIDS unit. Every day she arrived in the early afternoon and stayed with a different young man until he'd fall asleep. She brought the guys pastries from the neighborhoods she visited. I remember because most of the guys couldn't eat them, and the sweets ended up at the nurses' station. When the week was up, she told me she didn't have a lot of money and asked me how she might extend her stay without paying Boston hotel prices. She'd befriended one young man who I also liked. He'd convinced himself he'd get better, get out, and feared he'd lose his lease if he didn't get well enough, soon enough. It cost a fraction of a hotel, and I asked him if he'd sublet it to the lady from Kentucky. Without hesitation, he said yes."

As his mother told her story, Thomas watched her hands. She chopped and stirred, mixed and watered: a shallot, a sauce, a houseplant. He'd woken up with the familiar fatigue. Last night's outrage birthed this morning's numbness. Those hands belonged to someone he hadn't quite seen. He always saw Maddy as his mother, and up until this moment, listening to her, he hadn't seen her for what else she'd always been. A person, and a brave one. Thomas touched her shoulder. "So. You went from liar to a real estate broker?" Thomas asked, and the microwave beeped again. Thomas sautéed the now-thawed zucchini until most of the moisture had evaporated. He added olive oil, salt, pepper, and mint to the pan.

"Ed the librarian, that was his name. From then on, the lady sat with Ed. The two were often told to quiet down. They'd crack up watching Benny Hill or argue over the merit of a book she'd bring him from his apartment. Ed had been an only child, and his parents had both died before he finished grad school. He told me they knew he was gay, and they loved him."

"Did Kentucky try to save his soul? Get him to accept Jesus or something?" Thomas asked. He added a bit of vinegar and turned down the heat to get a good caramelization.

"No. One day, we lost three men by noon. That's what it was like back then. You might go a few days without a death, and then, bam, three, four, five, six guys on the unit would die on the same day. The lady from Kentucky arrived with her bakery box tied with a crisscrossed string. She used a plastic knife to cut the string and the pastries into quarters, and then she passed them around to the deceased patients' loved ones, who, that day, out-numbered the hospital staff. Later, Ed, who, by then, weighed about one hundred pounds, held her as she cried."

Thomas put down the wooden spoon. He recalled Tony, pictured his first love each time his mother used Ed's name, saw Tony in that bed, on that ward—or one like it—and hoped, prayed even, that Tony, too, had been the recipient of someone's compassion. Regret poked at Thomas; he felt it from within, between each rib, a regret that he ran away from San Francisco. His fear of reality came at a price. The richness, the layers, the complexities, the opportunities to be of service, the kind of messy relationships his mother described—he'd missed out. "What happened to her?" Thomas asked.

"I don't know. I left Mass General when hospice reassigned me to a different facility. In my mind, the lady never went back to Kentucky. Instead, she planned Ed's memorial, kept his home after he died, dusted his knickknacks, placed Ed's and her son's urns next to each other, and read the books Ed brought home from the library after she spent every afternoon holding hands with those men."

Once, a colleague asked him if his parents named him Thomas after the one in the Bible. "No. My great uncle, I think," he told her. She had said, "I love Thomas in the Bible. Like a lot of us, he came to a certain point and stopped. He was a good dude who gets a bad rap. His lack of imagination was his big mistake. He, like the others, wanted to believe Jesus could resurrect but he couldn't get past his fear, his doubt."

Thomas leaned against the cool tile of his mother's kitchen counter, felt it push into the flesh at his hip. He closed his eyes and took a deep breath, remembered Chad's bright blue eyes, the blood on his face. He imagined Chad offering him his palms, taking them, Chad saying: put your hand here, then guiding Thomas's thumbs to the empty place in each.

They finished setting out the jars for the vegetables and sauce, and Thomas went for a run, took a nap, and that evening, he and Maddy watched TV. She'd bought a huge cube of memory foam from a mattress factory and then took it to the home store to have it divided at the diagonal. The two lay in flannel pajamas in her bed, backs against the foam triangles, watching *The Good Wife*.

Thomas reached into his bag of microwave popcorn.

Neither Jake nor James had ever hung out with Maddy, at least not like this, in her bed. Perhaps the desires and impulses that made them sleep with women other than their mother kept them out of their mother's bed. Thomas wished that they would or could spend an evening on the other side of Maddy's closed bedroom door. As boys, the brothers couldn't help but feel they caused Maddy to retreat to her room. The three of them had worked so hard to determine, then avoid, the magical combination that would send her into hibernation.

They never got it.

Whoever did or said the last thing before she disappeared would get blamed by the others. You sent her up, so you're the one who has to cook. You made her go, and now I have to bike to soccer practice. You were too loud/too soft/too hyper/too silly/too serious, so now we're on our own.

If Jake and James could have spent a few hours with her, in her room, watching Maddy's face as she read her book or watched her show or sipped her beer or ate her popcorn, they'd understand, too, as Thomas understood. Maddy wasn't trying to escape her children as much as she was trying to create a place where she could have space, feel good. Happy, even. In control. Her coaster lay on the exact spot on her bedside table as it had for Thomas's whole life. She also had an exact spot for the television remote. An exact spot for her popcorn bag and the exact moment, every time, when she needed to add salt.

Now, on each of the two bedside tables, a small glass of beer rested on those coasters. Family rule was you only crunched during commercials, so in addition to popcorn, they also emptied a bag of Gummi Bears. The television episode ended, Maddy took the last sip of her beer and said, "I'm early to bed and early to rise these days," then grabbed the remote control. "If you want to go out, or back to your brother's to kill him in his sleep for being so dense, the house keys are on the hook by the door."

The whole house now smelled of the food they'd prepared. The tomato sauce still bubbled on the stove in a giant aluminum pot over a flicker of blue flame. Thyme and marjoram, oregano and basil, onion and garlic, all from her garden, filled her home with the aromas of Thomas's childhood. In the morning, they'd divvy up the jars and deliver them to her neighbors who'd helped with the garden when Jake was sick. She wanted to wish them happy holidays.

෴ ෴ ෴

Thomas typed a text to James from under the covers of the guest room bed. *Having a nice visit with Mom. Junkels won at April Fools. Wish you were here. Love you.* He looked at it for a few seconds before deleting it. The moment after, his phone buzzed.

Thinking of you. I'm back in SF! Merry Christmas!

Manny. Thomas felt a surge of excitement, blood to his groin. *In Colorado Springs,* he wrote back. *Visiting Jake and Sheree and Maddy and Max.*

Send my love, Manny wrote. Then, *Goodnight.*

On her refrigerator, among dozens of pictures of her four grandchildren and three sons and a 20 percent off coupon for the big home store, Maddy had a magnet. It read, *Everything we do is futile, but we must do it anyway.*

The fantasy about getting back with Manny morphed into regret. Two trickles of sweat slid into the sheets, one from his forehead, one, his armpit. His mother had just washed them, then hung them on her clothesline. Even in winter she gave sheets the Rocky Mountain air, because to her, those small offerings: herbs from her garden, a jar of sautéed squash or homemade tomato sauce, sheets hung to dry in the tiny slice of December sun, were love.

Thomas closed his eyes, made a decision to see more and focus on small offerings, not to let the damage of his past get him—at least not every day. He had recalled Chad in many quiet moments since leaving that Massachusetts high school. Not just recently. Guilt had turned Chad into a ghost that liked to haunt. Thomas would remember the place where he hid in dusty corners of the classroom while bullies split Chad's face open on a band room locker. In those moments—like now, on his back in the pitch blackness on the bed in his mother's guest room with the familiar quilts covering him—he'd feel a complete emptiness. In it, he'd understand how tender that made him, how imperfect, ungodly.

Bundled in layers of cotton and wool and goose down, the McGurrins rang in the New Year with giraffes and hippos, mountain lions and monkeys. After dinner at the Grizzly Grill, they walked the grounds of the zoo, which were lit up by hundreds of thousands of tiny Christmas lights, and toasted each other's health in a crook of the Rockies. Like winter ravens, they soared up Cheyenne Mountain in pairs, legs dangling beneath the chairlift, looking down at the lit-up view of the Springs which brightened an aura around the dark expanse of the eastern plains.

Maddy's neighbor and best friend Frank, the garden landscaper at the zoo, let them sneak in sparkling apple juice and champagne. Thomas and Maddy were the only ones who drank the champagne, and Maddy barely any at all. Thomas, drunk and happy, rode the Mountaineer Sky Ride with Jake. He could hear Max and Sheree laughing from the chair in front of them. Frank and Maddy waved from the chair behind. Overcome, he grabbed Jake and hugged his neck. "I'm glad you're still here," Thomas said. "I don't think I could have gotten through this last year without you."

"I love you, too, Tommy," Jake said, resting his head against Thomas's shoulder. "Now shut your drunk pie hole and let me enjoy the view."

Thomas returned to San Francisco fatter by five pounds, but he felt lighter than he had in years. Just before leaving, he and Jake and Sheree, Maddy and Max had gathered around the computer to video chat with Stuart and Dot; then James. They still hadn't spoken, so Thomas said hi but focused on Joyce, and all three nieces. Silvia broke through the din of voices and gave him the hardest time—not for leaving at Thanksgiving, but for leaving without taking her sneaker shopping like he had Max. "He's not even in the Middle Kid Club, Fluff. WTF?"

"I'll make it up to you. I promise," Thomas said.

He'd used the suitcase he'd emptied of gifts for Max to pack the ones he'd received from Maddy and Jake's family. He got busy unpacking the pod that had finally arrived from Portland. As he decided on the angles in which to place his furniture, he imagined the guests he'd soon receive.

Why hadn't Thomas called Jake after the accusation? After Tony died? After Manny left? He could've used a brother. Perhaps he'd been shortsighted with Sheree, too. Sure, they always got along great, but truth be told, Thomas often felt, with their mutual love for witty barbs and comebacks, like they fell into this weird fag/fag hag game. They did something that resembled a Black woman/gay sidekick sitcom for the rest of the family—trash-talking the religious right and Republicans, elevating their own charms.

Jake talked about homophobia and racism as if it were the same thing—and drew parallels to his own life as an addict/outsider. At Barbara's first communion, the whole family had gone to New York. Jake and Sheree sat down next to Thomas in the church. Jake asked, "Is this the pew for the queers, crackpots, and fallen women?" Thomas didn't see his attraction to the same gender as equal to or related to the plight of living with addiction—beyond basic societal misunderstanding—and he felt like a fraud for not chiming in every time one of their family conflated the struggles. Nor did he think being white and gay as parallel to being Black and a woman, and always assumed Sheree felt the same. The true kinship he felt to his sister-in-law had nothing to do with their identities—but at the same time, it felt related to the fact that each had lived through experiences that others in their families hadn't.

He loved spending time with Sheree, even when they fell into weird patterns in front of the family. One on one, they shared their love of books and cooking, their belief that future generations might affect change if mentored. Sheree had opened up to Thomas several times about her complicated relationship to Maddy, her own health, her joys and fear when parenting Max, her abiding spirituality, and her difficult relationship with Reggie. But there was still some distance. While he listened, he did not dig in, probe like he would with Dana, go deep. Instead, he either joked or remained silent or tried to make her feel better. He also didn't confide in her the way he did in Dana, even though she'd completely earned his trust. His hesitation seemed less logical and more out of fear of what Jake might find out. He had never been able to resist the desire to be seen as the rock, the unwavering presence in Jake's life, and he began to see the selfishness in this choice, the very limits of it.

Thomas removed the tape he'd used to keep his dresser drawers closed for the move. He couldn't wait to invite Jake and Sheree to stay. He could picture everybody chilling in his new living room. He'd tell them how stupid he'd been to overreact to their joke, how much he appreciated all of the ways they made him feel lucky. He wanted to go deeper, get closer.

After he dug into the box marked *Desk* Thomas pulled out and unwrapped the newspaper around his wooden Pinewood Derby toy car and placed it on the new desk, one he'd bought for the guest room. Not office. Guest room. He'd insist they stay.

Soon, Dana would come over for the supper he already had cooking in his new crock-pot, Jake's gift to Thomas for Christmas. Green chili and tortillas, with Sheree's recipe which Thomas had brought back from Colorado for Dana. He checked his phone, opened an email from James, who'd already signed up for the Thanksgiving 5K next year in New York. He forwarded his confirmation to Jake and wrote, *Your turn to sign up!* And *You both better start training now.* A few minutes later, Jake's confirmation chimed into his inbox. *5K?* he wrote, *Is that what you think of me? Isn't there a marathon? Something serious?*

By the end of the weekend, Thomas had broken down and recycled every box, hung all his frames, and planted an herb garden that he put on his fire escape only to be told to take it off by David, the property manager. "Fire hazard," he said into the phone. "We don't want that."

He sent thank you cards for each of the gifts he'd received at Christmas, shopped the after-Christmas sales for future birthday presents for Max and the nieces. Thomas even sent out a few resumes and cover letters for retail jobs to keep him busy and followed up with the name of an attorney who specialized in setting up philanthropic trust funds.

Sheree had called every day to say she missed him. Manny called, too. He and Thorsten had made an offer on a condo three blocks north and five blocks east of Thomas's place, smack dab in the same corner of the city. Manny and Maddy had reunited by text and had a game of online Scrabble going.

Mercy called and left a message saying she'd been thinking about Thomas nonstop since Manny had contacted her, that she wanted to make things right between them as friends. He'd been procrastinating about getting back to her, missing her friendship, but just couldn't bring himself to call. The same week she'd sent a small package in the mail. He tossed it down the garbage chute, then retrieved it, cleaned it, put it in a drawer unopened.

He kept vacillating between fury for her participation in the fiasco—a fiasco that had destroyed his career and driven him out of Portland—and knowing how many ways her hands were tied. It had been hard enough for Mercy to earn the autonomy to have such an influence over the education of the students. The innovative ways she'd overhauled the curriculum. The number of schools across the nation who modeled their curriculum after the initiatives she'd proposed. The research. The conferences. The willingness to experiment and fail, to try something new. The equal emphasis on art and science and math and robotics, for everyone, but especially science for the girls and humanities for the boys. Required. Not optional, until twelfth grade. She changed social studies or history to "our stories." Whenever and wherever possible, students studied first-person accounts.

Thomas remembered his history teacher, Mr. Whittaker who said, "Now that you know what they say, your job is to look for and find what they didn't." Mercy eliminated "they," looked for and found what "they" hadn't, assigned it, and trained her staff to do the same. After years, Mercy had finally managed to get rid of the standard textbook at Country Day. Mercy chose the people who came to the school to discuss their ancestors, their lives, their careers battling injustice; people who developed water systems and planned cities and engineered stadiums. She eliminated gender as a factor in who got to train and play which sport. The list went on and on. While a student, Mercy saw Country Day as the ideal environment to learn. She thrived and created a vision to double the school's good use by overhauling what got taught. Without Mercy's influence, Country Day would be nothing more than a paradise where rich people could deposit their children for the majority of the day for the majority of the year. She already knew how he felt about everything she'd done. He'd told her so many times. Thanked her.

The PFA and board's votes to fire him would've outweighed hers, even without the petition, even if she'd wanted him to stay. He'd never know how hard she did or did not fight behind the scenes to convince the PFA or board. Once, it even occurred to him to thank her for getting him out of there, but he wasn't ready to hear her voice. He knew these conversations were better had in person. Face to face. But he wasn't ready. So, he texted.

I can tell how guilty you feel and my sincere hope for you is you'll find someone to talk to and forgive yourself. But that person is not me. Not now. Not yet.

Chapter Twenty

Sunday
March 23rd, 2014

Just before the second call came in, Lindsey Buckingham played
guitar as Stevie Nicks sang "Landslide." Thomas turned it up,
hummed along, high on his productivity. He'd made it to the
farmers' market before the rush at Fort Mason and had already
knocked out an arugula pesto and washed the rest of the greens
for salads. His first day off since landing a job selling mid-century
furniture at a shop near Dana's place in Noe Valley. Now he stood
in his closet in front of the small pile of sweaters he'd kept,
deciding which to wear under his motorcycle jacket.

Thomas was one of nearly twenty guys who, on the last Sunday
of the month, rain or shine, took a motorcycle trip up or down
Highway One to have a late lunch at a spot not far from the scenic
drive. They called themselves "Homomoto." That Sunday, the plan
was to meet at the Marina Green at ten thirty before heading two
hours north to Tamales Bay for lunch in Inverness.

Thomas had just hung up with Dana. He'd convinced her to
try the free music app Max used. "They're playing all these songs
I haven't heard in years. The lyrics seem like they were written
just for me."

The second call came in at 12:13 p.m. on that last Sunday in
March. Thomas fished his phone out from his back pocket.

"James?" Thomas said, while grabbing the sweater Joyce had bought him in Scotland. "I thought for a sec you were Dana calling back."

"No," James said.

"Tell your wife I'm wearing the sweater from her Glasgow trip."

"I need to talk," James said. His brother's voice sounded thin, too quiet.

"Jimmy?" Thomas said. "You okay?" He walked out of his closet, put his sweater on the bed.

"Jesus, Tommy," James said.

"What's wrong?" Thomas said.

"It's Junkels," James said.

Thomas sat on the bed next to his helmet. He'd spoken to Jake on Friday. He'd gone in for his monthly tests. Everything excellent. Tip-top, he'd said. Zero uptake.

"Jake and Sheree were in an accident," James said, his voice barely audible.

"Accident?" Thomas said. He felt his chest tighten. "What kind of accident? And I swear to god, James, if this is April Fools, you're already on thin ice."

The steady beat of a tambourine and a simple guitar riff gave way to Bruce Springsteen's voice. He sang, "I'll wait for you, and should I fall behind, wait for me."

"Not April Fools. Collision with a truck on I-25. They think the driver fell asleep. No joke."

Thomas stood up. "Max?"

James said something Thomas couldn't make out. He could barely hear his brother.

"Can you speak up?"

"Max is safe. He was in the back," James said.

"What hospital?" Thomas asked.

"Children's Memorial."

"Jake and Sheree?"

Muffled sobs.

"James?"

249

Thomas leaned against the refrigerator in his dead brother and sister-in-law's kitchen. He tried to concentrate on the coolness of the stainless steel against his scalp, and the vibration of the motor on his spine. He fingered the keys to his mother's hybrid and waited for Max, who was locked in the bathroom of the home he'd soon vacate for good. The kitchen smelled of burnt coffee. Jake and Sheree's friends from Alcoholics and Narcotics Anonymous were in the basement at four o'clock on a Wednesday. Always a steady stream of friendly weathered and tattooed workers who took off work to help out. A coffee crowd. So quick to finish one and eager to brew the next pot, they forgot to wipe the burner down.

Jake and Thomas had chatted a ton, both online and by phone, since Thomas's Christmas visit, but leaning there, he could only think of the one call that had devolved into an argument. Jake got pissed that Thomas had told Maddy about the big gift Stuart gave them. "A car?" Thomas had said.

"An emergency," Jake had replied, defensively. "After a burst water pipe in the same week that Sheree's cylinder failed."

Thomas only mentioned the car to Maddy because she'd been bitching about Stuart. Thomas, sick of her complaining about his father, countered her negativity with mention of his generosity, citing the car as the example. Thomas had no idea, until later, that Maddy lit into Jake and Sheree for their trip to Walmart for a huge new television and stereo system, birthday gifts for Max that would elevate his status among his gamer friends. They'd installed surround sound in the walls right before a balloon payment was due on their mortgage. Apparently, the call sent Maddy into her tough love, post-rehab mode.

Jake always reacted negatively to confrontation. Instead of giving it back to Maddy, he chewed out Thomas for innocently mentioning the car.

"Sorry, Jake," Thomas said. "But don't pin this on me. I didn't know it was a secret. You live in the same town as Mom, so she's bound to see the car. I was merely mentioning how sweet . . ."

"No," Jake interrupted. "You don't have a kid, so you have no idea what it's like. Since you stopped teaching, you have nothing to do except lick your wounds. Now you're all up my alley? I work fifty hours a week, Tommy. I don't have some lawsuit settlement to keep me up to my fucking ears in cashmere sweaters. You and Mom gossip like a couple of old ladies."

"Don't chastise me, Jake. What do you even know about what I do with my time?" Thomas said. "Mom babysat for you, for free, for years, while pulling you two out of the gutter. You talk about your family like it's a burden. Do you hear yourself? I am so fucking sick of you people talking about having children as if it's a disability."

Jake's and Sheree's friends started to come out of the basement doorway into the kitchen. Gerard, the queen bee leading a hive of workers, smiled, led his group of volunteers out the door of Thomas's brother's house. When Jake had cancer, Sheree's program girlfriends had dropped off Tupperware containers stuffed with meatloaf and giant Ziploc bags full of soup. Jake's guys did the yard work. They all helped drive Max to and from school and sports. Not just the first week. But week after week after week, for months. They'd just finished emptying all the junk stored in the basement.

Gerard, who had been Jake's sponsor, walked into the kitchen from the basement stairs holding a box he rested on the counter. "See you later?" he said, reaching out his arm.

"Yes," Thomas said, shaking Gerard's hand. Gerard wore an expensive dress shirt and ironed slacks. The wooden soles of his Italian shoes clicked on the linoleum. With his tailored jacket and silk tie and calm, reassuring voice, he looked and sounded like a man who could run for president.

The day before, at the service, Thomas found his father squatting, torso facing the wall in the corner of the funeral home's lobby. Dot stood near him, signaling to Thomas to come over.

"Dad?" Thomas held a piece of white paper, folded in half, with a photocopied image of Jake's and Sheree's faces. Thomas had taken the pic with his phone on New Year's Eve at the zoo.

Dot said, "The outlets don't work back there, but he won't give up."

She wore more makeup than he'd ever seen on her, foundation and powder that Thomas could smell.

"I can't find a goddamn plug in this place," his father said without looking up. "I need to charge my phone."

Thomas lifted his father and took him into his arms. Stuart wept. When the first wave of it ended, Thomas led his father and Dot to the chapel, already packed with friends and coworkers, and left them in the first of two rows where James's family sat.

On the way back to the lobby, Thomas saw Reginald and Charlotte across the aisle, sitting with Sheree's colleagues from the salon. As Thomas approached, Charlotte stood up. The small, bright lily she wore pinned to the lapel on her black blazer perfumed their hug. Reginald kept to his seat, but shook Thomas's hand. "I'm sorry," Reginald said, "for your loss."

For the first time since the death of his brother, Thomas felt like he might cry. "And I'm sorry for yours," Thomas said. "Come sit with the family," Thomas said, motioning to the other side of the aisle.

"We're more comfortable here," Reginald said.

The memorial began and passed in a combination of hyperfocus and blur. Thomas sat down next to Max and Maddy and wiped his shirt with a Starbucks napkin. It was wet with his father's crying, so it left little gray-brown specks of paper that looked like roly-polies around the buttons. When Francine, Sheree's best friend from the salon, sang "Amazing Grace," Thomas worried his dad might choke on a new wave of sobs.

James lumbered through the service with slumped shoulders. The girls leaned into each other as Joyce moved one palm slowly over James's back, as elegant as she was forlorn. The five of them, in the second row of chairs, seemed held within an invisible force field, one that enabled them to navigate the weekend by keeping everyone else out. Thomas stayed as present as he could sitting next to Maddy, and Max, who kept his head down. Thomas took a cue from Joyce and rubbed his nephew's back. Maddy's face seemed both tight and slack. She did not cry in public, and her eyes held no hint to how she felt. Thomas held her hand, stared at the framed picture of Jake and Sheree on the table between their closed caskets. Addiction, HIV, interferon treatments, HEP-C, cancer. One or both of the two had survived it all.

In the kitchen, Thomas put his mom's key in the pocket of his chinos and closed his eyes. A few minutes ago, he had backed Maddy's car into the empty spot in his brother's driveway. He hadn't wanted Max to come, but he'd insisted. "It's my house," he said. "I helped Gerard pack, and I know which boxes are yours."

Colleen, The Kid Shrink, as Max called her, because of the dolls and finger-paints and mini-chairs in her office, said it was healthy to allow him to participate in the various rituals of closure. While Thomas disagreed, he deferred. Maddy agreed with Colleen. Maddy had inherited the house, and put it on the market immediately, as real estate had been leaning toward a sellers' market in Colorado Springs for the first time in years, and she wanted to make the most of it for Max's future.

"Shouldn't I stay there with him for a few weeks? Let him sleep in his bed instead of making him pack?" Thomas had asked the night he arrived.

"No," his mother had said to him in the kitchen, calmly and quietly, as Max watched TV in the next room. She put her hand on the side of Thomas's face and met his eyes with hers. "I want this done. You can't understand what it is to lose a child."

Standing in his brother's kitchen, he thought of his students' parents over the years, how they frequently said to him, "You can't understand," preceded by, "You're not a parent . . ." and followed by, "I'm sorry, I know it sounds bad, but unless you're a parent . . ."

Jake, and Lisa Jay, and how many others had said that to him?

The toilet flushed. The faucet stopped running, and the door opened. Thomas watched his nephew walk across the kitchen. His body, solid and lean, already so tall, and the hairstyle he called a mini-afro—which puffed out from the sides of the stiff baseball cap floating on his head—made him seem even taller. A shade lighter than his red hat, the pinkness of his lips brightened the lower half of his tanned face, which had darkened in Colorado's springtime sun. Max's arms hung long at his sides, and his shoulders and upper arms were starting to show the muscle he'd built practicing Capoeira every day in the after-school program. After he'd crossed the full length of the kitchen, Max reached his arms around Thomas. "My parents are dead," he said. "I'm fucked."

Thomas wanted to kiss his nephew's face, squeeze him tight. Instead, he stood stiff, barely touching Max's shaking shoulders. Thomas stared at the bathroom door that Jake and Sheree, three months before, had held closed as Thomas tugged. He suddenly pictured Toby Jay coming back from the bathroom. If Thomas would've let him be, let the kids laugh, let Toby figure it out, pull up his own pants, he could hold his nephew now without worry, comfort him, like he'd comforted Jake when they were both children.

Thomas felt tingling in his cheeks and fingertips like he might faint. He'd been standing too long. Max finally released his grip and led Thomas to Jake and Sheree's bedroom. Five cardboard file boxes were lined up on the floor by the lower half of their bed, stripped of its sheets. Gerard and the others had packed the clothes into plastic donation bags and left them on the floor. "Look at all this shit," Max said.

"Language, Max," Thomas warned reflexively.

"Sorry," Max said, and sucked his lower lip into his mouth, rested it under his top row of teeth.

"Fuck it," Thomas said. "Swear all you want."

They laughed a little. Thomas plopped himself on the upper half of the bed first; then Max did the same. Dust floated in the light squeezing in from between the windows' metal blinds.

"Colleen told me that I shouldn't feel bad for laughing."

"She's right," Thomas said. "We need to laugh."

Max ran his fingers through his uncle's hair. "White people hair is so sad—so thin and straight, yours and Dads—not cute and curly like mine and Mom's. I miss them so much, Uncle Tommy."

Thomas pulled his nephew to him, held him tight as he cried.

God help the person or people, anyone, anywhere, if they ever questioned him about the way he touched his nephew. On the plane from San Francisco to Denver, Thomas had read and re-read his older brother's email, *Dear Thomas, Jake and Sheree requested that you take full custody of Max. Do you think this a good idea? I can't imagine how the timing of this—what it must be like for you—but you know my imagination has always had its limits. Of course, we're here to help. Please call. All Best, James.*

After a few minutes, Max moved, then stood up, grabbed a tissue from the box on the dresser, and blew his nose.

Even with its walls painted a warm sienna orangish-red, the room appeared sad without the bright comforter that Sheree had sewn out of the gold and blue kente cloth she'd purchased on "the dream trip" she'd taken with Maddy to Ghana.

"Those are yours, too," Max said, pointing to a stack of four white file boxes set off to the side.

Thomas grabbed the top box. Jake had assembled them when he thought cancer would win. One for James and each parent, two for Thomas, who couldn't stop thinking that Jake had been right during their argument. What a selfish indulgence, those months in San Francisco. He should've stayed with Jake and his family, moved to Colorado. *I could've been useful,* he thought, *helped Mom in the garden, Sheree in the salon, taken Max snowboarding, tutored him with his homework, helped Jake with his landscaping.* The boxes had all been neatly marked with a name in the blank square under the word CONTENTS. On one, Jake left out his *H. T O M A S,* like Manny had spelled his name when they first met. Thomas opened it.

There were old photo albums under a plastic bag full of loose snapshots from a ski weekend they'd shared right after the rehab, the one to celebrate Jake's engagement to Sheree. He opened the second box. A tracksuit. Several pairs of sunglasses in cases. A pocketknife and a couple of notebooks. Thomas opened the green spiral. Its cover contained an inside pocket holding an envelope. Thomas opened that, too, recognizing his own handwriting.

Max said, "My dad loved that letter."

Thomas looked at the address. A rehab in Minnesota.

"He read it to me about ten times. To me, it doesn't sound like you."

Dear Jake,

Remember our parents' creaky bed? In that house on that unlit street? I do. One night we were alone, holding each other tight in the middle of the coldest night of winter. Your ten-year-old body was all elbows and knees. You'd chewed and stretched the elastic cuffs of your long johns at the wrists. Chewing is what you did with worry. We worried Mom would not come home from work; worried that Dad and James had forgotten us since they each found new girlfriends.

That morning, while Mom slept, I'd layered you: thin socks under thick, cotton then wool then down. The small red needle in the thermometer buried below zero—bolted to the deck overlooking the yard sloping down to the stream where a bridge led to the woods—I can picture it all even though I left it so long ago.

There was talk of this cold breaking the record held in '81, when it'd reached thirty-five below. We hurled snowballs at the Ryans' mailbox while waiting for the bus.

I remember your eyes, like Dad's eyes, facing downward, you pinching your lip as you got on the bus.

That afternoon, the paperboy arrived after Mom left for work. He said, "Town Lake froze all the way to the bottom. No current, even underneath. Like a cube in an ice tray. The fish froze solid mid-swim!"

You gasped.

He said, "Don't worry, Jake. Come spring they'll thaw and swim again as if they'd only missed a blink."

Remember?

At bedtime, it was so cold, all we could do is huddle, hang on to each other. You gripped me so hard it hurt, and I prayed for summer to return, so we could swim at Town Lake, click rocks underwater.

Your hair smelled of wool cap. I rested against you, my front to your back, my mouth and nose against that triangular dip between

256

your head and neck. The same spot where Mom, when you were an infant, had taught James and me to protect your skull with a hand—said it was your soft spot, the place where your bones had yet to come together.

You woke up and couldn't get back to sleep.

"Think of summer," I said, "When we went swimming, clicking our rocks. Remember? The two of us, brothers underwater, where sound travels fast? Click click click, like I'M STILL HERE?"

Jake, I know I didn't say goodbye when I left for California. I know I haven't been a good brother. I still imagine us huddled together to keep warm in winter, clicking rocks underwater in summer. Do you?

I'M STILL HERE.

Get well soon. I'M STILL HERE.

Love,

Thomas.

Thomas folded the letter, slightly ashamed. Of what? The fact that he'd tried to be so poetic? Or how easy it was to see his own not-so-hidden plea—please Jake, stay alive for me? Or his earnestness? As an adult, Thomas had only been able to muster the courage to express any tenderness toward Jake if he were next to death. And even then, only in letters and texts. He put it back in the envelope, and then back into the pocket of the green notebook, and then back into the box on the bed. He looked at Max, who stared up into his uncle's face, just like Max's father had once done, just like Toby had done.

"Ready?" Max said.

Thomas took the keys out of his pocket. Placed them on top of the boxes, which he grabbed to bring to the car.

"I'm ready," Thomas said, remembering Town Lake, remembering writing the letter and running it to the mailbox in a fury, as if his brother's recovery had depended on it. Thomas remembered all of this, and Jake's birth, and Manny spelling his name without an *H*. He remembered all of this as Max stood there, as if waiting. Waiting for Uncle to say it again, this time to him. Say, I'm still here.

Chapter Twenty-One

Friday
March 28th, 2014

Sheree's brother Reginald called at six, startling Thomas awake, and invited him to meet at the King's Chef Diner at nine. Thomas had first met Reggie at Jake's and Sheree's wedding more than a dozen years back, but struggled to get to know him, and so Thomas was both delighted and surprised that he'd reached out. Before the memorial, it had been Christmastime the last time he'd heard from Sheree about her brother. A sink had gotten clogged at the salon, and Sheree complained that she'd lent her expensive electric snake to Reggie, but never got it back. Reginald had arranged with Maddy, not Sheree, the days and times he and Charlotte cared for Max during the cancer months, mostly when Thomas was in Portland. Max had spent the night with Reggie and Charlotte once in the few days that had passed since the memorial, but Maddy drove Max to Denver.

Thomas approached East Bijou Street. Compared to San Francisco, the streets in Colorado Springs spread wide, the sidewalks lacked pedestrians, the sky seemed enormous. He couldn't shake a chill, even after he'd zipped his hoodie over his thermal.

Reginald sat in a booth, his coffee cup blocking the lower half of his face. Reginald must've been in his early fifties but looked at least ten years younger with his full head of hair and taut skin.

A plate of toast and fried eggs sat in the middle of the table. In front of him, a waffle covered in syrupy strawberries and whipped cream. "Sit," he said as he got up and shook Thomas's hand.

As Thomas slid closer to the window in the booth's opposite bench, Reggie swallowed a bite. "Sorry," he said. "I hope you don't mind I ordered. Got a bit of everything. Happy to share."

"I'm sorry about your loss. About your sister," Thomas said, wanting to hug him. "I wish we could've spent more time together at the memorial."

"And I'm sorry about your brother," Reggie said, and stopped chewing. He looked up at Thomas; a constellation similar to Sheree's freckles followed the lines of his cheekbones.

"How's Charlotte?" Thomas asked about Reggie's wife. Thomas liked her too, but whatever tension Sheree had had with Reggie carried over.

"She's worried about Max like I suppose we all are. Working too much," Reggie said with a tone Thomas couldn't read. "The hospital always wants more for less," he said. Reggie cut through the golden waffle and dragged the forkful through the syrup. "We appreciated the memorial."

Thomas looked toward the counter. "Everything's a blur," he said. "Those two touched so many people's lives. I couldn't wrap my brain around it. I couldn't feel anything. Still in shock, I guess."

"Believe it or not," Reginald said, "I loved my sister." His eyes held light like topaz. Ice clinked against a glass somewhere, and Reggie's neck moved his head in a subtle *no*.

"I have no doubt," Thomas said.

The server, a woman with long blond hair in a net, interrupted, asked Reginald, "Did you order the eggs for your friend?" Then to Thomas, "Or can I add to the order?"

"Would you like a plate?" Reggie asked.

"Just coffee for me," Thomas said, his mind lingering on the word *friend*.

When she left, Reginald said, "I helped Sheree a lot before she met your brother in rehab. Before that, I picked her up after relapses I don't know how many times. Let her live with me.

Charlotte took care of her, too, you know. That's how I met Charlotte. During nursing school, she worked as an aide at one of Sheree's detox centers, way before your brother came onto the scene. Once Sheree got it together, she dropped us."

Reginald pushed the waffle plate into the middle. "Not that I could blame her. It's rough enough out there for everyone, but always being the newbie in school, sometimes the only Black kid and such. Sheree needed our mother. Our mom was sweet, they were close, and after Mom died it was hard for us to find sweetness. I used to believe in the tough love approach. It's how I was raised, military family and all. That didn't help me win her affections."

The whipped cream, which he'd scraped off the fruit, was slowly turning the syrup a caramel color. "Me and Charlotte have been married fifteen years. She's a nurse, like your mom, but Charlotte works in pediatrics. We live in a part of Denver that the white folks call 'up and coming,'" he said. "And it just so happens our district high school is in the top ten in the state."

Thomas already knew about Charlotte's job. "Sheree talked a bit about your mom," Thomas said. "I can only imagine how hard that must have been. But I'm not following your point about the neighborhood and school district."

"My point is that our apartment has an extra bedroom. And a courtyard with a lawn and benches and flowers. We know you've been named guardian. We know Sheree thought of you as the good uncle. Saint Thomas."

The syrup on Reggie's discarded plate looked so sweet, Thomas had to resist the urge to wipe his finger across the plate and put it in his mouth. Thomas tried to locate how he felt now that he understood why Reggie had called. Thomas picked up his napkin, unfolded it, placed it in his lap, took and released a breath. Calm. He felt calm. Relief.

The server arrived, placed the coffee and a tall glass of ice water on the table.

"We know about your unfortunate work circumstances," Reginald said.

Now, a swelling of nausea returned, under his ribs, above his guts. "We?"

"Charlotte and I," he said. "Did you get asked if the kid had a tight ass?" Reginald asked. Strawberry sauce made his lips shine.

Thomas's sight blurred at the edges, making Reggie's teeth seem less like several individual things and more like one: an oval, an aura. Since his move, Thomas started each day not thinking of Toby, the Jays, Country Day, his past. But each day something happened: a package, a phone call, a text, an email, a comment— shoving him back into it. Today it was Reggie's question. Its directness, seemed, on the surface, confrontational; but the tone carried more sympathy and curiosity—at least toward Thomas— than judgement. "Practically," Thomas said. "And a dozen or more questions just like it. How did you know?"

"Cops hate me most. All other brown people second. You third."

Thomas thought back to Sheree's reaction to Trayvon Martin, and each subsequent reaction to each subsequent murder, and how Thomas failed each time to offer his sister-in-law comfort. Now, sitting across from Reggie, he learned what he should've done all along: say the truth. "It's so fucked up. I got by for a long time, because, well . . ." Thomas hesitated. "Look at me. But after the ordeal, I thought about what the Stonewall rioters—Black, brown, trans, queer—must've endured."

"Passing is a double-edged sword. It gives an illusion of acceptance. Even with all that shit, Charlotte always wanted kids," Reggie said. A tiny clank of his knife sounded against the porcelain plate. "I thought I did, too—but not enough has changed—and I'm too mad. Can I ask you a question?"

"Of course," Thomas said.

"First let me say, Charlotte and I are married for insurance and tax reasons, but we don't believe in the institution. That's a white man's game, to think he owns another person or that another person needs to take his name. So, my question is, knowing what this world is, why would you ever become a parent or teacher? And married? Don't gay people hear the anti-gay-marriage

261

people's message? They're saying you can't have what we don't want. It baffles me to see gay men squawk about wanting the freedom to marry," he said, with a slight chuckle. "I get the equal rights part, but the rest of it? It seems everything is backwards. Fat geese are feasting on pâté as the pigs eat bacon. It's a mad fucking cow world."

Thomas smiled. "You can't have what I don't want. That's genius."

"Gay dudes and lesbians I knew back in the day were radical. They thought of kids and marriage and monogamy and suburbs as the trappings of the institutions that confined them. Little known fact: the first gay guy I knew? I caught him fucking my girlfriend. When I tried to beat him down, he floored me with some martial arts-style headlock and laughed. 'Yeah I'm a punk,' he said. 'But she likes me, and I like her and she's not yours.' When other guys called him a faggot, he said 'yes, and?' The 'and' wasn't a question. It was a statement. That man was downright badass. Not like those queens that Sheree has working at the salon with their neck rolling and tongue popping. Not that I mind that, either. I mean, I've met feminine gay men and transsexual people who are also radical, but most of the gay guys I see today? They all seem to me to be imitating Black women, but a version that doesn't even exist except for white people. That trope on what they call reality TV. But whose reality is it?"

The server appeared with a full pot of coffee, smiled at Reginald, balanced it over Thomas's cup, saw that it was already full, and left. Reginald pointed his fork at Thomas. "You had a Black boyfriend, didn't you?" he said. "Didn't Sheree tell me he was European? Your whole family got jungle fever?" He laughed quietly. "She does," Reggie said. "Miss Waitress over there was flirting up a storm before you arrived. I don't get how my sister could live here. This whole backassward town is full of women who want to fuck me then watch their husbands kill me for it. She's that KKK-type Christian. She'd burn us both at the stake."

Thomas sat still, thinking of Manny, of marriage.

"Back to Max," Reggie said. "Charlotte mentioned that you

might not need the responsibilities of a parent right now. You know," he said. "With your concerns. Charlotte is a good person, and that's the reason she believes that you're innocent. I'm an informed person. Openly gay men do not molest fourth graders, so that's how I know you're innocent." He took a bite of his toast, soaked at the center with butter. "But Max? He's already been through the wringer."

Thomas said, "When Jake told me he planned to designate me the just-in-case guardian, I agreed you have more to offer—even before the accusation had happened—but back then, it didn't seem a real possibility. Sheree had a scare here and there, but she was one of the healthiest people I know. It didn't seem possible." Thomas remembered the call from James telling him about the accident. "Jake thought . . ."

"I know," Reggie said, after taking a sip of his water, "Sheree insisted. I know Jake liked me. He and I could've been friends. But if you have any hesitation, and want our help, I think we could convince a judge," he said, "to have Max come to us. You and your mom would refuse custody. I'm Black." Reginald broke the egg's yolk open with his fork. A tiny bit of liquid leaked out from the orange circle. He dipped the triangle of toast in it.

"And?" Thomas said.

"Tell me a nice Christian judge is going to have a problem allowing Max, also Black, to live with me and Charlotte. In his eyes, you're a gay dude who got fired for child fondling, and I'm a married, employed Black man with no criminal record. He'll think I'm the guy who will protect Max from a menace like you. Just like he'd think you could protect your nieces from a menace like me. You can't escape this shit. Sorry, Thomas. I guess I'm concerned how the past will affect Max. Do you think you can keep a lid on the accusation? Keep his friends from finding out?"

"Well," Thomas said, "I have all the documentation that shows how hard they tried to find something, if I ever need to use it as a way out."

"Must be nice to have a way out," Reggie said. "Sheree believed there was a way out. She loved your brother and mother, but she also saw them as a ticket out of the shit of her childhood, which is just the shit of this nation, Black president and all. She often thought she was winning, but each time something broke through the illusion, she'd put it on me. I know she cast me as the troubled, angry, no-good brother, but I wasn't. Without drugs, without me, she'd have gone nuts. She needed a place to put her pain."

Moments from those town halls at Country Day came to mind along with too many metaphors. How awful to be a scapegoat or, as Jerome said, the pariah, a dumpster for others' confusion and pain.

"Liberals think that we're post-race now because of Obama—and there are things to appreciate about him—but no single individual is a savior. His cabinet is made up of people for whom the system worked. Few of the people who were truly suffering before. And they're suffering less now."

"Reggie?" Thomas asked. "Do you and Charlotte want to adopt Max?"

"No," Reginald said. "And I don't want to run for office either, so I need to quit criticizing. Mark my words, though. Almost every African American and homosexual I know thinks we're in a moment of progress. But you watch. There will be backlash, my friend."

"Then, what?" Thomas asked. "If you don't want to raise Max, why did you bring me here?"

"It's not that we don't want to, it's that we understand the complexities, and so we're here to offer. To give you choices. To let you know that if you do adopt him, it's not because you're some hero, or that you must. And to warn you about what will likely happen in case it hasn't already occurred to you. If you succeed in adopting him, Charlotte and I insist on being a regular and central part of his life. Sheree's old beefs need to be buried with all the rest." Reginald wiped his forehead and mouth with the paper napkin and placed it in the center of the table. He took another bite of his toast, which he stacked with the rest of the fried egg. "I'm still pissed at my sister for her shitty treatment of me. It makes it difficult to grieve, but I like to imagine that if she had lived long enough, I would've received my amends, too. I want a regular relationship with her son."

"Makes sense," Thomas said. "You've given me much to think about. You're generous. I didn't ask to be Max's godfather," Thomas said. "But I am. And I promised my brother and your sister."

Reggie motioned to the server to bring the check.

Chapter Twenty-Two

Saturday
March 29th, 2014

Yesterday, as the sun climbed toward the middle of the sky, Thomas had stood in the King's Chef Diner parking lot and wondered about his limit. What, exactly, would constitute too much? He stood by the door of his rental car and watched Reginald take a left out onto East Bijou toward I-25 where a truck driver had fallen asleep and killed his brother and Reggie's sister. Thomas had walked back into the diner. Sat down in the same booth. Ordered two plates. One with eggs over-easy, hash browns and white toast, and also a waffle with strawberries and cream.

The next morning Reginald called. "Tommy?"

After they'd spoken, Thomas walked to the bench in his mom's garden. A branch fell from the tree above him, and hit him on the head, like the acorn from Chicken Little.

The sky was falling down.

Reggie's voice and cadence brought back a visceral memory of Sheree. He had said, "Hard to believe they're gone for good."

The phrase *my brother is gone for good* kept playing.

Language always failed.

Having seen his brother's body bounce back from heroin

addiction and cancer treatment, Thomas couldn't help but believe Jake invincible. How could he be gone for good? Earlier, Maddy had got up from bed to make oatmeal but didn't eat any. She returned to the infomercial playing on mute from the TV, her eyes wide, staring not at the TV, but at the ceiling, occasionally blinking.

Thomas changed her water glass on the bedside table next to the photo of her as a little girl on her family's farm in Wisconsin. Maddy had always been the supreme realist, a woman who grew up with scorched and flooded crops, livestock diseases, and low yields. Not only could she cope with life's challenges, she often imagined and executed brilliant contingency plans. And yet she suffered periods of depression so intense that the only thing she could do besides work was sleep or lie on her back and stare.

Thomas always got up.

This morning he had made coffee and warmed the oatmeal Maddy left covered on the stove. He called Jerome. He'd slept through last night, a gift, the privilege of options. As he brushed his teeth and washed his face, he'd conjured do-over scenarios of what he would've said to Reggie at the diner. He wished he would've interrupted Reginald to say, "You're right. You're right you're right you're right." He closed Maddy's medicine cabinet, went downstairs to the basement, where Max had a room, a TV, and a video game console. "I don't want to leave The Springs," Max said, video-chatting with his best friend.

"Tell them," his friend said.

Thomas listened for a while before sneaking back upstairs with a pit in his stomach. Then he went to the garden. Then the branch landed, hard, on his head.

The sky is falling down.

Now as he surveyed his mom's plot, a mountain bluebird landed on the top of a PVC pipe caging her tomato vines. Electric blue with black eyes, it appeared to stare at Thomas. The smell of loam and the abundance of the ripened tomatoes, thriving, despite their neglect, all so gorgeous. Evidence of the indifference of the natural world, which continues, no matter who dies, loses a job, becomes a dad. Thomas checked the charge on the phone.

Opened his photo folder. Looked at the first pictures he'd taken of his new place in San Francisco. His new desk and old desk chair looked so good before he had decided to forgo an office for a guest room. He closed the file and checked the ringer to make sure it was on.

He rested his head against the tree, closed his eyes, and listened to the birds and the sound of a car passing.

The phone rang.

Jerome said he'd reviewed all the documentation around his brother's passing and said it should be a smooth enough ride to adopt Max. He asked Thomas how things were going.

"I'll tell you, but first ask me any other question. Anything at all unless it's about dead siblings."

"Meet or be: Diana Ross and Hillary Clinton?" Jerome said.

"Easy," Thomas said. "Meet Hillary, so I could be Diana the day she sang in Central Park in the rain."

"Gandhi or Jesus?" Jerome said.

"Neither," Thomas said. "I wouldn't want to meet or be either. But I'd go to hear them speak publicly then send them thank you notes after, and hope they'd write back."

"That's not an option. You have to choose."

"I have one for you: Gloria Steinem or Gloria Allred?"

Silence, except for a pair of bluebirds. A second had just landed near the first, and the two engaged in soft, repetitious warbling.

"Meet or be?" Thomas said.

"Wow," Jerome said. "This is intense. Meet Allred and be Steinem."

The second bluebird now pecked at the plastic covering the PVC as it inched closer to the first. The newer one let out soft nasal notes, which sounded like *tew*, and the tomato defender released high-pitched tink tink tinks. "Too late. You're already Allred. I'm no fool. No one has ever seen you two in the same room."

"There's no hiding from you," Jerome said, and laughed. "Now tell me how you're doing."

"I've been better," Thomas said.

"What's up?" Jerome asked.

"My sister-in-law's brother Reginald was left nothing, including zero custody of Max. I had breakfast with him yesterday and a long talk with him this morning, and I think we should work in a clause in the adoption. Something that offers them extended periods of time, names them as capable and willing to have full custody as well as be guardians in case something happens to me. They don't even want it to be mandatory. They ideally want Max to choose, but I think it should be written in somehow, so if Max wanted to spend the summers with them it will appear in documents." The birds flew away; the sounds of their argument had been replaced by the slap of plastic in the wind. "To be honest, I'm thinking of asking them to raise Max from the get-go. Not just because they offered. Because Reggie might be a better-suited dad. Of course, I have to talk to Max."

"Are you kidding me?" Jerome said.

"Max is Black," Thomas said.

Pause. "Thomas? You there?"

"Yes, I said Max is Black."

Maddy's neighbor caught Thomas looking in his direction and waved.

"Yeah. So?" Jerome asked as Thomas waved back.

"I remember when the report of Trayvon Martin first broke," Thomas said. "Seeing that picture. The image of him wearing that red tee-shirt—a happy kid with the grin and eyes of a person who knows he's loved. I imagined him on Country Day's zip line, flying through the air, laughing on his way to meet his classmates. I read somewhere he loved airplanes. Max will be Trayvon's age in four years. Max is so damn tall. He already looks like a man. He wears hoodies and those slouchy pants and carries a skateboard everywhere he goes." Thomas looked over his shoulder toward Maddy's side door, making sure Max hadn't come outside.

"Trayvon had a Black dad," Jerome said. "It's so awful to say, Thomas, but there are no guarantees. You should know that. We don't transcend difficulties by avoidance. We fight. We build. Bridge communities. No doubt Max needs Black role models. Of course, you've got to ask for help."

"How is a child supposed to transcend the truth of history? A loaded gun? With community and role models?" The sunlight got caught in the mirrored discs Maddy had hung in the lemon tree to repel woodpeckers. "I've been researching. San Francisco is more segregated now than when I lived there last time. Manny just started a job in the city. He wears a lab coat with a photo ID pinned to his chest that states clearly, he's a goddamn molecular biologist. An immunologist. And a white colleague wearing the same coat asked him to take out the trash. Whenever Manny was late, I worried," Thomas said. "And he's a grown man. How will I protect Max? Me? A single white guy? Gay? With a teenage Black kid? He'll grow up to hate me. What if he suspects I touched Toby? What if he's ashamed of me?"

"Country Day has taken its toll, Thomas. That's expected. But you're doing exactly what they want you to do, and that's optional. This culture wants us to give up on each other. Step aside. The country is racist. I can talk to Sheree's brother and his partner, and we'll work something out, but there's no reason not to adopt your nephew."

Thomas got up from the bench, made his way to the end of his mother's driveway as he pictured Max walking through San Francisco wearing earphones and a hoodie and wished he'd been a better brother-in-law to Sheree. Now that he faced the responsibility for his nephew, he could see. The range of the Rockies spread across the horizon, with Red Rock Canyon in the foreground. Somehow, he wanted to believe it could protect his brother's son.

"I made the choice to leave Country Day, Jerome. I made the choice to leave. It had nothing to do with them." Thomas wondered what would happen if he dug in the garden, if the soil in this dry town held any moisture at all, six thousand feet above sea level, six thousand feet closer to the sun than San Francisco, where a patch of dry grass could not be found.

"You can say that to me," Jerome said. "You're paying me, so I'll listen to whatever you want to say. The clock is on, and I'm billing you. But don't fool yourself. You're terrified of Country Day folks and the others like them. You sat in that room, staring up at the Jays, looking like a kid sent to his room by his parents. From the start, we both knew the only reason she accused you of molesting her kid. He was more certain of your silence than her loyalty, Thomas. I had that other guy ready to testify about Conrad Jay."

"I was thinking about Toby," Thomas said. "Of my students."

"No. You were thinking of yourself. I sat next to you every minute of those meetings and that asinine town hall. You and the rest of them convincing yourselves you were all protecting children. Do you know what you all were doing, Thomas? You were helping those kids form the belief that gay people molest children by nature of being gay. You helped them create yet another generation of bigoted idiots."

Thomas felt light-headed, staring at the red rock against the mountains, just like when he climbed those five thousand stairs up to the peak of the Manitou Incline with Jake. He'd planned on running, but couldn't, because of the altitude, and had to walk. Jake had said, "Mother Nature is stronger than all of us."

Thomas said, "I have a family who loves me, worries about me, as I worried about Manny. And I have a nephew who has a life here in Colorado who doesn't want to move. He's almost a teenager, and he wants to be here, with his friends. He's already lost so much. Now I'm supposed to make him move? When I'm not even sure I want to take him?"

"Thomas," Jerome said.

"No," Thomas said. "Don't give me another lecture. I'm sorry if your family disowned you. I am. I admire you. I've finally come to realize how conflicted I've always been, not about being gay. I may never be a Larry Kramer-type—we need him, and we need you, and I love him, and I love you—but you're not me. And not because I hate myself but because it's not my nature. I'm starting to see myself clearly. I've spent a lot of time with my mom, and a lot of people think she's a recluse or a badass. She's not. She's gentle and complicated and conciliatory. She loves her family. She forgives. She wants individuals to go about their day the way they want to go about it. I want to be like her."

A long pause. Thomas pulled his phone from his face to see if Jerome had hung up, but the counter that logged the duration of the call continued ticking.

"Jerome?" he said.

"I'll write something up, send it over."

Thomas turned off the phone, closed his eyes, and remembered the rest of that day hiking with Jake. The two had run down the incline. Jake had warned him and offered to stop at the shoe shop to buy a pair of trail runners with traction, but Thomas refused. "I'll be fine with these," Thomas said, pulling on his street runners.

At the top, Thomas told Jake to take the lead. Halfway down, Thomas slipped, fell, and rolled quite a distance. By the time he stopped, he was pretty scraped up. Rocks and earth, pressed in deep, at least through the first few layers of skin on his knees. Thomas hoisted himself back up, his knees looking like water balloons. Just as Thomas had finished pouring what little water he had left onto the worst part of the wounds, Jake appeared around the bend.

"There you are," Jake said. "Shit. We should've gotten the shoes." He put one arm at Thomas's neck and the other under his knees, picked him up and walked him down the side of a trail. The Springs spread out in front of the brothers, desert-like, as the sun hit the dusty haze. In Jake's arms, Thomas could see the red earth in the creases in his brother's neck around the greening-black tattoo script spelling his wife's and son's names. Sweat had dampened his scalp and separated his hair into little spears. Jake had fewer freckles than James, but ten times the number as Thomas. They spread out on Jake's shoulders and upper back like fistfuls of pennies that had been thrown into a shallow fountain.

Thomas weighed nearly a hundred and ninety pounds, and it took a good five minutes to get to the clearing near the base of the mountain. They'd jostled, but Jake never lost his balance, never let Thomas down. At the car, Jake leaned Thomas into the driver's door, pulled a packet from his glove box, unfolded the small square until it became a rectangle. He used it to wipe the larger pieces sticking to Thomas's broken skin.

Thomas couldn't bear Jake touching his body and blood. It felt too close, too intimate. If he allowed himself to be that vulnerable, if he opened that hatch, what else would come out?

"Stings that bad?" Jake asked.

"Worse," he said. High from pain and lack of oxygen, Thomas had said, "I'm good," and ambled to the passenger door alone.

When he came inside, Thomas was surprised to see Maddy up and about.

"Your turn," Maddy said. "I heard you on your phone out there. You look like shit. Lie down, and I'll bring you something cool to drink. Max is going to Corey's house."

"He wants to stay here," Thomas said, looking at his mom, the light of the refrigerator glowing off her white bathrobe. "In Colorado Springs."

"That's not yours to worry about right now," Maddy said, putting the two-liter of soda on the counter next to the ice tray and glass.

Thomas made his way to Maddy's guest room. Fully dressed, he squeezed into the twin bed, its sheets tight. Soon Maddy came in, holding a glass sizzling with carbonation. "I only had diet, but thought you might like it," she said.

Thomas finished the entire glass.

"Be or meet?" Thomas asked, as Maddy squeezed onto the bed next to him. "Jesus or Gandhi?"

She fished a piece of ice out of the glass. "Meet Gandhi and be Jesus. Definitely," she said, putting the ice cube into her mouth. "First," she said, her cheek bulging, "I'd listen to Gandhi's advice, and then I'd use my Jesus powers to enact it."

"What do you think Gandhi would tell you?" Thomas asked.

"Who knows," she said, slowly. "Probably to laugh."

"Come on," Thomas said. "You don't need a miracle to laugh."

"You don't?" Maddy said. She crunched the ice and swallowed.

Chapter Twenty-Three

Friday
June 13th, 2014

He could hardly believe that they had almost finished packing, had a date, and bought the tickets, the decision final. Max would move to San Francisco.

A couple of weeks ago, while going through piles of his parents' stuff, Max found one of his dad's journals, and he gave it to Thomas, saying, "I don't think I'm ready for this."

Thomas wasn't ready either and put it in the drawer in the bedside table in the guest room at Maddy's, where he'd just found it. He opened to the first page.

August 20th.

The speaker's name was Sky. Pretty. In that too-skinny way. With raccoon eyes. Her mascara looked like she started applying it years ago and had been adding a layer every day since. She talked about God not giving us more than we can handle. "He didn't bring me this far to drop me now," she said.

Of course, I want to believe her. My MRI is next week.

She looked familiar. My best guess is the 7:30 Clean and Serene NA meeting at the Presbyterian Church on 10th and Pueblo, a meeting I attended years ago.

She talked about being sober sixteen years when she decided to use again. The same old story: addict gets sober, gets her life back, makes money, falls in love with a user, stops going to meetings. While doing laundry, Sky said, she fished a baggie of coke out of her boyfriend's jeans, just a couple bumps, and snorted it, without thinking, standing over the washing machine.

Thomas looked out the window of Maddy's small guest room, past the open slats of the blinds, past the neighbor's fence, over his roof to the streetlight that had just turned on.

On her drive to score more, she hit a pedestrian and killed her. It would've happened to anyone, using or not, Sky said, because the lady jumped suddenly into traffic. There were witnesses.

The cops saw the empty baggie on her car's dash and found more empty bags in the ashtray. Sky admitted to being under the influence of an illegal narcotic before thinking to call a lawyer. Two priors for possession and a third for solicitation.

Now she's one year clean, and waiting for her trial date for manslaughter, not criminal negligence. "The victim's family has a good attorney," Sky said. "Being high may not have caused the accident, but I would have never taken out the car without the phenomenon of craving."

Thomas felt. He felt for Sky, felt for his brother who'd listened so carefully to this woman, felt his own missing. He missed his brother, missed all they never spoke of, missed parts of Jake's life.

Sheree and I haven't relapsed—at least since we met—but we could, either one of us. Our histories prove that. Max, has never seen either of us drunk or high. Still, we've gotten grouchy with the meetings and people in them. The saintly & idiotic addicts in those chairs in those church basements are either driving us nuts or saving our lives. And it's hard to tell who is who and which is which.

Sky's share snapped me back into place, made me grateful that

I'm not facing active addiction and cancer at the same time. But something about her seemed phony.

The speaker-seekers love stories like hers. The ones awaiting trial. Or like mine. Sober addicts with cancer. Or Sheree's, because she's got HIV. Is it human nature to get off on others' suffering? The more extreme and/or imminent, the better the story. Good stuff for newcomers.

I've been asked to speak at a lot of meetings lately. In NA it's tough to distinguish between someone undergoing chemotherapy and someone just back from a run on crystal or crank or heroin. People come and welcome me like they did when I was new. Give me their numbers. Ask me if I have a sponsor. When I get up there and say I have thirteen years clean time and that I'm in treatment for cancer, jaws drop. After I catalog my treatment woes and wax on about how "you people show me I don't have to pick up a drug or drink no matter what," men with their gang symbols tattooed on their faces and women who knowingly let their dealers fuck their own children start to cry. Then, high from playing hero, I come home and sign on to CaringBridge, and say that each step of my cancer treatment is a minor hurdle to jump over because of "your loving support."

The truth? I refused to drink water after the doctor warned me that dehydration caused kidney failure. I threw sliced cantaloupe across the kitchen at Sheree. I flipped off my own son when he told me to man up and do what I'm told. Forget how I've treated my mother. There's a special place in hell reserved for assholes like me who put their mothers through the worry I've caused Maddy.

After I got home from the meeting, Sheree came and pulled the plug from the computer monitor before she left for work. She said, "I'll fucking blow up the internet if you don't' get real and start showing those outside your inner circle your cowardice and self-pity. We deserve some of the goodness you give them, and they can have some of the bullshit you save for us."

Thomas looked up, felt in the tightness of his neck and throat how much he missed Sheree. What an exceptional sister-in-law he'd had. He thought of Reggie, how much he would have liked his sister, and how she would have appreciated her brother's mind, his thoughts. Thomas had seen Reggie and Charlotte, too, a handful of times now, when he'd dropped Max at their place and stayed for breakfast or lunch. A day didn't go by without Thomas thinking about his and Reggie's talk at the diner. After each visit, he wondered just how incredible their bond could've been, Reggie's and Sheree's, if their histories hadn't blocked them from knowing what was good about the other. He rubbed his palms on the afghan, then continued to read.

I called a family meeting and told Max I was afraid the cancer was winning, that the treatment would kill me. I told him how badly I wanted to see him grow up. That I was proud of him. Poor kid. He took my hand.

Sheree told me to save the come-to-Jesus speech I'd prepared for her and stop acting like an a-hole. "If you're sorry and want to show it, take your medicine when you're constipated. If it hurts to drink, hook up your IV. And if you're so worried what'll happen if you don't make it, write a will."

That's what got us thinking about Thomas. While it didn't alleviate all my fears, it felt good to get it down on paper. That we wanted Thomas to raise Max if something happened. Now it's signed and sealed. On his last visit, Thomas let Max read him his last three school reports—word by word. He took him to the Cadet Chapel at the Air Force Academy (again), and to the zoo (again) to see the elephants and giraffes.

Who am I to judge? I wished Sky would have broken down. Screamed "why"? Thrown rocks at the church's stained glass. Admitted that she has no idea if God exists. To me, that would be more honest than her measured monologue, her healthy and groomed hair.

When Sky finished, everyone else was crying. Sheree leaned over, whispered into my ear, "Wow. Look at these suckers. That was the least moving pile of happy horseshit I've ever heard."

Sheree went up and got in line to thank Sky for her share. I

*went out to the parking lot to call Thomas. I got his voicemail.
Left him a message to call us back.*

*We just got home. I'm writing this instead of posting on Car-
ingBridge. Sheree's right. I need to talk about being scared, and
when Thomas calls back, I will.*

Thomas closed his brother's journal, got up and went to the
kitchen.

"Can you do it?" he asked his mom, who was drinking coffee
and playing online Scrabble on her tablet at the table.

"What?" she asked.

"Raise Max. It's only five years. If he stays here, he won't have
to make new friends. Or switch schools. Or choose between
uncles. Reginald and Charlotte are close by. I can stay, get an
apartment."

"No," she said, looking up from her game. "I can't, Thomas.
What makes you think I could do a better job than you?"

"For one thing," Thomas said, sitting down next to his mother,
"you're straight."

"Oh, Thomas. Stop acting like some wounded child just because you're gay," she said, reaching over and taking his hand for
a moment. "Somewhere along the way you conflated your self-
imposed exile with others' banishment. My lesbo aunt raised a
household full of kids. Besides, it's said and done and signed and
in motion. And I'm tired of raising children. I never wanted them
in the first place."

"Ouch," Thomas said.

"For Christ's sake, Tommy, I'm not saying I'm sorry I had you,"
Maddy said, grabbing her coffee mug. "I love you, okay? Is that
what you want to hear? Because it is, in fact, true." She took a
sip from the mug. "But it's also true that I hated being a suburban
housewife and soccer mom. And it has taken me all these years
to forgive myself for living the life I was expected to. Now I'm
trying to forgive myself for getting on that roller coaster praying
Jake would've never been born. I've spent my life superstitious
and guilty, believing his addictions were caused by my wish to

278

miscarry. I'll be damned if I'll sign up for another five years of the duties of motherhood. I love Max, Thomas. As much as you do. But I don't want another high school kid in my house. I get dizzy now, and my eyesight is going. I live with the dark periods because the medication flattens me out. I don't feel safe driving at night. I've lived with addicts for twenty years now, and with his parents' genes, Max might develop problems."

"What if Jake had said he wanted you to raise Max? Then what?"

"He asked me. He's the only one who ever asked me anything, Thomas. I told him I didn't want to, and he listened. Why do you think I'm so upset that he's dead?"

Thomas looked at his mom's face, the space between her two front teeth, the pale blue of her eyes, and the rounded tip of her nose.

"You need to buck up," she said. "You're the one who has always wanted a family and to be a parent. Jake was a great dad, but Max was an accident. And James? He's done well to provide for the girls, but you're the one who has always loved kids, Thomas. You became a teacher. Some of us are meant to be parents and some of us aren't. You are."

"I'm afraid," Thomas said.

"Welcome to the club, kiddo," she said, swiping her tablet's screen. "Of course, you are. I was terrified after I got pregnant. Each time more afraid, not less," Maddy said, looked at Thomas. "You should be afraid. You have to squeeze out a thirteen-year-old."

"What about the accusation?" Thomas asked.

"What about it? You act as if it's a person. Or a thing. It's not. It was an event. A misunderstanding. It's over."

"Aunt Eunice was a lesbian?"

"She had a lifelong affair with her childhood best friend. The two were a couple for sixty years. Both had families and husbands. They needed kids to help on the farm and to care for them when they got old. They were good to their families but loved each other. It was simple. People talked, but they didn't look for the neighbors or their husbands' or their kids' or the church's approval. Others fell into place."

"If we all did that, there'd be chaos," Thomas said.

"There's chaos anyway, Thomas," Maddy said. "Everywhere. None of us counted on this mess. You've waited your whole life to be chosen. Time to step up."

A Spiderman action hero slammed into the support beam and fell to the floor. Max picked it up, walked across the room, and refastened its hand to the higher end of the zip wire mounted to a second beam. It slid down the taut wire and crashed again.

Bruce Lee was up next.

Thomas said, "Did your dad put that up?"

"No," Max said. "I did. Grandma helped." He molded clay into what looked like snow boots around Bruce Lee's feet. "Makes him go faster."

"How do you keep from decapitating yourself at night?" Thomas asked, stacking giant Legos at the base of the beam where the lower end of the wire was attached.

"It unhooks," Max said. "I take it down before I go to bed. Don't lock the Legos. If you want to be useful, stack them on their bare sides."

"How was your first official day of summer vacation?" Thomas asked, unlocking the Lego pairs, restacking them as instructed.

"Fine. Corey's mom took us to the movies. At least she lets us see the action stuff. You're always trying to get us to go to your depressing documentaries."

"Hey," Thomas said, and smiled. "I thought you liked the movies we see."

"No one does," Max said. "My dad and mom hated them but went because that's what you do when you love someone."

Thomas looked at his nephew, so comfortable speaking to adults, so nonchalant, so much like his parents, so unlike himself.

"I overheard you talking to Corey," Thomas said. "You said you didn't want to go to San Francisco. Is that why you're angry?"

Max sat on the braided rug spread out on Maddy's basement-turned-Max's-room floor and leaned into the couch with the action figure and clay. Thomas stood with his back to the television.

"Try and stack them higher than the place where the wire goes in," Max said. "Why were you spying?"

"I didn't mean to," Thomas said. "I came down for something else. You didn't hear me."

"You could've announced yourself."

"Maybe you're right."

"What do you expect? Of course, I want to stay here. All my friends are in the Springs. So is my shrink."

"I know," Thomas said. "But school doesn't start until the end of August. We can trade the tickets if you're not ready. You can stay here for the rest of the summer. We can bring you to Dr. Colleen as many times as you want before we leave. There's already a computer at your desk in San Francisco for video sessions."

Max didn't look up from the clay. Now he was molding the doll's second foot. "I have my own laptop." Max got up. "I can tell you don't want me to come." Spiderman's torso was hidden under Max's tightened fist.

"I have doubts, but not about you. About me," Thomas said.

"I'm like, twelve. You're worried about you? You do realize that both of my parents are dead?" Max struggled to get the paper clip out of the hole he'd pierced through Spiderman's hand, but he persisted, not looking up. "Corey's folks were foster parents. He thinks they're still licensed and everything. They could use the money, and I'm already over there all the time."

"It's not like that," Thomas said, fixing his stare on Max.

"I know why you left Portland," Max said. "Dad told me. Grandma says you're acting like you did it when you didn't. And now you don't want to be around kids anymore." Max tried forcing the paper clip but couldn't get it to go through Bruce Lee's palm. "You've been different around me this last year. Like you're a big coward."

For the first time, Thomas felt powerlessness in the face of a child. He started toward Max's corner of the room, forgetting about the wire. It startled him, the feel of the wire across his cheek. He tasted salt and felt a sting on his lip.

"You're not bleeding," Max said. "But my zip line. Please tighten it?"

Thomas did what he was told. He dropped the Legos he had pressed to his chest and went to the hook near where the wire now slacked.

"Oh my god, Fluff. Were you coming for me?"

"You think I'd do that?" Thomas said, winding the wire around a screw.

"That would be awesome," Max said, smiling like he'd just landed a new trick on his skateboard.

"Your Uncle Reggie and Aunt Charlotte will adopt you before anyone would let you go into the foster system. There's a pin over there," Thomas said. "By the newspapers."

Max went to the fireplace and took the safety pin from the stack of newspapers under the mantle. "I love Uncle Reggie. Aunt Charlotte is nice, but she works a lot and is close with her own nieces and nephews. They caught me surfing porn on Uncle Reggie's computer and freaked out."

"Porn?" Thomas asked.

"I saw something that made me curious and clicked. Unks, I'm not afraid of sex," Max said. "Kids my age get STDs. Every year there are pregnant girls in the sixth grade. My parents told me about sex in the first grade, taught me how to protect myself from predators."

Thomas cringed, waited for the feeling to pass. "What about a gay parent?" Thomas asked, moving away from the finished stack.

"You're my uncle, not my dad. You wouldn't be my parent; you'd be my guardian." Max pulled the safety pin out from Bruce's hand and threaded in the paperclip. "One of my friends has two moms. It's not like you're the only gay person on earth."

"True," Thomas said. "On both counts."

"Think about it, Uncle Thomas. My mom had HIV, and I grew up in a hair salon."

"You're way ahead of me," Thomas said.

"Move over," Max said, waving Thomas away from the Lego tower. "Now start the countdown!"

"Three," Thomas said. "Two. One."

Max sent Bruce Lee sliding. A much more satisfying crash sounded than Thomas expected, and the blocks went flying. "You have more reasons to love yourself than anyone I know. You got money, your family adores you. Shit, I adore you. I love the hell out of you. My dad thought you were a superhero, but can I be honest?"

"Thank you. But?" Thomas said.

"A superhero turns their freak into strength." Max looked up. "They don't hide."

The light from the small basement windows started to fade. Thomas reached for the switch on the wall, turned on the lamp. Never had he seen things so clearly.

Thomas arranged for Nesta to move, too, but his bones protested, and Max thought it better that he stay. The first Wednesday evening of July, Corey, Gerard and Nesta waited on the front steps of Max's house when he and Thomas arrived to say good-bye. Nesta lumbered over to Max, who squatted down to let the old dog lick his face in front of the FOR SALE sign. "I'll take good care of him," Gerard said to Max. "I've known you both since you were pups."

Corey held a blue and white neck pillow that he extended toward Max. It had *COLORADO* written across it, a red *C* with a big yellow dot in the middle.

"See you guys in an hour."

Thomas parked close to the sports field for the Colorado School for the Deaf and Blind, which took up several lots across from Jake and Sheree's. As Thomas shut the hatchback, he saw a lone runner circling. A yellow handrail ran the length of the track. When Jake and Sheree had first moved to the house, Thomas, not knowing anything about the school, had used their track for an afternoon run, but didn't register the rail as anything but a design choice. When a second runner veered slightly too close to his lane, threatening to cut him off, Thomas said "Hey," to the young woman. "Watch it."

"I can't," she'd said. "I'm blind."

Later, in Boulder Park, on Memorial Hospital's campus, Thomas walked by the swing where he'd pushed Max as a baby. How he missed his baby brother Jake. He sat for a moment on the bench and looked up at the Cancer Center, took out his phone, made a donation in Jake's name. The Rockies looked too beautiful, like a masterfully painted backdrop on a theater set. Max texted that he'd broken into the house to see it one last time and that Gerard would take them to Taco Star, then meet him back at Grandma's.

Chapter Twenty-Four

Early to Mid-July, 2014

They now lived on a fault line.

James rented a fully furnished apartment two blocks from Thomas's place, then sent out an email with a link to pictures and invited everyone on "Team Max" to come and go as they pleased.

Everyone came.

Reggie, Charlotte and the McGurrins ate a cow's worth of hamburger during their first week in San Francisco, starting with their unplanned, accidental July 4th barbecue. Only after hearing firecrackers go off did they realize. The next morning, Thomas tacked a huge calendar to the wall behind Max's desk, a hard copy of the Team's online version of Max's SF agenda. Sundays were his day off. Monday through Saturday he was entitled to one "I can't today." He could use it for any reason: to sleep, to stay home and veg, to space out on video games.

When he cried, Max either wanted Maddy or Thomas to hold him, stay close until it passed—or he didn't want to be touched at all. Max's sobs shook his body, and Thomas would rub his back or pace outside his room, worried his nephew might choke. His cousins nudged Max until he joined them on ranger-guided tours of Northern California's state parks.

Charlotte and Reggie insisted on booking their own hotel but came around every day. Twice a day, on average, Thomas regretted the choice to live with Max, missed his life and the freedom that had come with it in Portland. Max's teenaged moodiness, his defiance, the testing, all the acting out—it reminded him too much of the chaos of sharing space with James as a teenager. The past seemed more tolerable than the present, with the sock-soaking puddles of water on the kitchen and bathroom floors, the towels not hung up to dry and their musty, level-ten stink. Stench everywhere: Max's shoes, socks, hat, bedroom.

Thomas confessed his frustration to Reggie who laughed and said, "It's hard enough to deal with walking a dog four times a day, let alone a human in your house. Let us entertain him tonight." Reggie and Max took long walks to the water while Charlotte and Maddy shared opinions of male doctors.

Mel booked time with Max for a day trip to her studio, where one of the animators asked to capture video of him running. "My first paid gig as an actor," he reported. "They wanted to capture the movement of my hair!" In the sound studio, Max read real lines of an actual script for a real director. After coaching Max, she said he had some skills.

Stuart took Max to The Exploratorium. After a full day at the exhibits, they dipped sushi into wasabi and soy and cleansed their pallets with pickled ginger in the museum's fancy cafeteria overlooking the Bay. "Grampa bought me, like, eighty bucks' worth of rolls," Max bragged.

Dana had befriended stepmom Dot, and the two took Max to gather stuff to design his room. Reggie and James brought Max to the rodeo at the Cow Palace, to a Giants game (Max talked more about the nachos than the baseball), and to Golden Gate Fields in Berkeley to watch horse races. Thomas took James out for Indian food at his favorite spot on Chestnut. The brothers toasted Jake with cheap, sweet wine that cut the heat of the fish curry and ginger mussels and vegetable vindaloo that they'd spooned to their plates from silver bowls.

"Listen," James said, a bit drunk. "I wondered about you taking Max. Not because of the shit that went down at Town and Country."

"Country Day," Thomas said, sipping his wine.

"Shit," James said, and laughed. "It's just you were so used to a certain kind of life, and I always envied your freedom. Over the years of your summer visits, just hearing about what you'd do during the day, watching you travel with Dana. You had it made. You'd sweep in, collect the admiration of everyone, and sweep out."

"Swoop," Thomas said. "I'd swoop in and out."

"Wait. You never swept?" James asked, and they laughed again.

James's eyes were an intense blue, like Thomas remembered his high school mate Chad's, but softer, a blue easily found: water, sky, morning glories.

"Here's to fatherhood," James said, and the two clicked glasses.

"Max made it very clear I'm not his father. Sometimes I can't fucking stand him. Any advice?"

When he asked, Thomas expected the usual: something sarcastic, something James. Like, hide the good whiskey. Like, start saving for rehab now.

Instead, James, with a single grain of rice balancing in the tiny triangle joining the left side of his top and bottom lips, looked at his younger brother, said, "I'm sorry about asking you if you did it. I don't know how to say what I want to say. It's fucked up."

"Say it," Thomas said.

"For a minute I forgot you were my brother and thought you were just a fag."

"That is fucked up, Jimmy," Thomas said. "And I hope you never forget that that's exactly how you made me feel. Not like a fag. But brother-less."

"I'm sorry."

"I know," Thomas said. "But I'm not going to make it better for you. That's your mess. Now tell me your best advice on having a teenager in the house."

"You can't be his buddy, Thomas. You can't be his friend. Jake and Sheree understood this better than anyone. They're the ones who taught it to me and Joyce. That's why Max is such a great kid. His welfare is more important than your desire for accept-ance. And your need for acceptance?"

The grain of rice fell into the wine glass, still raised, and the brothers drank.

Thomas invited Reggie and Charlotte for breakfast on their last day so everyone could say goodbye. Nephew, aunt, and uncle shared a veggie scramble and sourdough toast. Watching their exchange made Thomas sad. In her desire to slice out the uglier parts of her past, Thomas wondered if Sheree had made a cut too deep.

After Reggie and Charlotte left, Max said, "You know that he's a math genius? His stupid guidance counselor didn't think Black people could be scientists, so he sent him to the technical high school. If they hadn't, he'd probably be Uncle Manny's or Uncle James's boss at some fancy science lab or hospital."

Joyce and the girls were next; they followed their dad back to New York, and Thomas and Max settled into a calmer routine.

Jerome had been calling every single day. When he found out Thomas had been interviewing other lawyers to set up a trust, Jerome flew in, planned to stay a whole month, vacation a bit while working remotely. Thomas insisted he stay with the family. His plane landed just before noon. Thomas offered to catch a cab to the airport and meet him, but Jerome refused with his signa-ture steeliness. He arrived with a huge suitcase, asked Thomas about Max and Maddy, their whereabouts, what time they'd be home, if he could shower. "They're with Dana and Mel and won't be back until after dinner." Thomas went to his desk, gathered the last of the paperwork Jerome had requested to start the trust.

"Could you come here?" Jerome called from the bathroom. A bank statement finished printing. Thomas took it from the tray and added it to a folder, then went to the bathroom.

Jerome stood naked in the steam. "The water's lukewarm or boiling, but I like it hot," he said, indicating the faucet. He'd set up his razor and mini shaving cream on the vanity. Thomas cringed, remembered how humiliated he'd felt that time he misread Jerome's cues. So much so, he willfully ignored the sight in front of him and decided to forgo wordplay and innuendo, no matter how tempting.

Before Thomas could instruct him on finding the faucet's sweet spot, Jerome pulled Thomas to his chest with the same combination of gentleness and forcefulness as he had that day at the town hall. This time, he kissed Thomas, pressed against him. The kiss, like the pull, was gentle and forceful, and Thomas decided, for the first time since Tony, not to lead, only follow.

Max welcomed Jerome by saying, "Isn't it crowded enough in here? Don't we all have to wait too long for the bathroom as it is?"

At first, Jerome tried reason. "We can make this difficult on each other if you want. But I prefer to get along."

When that didn't work, Jerome asked Thomas how far he could push back. "Believe me, I have some tricks up my sleeve when it comes to dealing with brats."

Thomas asked Jerome to wait. "We both know he's not a brat."

Max pushed hard. Jerome booked a hotel for his second week, only stayed for a few hours at a time, and worked up strategies to sense tension, then go on walks, or work downtown in a colleague's office, or go to the gym so Max and Thomas and Maddy could share supper without him.

On good days, Thomas visited schools in the SFUSD in the early mornings then sold womb chairs and Noguchi tables to gay couples and tech bros for a few hours a day while Jerome hunkered down at Thomas's desk, taking all the calls from Jake and Sheree's insurance and their real estate lawyer. After the sale of Jake and Sheree's house, Jerome helped Maddy set up the college fund, signed and sealed and notarized the first and most challenging round of adoption paperwork. Soon he started to account for how much and where Thomas could donate his Country Day settlement to enrich the programs or improve the lives of kids whose parents were committed to public schooling. It was Max's idea to place an emphasis on helping students who called themselves Black or queer or both.

When Dana came to Green Street to finish up the last of the bedroom design details, she needed help lugging a massive beanbag up the stairs. She had been sick for a couple weeks, and Thomas hadn't seen her. When he opened the door, he took one look at her face, and said, "You're pregnant."

She walked by him, plopped down on the sofa. "Remember when Mel's brother came to visit?"

"Did you finally use the turkey baster?" Thomas asked, sitting next to her.

"A syringe is the preferred method these days," she said. "I didn't want to tell you until after the third month," she said, taking Thomas's hand, placing his palm on her tummy like Maddy had all those years ago when pregnant with Jake. "But fuck it. Max is going to have another cousin. And for what it's worth, I wanted your sperm, but didn't dare ask with all you already have going on."

When James left, Dot took over at Franklin Street. She attended cooking classes in the mornings and, attempting what she'd learned at home, kept the refrigerator packed with food. The gang could just reach in, grab, and then eat. Once, Thomas found Maddy and Dot in one of the bedrooms. Dot sat at Maddy's side as she lay on the bed next to an uneaten plate of food.

Thomas had gone to the refrigerator and stood in the open door until he felt the Freon breeze on his face. When Dot came out, she asked Thomas if he minded if she stayed in town a bit longer. "I talked to James," she said, "told him I'd be willing to keep taking cooking lessons until your mom gets back on her feet."

"We don't know what we'd do without you," Thomas said, shutting the door. "But you're not allowed to stay here anymore. I want you to stay with us. Max can use the air mattress in my room. You and Maddy can have the bunks."

Dot smiled. "Can I have the top?"

"I don't think you're going to get too much argument on that one," Thomas said. "Do you think she's going to be okay?"

Dot had shrugged. "Jake was her baby boy."

When he first started teaching, Thomas had begun every single day tense and ended it exhausted. Then, one morning, about four or five years after he started at Country Day, he woke up excited. He didn't register it that morning, nor did he detect the shift that happened at the end of that same day. He finished work invigorated. What had happened? As the days and weeks and months and years continued, the bell curved back down. After proving himself, and achieving his yearly goals, his work, in itself, proved neither exhausting nor invigorating.

Then, Manny came into his life and encouraged Thomas to be himself. Thomas, in turn, stopped trying to fix or improve his students; stopped trying to mold or change them. He didn't know what a gift Manny had given him, so he wasn't able to see what a gift he passed on to his pupils. The students and their parents, he thought; the school and Mercy; Country Day. What an error in judgment. What a misread of what had been exceptional about his life.

After Manny left, Thomas's best days at work didn't lessen the shock of loneliness nor quench the unexpected misery he'd endured. The breakup felt like a seven on the Richter scale; and then, so soon after, Jake's cancer diagnosis, an eight; and the accusation and resignation, a nine. Jake and Sheree's death, a ten.

How do we live with so much grief? Maddy had told him stories of her days as a hospice nurse on the AIDS ward, and Thomas had listened, tried to forgive himself for abandoning his community during its roughest years. The effect of AIDS was brutal. Relentless. People lost dozens of friends and loved ones. Hundreds. The nurses, like Maddy, thousands. Back then, Thomas didn't think he could bear it. Frightened, he had left. He successfully avoided most of the pain. But he had also missed out on what happens when a group of people survive something unimaginable.

Dana said, "If you wrote a book and called it 'A Year in the Life of the McGurrins,' editors wouldn't buy it because too many bad things happen back to back."

"That's too bad," Thomas said. "For the folks who've lived through a year like ours. Or worse."

Max's psychologist, Colleen, helped Thomas see how the events—wounds, she called them—back to back to back, one subsequent wound on top of the previous, made it difficult to heal. "Difficult," she emphasized.

"Difficult, but . . ." she said.

But?

"Not impossible. It's important to remember: Tens on the Richter scale mean total and complete destruction. No one and nothing left standing. So, don't exaggerate. You and Max and the rest of your family. You're still here."

Before leaving Colorado, Thomas had held half a dozen meetings with Max's last two teachers and principal. Charna had come to one of the meetings with Max's teachers. As flaky as Jake had made her sound, Charna, Max's visiting poetry teacher, was, in fact, as brilliant as she was encouraging. "When he wouldn't write anything other than drivel, I made him the class's town crier. Max read the poems his classmates were too shy to share themselves. He's so empathetic. He added real emotion and nuance to the pieces," she said.

Thomas set up meetings with the High School of the Arts while researching middle schools. Stuart and James both volunteered to help pay private tuition, but Thomas refused. There was a public school right in the neighborhood that everyone on Max's academic team agreed looked good. Thomas enrolled him for fall.

In their last in-person meeting, Colleen asked Thomas how he was doing. "And I mean how you're really doing. I'm not asking as a formality, and I'm not asking about Max."

"I feel oddly relaxed," Thomas had said. "Part of a well-oiled machine. And I don't take shit from moving or cell phone companies anymore. And I hate the gym now. I just want to be outside all the time. With Max."

"That's good," she said. "What else?"

"Walking into the schools and interviewing the principals for Max—the smell of pencil shards and the sight of teacher mailboxes—felt awful. New waves of fury and revenge scenarios aimed at Mercy and the Jays—but more than them, the PFA and the board. That kept happening until it didn't. Until it became what it is. A meeting about Max."

Colleen nodded.

"I'm most worried about my mom. I look at her," Thomas said, "in bed for weeks at a time, not eating. I'm not sure about her drinking or her pills. I wonder if I'm only a tiny step from crawling into wherever she goes and never crawling out." All along Thomas had thought he needed to be like his brothers. He didn't. He needed to be himself. More like his mom. Not the Maddy sick with grief, but the Maddy who lived her own life.

"Who knows what'll happen next? What a mystery," Colleen said, with an upswing. As if the word *mystery* were followed by an exclamation point. As if she were a child and Thomas's life the first ten pages of a good book.

"Hey," Manny yelled. The courtyard on Green Street had the acoustics of an amphitheater. "The call box is broken."

Thomas ran downstairs to meet Manny at the building's entrance. He opened the door to the chilly mid-July fog. A smiling Manny held flowers, two pizzas, a two-liter of Diet 7UP, and tiny, almost invisible dots of moisture on his cheeks and forehead. Thomas grabbed the soda and flowers and led him up the two half-flights of stairs, apologizing for his building's ugly common area. Back in the apartment, Thomas placed the bouquet on the entryway table. "I'll see if I can find a vase."

"They're for your mom," Manny said, not unkindly. The aroma of cardboard and cooked cheese steamed out from the boxes. "The soda is for you."

"I love diet soda," Thomas said, lamely, then quickly added, "Where's Thor?" as Manny looked around the house.

"Fighting with the contractor," Manny said, scanning the framed photos Thomas and Dana had hung on the hallway wall. Manny paused, placed the tip of his free hand's finger against the glass covering Sheree's and Jake's faces. "Your place looks good," he said. "Cozier than Portland. What's different?"

"Manny's here," Thomas called down the hallway as he took the pizzas. Then to Manny. "That wasn't my answer. That was just . . ." He tried to smile. "I have photos now. And Dana convinced me to get pillows."

Manny didn't seem to be listening.

Thomas called again, "He comes carrying dinner." The boxes were hotter, heavier than he expected.

"Take off those damn earphones," Thomas heard his mom say. "Uncle Manny's here."

The bedroom door opened, and both came out, Max with his giant earphones around his neck and a pair of basketball sweats so wide-legged and long he almost tripped on the extra fabric when crossing the room to hug Manny. "Long time, no see," Max said.

"You're so tall," Manny said, and the two looked at their reflection in the hallway mirror. "Jeez. It's usually the whiteys who think we look alike," Manny said. "But we could pass as father and son."

They ambled closer to the mirror.

"Maybe it's our eyebrows," Max said, making a face. "Look." Max touched both his and Manny's reflection. "I could use your ID to get into the clubs," Max said.

"Slow down, Mister," Manny said, and turned to Maddy.

Maddy nudged in between the two, grabbed Manny. "Do you miss my cookies?"

Manny grabbed the now much leaner version of Maddy's body. His mom looked skeletal, Thomas thought.

"Grandma sent Uncle Manny a huge batch of cookies every month when he was doing his research studies in Portland," Thomas told Max.

"You never sent me cookies," Max said, now back in the kitchen, lifting the pizza boxes' lids.

"You lived down the street," Maddy said, taking a seat at the kitchen table. "I baked for you all the time."

"Grammy never sent them to me either," Thomas said, gathering the new plates from the built-ins that separated the kitchen from the dining room.

Even when Manny was in the furthest reaches of his periphery, Thomas could see the circle of platinum he wore on his left ring finger. Thorsten, his fiancé, the sports medicine doctor, hadn't quit Portland or his work with the Trailblazers; he had expanded his territory to include San Francisco. The two rented a temporary apartment in Mission Bay near both their new offices while they remodeled the condo they had bought in the neighborhood on Vallejo. They planned to elope to Hawaii, fingers crossed, hoping gay marriage would pass in June, so they wouldn't have to wait for California.

Thomas gathered napkins and glasses.

"Before we eat," Manny said, then stopped. Then he said, "I need to offer my condolences." He looked at Thomas, then Maddy, and finally Max. "I'm not good at this kind of thing, but I am so, so sorry, guys." He placed one hand on Maddy's shoulder and the other on Max's neck.

Thomas stood back looking at his three, the light from the courtyard silhouetting their bodies. He closed his eyes and concentrated on the tableau. He imagined a file name for the image: *The San Francisco Years. Part 2. Family.*

Things You Can't Do in Colorado/Things You Can Only Do in San Francisco. In the morning, Max and Thomas hopped on the motorcycle. Off they went to cross another thing off a list. They had parked the bike at the base of the Lyon Street steps and raced to the top before riding through the Presidio to the cliffs over-looking China Beach. They parked the motorcycle again, and Thomas used Max's phone camera to freeze his nephew midair during a jump. In the photos he posted, Max looked like he was floating over the Pacific Ocean. His cousins and friends in Colorado piled on the likes.

The day before, they had geared up and taken Highway One north, walked under the redwoods in John Muir State Park. When they were done with that, they tossed rocks off the over-look while screaming, "Fuck You."

At first, Thomas had wondered if he should take the kid on the bike. But Max said, "Seriously, Uncle Thomas?"

So they headed toward Sausalito, where they ate overpriced ceviche in a restaurant on the pier, then ordered ice cream in the charming town center, before strolling on the promenade to snap shots while making peace signs over their dripping waffle cones in front of the international orange backdrop of the Golden Gate Bridge.

They lived close to the water, and because of that, the tide would occasionally suck them each in. Luckily, it never got all of them at once. When it carried one of them out, the strongest among them would toss out the old orange vest they'd all been using since the accident. And after Maddy went back to the Springs, the two McGurrins had Jerome and Dana and Mel and Manny close to shore, waiting.

Chapter Twenty-Five

One Year Later
Sunday
Mid-August 2015

Blue and humpback whales were breaching the waters near the Farallon Islands just northwest of San Francisco.

At least that's what The Marine Society's website said.

Just back from a month with Reginald and Charlotte, Max packed a backpack of protein bars, peanut-butter-and-honey sandwiches, and apples. To welcome him home, Thomas had booked the tickets to celebrate Max's rejection from the High School of the Arts. He'd been wait-listed after finishing eighth grade with a B- GPA. He'd racked up more absences and dismissals than the admissions panel liked to see. He'd also been suspended once for getting high on school grounds, an offense for which they usually expelled students.

Max and Thomas hoped and hoped, but the slot didn't become available. During the wait, Thomas used his past as an educator to schedule an appointment with the chief of admissions. Once there, he told her about Max's losses, why his grades were a bit low, that he'd stabilized. He promised her Max would succeed, be an excellent citizen of the classroom. Thomas even told her that he'd be a good financial donor, and that he belonged to a network of others in a position to donate.

"Get out," the woman said. "That shit don't fly here."

And so, the two decided they'd celebrate their failures. It seemed perfect to pair "Failure Day" with a remembrance of Jake and Sheree, as they'd been the two people on earth who Max and Thomas loved the most. And, according to some people's logic, they'd failed and failed and failed while being the most successful couple and parents and sibling the two had ever known.

Thomas had invited Dana and Mel on the adventure, but Mel was working, Dana too busy with a colicky Shay (Max's new cousin, the green-wearing gender outlaw).

The duo joined the other whalers at the Marina Yacht Harbor at the end of Scott Street at 7:30 sharp. At eight, they set sail on *The Salty Lady*.

Five hours into the boat ride, the initial rush of excitement and anticipation had faded from bright to dim to dark. Neal, the guide, said the type of sea lion they spotted was rare, but Max said it looked just like the ones at Fisherman's Wharf.

Both cold and nauseous, Thomas and Max stood too long in a circle of loud-talking optimists whose tones and cadences felt like a soundtrack for their regret. Every once in a while, there'd be movement on the water, or a passenger who'd yell "Look!" The first few times, a spark ignited, but the hope quickly receded into the miserable drudgery of getting back to shore. The cold had penetrated all their layers and won. The Dramamine kept them out of the restroom, but a weariness had set in, and uncle and nephew had hunkered down and sat quietly to endure what would be another three hours before they could get back on Bull.

Just then, Neal came to the top of the cabin's stairs and said to Max, "Come here, kid."

Max eyed him, suspicious, but got up, wobbled from his coveted seat in the cabin toward the door. Thomas followed.

"Looks like a Right!" Neal yelled, one arm over Max's shoulders, the other hand holding binoculars. "Starboard."

She headed inland. Neal said, "Rights like peninsulas." The whale swam close to the surface. "And are among the rarest," he said, elated. "I've only seen one in twenty years. Most peaceful creatures on earth."

As the whale and the boat closed in on each other, and Neal got his binoculars set to focus, it turned out to be a Blue, not a Right. "Must be a teenager," he said. "It's small for a Blue. But what a beauty."

Neal gathered the rest of the passengers who joined them against the starboard rail. Thomas stared through his binoculars as the whale started rolling, almost flirting, as if she could sense a boatload of admirers. He could not have imagined the enormity of the animal so close. She breached the water, mouth open, and turned and submerged her face. Her mouth looked as though it could swallow the entire boat. Almost a full minute later, her tail appeared.

He listened to Neal tell Max that whales don't eat boats, only tiny fish called krill. "First they swallow a ton of water and force it back out. They chomp up about forty million of those suckers a day. Calves drink fifty gallons of milk."

"Do they have friends? Where's her family?" Max asked, holding on. Thomas watched his nephew watch the whale. In profile, with his hair close to his skull under the knit hat, he looked so much like Jake.

"They never travel in groups more than two. Often solo," Neal said. "Looks like this lady likes to go it alone."

"Maybe she's looking for a friend," Max said.

"Could be." The grooves around Neal's eyes spread down his sun-worn face. "Blue whales have powerful lungs. One in California can talk and listen to one in Hawaii. They're communicating all the time."

Thomas remembered he and Jake as boys, swimming together at Town Lake, how they'd swim in different directions, go underwater and click rocks. Her tail fluke rose out of the water, waved to the boat. Most of the people on board held fancy camera equipment with long telephoto lenses. Max had brought Ziplocs to protect his and Thomas's phones, and snapped a few shots, but the splash was high, and so were the winds. Those on the boat needed to let go of everything extra just to stay standing.

"Just her tongue weighs as much as an elephant," Neal said, as he held the rail. "And her heart is as big as a car."

Thomas closed his eyes, felt the tug and pull of the ocean, the push of the wind, the shifting of the boat's deck. He imagined hearing the whales' songs.

Back on shore, Max said the pavement seemed to be moving under his boots as they walked to where the Bull was parked. "By the time Ms. Blue went too far under to see, I got used to standing out there."

"Me too," Thomas said. "Neal said the ship's floor is called a sole, and a person becomes a sailor when they can stay standing no matter what the ocean dishes out."

Thomas was scheduled to start full-time at the furniture store. He liked the job for now, how uncomplicated it was, and he appreciated it for keeping him busy, but would look for something different when school started. Before Max had left to visit Reggie and Charlotte, at the very beginning of summer, Max's friend Corey from the Springs had visited, and while they were mostly a joy, the two boys got caught, twice, with cigarettes and booze. They had to cancel their trip to New York as a consequence. It was hard to do, and Thomas, putting on his helmet, thought about telling Max that he'd already bought their tickets to New York to reunite with the cousins and uncle and aunt and grandparents at Thanksgiving.

"Can I drive around the parking lot?" Max asked.

Thomas remembered the lesson the flight attendant had given him soon after he left New York in the middle of the night. It seemed like a lifetime ago.

"I don't even want to think about what your mom would do if she found out," Thomas said.

"She'd freak," Max said, kneeling down to pull the tongue of his leather boot from side to center. "But I'd win," he said, looking up, "because I'd ask her if she did it at my age."

"Well," Thomas said, as he put the key into the motorcycle's ignition. "That may be the exact reason we sell Bull and get a car."

Max tightened the chinstrap on his helmet and said, "Is Jerome ever leaving? Or are you guys getting married?"

"That's a weird segue," Thomas said, mounting the driver's seat.

"You're already a couple. I know you play it cool around me, and he got his own place because I acted out. But I also know you guys have sex," Max said, getting on the back.

"That's none of your business," Thomas said, slowing down, driving to the edge of the parking lot, remembering when Jerome came to help him pack, what a fool he had made of himself.

"That means yes," Max said, grabbing his uncle at the waist.

Go to Half Moon Bay was the only thing left on this summer's *Only in San Francisco* list. The public high school in their neighborhood used to have a good theater department before cutbacks, but it hadn't been the same since. The guidance counselor said an arts ed org had just partnered with them to try and revive it, but it would take time and much more money. "This outfit usually has real theater artists who conduct extensive residencies, but we only have enough funding to get them here once a week. At least it's a start?" he said, sounding unsure.

After deducting enough for motorcycle and medical insurance for their foreseeable futures, Jerome had set up a trust with a bit more than half the settlement money. He talked Thomas out of using all of it. "Don't be a martyr. You can add more if and when you're in a more lucrative career." Thomas obeyed, even though he'd become keenly aware of his and Max's uncountable advantages.

It was in that guidance counselor's office that Max had seen a poster, of the ocean with the town's name, hanging, and Thomas, after grilling the counselor about the non-profit, went home and researched their work. Impressed, he met up with their program manager and executive director, then decided they'd receive the first annual grant he'd make from the new trust. The money would allow Max's school, along with two others in the district, to have a fully funded afterschool theater program two hours a day, five days a week. It gave Thomas an endless amount of satisfaction to think of the grant as paid for, in part, by Country Day's parents and scholarship fund.

Driving fast down 101 South, Thomas still felt like he did on the boat. Neal, the whale watcher, may have been right. The whale with its sonar may not rely on the company of others for her contentment. As Thomas watched her dance, she had performed a convincing argument for going it alone, which comforted Thomas as he thought of Maddy. Just after Dot had bought her ticket home, Thomas talked to Maddy, and said, "Stay."

She had said, "My life is there," and went back to the Springs, where she began tending to her garden, filling her freezer for Christmastime, making a life by sharing the bounty with Frank, the zoo's gardener, and other neighbors.

"Sorry, Uncle Tommy," Max said.

Thomas had finally outfitted their helmets with the walkie-talkies and couldn't believe how deep his nephew's voice had gotten.

"Why are you sorry, Maxipad?" Thomas said, speeding toward the last of the afternoon light.

"You know," Max said. "That you were screwed out of your job. That you had to move. That you have to look after me."

"Where in the hell is this coming from?" Thomas asked.

"The walls between our rooms are thin. I heard you talk to Jerome."

"You are a snoop," Thomas said, leaning into a curve.

"Sorry," Max said.

"Stop saying sorry," Thomas said. "They were never my family. It has always been you."

Soon they'd arrive in Half Moon Bay.

"You sure?" Max asked, tightening his grip on Thomas's waist.

"Positive," Thomas said, accelerating, remembering when Russ the flight attendant had taught him how to ride the motorcycle, how clunky it felt then, how self-conscious and aware he'd been of clutch and brakes. "Now hang on tight and no more talking. Can you close your eyes? Just until we get through this traffic?"

"Why close my eyes?"

"Because," Thomas said. "We're a team. And Momma needs to fly."

Acknowledgments

The help I've received in my life—as a person and as an artist—is too much from too many to be contained, but I must try and fail. Forgive me for not mentioning all of you.

This book is dedicated to my parents and brothers. Thank you for your love, for sticking with me. What a gift, what a joy, the closeness we have now, cultivated with three thousand miles between us.

Thank you, Janice Mirikitani for asking me what was in my notebook and inviting me to a writing workshop with you and June Jordan. You changed the trajectory of my life.

To every queer(-loving) author, editor, agent, and teacher who paved the way. Thank you. Thank you. Thank you.

Thank you, Cheryl Cox, Michael Mullen, Nan Peletz, and Gerard Westmiller for listening and sharing your experience.

Thank you to every single person who signed up for "The Lab." I wrote into each and every experiment I suggested, right along with you in our Tuesday night writing workshop. Your results inspired mine.

Thank you, students and colleagues and teachers

from SFSU for years of engagement—especially those who came to campus from less traditional academic backgrounds. So many of you have, so often, made this former teenage runaway and high school dropout feel at home.

Thank you, to the late "Labber" John Trout for his friendship and for introducing Thomas (and me) to writer/editor Michael Nava. I will remember you, always.

Thank you, Michael, for your bighearted guidance and friendship. Given who I am, where I come from, what brought me to writing in the first place, and what this story examines, it is so appropriate to be making my fiction "debut" with Amble Press. I remember your first editorial suggestion: "I feel Thomas could be angrier. And queerer." I didn't know until you said it that I'd been waiting my whole life to hear that comment.

Thank you to the whole Bywater Books and Amble Press family and to Ann McMan for the gorgeous cover.

Thank you, Mackenzie Watson Brady and Beth Vesel for your generosity and feedback on earlier versions of the manuscript; and to Victoria Skurnick, my agent, for your enthusiasm and support. Thank you to all the editors who carefully considered and said no. Your comments showed me where the story needed work and inspired me to do it.

Thank you, Gregory R. Miller and Michael Wiener for summers and space to research and write inside the most loving and celebratory queer family enclave. Thank you, Jetson, Frisbee, and Mukti Miller-Wiener for keeping me company while writing, and Lucas for entertaining me on breaks. Thanks for introducing me to the whole Firefly family, including Casper, Alan, and Lyle.

Thank you, Casper Grathwohl for your sensitive comments and suggestions on early drafts of *Doubting Thomas*, and your unwavering belief that he'd find a home. You set up and lit fireworks around the pond and you set up and lit fireworks around Thomas.

Thank you, Lyle Ashton Harris for your example and mostly hands-off mentorship-by-example with an occasional come-to-Jesus moment. You have what I want and I'm willing.

Thank you, *Foglifter*, *Lumina*, *Per Contra*, and *Fourteen Hills* for publishing early excerpts of *Doubting Thomas*.

Thank you, Alice LaPlante, Mieke Eerkens, and Zulema Renee Summerfield for reading and for the encouragement during various in-between states, and Terese Svoboda for the love, edit suggestions and Pushcart nominations.

Grecia, David and Patrick, thank you for sharing your ESH as openly gay teachers of young kids.

Thank you, Dennis and Brianna for your help with legal questions.

Thank you, Michelle Carter for keeping a candle lit for me from the day our paths first crossed. *It has taken me all this time . . .*

Thank you, Zach Grear for making Momma proud. I needed every one of our summertime talks and strolls through museums and galleries. Thank you for providing inspiration for the cover art. We will make a family collab happen sooner or later. Meanwhile: *God bless* and *heart of gold*.

Thank you to my sisters-in-law Victoria and Teresa and to my nieces Madeleine, Isabelle, Teresa, and Amara and to my stepmother Peg. While we are all so different from Thomas and his family, I hope I gave Thomas a fraction of the depth of relationship you all have given me.

Thank you, Emily Fitzloff for being my sisteria and for help with all things Portland, and to Buggie and Rolfie for putting me up when there to research and again to Buggie for the binder.

Thank you, Rick Rochon and Janet Rikala Dalton for years of friendship and for bursting into tears. Your joy acts as a locator for mine.

And finally, before I switch to invisible ink to continue this list with your name, one more:

Philip Ansumana Munda Hull—Ansu—BZL1—numba—huzzleone. You found the key and unlocked the rusty old box. Thank you for keeping the faith. I love you.

About the Author

Matthew Clark Davison is a writer and educator living in Oakland. He is creator and teacher of The Lab :: Writing Classes with MCD, a non-academic school that meets both online and in person. It started in 2007 in a friend's living room on Douglass Street. In 2022, W.W. Norton & Company will publish a book partially based on *The Lab* by Matthew and co-author Alice LaPlante.

Matthew earned a BA and MFA from San Francisco State University, where he now teaches full-time in Creative Writing. His prose has been anthologized in *Empty the Pews* (Epiphany Publishing) and *580-Split*; published in *Guernica, The Atlantic Monthly, Foglifter, Lumina Magazine, Fourteen Hills, Per Contra, Educe*, and others; and has been recognized with a Creative Work Grant (Inaugural Awardee/San Francisco State University), Cultural Equities Grant (San Francisco Arts Commission), Clark Gross Award for a Novel-in-Progress, and a Stonewall Alumni Award. He is now at work on a second novel and a memoir.

Amble Press, an imprint of Bywater Books, publishes fiction and narrative nonfiction by LGBTQ writers, with a primary, though not exclusive, focus on LGBTQ writers of color. For more information on our titles, authors, and mission, please visit our website.

www.amblepressbooks.com